Josephine Humphreys is the author of three novels, and has won both popular and critical acclaim for them, one of which was made into a Hollywood movie.

She lives on the coast of South Carolina.

NOWHERE ELSE ON EARTH

In the summer of 1864, the citizens of North Carolina's Robeson County have become pawns in the devastation created by the Civil War. Rhoda Strong is sixteen, the daughter of a Scotsman and his Indian wife; she is the first of her family to have learned to read, and her parents have plans for her. But with the coming of the Civil War, her brothers become outlaws to evade conscription by the Confederacy, and when Rhoda falls in love with the outlaws' leader, Henry Lowrie, her mother fears the relationship can only lead to tragedy . . .

JOSEPHINE HUMPHREYS

◆

NOWHERE ELSE ON EARTH

Complete and Unabridged

ULVERSCROFT
Leicester

First published in Great Britain in 2001 by
William Heinemann
London

First Large Print Edition
published 2002
by arrangement with
William Heinemann
The Random House Group Limited
London

British Library CIP Data

Humphreys, Josephine
    Nowhere else on earth.—Large print ed.—
Ulverscroft large print series: general fiction
    1. United States—History—Civil War, *1861 – 1865*
—Fiction 2. North Carolina—Social conditions—
19th century—Fiction 3. Love stories
    4. Large type books
    I. Title
    813.5'4 [F]

    ISBN 0–7089–4748–4

Published by
F. A. Thorpe (Publishing) Ltd.
Anstey, Leicestershire

Set by Words & Graphics Ltd.
Anstey, Leicestershire
Printed and bound in Great Britain by
T. J. International Ltd., Padstow, Cornwall

This book is printed on acid-free paper

For
L. C. M.

With gratitude to those who inspired
and encouraged

ROBESON COUNTY

Union
Chapel

Floral
College

Burnt Swamp

New Hope
Chapel

Shoe Heel

Bear Swamp

Saddletree Swamp

Red Banks

Pate's

Raft Swamp

Moss Neck

Big Swamp

Lumbee River

Lowrie's
Cabin

Back Swamp

Lumberton

W. C. & R. Railroad

Lumber River

North Carolina
South Carolina

Robeson County

Columbus County

Marion
District

Lumber River

N
W   E
S

0   6
Scale of Miles

© 2000, Mark Jam Studio

Prologue

November 3, 1890
from my hidden town on the Lumbee River,
Robeson County, North Carolina

What happened here twenty-five years ago could not have happened in any other place or age. Maybe it will be told in full someday, and all the secrets known.

But my guess is nobody will ever roll back the curtain to show a true picture of us and our land in those times, just as a soldier can never describe a whole battle — only his little piece of it, the tree and fence and field he saw, his own wounds and the wounds he gave. He does his best, telling what he knew and what he supposed and what he heard later from the others, but always wanting to tell more, always wishing a view would clear and the whole scene — not just its deaths but its explanation and design — would suddenly lie open before his eyes on the green field, revealed in a dazzling afternoon light.

★ ★ ★

1

One time a newspaper said, 'The Queen of Scuffletown cannot read, or even write her own notorious name.' Which may show something about newspapermen, how easy they are to fool, because of course I read the remark. But it was no slander, it was what I'd led them to believe. In those days I found it an advantage to hide many things. The first time I had to sign a court paper I was inspired to put an X instead of my signature.

Now, though, in my old age (well, forty-one isn't ancient but I can tell you it is well past all the excitement) I am ready to drop my disguises. Mine is only a single and limited testimony, one woman's version — as much of the truth as I know or can guess, but not guaranteed pure, not unswayed by certain passions. Love, for one. I have loved this place as much as I've loved any human soul.

Since it is somewhat changed today, I'm describing our geography from memory. The county has more farms and towns now, more ditches, more roads and bridges and railroad tracks. But back then everything not pine-woods or fields was swamps, fifty of them labeled on the map and more whose names were never known to mapmakers. Some were pocosins, shallow egg-shaped basins land-locked and still, scattered northwesterly as if a clutch of stars had been flung aslant in one careless toss from heaven, leaving bays that sometimes filled with rain and sometimes dried in the sun, growing gums and poplars and one tiny bright green plant found nowhere else on earth, the toothed and alluring Venus flytrap.

In the bigger swamps, miles wide and inches deep, a slow current drew toward the river through thickets of briar and cane and bottle-neck cypress, each tree rising from a little island of its own making. The roots caught silt from the drifting stream, and slowly built a solid ground where none had been before. Some of the roots came up as knees all around, to steady the tree.

And directly through the middle of the county ran our narrow zigzag Lumbee, choosing any course it wanted, swelling with freshets, washing out bridges, carrying off sheep and pigs and sometimes human beings. Its other name was Drowning Creek. The result was a sodden, hard-to-travel territory of which our little part was always the worst (as they said, but we said the best), the hidden, tangled, water-logged heart.

★ ★ ★

My father was born a Scot in Portree on the Isle of Skye, and shipped as a boy to

Pennsylvania in service to a dairyman. But before his term was up, he fled the cows for a career of escapade. In Virginia he spent his youth (spent it all out, I mean, carousing), and eventually he roved down across the state line and south to Alamance, where he was leading a rowdy existence and drinking himself into difficulties around the same time my mother was roving up.

The daughter of Dorcas and Malcolm Sweet, Americans, she was raised on the run from one hard-labor turpentining camp to another in and around this piney lower corner of North Carolina. Malcolm was a native of here, his mother a Lowrie. Dorcas had come from the Marion District, the part of South Carolina that touches us and, a newspaper once said, could be sawed off along with us and dropped into the sea with no loss to either state except for the turpentine.

From the day Malcolm first went out as a chopper he kept his family with him. So his daughter, called Cee for Celia Ann, learned turpentining at his side, watching and helping as he moved from chopper up to dipper and puller, then teamster, woods-rider, and at last stiller, hired to run the works at McRaney's when the owner, McRaney Senior, became infirm and the junior was still a boy. There at

4

the stillery Malcolm finally had a chance to stay put on home ground. He trained his daughter as a grader, teaching her the colors that would decide the price. Her eyes were sharp and her mind was quick. In the spirit room, she watched the vats and graded the batches. Top quality was the clearest, nothing but a gleam of no color at all. Extra, that was called. Then came Waterwhite, not quite so clear; Windowglass, starting to cloud; Nancy, tinged but acceptable; and the lowest grade, Betsy, too darkly gold for shipping, sold locally at a low price.

The family might have prospered then, as a stiller was a high-paid man, and Dorcas had only the one child because of medical disturbances preventing more. But Malcolm died in a still-bang, his legs blown off before his daughter's eyes by the new machine he had warned everyone was dangerous but no one listened. It was a fire-still, the first in the state. The explosion made them change their minds — *maybe old Malcolm was right* — and they perfected the fire-still the way he had suggested.

North Carolina in those years had changed its mind about a lot of things and changed its laws too. It put in new rules for who could vote and who could own a gun and who could go to school. Yet those you'd think would have left the state then, didn't. Either they couldn't afford to move or else they loved the place too much. But Cee had an added motive for leaving. She hated turpentining, for killing her father, and she blamed it also for the death of her mother, who declined into a widow's despair and one year later shot herself at the bunching ground. The day after Dorcas was buried, Cee struck off on her own, age sixteen, aiming north for Baltimore or beyond, and hoped to never smell the smell of gum again or see a spirits vat.

The same for men. She could do without the sight of them too, and the aroma. My mother was big and dark and beautiful when she was sixteen and she was trying to learn a tough style that would keep men at bay. Fending them off, she worked her way up the state in kitchens and taverns, fields and sawmills, wherever she could make a dollar to finance her escape from North Carolina. She tried going as a boy, for safety's sake, with a punchbelly file always in her pocket. But her figure was the kind not easily disguised.

In Alamance, one county short of Virginia, she met Daddy. He was in straits, of course, and not the sort of man I'd have predicted to catch her eye. But he did, one night in a tavern, when he took on a fellow who was making remarks to her along the line of that old question she hated: *What are you?* They fought no-holds-barred and Daddy won, but the insulter turned out to be a squire. Holding his bitten-off ear-lobe in his hand, he swore to have Daddy pilloried and lashed for maiming, but Dad spit out a Gaelic curse and made a lunge for the squire's other ear. Cee held him back, and by the time a sheriff got there, both she and Daddy had hightailed it. A paper printed his description, 'clean-shaven red-headed buckskin Scot, lame in the leg and foul in the mouth,' but by then he was in the custody of a higher power. Hers.

She was tired of the dangers of the single life. And maybe she saw promise in him, which no woman had seen before. Once she got him into the hills, she decided to give up her northward progress in order to reform him. The bribe she offered was herself. If he would become a sober family man — and also grow a mustache, change his name, and watch his tongue so he couldn't be matched to the description — she would throw in with him. He accepted, and they were married. Did she love him or did she only prize his lack of meanness? For despite the chomp he took of the squire, he was, when sober, the sweetest of men. Whatever it was, she declared it love, and so it was.

7

The first morning of their wedded life, she poured a teaspoon off his daily pint and put back in a teaspoon of water. The second morning it was two spoonfuls out and two in, and so on until at the end of three months he was drinking nothing but pure well water. They worked together awhile ditching, till they found a little one-horse place to farm for thirds, handing over an ear of corn for every two they kept. But after we were born she began to see they'd never make a life for children in Alamance, the way Daddy was. He couldn't get a foothold, still owed debts, and — something she had not anticipated — once free of the demon Rum, he was subject to the hellhound Gloom. He had bad spells of fear and dread. He dreamed the squire had bled to death from the ear, and all of Alamance was out to hunt the culprit. So at last, unable to think of anything else to help him, she brought us and him back down to the only place she knew as home, the hidden town in Robeson County where her relations still lived in spite of it being a time when they might ought to have gotten out.

By then even the people who loved this section were leaving in droves, following the turpentine trail into Georgia, where the camps were new and the law had not yet gone against us, or heading west for Tennessee,

8

where it was rumored there was no law at all. But Cee brought us here, where she believed she could give her husband the security he needed.

To call the place a town might be misleading. It was more like a fishnet. Or a cobweb, a lacy swatch of tatting, a snare of mesh. Two hundred houses spread through miles of swampy woods, threaded together by footpaths and narrow oxcart lanes of sand. On its southern side between the swamp and the river, Cee rented a one-room house of logs from her cousin Allen Lowrie. Daddy took it easy for a while, and she went back into turpentining.

Robeson County was then on its way to becoming the turpentine capital of the world. We had eighty stilleries going strong, some of them big slave operations and some a single family's livelihood. You could sharecrop a rich man's stand of timber, or hire out to a woods crew, or you could do like my mother, become skilled in one difficult thing and always have steady work. Walter McRaney Junior wanted her right away, remembering how good a grader her father was, and she agreed to hire on in hopes she could wangle Daddy a ditching job later on.

It was all part of her plan to save him once

and for all. In gratitude, he became a new man. He fit in. In this secret place, like none he'd ever known before, he grew to be honored as a man of many talents, Cee's husband and therefore one of us, no questions asked. The name of the place was Scuffletown.

She was a Lowrie through her father's mother, and the Lowries are Indians. The whole place is Indians. And that is the answer to what we are, in Scuffletown.

It is an answer the rest of the world don't like.

Whites and blacks and even the smilings who lived under a question mark themselves will draw up their mouths in a purse when the subject of Scuffletown arises. The Cherokees deny us, I'm told, although from ten counties away they don't exactly have a front-row view, and I might point out that their Principal Chief Ross was one part Indian to seven parts not.

But nobody of any sort wants us to be what we are.

Some say we are too dark to be Indian. Some say too light. And we do vary. 'What can I do about that?' my mother used to say. 'To hell with them.'

Where's the proof? they always want to know. *Where's the language and the relics?*

Even Dr. McCabe, a friend to us and a man reputed to be a genius of knowledge, would ask these questions. We were lucky he took an interest, for otherwise we'd not have had a doctor. He would come in when called by the grannywoman, Mrs. Revels, and after doing what he could, he would sometimes stop to talk with Cee. His wife was dead, and maybe he found in my mother a brain to match his own. Cee didn't look forward to his visits, but she allowed them.

'Rhoda, listen,' she said to me. 'He's a harmless coot, and I owe him a debt of gratitude. He helped my mother not to die when I was born. We need him, time to time. Be nice to everyone is the rule here because you don't know whose help you'll want someday.' But Daddy usually would leave the house and find something to do in the yard during the doctor's visits, saying McCabe was the talkingest man with nothing to say that he ever saw.

I remember a morning when the doctor stayed a good long time, asking my mother the same old questions. Did she recall old folks in the settlement speaking an Indian language? Did she have any old papers like land deeds or government letters? Was anyone in the family tree part Portuguese, or maybe Gypsy or Turk or Italian? And how did the first James Lowrie get all that land he'd owned?

She was churning, working the paddle so hard it screeched, and he didn't notice the gathering frown of annoyance that was the one she used on gnats and bothersome children just before the swat. But Daddy's bum leg was hurting him worse than usual, and she wanted the doctor to look at it. So she sucked her breath and held her temper.

'I've heard Lazy Will Locklear talk in what I took to be the Indian tongue,' she said. 'Elizabeth Locklear too.'

'His wife?' The doctor was writing the names down, and his pocket notebook caught my eye. Green linen-covered boards. Thin white whispery pages tipped along the edge with gold.

'No, and not his daughter, either — those are the Prospect Elizabeths. I'm talking about Ma Bet. Bettie Locklear, Bill Lowrie's wife. Allen's mother. She's one of the New Hope Elizabeths.'

He scratched out what he'd written. 'I don't know how you all keep yourselves straight,' he said. 'How many Elizabeth Locklears have you got anyway?'

'About as many as you got Neil McNeills, I guess.' She was breathing heavy, pumping her big arms, beating harder than she needed to.

'Well, I'll need to see this Lazy Will and Bettie,' he said. 'Can you arrange it?'

'You'll get nowhere with them.'

'But they all trust you. 'Mayor of Scuffletown,' I'm told. You could introduce me, explain I'm trustworthy — '

'If there's a mayor here, it's Allen Lowrie. I'm not gray-haired or fair-minded enough, and I don't have the right last name for it. All I do is visit the sick and let them tell me what they want to tell. People trust me all right, but those particular two I haven't got much sway with, Doctor.'

'The tight-lipped sort? Standoffish?'

'You bet. In the grave.'

He shut his notebook, and the pages made a golden bar between the covers.

'All right,' he said. 'Where history is dark, we must cast a searching beam. Archeological evidence is what we need. If there were real Indians here, what's left of them? A pot or tommyhawk, some sort of beadwork or headdress . . . '

At that she lost her patience. Dropped the paddle, rose from the bench, and opened her arms in a gesture of display.

'What's left of them? What's left of them is me! Me and the Lowries and the Braveboys and the Oxendines and the Locklears and all

13

of us. The relics is standing before you in person alive and kicking. The relics speak for themselves.'

The doctor said, 'But we can't have history by say-so.'

And she said, leveling her gaze at him, 'Depends on *whose*, it looks like.'

He studied her face. He was always studying something, always mentally whirring. Some days he might stand two hours at the edge of a swamp to count the parakeets, a scientific curiosity as the only ones of their race remaining in America. Jungly, remote Robeson County was their last stand, but they were sociable and fearless in spite of their diminishing numbers, and allowed themselves to be observed. The doctor would note their habits of flight and feeding and mating, then shoot a couple to study at close range, stuffing the little green-and-yellow bodies into his frockcoat pocket and sometimes forgetting them until his daughter found them days later much declined in condition.

'The human relics, then,' he said to Cee, musing.

'Yes, and why not?'

★　★　★

14

My mother was nice right up to the line where niceness became impossible, and then she wasn't afraid to stand up to anyone. She had learned early to claim her ground and take her stand. The only time I saw her bullied into something was for my sake — when she gave in to Miss Amanda McCabe and let me have lessons from her.

Cee couldn't read, but she knew a lot. I am sure she had the biggest brain in Robeson County. Her head was twenty-five inches around, more than any of the others measured by the Government the time they sent down a scientist at the request of Dr. McCabe. The doctor said Cee had given him the idea, and she could expect to see her name in a footnote to the paper he meant to publish with the help of this scientist. The paper might mean government schools would come in or maybe even the Quaker teachers who liked to go to Indians. So a good number of settlement families went to the courthouse and, one by one, stepped into a closet and took off our clothes, and the man measured us to see what we were.

Some came out Indians, he reported in his report — my family not among them. Cee's skull was too big. But by the time we heard that, she said she didn't give a damn what Science or History or Government thought, and she regretted she had talked the families into getting measured.

'Whoever's here is one of us,' she said to me and my brothers. 'Those with the right-sized head, plus the thousand rest, including my babies. Your daddy might be a orange-haired Portree man, but never forget you are all one of us.'

'*Might* be?' my father said. 'Their daddy *might* be a Portree man?'

'To the best of my recollection. A withy little buckskin. My recall is foggying but I think I'm right on that. Funny-looking fellow.'

As always when she joked with us, there was no smile on her lips, but there was a glint in her eye as sharp as her power of recall. She was famous for her memory, which included not only the events of her own life but the entire history of who had married who in Scuffletown and what they named their children.

'I do remember the mustache that rascal had,' she said.

Daddy waggled a finger over his lip. 'Like this one,' he said.

'Redder,' she said. 'Younger.'

This was their game, their signaling. After a while they went out for a long walk.

She decided to quit answering the question *What are you?* Because the bigger question was why they asked. Our answer never satisfied, and they kept on suggesting something else until we learned to keep quiet. We were called many names but publicly it was Scuffler or Scuffletown Indian, meaning Not-Indian, No-Person, Nothing. But she always said, 'Remember the bones.'

She was thinking of her ancestor Rafael Kersey, who shot to death the first Government man that came in, a surveyor who climbed a tree to take a sighting with his instrument across Mr. Rafe's field. Not far behind a surveyor there was always a land grabber, so the man was not welcome. He stayed up there in the branches a right long while before his bones started falling one by one; but the oak tree was said to be still standing somewhere in the woods between Raft Swamp and Moss Neck with an arm bone lodged in its crotch.

She didn't like surveyors. Didn't like any outsiders, whether they were census takers, newspapermen, teachers, or preachers. The paper had once reported the visit of a famous bishop in Lumberton. Sermonizing on the number of heavens, the bishop explained there must be three, as God in His wisdom had created white souls and black souls and red souls all with different needs. The only snag was the puzzle of those who nobody knew exactly what they were, the 'mixt crew.' To which heaven would they go? This was a knot the bishop could not untie. But one thing was certain, they wouldn't be going to white heaven. It was impossible that blood of the early white colonists might run in the mongrel Scuffler veins, as some had claimed, because of 'the Christian Britisher's propensity to mate only with his own kind.'

So why did he bother to preach a special sermon on the subject of us at all? I always thought that those who were so disgusted were also fascinated. They were drawn to us, they couldn't help themselves.

For one thing, we were good-looking. Dr. McCabe said North Carolina's prettiest girls and handsomest boys were to be found in Scuffletown. The macks (MacThis and McThat, the big Scots planters) all thought so. For another thing, they knew, deep down, the truth: that when their own Gaelic-talking ancestors first arrived, having fled their original wild poor country to continue their bickering in another, and finally chopped through to the banks of the Lumbee, they found us already here talking English and wearing English hats in houses along the English plan. They knew of James Lowrie, who played the mouth harp and ran the first ferry and married Sally America Kersey, because Mr. James once owned two thousand acres, more than half of which had by now passed into the hands of the macks instead of his own descendants. 'Allen Lowrie lost his granddaddy's Indian land,' Dr. McCabe once said, as if Mr. Allen woke up one morning to see a great big hole in the ground. But Mr. Allen knew where the land was. Its papers had been shifted into someone else's pocket, is all.

Why does a language fade away? I don't think that is a hard-to-answer question. Truth is a curing power, and they had it in their reach. They might have recognized us. Instead, they declared we were a mystery.

'There's people in North Carolina that can't count no higher than two,' Cee said. 'White and black. Anything else they ship out or won't see.' And so, 'Hell with them.' She said that, not me, I hadn't gone that far. It seemed too many people to send to hell, and some of them I personally liked. Stupidity is no sin. But when something's clear as day and they deny it, well, as she said, what can you do about that?

It would have surprised them all to know,

we didn't spend our waking hours wondering who we were. We knew.

What we wanted was the life before us. To do the work, to fall in love, survive the sorrows, stay put. Like anybody.

1

I begin with an afternoon in the summer of 1864, a season of bad heat and rain. War raged somewhere and probably love too, but I was safe from both, I thought. I didn't know they were sneaking up to storm me by surprise and wreck me. There had been signs — mud snakes in the well, thunderbolts cracking our nights like warning shots — but I was fifteen. I read things wrong.

We had spent the morning sweltering behind a barred door, with daylight only through chinks and our one high window in the gable. The Home Guard was on a tear again, so Cee wouldn't let us out. She was the kind of mother who might sometimes risk her own neck but never ours.

I was sick with the heat and confinement. After six hours of it I broke.

'I can't breathe!'

'Lie down by the cat hole,' she said.

So I got some air there, with my nose next to the little cutout square at the bottom of the door, hoping Cee would say, *You poor thing*, which she didn't. Under the floor our gold dog, Girl, snuffled and whined, scratching out a hollow to lie in. Through the cracks I could smell the turpentine we rubbed on her for fleas and yellow flies, and probably she could smell me, I was so sweaty. Whispering down to her, 'Poor thing, poor you,' I spied out the cat hole, but all I saw was a patch of the ordinary world.

Nothing moved in the drowned cornfield. Rainwater stood in pools like flat tin, and no birds flew. It didn't look like danger, it only looked like home, still and beautiful and scorching green. Now and then a dry pod snapped in the chimney vines, flinging seed across the roof like sand. Deep in the matted honeysuckle on the porch a lizard hid, and suddenly his throat bubbled red.

I said, 'There's nothing out there but the usual.'

'What did I teach you? Before you take a chance, you figure your what?'

'Odds.'

'You mean to tell me they turned in our favor?'

'No, ma'am.'

'Sit tight then.'

In the early afternoon Henderson Oxendine came to tell us the Guard had been seen on the Lumberton Road heading our way. Eleven horsemen riding hard, Brant Harris in the lead. Henderson said we better let him take Boss and Andrew out to the swamps to hide with the young Lowries. At first I wasn't paying close attention to what he said, I was noticing how both his pants legs were worn through to his scrawny knees.

Cee thought Andrew and Boss too young to let go, only seventeen and fifteen.

'And if I can't protect my own boys against a half-blind bunch not even fit for the Rebel army then what am I good for?' she said to Henderson, still a boy himself not yet twenty but serious as a preacher, born that way. I'd known Henderson all my life, he was my childhood favorite up until I was thirteen, when Margaret Ransom came along, frisky and pretty and down-to-earth as a turnip, and a lot easier to talk to than Henderson. Besides, Cee thought it was time I had a girl for a best friend instead of running down to the fish traps with that boy every day, so Henderson and I drifted apart, me with Margaret and him with his brother Calvin.

But when I saw him again, with his bare knees and his knowing eyes, I was a little sorry I had swapped him for Margaret in the first place. If I'd stuck with Henderson, I told myself, things might have turned out different. His appeal went beyond the ordinary, to something in the spirit realm. He had a gift of music that could move the doubtingest heart. Whenever there was a brush-arbor preaching, or a husking or a picnic, someone would call on Henderson for a hymn. His face was narrow and bright, his eyes deep with the true, mysterious, hopeless love of things that can't be seen. The times I heard him sing, I said to myself it was too bad a boy like that couldn't be traveling the world, singing the praises of the Lord in his sweet, sad voice to the heathen.

But under the present circumstances — hunger and peril — Henderson wouldn't be singing for a while. He and his brother Calvin and their cousin Steve Lowrie and some others were trying to dodge the Guard and not get conscripted to Wilmington for forced labor at the salt factory or the Fort Fisher earthworks. The macks had decided they'd rather not send any more slaves for work that broke them or even killed them, so the solution was 'Send Scuffletown.' They wouldn't have our boys as soldiers but they grabbed them quick enough for slave labor. Word was that Steve Lowrie's brother Henry — the great Henry, who nobody could outrun — had been caught and sent.

But the truth was, when boys went missing like that you couldn't be sure what had happened. They would vanish off the lane on a quiet morning, and no one knew their fate or if we would ever lay eyes on them again. It is terrible to hope your boys are slaving somewhere, but that was what we had to hope.

'There's no end in sight,' Henderson said. 'And Harris is taking boys younger now, to fill the requirement. Somebody's helping him, writing up a list and telling him where to hunt. We think it might be the postmaster.'

'James Barnes?' Daddy said, and Henderson nodded.

The postmaster knew us. He lived down the river half a mile.

Henderson offered to take Andrew and Boss to where the Lowries were lying out, but he wasn't allowed to say exactly where that was, for our own safety. Nobody was to know, not even mothers, not even Preacher Sinclair, who was passing information to the lie-outers. Sinclair and Dr. McCabe and Lawyer Macmillan were three among a handful of macks who took an interest in the settlement — all of them good-intentioned but one way or another troubled in mind and therefore not to be confided with the whole story.

'I brought a little something,' Henderson said, and he put three eggs on the table. I never had seen anything so pretty. Eggs! I'd forgotten how they looked. The way they sat there, smooth and perfect, gave me a shiver of pleasure.

'Did you get you one?' Cee asked him.

'No'm.'

'Well, here.'

But, thank goodness, he shook his head.

'And how did you come by these eggs, Henderson?' she said.

'Some folks still has hens. Mr. Allen's got his underneath the floorboards, trained to hush when someone comes. He closes the trapdoor, and there's not a peep.'

'Allen's playing you along,' she said. 'Chickens don't fuss in the dark anyway. They think they been swallowed, they think it's doomsday.'

From my corner I said, 'Swallowed alive. Never again to run free or see the light of day or breathe the sweet air of God's green — '

'You didn't swipe them, did you?' Cee said.

'No'm. They were given to me to give,' Henderson said.

'By Allen?'

'In a way of speaking.'

' — swallowed into the pitch black dark, no ray of hope . . . '

Finally she looked at me and saw my puffed face, my damp curls clinging to my neck.

'Bless your heart,' she said, and meant it.

She held out an arm and I went to sit by her knee so she could fan me.

Daddy said let Henderson take the boys. 'I've done some lying out myself, in my time,' he said. 'It ain't nothing to be ashamed of when your life is on the line.' He told Henderson, if the Lowries were at Devilsden in Back Swamp like he'd heard, and if they had as many guns as he'd heard — he paused but Henderson didn't say yes or no — then Boss and Andrew should go.

'It's Lowries and you two Oxendines out there, I believe, along with one white one, McLaughlin, and one black one, Applewhite. I have it on good authority. Am I right, Henderson?'

I smiled to hear Daddy quote me as a good authority.

'I've given my oath not to say, Mr. Strong,' Henderson answered.

I said, 'I guess Steve Lowrie didn't give his or if he did it's bum. He came in Pate's last week telling everyone Henry was taken off to Wilmington but Applewhite joined in his place. Steve said they have five revolvers, ten shotguns, four Union rifles, and a plan to get a bunch more.'

To gain Henderson's attention I may have left the impression I'd been at Pate's store myself to hear this when really it was something I had overheard said between Cee and her friend Nelly Gibson the day before. I thought I might impress Henderson with my up-to-the-minute knowledge. But he was keeping his eyes off me. I wasn't playing the flirt, all I wanted was to be seen as another human being in the room. I wanted to say, *It's just the same old me, Henderson,* but suddenly I wondered how true that was. Time had been at work on me since our childhood days.

Looking at his shoes, Henderson said, 'If Applewhite's with us — and I'm not saying he is or he isn't — then we're lucky to have him.'

This was George Applewhite, who had once been a slave in the Marion District but found the life not to his taste and made his way to us, dodging the catchers for so long now — five years at least — they would soon surely have to declare him dead or northernized.

'Ap can keep the boys safe,' Daddy said.

Cee said, 'And I can't?'

'I don't mean you aren't a strong woman, Celia Ann,' Daddy said, his tongue rolling with the sound of his childhood home. His Gaelic was long gone, since Cee never let him talk it, and sometimes you could have thought he was settlement-born, he came so close to what was called the long talk, the Scuffletown sound. But his burr crept back when he was anxious. Then you heard Isle of Skye coming through.

'You're the strongest in the world,' he said to her ('sdungest in the wudduld'), 'but how could you hold off the Guard? Or how could I? And suppose Harris starts thinking, 'Well, he's halt but he's a digger, ain't he?' Barnes gave me a hard look at the post office last week, he might put my name down. But I don't want to be took, Cee. My knee, my constitution . . . Maybe we all ought to go with Henderson and lie out till the war ends. Wilmington would be the end of me. I'd not survive the climate, I don't have the strength of the rest of them — '

'Johnny, that's why you won't be took.'

'You don't think they'll come for me?'

'Not an old bustard like you. You got my word, it's the truth if I ever told it. Besides, you forgot, you're not the shade of color that's preferred for fort work.'

That settled his mind, and he quieted down. Half her time was spent calming him, keeping his thoughts off the subjects that could plow him under (jail, death, and my bleak future). Ever since the day they met she had been his guarantee against despair, and if she had her own share deep down, she hid it.

29

I wondered if other marriages worked by the same arrangement, wives shooing off husbands' gloom by teasing, soothing, badgering, any trick in the book to bolster them.

Cee said thank you to Henderson but she would keep Andrew and Boss at home, and he could have the pail of potatoes by the hearth. They were resin-baked, a specialty from the old days when Dorcas, my grandmother I never met, cooked for the turpentine woods crew. You dig a hole and bury the potatoes under a thick layer of wet moss, add your lightwood and a ladle of gum, stand back and throw in a match. This is best done at night, to see the flare whoosh up toward the stars and then settle back to a long steady burn. By the time it's down to a flicker, the potatoes are done, and you spoon them out of the ashes. Then you cool and peel and eat them. The taste of the resin isn't strong, it's more like a tinge, a *something*, that bumps your memory back to other times and your thoughts back to times even before memory. Resin-baked potatoes was my only knowledge of Dorcas Sweet aside from her death by suicide.

Henderson looked in the pail, and I hoped he would decline but he took out two — my mouth watered just to see the charred papery skin and orange flesh showing through popped blisters — and he lingered by the door with the potatoes in his hands. He seemed to have something else to say, or maybe he misunderstood my longing gaze. *Don't take them*, I was thinking, even though his bony knees proved he could use some fattening up.

I wasn't as generous as my mother, and I hadn't yet learned how to kill hunger by force of will, as she could, or the even better trick of holding it and using it as a power. I was always famished. But sometimes my belly wanted something more than ordinary food. It wanted a food like fire, like iron, or earth itself in fistfuls. People do sometimes crave things that don't make sense, they will eat clay and swallow swords for no earthly reason. But it could be they've learned food only *feeds* hunger. To kill it, you need something stronger.

Suddenly I noticed, and my mother noticed, how Henderson was looking at me now. He started to say something, but then he thought better of it. He took his leave and backed out, and Cee bolted the door with the new iron rod Boss had just added to replace the thumb bolt he said was too puny now, in these times.

We had a new key lock, too, that Boss had put together from parts collected off the locksmith's trash pile in Lumberton. Boss was the promise of the family, the one I put my hopes in. We were close, Boss and me, less than a year apart, alike in features and complexion — but he was slight for his age, and I felt motherly to him more than sisterly. I had decided I wouldn't give him up to the Lowries or the Home Guard. The Lowries would have to take me too if they took him, and the Guard would have to kill me. Boss was my darling, my little man. He didn't let me cuddle him anymore, but I could at least throw my arm around his shoulder and he would lean against me. He was who I loved most on earth.

Others loved him too — his blue-gray careful eyes, his slow deliberate talk, and his singing voice, second only to Henderson's. But Boss's own passion was for locks and clocks and springlatches, anything that had a mechanism of little parts. He could make gadgets work after other people had given up, using needles and a punchbelly file to fix the inner workings, those springs no bigger than a grain of rice and cogwheels smaller than a wedding ring. For our lock, he made a key from a spoon. He was an uncommonly directed boy. The pleasures young men often care for, drink and revelry, shooting and whoring or knocking women about, Boss showed no interest in. He never even wrestled Andrew — I did, and I was good at it.

But I don't mean Boss was scaredy or girlish. He only had his mind on other things, and his way was to watch and listen. Someday, he was going to be — well, I hesitate even now to say my plans for Boss. I had hopes for him so high that to tell them then would have made me sound crazy and still might. He was born for something more than ditching and chopping — and the future I dreamed up for him was work I'd never known anyone to aim for. I wanted him to be a poet. I wanted him to adventure out into the world and learn its ways, not losing himself in the jumble of life but seeing it with a poet's eye, and withdrawing later to a library room where he would write his poems of revelation. He would tell what he had seen. This was my big plan, one that today seems both a pipe dream and a prophecy. Boss never wrote a word in his life. But he did see.

★　★　★

Margaret Ransom, once I got to know her, had turned out to be the best friend I could have found for myself. She was three years older than me, high-hipped and long-legged, with the round Ransom face and freckles on her nose. She could read, and she ran her own household, minding four younger brothers after her parents died in the big yellow fever. We had the same dream of life, Margaret and me — of going to school, even if we were grown by the time one opened up, and raising our families in houses by each other. We made a plan to marry brothers if we got the chance, but I already thought of her as a sister, an older one whose life unfolded a step ahead of mine and showed me what might lie in store. To me Margaret proved that no matter how bad things got, a Scuffletown girl could take care of herself and make her own way. She kept biddies and sold the eggs in Lumberton, and she farmed two acres with the help of her neighbor Mr. George Lowrie and his sons. And she taught me to read. We pretended we had a school on her back step, and if I made it through a Bible page without mistake I could rise a level. Margaret was my idea of what a girl should be, and I didn't mind the prospect of following in her path all my days. But we had a falling out when I was sent to the McCabes.

I thought she'd be glad when I told her Miss McCabe had made Cee an offer to take me in and tutor me. But she felt cut. I begged her to come use my books and lessons when I was home on Sundays, and for a while she did, but I could see her drawing off from me.

'Mrs. McCabe said I have promise,' I tried to explain.

'You think I don't know that?'

'And all I need is schooling.'

'I don't call it schooling, going to Miss McCabe,' she said. 'I call it letting yourself get used for somebody's little toy. Like a doll baby for her to dress up, and change the way you talk. You'll end up like Donohue McQueen, a sorry wandering soul.'

'Me?'

'He got to thinking he was something, didn't he? Just because some McQueens adopted him away from his Scuffletown home. But come to find out they didn't want him for a real son, they put him out for wages ditching. And now look at him, hanging around trying to weasel back in. He's decided to be Indian again but he don't fit.'

'Margaret, you know I'm not like that.'

'And besides, your Miss McCabe didn't even go to school herself, so how can she be a teacher? A real teacher wouldn't make you scrub the kitchen.'

I had always trusted Margaret's judgment, she was quick to see what's what.

But I told her this time she was wrong.

'It's not Miss McCabe's fault Floral College got shut down by the war,' I said.

'Anyway, she didn't need it, her daddy's her professor.'

Dr. McCabe had taught his daughter reading and arithmetic to prepare her for the female academy, but then it closed before she could enroll so he just kept on teaching her at home. Maybe his program was a little lopsided — no spelling or music or literature — but he did cover the scientific laws, the history of Scotland, and all the bones of the body, and in secret she read the love stories and poems she liked so much. Anyway, what choice did I have? There was nowhere else I could get books. And I didn't mind Miss McCabe's moods because I recognized their cause. She was a lonely person — in her twenties, with a plain face, square pretty teeth, and brown hair she called muckledun, making some fun of herself. She wasn't as high and mighty as some thought, only impatient.

Yes, I was supposed to clean the kitchen. 'Nothing's free, you know, Margaret,' I said. 'I have to earn my keep. But it's not like I'm just her kitchen girl, I'm her *pupil*, and she promised we would be like . . . '

'Like what?'

'Well — friends. Not the same as me and you, but sort of.'

Margaret snickered. After that, she was

36

close-mouthed around me. She started skipping her Sunday visits, saying she had too much work to do. And then she dropped me flat. I saw her at Pate's store one afternoon and we visited a minute, but the last thing she said was by the way she wouldn't be coming around to my house anymore, she had fallen in love and didn't have time for 'a little thin old white girl and some fake schoolbooks.'

I was so surprised, I didn't have a ready answer, my mouth dropped open. 'I'm not the first Scotsman's daughter in Scuffletown,' I should have said. But she had turned her back on me, like I was nobody she ever saw before. And then she was gone. It must have been a great romance of passion she had fallen into, I thought — the kind that fills your life and makes you act hateful to your old acquaintances. She never even told me who she loved, she left me in the lurch. I started spending my Sundays with Clelon Barnes, who was a mute and couldn't speak a word, and Mr. Allen Lowrie, who was older than me by a whole half-century.

As it turned out, Miss McCabe and I became what she'd said: 'like friends.' But that is not the same as friends. And all that year I kept Margaret in my heart, planning how I could make up with her and prove I was still myself and she was still my ideal.

But by the time I was through with Miss McCabe and home for good, Margaret was gone. My brothers told me she had hired out, but from my mother's glare I guessed different. Most likely when Margaret showed up again she would be riding a baby on her hip.

She was so far past me I might never see her again, and it broke my heart to think of our bygone days together. But the worst was, I needed Margaret *now*. I needed to know what a girl was supposed to do when there was trouble like the trouble we had.

My mother said trouble wasn't new to Scuffletown. But for me it had started that winter, the day Mr. George Lowrie couldn't find his sons Wesley and Little Allen. He was worried sick because he'd already lost one boy, Jarman. Brant Harris had killed him — 'accidentally,' Harris claimed, which I guess was true since when he pulled the trigger he fully believed he was shooting Wesley. Harris bore Wes a grudge and wanted him out of the way, but most of the time he couldn't tell the Lowries one from another, and he said there were so many of them he didn't know or care who was who but the fewer the better.

So when Wes and Little Allen vanished, we prayed they were in the labor camp. And it turned out that's where they were, held with slaves almost three months until one day they escaped from the work gang and fled, slowly making their way home by sneaking north along the Cape Fear River and east through Big Swamp.

The day they got back, a thin snow covered the ground. My brother Boss was crossing the trestle bridge at the mill pond when he spotted them on the bank, but he couldn't be sure who it was until he climbed down and cleared their faces. They were handcuffed together, dusted white all over by the snow, their skulls cracked by a lightwood knot.

At the inquest Harris said he stopped them on a suspicion.

'I asked them weren't they supposed to be at Fisher, didn't I load them on the train myself? They couldn't show me no leave papers, so I placed them under arrest but they put up a fight and tried to kill me. Case of self-defense.'

And that was the end of it, the court said. There were no witnesses. No question raised about how could boys in handcuffs put up a fight. Harris got off scot-free.

Boss saved that knot, though, a long twist of greenheart, the part that's left after a fallen pine rots down to the bone, so fat with resin it will flame at the touch of a match. And on the night before the boys were buried, he nailed it to the bell house above the gable at New Hope, as a gnarled yellow steeple.

After the funeralizing, Mr. George was asked if he would like to speak. He shook his head, but then he changed his mind and was helped onto the little porch of the church. From there he faced into the late-afternoon sun and put a hand up to shade his eyes, looking out at the crowd of a hundred, which included a good many white and black faces as well as ours. The Lowrie family held a high position in the settlement, and even some of the macks would say, as if it was a big surprise, that Mr. George and Mr. Allen were 'true gentlemen.' But every single person there that day knew Mr. George's boys had been killed in cold blood, and that nothing would be done about it. Harris was too strong and too mean. He had something on everyone.

I was standing halfway back, but I could see Mr. George's wife, Ma Silla, up front with Mr. Allen Lowrie and his wife, Mary Cumbo — and Mr. Jack Oxendine, with his wife, Christianne Cumbo, Henderson's mama and daddy — and then a bunch more Lowrie and Oxendine cousins, and the rest of Scuffletown. Behind us stood the macks, including Preacher Sinclair, who had been a Rebel colonel before losing New Bern to the Yankees (some said on purpose, as he was Ohio-born, torn between abolition on the one hand and his McQueen wife and her rich daddy on the other). Postmaster Barnes had showed up too, claiming he was a friend to his Indian neighbors but his hands were tied when it came to the labor conscription board, even though he was the head of it. His brother, Clelon, had drifted back to where the black people were. He sat on the ground with the Bethea children and cooed while they climbed all over him. Ben Bethea had just bought his freedom from Dr. McCabe and was farming a plot of Mr. Allen's land for the rent of one peppercorn a year until he could get his stake and buy it outright. He had his wife with him plus old Free Tab, the asylum cook, and her husband Free Jack. And behind everyone lurked Donohue McQueen like a gimp dog outside the pack.

Mr. George, grown frail overnight, stood there in silence, craning his neck and searching our faces. I thought grief had snapped his mind and he was looking for his boys. The wind blew his hat out of his hands, and Cee went to ask if he wanted help to sit back down but he waved her away and kept on casting his eyes one way and then another, as if he didn't quite recognize anyone in the whole crowd.

'Neighbors,' he said at last, in the humble-sounding voice of a man made both wise and doubtful by a long life in a rough time.

But nothing followed that one word. It hung alone in the winter air for a minute, until his eyes fell on someone standing right in front of him, almost in his reach. I knew who it was by his hair, long and black with a reddish tinge like mine. Boss.

He was a boy that old people always liked. He paid attention, and everything he saw or heard he took to heart. Mr. George fastened on him, and talked like they were alone together.

'My daddy Bill had a bad left hand,' he said.

Some of the crowd started to shift on their feet and glance at one another. The sun dropped behind the pines at our backs, and a shadow inched toward the church.

'Well, it never could do much. Couldn't make a fist or even hold a cane pole.' Frowning down at his own hand, Mr. George traced a line from the middle of the palm around the base of the thumb and over to the back.

'Looked like someone tried to slice his thumb off!' he said, and raised his hand up toward Boss as if the scar were there to see. 'And I guess they aimed for more than that. The weapon was a saber sword. You know where Gilchrist's Bridge is?'

'Yes, sir.'

'Bill was there with Colonel Robeson when they met the Tories, and he got his scar in the fight. He carried it with pride the rest of his life. We children, Allen and Patty and me, we used to touch it and holler. You know what I mean, tease him, run away like we were scared. We were just little ones, fooling with the old man. But we understood it was a scar of America. Our daddy was a hero in the service of his country, even though he was no older at that time than you are now. He was a Patriot. He was a Revolution soldier. And we knew that, see, because he bore the mark.'

Boss nodded.

Mr. George went on. 'One thing that always puzzled me was, it wasn't an English who sliced him. It was James McPherson, who lived right there at Laurel Hill. His own neighbor! Because there weren't no English a-tall in that fight. We were neighbor against neighbor. But McPherson was on the side of the crown, and Bill Lowrie stood up for America.

'You know what else too? In his lifetime he voted for four presidents. He was a settlement

Indian man, but yes, he voted. His brothers voted, his nephews voted, and so did I and my brothers. But that was so far back — my one election day — I can't even tell you who were the men that got my vote. But I know they were the party of freedom. That is the side I have always favored.

'And Daddy told me, we used to love the English. Right from the start we took them in, the bad with the good, learned their language and their church. There was children born of the love between us. We fought for the English king against the Cherokee and the French and the Tuscarora — we stuck with that king a hundred years or more I was told. But when the time came, we fought to cut loose from him. Made the choice to be Americans and never changed our minds. That's what I want you to remember. Our choice was liberty. We stayed to live where we belonged. Nobody ever run us out, and we gave a home to many that was run out from somewhere else. But now, here are our young men, fine ones like you, carried off in the middle of the night, whipped if they make somebody mad, killed if they take a stand. Worse off than slaves, in a land where we were always free!

'I decided I would name my boys for the good-heartedest men I could think of. Allen my brother, Wesley the hymn writer, and a stranger named Jarman who rode me in his cart down the turpentine trail to Georgia when I was a young man in need of work, and he shared his meals with me. I picked names of charity, you see, not fighters, because I wished my boys to lead a peaceful, upright life — and they did do that. Never saw the inside of a jail. By the young people being good citizens, I always said, they might could get the vote back for us. And I told them what my daddy told me. Hang on, work hard, a better day will come, which at that time I believed to be true.

'But a worse day came, this one you and me are standing in now and my boys aren't. And they were just as good as you, so why? I grieve them, oh I do grieve them. But I'll say this, I rather they — or anyway I thought I would . . . '

He trailed off, gazing.

'Well, I was working up to a big oration here, to tell you a grand announcement. I was going to declare I rather have my own sons dead than in slavery. But now the moment is upon me, and I can't honestly say it. I was a too-loving father. They were the children of my white-haired years, the onliest ones I had left at home. You will find out yourself someday, how your sweet favorites may die but the love part has a life of its own. You can't knock it down, it keeps on rolling like a cart wheel flung off, and the fact is — the fact is — I rather have them back no matter what. Free or not free. I rather have them in my arms again.'

Everybody was still and quiet. In the high cold sky a single cloud turned red, catching the flame of a sun we couldn't see. Clelon put two little Betheas inside his coat. I noticed four young men had come out of the woods to stand near the church: one was Henderson Oxendine, but the others kept their collars up against the cold, and I couldn't see who they were for sure. But I guessed Calvin Oxendine and Steve Lowrie — and maybe Henry Lowrie, that everybody said was Mr. Allen's smartest son.

Or maybe I just hoped it was Henry. This was before he had disappeared. I couldn't make out his face, but having watched him many a time from a distance (from the woods while he plowed, from a crowd while he fiddled for juba dancers), I thought I recognized his shape and bearing. He stood tall and loose-limbed and watchful. Somebody near me whispered it was him, and heads turned. Donohue McQueen sidled over to get a better look.

I wanted a better look too, and I was

edging forward row by row when a hand reached out and snagged me and held me still.

'Settle down,' my mother whispered.

Mr. George leaned closer to Boss as if telling a confidence, but his voice hissed and his eyes bore down on Boss.

'And you know what? I call their names out loud. In the middle of the night in a empty room. I talk to them, each one, I say, 'Honey, I'm so sorry I didn't keep you from harm and I'm sorry I can't do nothing for you now, in your memory.' But they don't answer me back, they don't give me a sign. They don't forgive me. Because I can't do what I ought to do for them, because I got no fight left in me.'

He took a breath and straightened up. 'And that's all I can tell you. The truth is my mind is scattering and I can't pull words together like I want to. I guess I am nearly dead myself from this, very feebled, and it will only be a short while till I will slide off. So young man — I'll shake your hand goodbye now. You look like one who'll know what I've been trying to say. I'll leave it at that. I'll leave it with you, son.'

He reached down to Boss, but when Boss reached back, Mr. George grabbed his hand and opened it up. Before he was baptized Mr.

George had been a cup reader and a palmist, but if he read anything now of Boss's future, his face didn't show it. He looked for a long time, but all he said was 'All right then.' He clapped both his hands around Boss's and squeezed hard, stepped down off the porch, picked up his hat from where it lay in the frozen stubble, and started down the road home with his brother Allen at his side, the wives following at a little distance.

I took one quick look toward the woods, but the ones who had been standing there were gone.

Boss claimed he'd seen Henry among them.

'It wasn't him,' Cee said. 'Everybody just hoped it was, and a rumor got started.'

'But I saw him,' Boss said.

'Hope bad enough and you'll see what you want to see,' she said, but I couldn't tell if that was a warning or a promise.

A mack lawyer, Hamilton Macmillan, wrote down what Mr. George said that day, but I never saw it printed until years after. People who were there to hear it recalled it later in different ways. But we did remember it. We thought of it every time someone else's boys disappeared, and again when we heard that the dead boys' cousins began gathering themselves, and gathering guns, to prevent the disappearance of more.

But by summer's end, another dozen were in chains at Fort Fisher, set to an endless task. That fort, already the South's biggest, was not meant to reach a completion. As long as there was still dirt available and men to shovel it, the earthworks would keep spreading, broader and longer every day. And those who'd seen it said Fisher would never fall. At Charleston, Sumter crumbled to the ground in a shower of ten million bricks, but Fisher *was* the ground. It could not fall. It lay hunkered and solid as ancient hills.

★   ★   ★

Brant Harris and the Home Guard were not the only danger we needed a key lock against. It was a lawless, savage time, the war in its fourth year. I wondered how the Confederate Army could be holding up, if so many of its men had bolted and turned to independent roguery. There were of course Union robbers too, and sometimes a bunch from each side ganged up together to maraud their way across the state. For this career the armies both North and South had provided either direct training or a fine example. But mostly it was the mack towns and farms that suffered from traveling raiders. We were off the beaten path, and not worth robbing more than once anyhow. Our big threat came from closer to home, from people who knew us all their lives, whose forefathers knew our forefathers, back longer than anyone could say.

And it was not our goods they wanted, it was a chance to make us a donation of their own goods. Every time we came home from somewhere, we looked to see if they'd left us a gift, a suit of clothes or a pair of shoes, a valuable article of gold with their own initials upon it, a branded mule or earmarked pig. If you found something like that, you knew the law would soon arrive, and a search would be made, followed by a larceny charge, a lashing, a fine, and if you couldn't pay, a levy against your land, or if you had no land, then an auction of the only thing you did have — yourself. You would go bound to whoever would pay your fine in return for the shortest time of service. But ever since that had happened to Henderson's grandfather, old Mr. Charles Oxendine, we knew to be careful, to outfox them. Many a watch and fancy-knobbed cane had been thrown into the Lumbee River, rolling loose along the sandy bottom until it lodged on a snag, or maybe, as I liked to dream, carried along in the fast black current east to Lumberton where the river turns south, then down to join the wide gray Pee Dee, scudding across the flats, past bluffs and rice fields through the marshes of Georgetown to the white coastal lip and the great Atlantic. We fed their trinkets to the sea. Of course, when we could, we hid and kept some.

'They might know us but they don't *know* us,' Cee told me. 'Even ones that should, by now, don't have no more notion of us than of so many yard birds. Everything they think we are, we aren't. That's how we stay one step ahead.'

* * *

After she shot the bolt behind Henderson and darkness descended, we children and Daddy waited to hear what she would say, what she was thinking. Maybe she lacked book knowledge but, as I believe even the highest-learned men will admit, books are not the final word. She found her knowledge in other places. Yet sometimes she kept what she knew to herself.

'Well?' I said.

'Well what?'

'You're figuring something.'

'The only thing I'm figuring is, Henderson Oxendine wouldn't make a half-bad husband.'

Daddy looked up startled, and she said, 'Not for me! I got mine, don't I?'

This game of husband-hunting on my account was her new great delight, but I couldn't understand why. She never had told me the secrets of love, and I got my information on the sly from her friend Nelly, who told me a good deal more than I wanted to know. Yet all of a sudden Cee was saying things that made me blush. It wasn't like her. And the names she recommended could not have been her real choices for me. My guess was that the whole idea of my future with men made her uneasy, and Daddy even more so. They were torn, unsure which prospect was worse — that I might never find a husband, or that I might find one too easy too soon. Her jokes were meant to keep my mind on the subject, but at the same time make sure the subject was somewhat unpleasant.

About Henderson, for instance, I knew she wasn't serious. The story on Henderson was a case of mumps had made it doubtful he would ever father any children. Dr. McCabe, who told Cee the diagnosis and its likely outcome, didn't think this was such a tragedy.

'You people don't seem to understand that a passel of children guarantees a life of poverty,' he said.

'Doctor, if you already have that life, then

children are your only riches,' she said. 'And a man who can't make them is useless as a stump.' So I knew she couldn't really think of Henderson as a prize.

What puzzled me was how the mumps could have such an effect, unless the male anatomy was more outlandish than I already knew it to be.

My brothers hid themselves from me but there were some pictures, ink drawings, in a medical book belonging to Dr. McCabe, which when I saw them at the age of twelve caused me to bust out laughing. But I do admit I went back to the pictures for another few peeks when I had the opportunity. Later when I saw the real thing, it would turn out to be more appealing and less comical than the pictures — but still surprising. Always surprising. One of God's odder successes.

Cee didn't panic at Henderson's warning, but she pulled the stool into the middle of the room, where the most light fell, and sat Daddy on it to work at his Yankee passion, whittling. She gave the boys the look we called her evil eye, and without anything being said we knew we were going to be holed up a long time. It might be weeks or even months before we could again move freely in our own yard and field or visit with other folks — Cee out among the shut-in or gone to Hestertown to sit and smoke with Nelly, Andrew off to see the beautiful Flora Sampson, Boss hanging around at Mr. Allen's, and me reading stories to Clelon Barnes on his bench swing. We couldn't even sit out at night on our own porch. We were stuck in the hot dark with each other.

Ours was a small house. It was not like Dr. McCabe's, which was built for inside living at all hours of the day, with an airy parlor, a tall library, three sunny bedrooms and big dormer windows, a gentleman's study, even a dressing room for Miss McCabe's wardrobe. The weekdays when I used to live there, my little budget of clothes looked pitiful and meager folded on the shelf. I felt meager myself in the McCabe house, flimsy and off my balance, whereas in our house I felt well-figured and steady. And though I had some regrets when I left the McCabes, I was happy to be finally settled at home again and not going back and forth anymore. Our one-room house served us fine most of the time because we spent our daylight hours outside. At night sleeping, all we needed was a roof against the rain and a door to bolt. No real windows, because Cee said we're only inside at night and what good is a window then? Just one more thing to lock up.

But with all of us in there on a burning

day, we could have used a window. The air was heavy with the smoky smell of wet ashes from last night's rain still dripping down the chimney and the smell of mildew on our shoes. Daddy was hunched on the stool with his knees together and his head down over a new pipe bowl, wood curls like feathers flying from his knife to the floor without a sound, and the boys sat against the wall dozing or just staring with the blank patience of penned dogs. Andrew now and then groaned and tried to pick a fight with me, but I just read, or tried to. I had to light a candle to see the printing. The book was one of a dozen Amanda McCabe had given me, *The Bride Betrayed*, a tale as foolish as the writer's name, Emma Dorothy Eliza Nevitte Southworth, and I couldn't work up any sympathy for the love-struck heroine and all her troubles. But Miss McCabe was a great fan of novels. She was writing one herself, although she hid it from her father and showed him only the daily journal he had her to keep, in which she recorded the weather conditions as a scientific exercise. I hoped her novel would not be so stupid as *The Bride Betrayed*, which eventually fell closed in my lap.

The room was so quiet I could hear the tick of Daddy's watch on its nail by the door. The heat started to pack my lungs and that's when I lay down to recover by the cat hole, where I soon filled up with thinking. I was a sprawly girl, I liked stretching myself out against anything low and solid, the floor or the oldfield meadow or the sandbank that curves in the river's elbow. I could sometimes be found laid out like a corpse in my own backyard, except I'd be face down, hugging the world. I got my best thoughts that way, pulling them up from somewhere deep. Often the subject that rose to me was the one that haunts young girls — untimely death.

So as I lay there, in the ticking heat with danger lurking and my still self flat, I planned my funeral. I would have Boss and Henderson to sing. I would have Mr. Jesse Oxendine, the coffinmaker, build a special box cross-shaped with room for outstretched arms, and I'd go in face-down. Who wants to spend eternity empty-armed when you can have the world in your embrace? One time, I found in an old Wilmington paper the account of a sea captain's young daughter killed by fever in the middle of a voyage. Why a father would take a child onto the high seas anyway, I couldn't understand. But when she died, then he got concerned with her well-being. Reluctant to toss her overboard for crabs and fishes, he tied her in a little straight-back chair and lowered her into a barrel of brandy in the hold. Two months later back in Wilmington he buried her in the Presbyterian churchyard still brandied and barreled. What was the captain thinking? I'm sure he loved his girl — gave her a stone that said 'Our Nance' — but I was horrified by that cruel form of burial. Sitting stiff in a chair more than five minutes was torture for me, and there's poor Nance pickled upright forever.

'Are you breathing now?' Cee said.

'Better.'

'While you're at it, listen out.'

Listening was a Scuffletown talent, down to the dogs. It was how we stayed alert and how we got our news — even the war news, which we overheard on the streets of Lumberton or got word of from the ones of us who went out, the turkey drivers or the turpentine choppers or others who had secret errands far afield. Our best source was Nelly Gibson, who relayed to us what she heard in her two lines of business, both services provided to the military: message delivery and female companionship. Each enterprise fed the other, making her the best-informed woman in North Carolina. Nelly crossed back and forth both ways between the army lines; she had no loyalties except to Hestertown, her adopted home. Later the newspapers would stupidly call her the 'Hestertown Wh-re,' but they never learned her name.

It won't matter if I tell it now. Nelly walked a thin line but she walked it artfully. She might deliver a basket of eggs to a certain officer at an appointed time and place; she would lift out the one he wanted, the one with a little hole at each end, and when he cracked the shell he would find no yolk inside, but tiny rolls of paper. 'Never sew dispatches in your petticoats,' she told me once while I was helping her punch and blow a dozen shells. 'Pickets and guards like nothing better than a chance to inspect petticoats.'

But after she sold those costly eggs, she might also sell her company, which was worth more than her information. Nelly was a cure for soldier's pain. Men of quality — and there were some, in both those armies — paid her to linger and share a fowl and a bottle of wine while they unburdened themselves of stories they could not tell in letters home. Many a soldier would be restored by that alone, the act of telling; and if more was called for, a bit of horizontal refreshment, the decision was hers. With one glance she could tell which men were to be avoided as dangerous, and she knew how to distract them and make an exit. She was halfway in age between me and Cee, with a face and figure that turned men into mealmush. Sometimes a beauty like that is safer than an ordinary-looking woman. Nelly Gibson could please men or unman them as she chose.

She never stayed on the road more than a few weeks at a haul, but came home to see her money and food gobbled by her neighbors, which gave her a great satisfaction because of her own origins. In childhood she had been a Christmas traveler, one whose family when they ran out of corn about the middle of December had to put their children on the road and hope someone would be moved by pity or a need for servants to take them in before they starved. Old Lovedy Goins was the one who found Nelly on the Whiteville Road and took her home to raise, which explains why Nelly was the only person I ever heard of who lived in Hestertown by choice and loved it. She was dark, but she didn't call herself Indian because she didn't even know where she came from. Dr. McCabe said she could have some Portugee or Turk in her, judging by her thin nose and love of silver bracelets, and some African by her hair; or maybe she came from Gypsy stock, he said, through the isle of Barbados to Charleston, or from pirates who ruled the coast and then snuck inland to retire. But Nelly laughed and said she wasn't anything but Hestertown, which covered all the possibilities.

★ ★ ★

For a while I fell asleep, until I felt the cat's cool wet nose touch mine and I had to shift to let him in. Girl wanted to follow, and didn't understand how the cat could slip his whole self through that little hole at the bottom of the door when she could only put in a paw and tap it around like a blind man's stick. I caught the paw and held it for a joke, tickling the hard gray pads under her toes, but she pulled away mad and trotted off, nosing the air. Then when I tried to love up the cat, he scratched and twisted out of my hands and scooted back out the hole, mad too. So that was it for animal sympathy. They cared less for me than for the business they had with rats and moles out there.

We ate the potatoes early, at three o'clock. The others ate more out of boredom than hunger, but I carried mine into a corner like Girl with a bone, chewed out the inside and sucked the skin to get all I could of that faint almost-pine taste that I liked so much.

By four o'clock even Cee was crazy for air and light, and she let us open the door for a minute as long as Andrew and Boss promised to hang back, out of sight of anyone who might be watching from the line of woods across the field. I stood in the doorway and drank in the color. Starved for it, my eye saw more than it might have on a normal day. And every separate shade was washed in green, green held it all together. Even the yellowing corn, even the brown tree trunks and the blue sky partook; and the rangy vines of summer sent runners out like feelers, looking for something new to swallow into greenery.

'Nowhere's prettier than Scuffletown, I say,' I said.

'Being a world traveler,' said Andrew.

'That's enough now,' Cee said.

I felt squashed dumb. It was true, my travels were limited to Shoe Heel and Lumberton and points between them on the railroad track, except for a trip to the seashore with one of the Scuffletown caravans that went every summer to bring home barrels of salted mullet. Of the more distant world all I'd seen was Rome and Egypt, in pictures hung in gilt frames over the sofa in Dr. McCabe's library. Yet it seemed impossible that any place on earth could improve on the beauty I saw before me from our door, and privately I stuck to my pronouncement. The ocean at first sight would make anyone gasp in wonder, but suppose you had to look at it every day? You would start to feel little. You'd start to think the world was gray and vacant, nothing on your horizon. As for those grand engraved civilizations, they were fairly well wrecked it appeared to me, their monuments all busted and lying about like trash. In the whole city of Rome I saw no trees, and in Egypt only a single dismal palm amidst the desert sands. Whereas we were green, we were budding. I said to myself the war had been like a dry spell, the kind that might hold back a vineyard for a while but secretly strengthens the root and sends it to a deeper source, teaching self-reliance, efficiency, endurance for the next time. The season was upon us, I wanted to believe, when we would shoot forth and leaf out and spread with a vitality no one had suspected we had. We would be the new civilization.

Cee put her hands on my shoulders and turned me around and marched me back inside. I thought of dungeon prisoners and how they pass the time by chalking a tally of days on the wall or reciting whole books from memory, but I'd been in for only half one day and couldn't think well enough to recall more than a few snatches of all that poetry I'd read for Miss McCabe about lassies and mousies and the sad battle of Culloden. I gave it a try and came up with *Fare thee well my only love and fare thee well awhile, and I will come again my love though it were ten thousand mile.* Which wasn't much to show for a whole year of reading. What good could my education be if it didn't return to me in an hour of need, or if the part that did come back was only a scrap of Scottish heartbreak?

To take our minds off the Guard, Cee made a show of going about her work as if nothing was wrong. She busied herself with a task she hated, removing candles from the mold. One after another the tapers broke, and she just put them back in without a word of complaint. Ordinarily she would have cursed the army to high heaven for taking the county's good beeswax and leaving us to make do with pine-tar tallow, but this time she let the army off. Instead she made jokes about me, eye glinting, mouth grim.

'It's starting, Daddy,' she said. 'We got a marriageable girl on our hands.'

He blinked and frowned. 'You don't think Henderson came for *that*.'

'They'll use any excuse.'

'My dear, those boys have their minds on surviving. A man can't save his hide and go courting at the same time.'

'You got a right short memory, Johnny.'

'This is different. Rhoda's not even growed up.'

I said, 'I guess I have a say in this. And I'm not looking for any man.'

'That's right,' Daddy said.

'It don't matter if you're looking or not, you're in for it,' Cee said. 'Sure as shooting, we're going to see boys coming around like randy hounds. I just want to be ready for the whole slew of them, so I can start narrowing down.'

'Ma, you don't have to pick me out a husband! Since I'm the one that will have to live a lifetime with him, I believe I'll be the one that picks if you don't mind. When the time comes.'

'Listen to that, Daddy. You watch, she'll fall for the first thing in britches.'

But this was the kind of thing she would not have said if she had meant it. It was all for reassurance, to comfort us with needling, as if all was well.

When it didn't work and we were still looking glum, she offered up some comforting news from Nelly. We'd heard it before, but it sounded good every time: the war was about done, a new day would dawn. Nelly was predicting a Union victory, based on inside information she had from soldiers. Life would go back to cropping, working, house-building, marrying. We would get coffee again instead of making it from parched corn or sweet potatoes. We would get sugar and lemons and milk and peaches — we'd 'cook up,' as Cee said, which meant spend all day fixing stewed chicken and pastry noodles, chopped collards, light bread. And creamed corn. Scuppernong pie. Salt mullet, pen-raised goose stuffed with onions. Ham . . . bacon . . . fatback, hocks, trotters, ribs, hogshead cheese, chitlins, sausage . . . oh, we would *eat* when the war ended, because turpentining would come back stronger than ever, it had only just hit its stride before the war, and once it picked up again it would transform the county, the whole state, beyond anyone's expectations. The great pine barrens and their endless supply of trees would be North Carolina's future. And ours too, as soon as Mr. Lincoln won his war, Cee said.

★   ★   ★

That night I dreamed Margaret lay with the lover who had spirited her away.

And while we slept, Henderson walked his circuit from house to house till all the settlement families from Back Swamp to Hogtown were notified and their boys accounted for. He made his way then to the lie-outers' camp in Devilsden, past midnight, where he found them already crept into the blinds for the night after their own rounds in other parts of the settlement. Henderson lay down in the open on a bed of fence rails with a saddle box for a pillow, and didn't sleep.

Thirty feet away, Donohue McQueen watched from the canebrake, his arms and face blacked with grease and soot, thinking if he could learn the Lowries' secret ways and signals, he might prove his worth and get in good with them.

Flora Sampson waited awake awhile hoping for Andrew's whistle under the eaves. Betsy Oxendine half dreaming reached out for Applewhite, but he had gone to the swamps, and the shoulder her hand touched belonged to her mother, Christianne, who let it stay. In the oldest bed in Scuffletown, built of ashwood by the ferryman James Lowrie a hundred years earlier, Allen Lowrie and his wife, Mary Cumbo, locked and pumped with an energy that surprised them both and surely would have produced — if Mary had not been a decade past the capability — an eleventh son.

James Barnes, the postmaster, quieted his moaning half-wit brother.

Dr. McCabe sat bolt upright in bed, waked

by the idea of an ice pack to cool the brains of women in difficult labor and thus clear the primitive channels of animal energy necessary in childbirth. He rose in his nightshirt and made a quick sketch and a note to himself: *Send, N.C. Journal of Medicine, call it McCabe's Cap.*

Raccoons pellmelled into the fields of the county under starlight and pulled down cornstalks. Rats scuttled in single file along the furrows.

The distant war continued.

Brant Harris, by now drunk to rage, nevertheless managed to stumble a mile to the postmaster's house, where he roused Barnes from bed and explained how unless he got good information leading to some Lowries he was going to have to send other men to Wilmington and the work there was such that didn't require brains, even somebody's afflicted brother could dig dirt.

And in a stand of McRaney timber, a swarm of summer pine beetles settled into one tree weakened by years of turpentiners' wounds, and started tunneling down the trunk, laying their eggs and chewing so hard a man passing by could have heard it, but no man did, and the only sign of the beetles — their calling card, a guarantee the tree would die inside a week before McRaney or

any of his crew had noticed, before they could
cut the infested tree and all around it to stop
the swarm — was a pitch tube on the bark,
high on the dark side of the trunk like popped
corn in a white cluster, the shape of a baby's
hand.

2

In the early hours while the rest were still asleep, I dressed and stole out for a look at the sky. It was just starting to lighten in the east, but ahead of the sunrise came the thinnest moon I ever saw, nothing but a silver hair. By the time I walked down to the end of the field it was invisible, lost in the light of day. I hoped Miss McCabe had recorded it in her weather journal.

But she had lost her enthusiasm for meteorology. On Fridays she would meet her father as usual, hand over the little red book, and stand there waiting. She knew he would say the same thing he'd said the week before. 'Coming along, Amanda! Coming along.' And then his thoughts would spin away to something else, and he would go back to his study, leaving her standing in the middle of the room. I thought he was wrong not to give her more encouragement, but it wasn't my place to tell her so. All I could say was that I myself admired her power of description.

'It's a waste of time,' she said, in a voice of scorn to hide her distress. 'If I were a farmer it might make sense to watch the skies. As I'm not, what use can it be? What does it add up to?' And she would throw herself onto the sofa with a Mrs. Southworth novel, which struck me as a greater waste of time.

She was too impatient. She expected she could scribble her daily observations and by the end of the week they would build to a conclusion. But a weather journal isn't like a storekeeper's ledger of accounts or a stiller's taskbook of so many barrels per man per month. It's more like a history, and history won't tally like a column of figures. Sometimes years might have to pass — or decades and centuries — before it adds up to something.

This day broke clear but slowly hazed until the sky at noon was white. By tea it cleared.

Five oclock pm. Thunderheads at the bottom of the sky. Showers thin as a mist, the sun still broadly shinning, but I see no arc.

A most Violent Gale in the dead of night. Lightening 127 strokes, forkt and double-forkt so frequent the yard below is lit as if by day.

One hour til dawn. The storm is passing over.

There might be no sum in those short notes, but I thought of them as bits of the atmosphere collected for storage. Her spelling was bad, but I agreed with her father that the spelling isn't important as long as the meaning comes across. And in time I was sure her journal would accumulate a meaning, or a hint of a meaning, or even the illusion of a meaning, which is not as worthless as it sounds. When I leafed through the pages, I thought I saw something already starting to add up. A grace and cleanliness beyond our reach, a purified level . . . and some of those phrases stuck in my memory better than poetry lines.

At five o'clock in that same parlor Miss McCabe would read over my written exercises. I remember the first time I managed to produce an essay of any length, three pages on the topic she had assigned, 'Loyalty, Our Duty.' I was proud of my great accomplishment, and I watched her face as she read my description of Margaret Ransom and the broken ties of friendship I hoped someday to mend. To my surprise I saw tears in her eyes.

'Coming along,' she said, handing the pages back to me.

So her tears weren't due to the moving sentiments I had expressed, but came from anger, loneliness, and longing. And I couldn't help her.

No young men ever came to call on her, and no young women either, no cousins or friends or neighbors. A pair of aunts from Shoe Heel came twice, urging her to move into their house for safety at least until the war was over. But the first visit consisted mainly of hands fluttering and eyebrows arching. Where were the servants? The doctor had sold Ben Bethea his freedom, and the aunts said one would think the ingrate darky might at least come weed the kitchen garden once in a while. And how thick with dust the curtains were!

'Have the girl take them down and beat them,' they said, but she never asked me to.

On their second visit, when they saw that conditions had not improved, they left in a huff; and a week later they wrote a letter to the doctor. When Clelon brought it, the doctor was napping, so Miss McCabe opened it and read it to Clelon and me.

It was the doctor's own business, the letter said, if he chose to live surrounded by swamp and Scuffletown and Union sympathizers and who knows what other horrors, but it was a crime to keep a young lady out there virtually a prisoner when she had been invited to refugee among cultivated Presbyterians. The dining-room chairs were disappearing, they had noticed. Was he burning them in the fireplace? (He was not; she was.) And where was the ball-and-talon table, the oval gilt mirror, the walnut armoire? (Burnt too, in the dead of winter, or sold to buy food; the doctor never missed them.)

''May we remind you, sir,'' Miss McCabe read dramatically, ''those items were the cherished possessions of our sister, who was taken by *you* to live in that hellish swamp where fever wrecked her health, just as we warned. The least you can do to atone for her death is to send her furniture to Shoe Heel for safekeeping before it is ruined, and her daughter.''

Miss McCabe laughed. 'It's curious that a place can be considered hell by some and paradise by others,' she said, tossing the letter into the fire. 'But you and I are birds of a feather, Rhoda.'

Right away she realized it was an odd thing to say.

'I mean, we both love it here,' she said. 'Living so far from civilization.'

'Yes, that's true,' I said, which was half a lie. I loved it, but I did not call it far from civilization.

'And,' she said, 'we share a taste in heroes. A love for the dashing daredevil.'

'Me? I never said that.'

'Oh, you have though, in your stories. Here for instance, this Silas you've invented, this racehorse rider. Quite a romantic figure. But I doubt any man could accomplish the feats you've made up for him. You should give him a few shortcomings. And the ending is overdone, too melodramatic.'

I didn't tell her that what I'd written was a true story well known in the settlement: how Silas Lowrie in 1780 tracked Colonel Cade's stolen Arabian, Whirligig, fifty miles down into South Carolina, re-stole him from a gang of Tory horse thieves, swam him back across the dangerous Pee Dee River and rode him home in time to win the Sunday race at the colonel's track near Ashpole. As a reward the colonel moved Lowrie and his family into the plantation house while the Cades fled to somewhere safer. But when the Tories came again to Ashpole, they remembered Lowrie, and they cut his head off and burned the Cade house to the ground.

How could Miss McCabe not know the Whirligig story? In the settlement it was told as an example of courage, to show how a Lowrie had saved the day. We children knew it by heart, and none of us missed its second lesson, either, of what had befallen one who dared to save the day.

'Some parts are convincing,' s̶
colonel certainly might have had
horses and a track, and I've hear
races at Ashpole back then. Fat
Tories were perfectly horrid, and ͏ͬ ͟
around stealing horses and burning down all
sorts of things. That's why he won't live in
Shoe Heel, too many Tories — of course you
can't really call them that anymore, can you,
but people around here don't easily forget old
battles. Father's people were staunch Patriots,
and so were the Cades.'

'So were the Lowries,' I said.

'Well . . . but your figure of the trainer and
his fantastic capabilities and his horrible fate
— you see, it just doesn't have the ring of
truth. You've made the hero too good and the
ending too bad. Also I'm sure a Cade would
never have entrusted his plantation house to a
Scuffletown man even if they were on the
same side. I speak frankly, Rhoda, because
you and I know each other well enough by
now. Don't you agree?'

I nodded. But she trusted her house to me,
the times the doctor was called away
overnight and she had to go with him to
make sure he got to the right place and then
found his way back home all in one piece.

And I believed the story of Whirligig to be
true.

ith full daybreak and the thin moon gone, I should have headed home but instead I turned toward the woods. I couldn't help it.

Ahead of me on the path, Girl crisscrossed, scouting. She led me down through the cane and briars toward the river's dark cool smell, and when we came to the bank she sailed straight out, ears fanned and feet splayed, to hit the stream paddling — the water-lovingest dog in the world. As long as her head was up she saw where I was on the bank, and generally stayed alongside me; but her great pleasure was to swim like an otter, beneath the surface. When she went under, she was carried along, and popped up a little farther downstream every time, beads of the river caught in her eyelashes, nose snatching puffs of air.

I followed on the trail, soft with black moldy leaves that made no sound at all under my shoes. Our bank was low, but across on the north side there was a low bluff holding in the river breeze. As a result, there were fewer mosquitoes on our side. Also I knew that if your mind is calm and your skin stays cool — 'If your conscience is clear,' Mr. Allen Lowrie said — mosquitoes will not find you. So I splashed my arms and face, and let my thoughts subside. On my conscience there must have been nothing of great importance, for the bugs let me alone.

We passed Three Brides Bridge and Wiregrass Landing and the path to the depot. Masked birds as small as moon moths flew back and forth across the water, and although in an open field their song was so soft you might not even notice it, down in the hollow of the river each note went ringing out. The river itself was running fast, and wild with bits of light. Bright dabbles bounced off the water onto the briar leaves that were dark and leathery and big as plates, and up to the higher leaves overhead — oak paw and gum star and cypress fringe — and down along the thick ropes of wild grape hanging back to the ground they started from. Everything flickered and brindled. Along the muddier parts of the bank where willows grew, their boughs trailed slender shoots like fishing lines into the narrow river as it rolled, past breakthroughs and over the sandbanks barely visible now, just a peculiar orange streak aglow under the tea-colored water wherever the river took a turn; and pretty soon we were all the way to Mr. Allen's.

The old mossy flatboat was tied up where it usually was, but I didn't see anyone moving about. From the landing, the Lowrie place stretched smooth as a blanket, every stump removed, an ash-colored field on one side already cleared of corn, plowed and ditched and cross-ditched for a crop of wheat, and a green fallow field on the other side, grazed short by four fat sheep in a circle of lounging dogs, who knew me and Girl and didn't even bother to raise their heads at us. The well had a newly shingled cap, the yellowish pink of new-sawn pine not yet weathered. The vineyard was spread with a fishnet to keep off birds. Everything was neat and spruce, including the cabin, which had been so improved and expanded by a century of Lowrie carpenters that you wouldn't call it a cabin anymore. Three rooms had been added, logs weatherboarded outside, and a scroll-work trimming ran along the eaves. The old stick-and-clay chimney like ours had been replaced by a sharp-cornered red brick one built by Applewhite. The whole place looked like a picture.

I loved pictures. When the *Illustrated News* came to Miss McCabe each month I pored over the sketches of ladies' gowns and hunting parties and battle scenes. At the same time I knew art is never true to life. Mr. Currier would have rearranged the Lowrie house to a more regular design and painted it white, put in some rosebushes and a horse-and-buggy and a lady in a hat, and labeled it 'Country Pleasures.' In other words, he would have missed its meaning.

Of all the houses in the county, including Dr. McCabe's and the even grander plantation mansions like McNair's and Mackenzie's, this was the one I liked most, partly for its looks but mainly because of who had built it, and how long it had stood, and who had lived in it. Allen Lowrie's sons were the settlement's pride, from Patrick, the oldest, who was now a Methodist preacher near Red Banks, down to Henry, at nineteen the youngest but the one they all looked up to. A family like that was what I wanted.

I loved my own family, but when my thoughts ran to the future — to the ideal — it was Mr. Allen's I thought of for a model. This family hadn't happened by accident, it had been *generated*. Some of its history I could half claim for my own, as I was an offshoot — but Mr. Allen's was the line with the name, the line of sons. It went all the way back to the scarred hero of Gilchrist's Bridge and the racehorse trainer and the musical ferryman. But the Lowrie family had more than a history. It had prospects — stretching out ahead through Allen's ten sons to a future of why not a hundred grandsons, a thousand great-grandsons, thriving with each new round. And all that family power, past and future, was laid out before me now in this one tidy farm, where there were still chickens and sheep, and nothing was run-down, where the corn had come in early and full and was already in the crib, the fodder pulled, pigs ripening in the pen.

I used to wander over here almost every day to see Mr. Allen. I adored him the way a girl sometimes does a kind old man. Tall and thin and bright-eyed, he could knot up a handkerchief into the form of a squirrel that would seem to play in his hands and then leap of its own accord into mine. When it did, I yelped, not from real fright but just to please him, because I saw that I could. He liked me. I wasn't his daughter but he took an interest in me as the daughter of Celia Ann, one of his favorites. And even though I loved my own daddy, there was something about Mr. Allen that brought me again and again to his porch, to his knee. When I was ten I said I would marry him when I grew up, at which he laughed and warned me I had overlooked two things: one, the fact that as I was rising to adulthood he was declining toward the grave, and two, his wife, Mary Cumbo, who he recommended I wouldn't want to tangle with. He was always joking like that, always making me laugh.

But over time my attachment to him had grown deep and serious. I got the feeling that he was my secret protector and my real teacher. Sometimes he would give me his advice for life, as if he had chosen me to receive what he had to pass on.

The day when I first came home from Miss McCabe, I spotted him out behind his house sawing shakes, and I crept up to watch for a while. This was a job he loved. At the Scots Fair he won the shake-sawing every year. He would chop the blocks out by hatchet, and then the sawing would start. At his feet a pile of shingles and sawdust rose. I always did love to watch a man at work, without him knowing I was there. It was a chance to see him as he really was, rather than how he was with women.

But Mr. Allen was not one you could ever fool or sneak up on. After a while he said, without raising his eyes, 'Quit your lessons, did you?'

'I guess so.'

He kept on sawing, so smooth and fast it was like a dance and a ceremony, and the shingles kept falling.

'Didn't I warn you, miss, if you're going to be worth five cents in this life, you better get yourself an education?'

I didn't know how to explain it to him

— how I had felt something pulling me home so hard I had to come.

'Well, never mind, you'll get your learning one way or another when the war's done. A light skin is nothing to brag on, but maybe you can use it to talk your way into a real school. Anything it takes. Remember that. School is what you need. Now you might hear people tell you, if you really want to 'make something of yourself,' get out of North Carolina.'

Here he hesitated. Stopped sawing, and held one shingle up to see if it was thin enough to lap and thick enough to nail. 'But I hope you won't, none of you young crowd,' he said, turning to me. 'I hope you'll stay to make something of North Carolina.'

Then his serious moment passed, and he went back to sawing and teasing.

'I suppose you've come to wink eyes at my boys then. Tell me which one you've set your sights on, and I'll put in a good word.'

I blushed because he was right. I did hope to catch a glimpse of one of those sons, or maybe two — Steve and Henry, who were the closest in age to me. I could count on Steve to clown around and tease, to make me laugh. He had stopped by our house a couple of Saturday nights, which my mother took to mean something, but he said he was there to play music with the boys. Henry didn't pay me any attention at all. I never had even talked to him up close. But he was the one I was hoping hardest to see, even if it had to be from a distance.

Mr. Allen pointed at me with one long finger aimed like a gun.

'Henry's the one you want,' he said.

Was he reading the inside of my heart, like his brother Mr. George read cups and palms?

'Oh, no sir,' I said, trying to look honest.

He laughed. 'I'm not accusing you, little cousin,' he said. 'I'm advising. You and him together — that would be something to reckon with. That would beat all.'

★ ★ ★

But I didn't see any of the sons now. The older four were all married and moved into their own houses: Sink, Cal, Jim, and Purdy; and of the younger five, Murdock was gone to Tennessee, Henry was who-knew-where, and Steve and Tom were lying out in the swamp. So I hoped William would appear, the one still living at home, or Mary Cumbo open the door and fling chicken feed, or Mr. Allen himself wave and greet me the way he always did. 'Hello there, little girl cousin, are you roaming loose again? Come on up, this old dog won't bite. Now, are you you? Or are you that brother that looks just like you? Come on and tell me something smart, come on and set with me a little minute.' And I always did.

So I waited now, but no one appeared. Maybe they had locked themselves in for William's sake. He had a combustible temper and more pride than was safe these days. It had been his idea to gather his younger brothers and cousins in the swamps, but once that was done he had a falling out with Henry. They argued — William wanted revenge for the murder of his cousins, he wanted to move against Brant Harris right away, torch his roadhouse and rob him blind so he'd be out of commission, but Henry said no. He said there would be a new court with a new judge when the war was done, and a chance for justice in Robeson County. A chance for regular life.

Regular life! That was a new idea, or at least one so long forgotten it might as well have been new. William laughed at the thought of it. They argued some more. When it was put to a vote, the rest stood with Henry, so William cut out and came home, and Henry took over. Mr. Allen and Mary were glad to have William back, they said they would put him to work, keep him busy and cool him off, let him lie low.

But if anyone was home now, there was no sign.

Even without a soul in sight the place had a hold over me. I loved it, and I'd have stayed longer just to look, if Girl had not dived again.

I could have called her back, and she would have come, but I didn't do it. She gave me an excuse to say to myself and to Cee later on: I had to follow my dog.

When I came to the postmaster's landing, I saw that Girl had climbed out and was trotting up toward the house. This was only habit. She thought we were coming to read stories to Clelon. He had two storybooks he kept hidden in a barrel as if someone might come to steal them, but he would bring them out when I visited, and we would sit and read awhile.

I liked Clelon. He was my only friend these days. But I admit I had another reason for these visits, too — and it was not a very honorable one. Curiosity is the polite word, although you could also call it spying. I liked to keep an eye on the postmaster, partly to try and discover if it was true he was the one who drew up the conscription lists and told Brant Harris where to hunt for our young men. But also, I wanted to get a close-up look at his life.

Except for a handful of girls who scrubbed kitchens, most of the settlement never saw the inside of a mack house. So it was a rare opportunity I'd had, to come and go so freely in two of them, the doctor's and the postmaster's. Those visits made my mother anxious, and she warned me to watch my manners, keep my mouth shut except to answer a question, and never disagree or call attention to myself — rules that would keep me out of trouble, she hoped. But they also helped me do my little bit of spying. One thing I found out was, James Barnes might not have as much control over the conscripting as everyone thought he did. His own slaves had been sent, and he lived in fear that Clelon would be the next to go. Barnes might have written and signed the lists, but someone else had the power.

His land was decent, a hundred acres with a one-story farmhouse, but the house was now graying and dilapidating, taking on the look of a sinner knelt in prayer because the porch roof had come unhooked and somewhat bowed down. In the years since their mother's death the two brothers had lived here alone. At one time I suppose James Barnes expected to become a well-to-do man, what with the five slaves he inherited, and half the farm, and for practical purposes the other half too, owing to Clelon's condition. And for a while Barnes did prosper, at least enough to make an offer of marriage to the widow Prevatte. But the proposal was a flop, she not being eager for a husband with an afflicted brother he had sworn to care for. After that rejection, his fortunes took a downhill swing. He sold two slaves to pay his way out of the army, then had to send a third to the saltworks and another to the fort — and the last one, seeing the fate of the others, ran off into Big Swamp with the Maroons. Barnes tried to make his crop alone, but two summers in a row his corn drowned in the war rains, and that's when he put up the farm to borrow from Harris. He was living on his pittance as postmaster at the Clay Valley Post Office, which was housed in a shed on the Willis P. Moore farm and received about six letters a week.

Just recently his second marriage proposal — revealing both his lowered standards and his need for another pair of hands, another strong back — went to a plump Irish cook who had fled the Union Army and was living in Hestertown. And she accepted.

If his mother had been alive, such a marriage would have killed her. A Hestertown Irisher! But Barnes got revitalized. Every time he returned from courting in Hestertown, he came walking with a jaunty step, whistling a tune. He mended his pig fence in preparation for the roundup of his hogs out of the woods, where they had been set out since March to forage on mast, acorns and hickory nuts and whatever else they could find. If he could get a little corn to ripen them off, he could sell some meat and buy next year's seed and by then the war would be done, and with his new wife's help in the fields, he could pay off Harris and get out of this hole of debt he was in. On the strength of that plan he sold one of his two mules to buy the feed and a better plow, and some little things he thought would please a wife.

I was there the day she arrived for her first visit, a week before the wedding date, with her hair curled in tight corkscrews close to her scalp and a pair of old shoes newly painted yellow, which quickly sank in the yard mud. Barnes jumped to assist her, and I knew he was genuinely in love, the way he reached for her.

'Bridget,' he said. I was surprised to hear him say her Christian name, and to hear how tender his voice came out. It was something close and secret, that I ought not to have heard. I felt ashamed, like an intruder.

But as usual he hardly knew I was there, and he didn't bother to explain my presence to her. She must have thought I was his kitchen girl, as I was barefooted and sleeveless that day; and she smiled at me. I liked her right away.

Gamely she stepped out of her shoes and climbed the steps in her stockings, but I saw her face fall when she surveyed the caving-in porch, the grimy kitchen and chimney with a hole in it, the smelly parlor piled with overalls, boots, traps, and guns. And then the bedroom, dark and airless as a cave, its only furniture one narrow rust-pocked iron bed covered with a sheet so new and white it seemed to have a leering gleam.

But she fought back her tears and didn't bolt. Though it was all filthy and gloomy, and surely frightening to someone who might not have understood how war had reduced us all, how even a slaveholder could be sunk in poverty to the very lips, still this house must have been better than anything she'd gotten a shot at before. She had a boldly pretty face, a jutting chin, and a strong gaze that might have been what attracted Barnes in the first place, and made him think she was up to the task of establishing a household in these ruins. And I decided if anyone could do it, maybe this one could. Certainly she was a better prospect than the widow Prevatte.

But when she opened the door to the little

dirt-floor room off the kitchen — Clelon's room — and saw him sitting on his cot, moaning and nodding away with his arms hanging between his knees and his hands spinning a pine cone on the floor like a toy top, it was the last straw. She closed the door. After a ten-minute conference outside with her intended, they departed both stone-faced in the wagon, and he delivered her to the depot. She fled back to her Union cookfires in New Bern, and Barnes requested a refund from Pate on the bedsheet and gold wire ring, the French soap, hand glass, Illustrated Family Bible, and little baby's bedcoat he had bought. But Pate said no — because he'd had to order the merchandise special, and who else would buy such things? — and Barnes told Clelon to tie the wedding gifts in a flour sack and throw the sack in the river.

In the two weeks since then, he had not mentioned her, and he became somber and withdrawn and careless, like a man who has received an injury he can't avenge, and he can't heal.

I could see him in the distance, just coming out of the stalls near his smokehouse. I went on up to the house, calling for Clelon. The ground in front of the porch was torn and muddy, tracked by wagon wheels and boots.

'What happened here?' I asked Clelon

when he appeared in the doorway. He stood aside for me to come in, and I saw that the house had been stripped. Everything was gone from all three rooms except the cot and bedstead. No mattresses, no bedclothes, no pots and pans, no traps or guns. Only some junk and worn clothing and empty boxes remained.

'Are you moving out?'

Clelon seemed to shake his head. But he ordinarily did that.

Barnes came in behind me, boiling mad, and slammed the door so hard it jumped open again. His face was purple and his hands shook, and he brushed past me to the other side of the room, then spun around and stomped back. I had the sense to get out of his way and slide up against the wall. He couldn't slow down, he bounced back and forth from one corner to another.

'Yankee fools, they think they busted me! Well, they don't know James Barnes.'

'Yankees?' I couldn't help asking. 'Do you mean, the Union Army's here?' But I knew it was too much to hope for.

'Hell, no. Thieving bummers that rather sneak and steal than to fight head-on a gentleman's way. Pulled me out of bed and tied me, or I'd have ripped their lungs out. They're long gone now, off for someplace where there's better pickings. They won't waste their time around here. It was their good luck and my bad that they happened this way, and right after I rounded up the damn hogs. If I had waited one day, I'd still have those hogs. One day!' He kicked at the empty sugar box and flour barrel. 'They got my last mule, the wagon, muskets they won't even use, and a good new plow they can't need. And every head of cabbage I had hanging in the shed — my peas, my corn from the cribs, sugar, blankets, brandy . . . They left me the bull-tongue plow and the ox and one hatchet, their idea of a joke. 'We don't want you Rebs to starve, you can either plow the ox for a winter patch or chop it up and get a bowl of soup off its bones.' Well, they don't know I plowed a ox and bull-tongue many a time in the old days. I'm going to do it again, with the Lord's help and yours too, Clelon, put on your boots.'

That ancient no-good ox, of the stunted variety that used to be the county's only work animals, not much bigger than donkeys, was the surviving half of a pair that had come with the farm. They had been old and useless enough to shoot even then, when Barnes brought in mules and got the farm going good; but Clelon begged and moaned to keep them. So the oxen became his pets, although a worse pet is hard to imagine. There was nothing affectionate or even responsive in their nature, they had no more character than blocks of wood. No one ever named them, unless Clelon did, in which case those were names we would never hear. The bull had died in January of age and freeze, and his yokemate couldn't have long to go.

Barnes pulled open the cupboards and the closet and then the door to Clelon's shed.

'Somewhere, I had another old harness off the dead ox — '

Clelon edged past him to the clothes barrel by the cot. The Yankees had thrown aside his ragged overalls and jeans pants off the top, but when they got down to where Clelon kept his pine-cone collection and his storybooks, they must have given up looking for valuables.

Clelon took out the cones one by one, and then lifted out a tangle of stiff and moldy leather straps.

'How'd that get in there?' Barnes said.

'He keeps all his special things in the barrel,' I explained. 'He saved her traces and her bell.'

'Why?'

'Just to play with, I guess, and remind him.'

As Barnes took the straps from Clelon's hands, something fell out of the tangle and

93

onto the floor at his feet, a little package wrapped in thin paper banded with a rose-colored label. Barnes stared at it, and then carefully he picked it up and held it in the open palm of his hand with his head tilted to one side and his brow in a frown. It was a bar of soap — the soap of the lost Irish bride.

I thought he would throw it away, angry it hadn't gone to the bottom of the river as he'd ordered. But he only looked at the label, which bore the picture of a dreamy-eyed lady with a tall hairstyle. Into the dank air drifted a too-sweet smell of roses, and Clelon sneezed. Barnes blinked. Then he handed the package back to Clelon, who set it down deep in the barrel and replaced the pine cones and the overalls and pants.

Barnes sat on Clelon's cot and dropped his head and maybe thought about his memories. I drew off to the front room, but Clelon stayed at his brother's side, untangling the traces.

I never could tell exactly what James Barnes thought of Clelon's capabilities. Two years earlier he had petitioned the court to declare Clelon insane, but that was because in order to mortgage the farm he needed legal control of Clelon's share. He did work him, and sometimes sent him on unimportant errands such as carrying letters to Scuffle-town. He talked as if Clelon could understand, and often he spoke to him almost in the tone of a confidant. Yet there was something off about it. It was more like the tone of a man confiding in himself.

My suspicion was that Clelon might well be full-witted, or at least three-quarters, and maybe his ailment had more to do with talking than thinking, plus a trouble with his neck that made his head wobble. People don't like to see that. They don't mind a wooden leg or a blind eye, both of which excite a certain sympathy and a thankfulness that the grace of God has protected their own legs and eyes. Blind or crippled, as so many were now from the war, a man still looks a man, and so he seems predictable. But a rolling head makes people think something lunatic and wild is going on inside it, like a murder plot or a mad rampage. It looks too *different*. They start to think maybe it doesn't qualify as human. That's what had swayed the jury of macks who declared Clelon incompetent, and that's what scared off the Irish cook.

After a few minutes, I heard Barnes stir from the cot. 'Well, come on,' he said to Clelon as if nothing had happened. 'We got a job to do. What are you dawdling for and looking so sorry-eyed?' But really it was

Barnes himself dawdling and sorrowing.

We followed him out to the stall.

I figured the ox must have been at least twenty-five years old. Her hooves were yellowed and chipped, her eyes cloudy as fish milk.

Pulling her out, Barnes started mumbling.

'They could have been the ones that were hiding out at Lowrie's. I bet they were. Yes, and when he couldn't keep his Yankees fed good enough, he sent them ham-hunting. To spare his own full sty. Clelon, who saw you going after the hogs? Who knew we penned them all? Somebody knew, or else it wouldn't make sense for them to come here. Somebody passed them the word, or brought them in and hid back in the woods while they loaded up. It was Lowrie, I know, or one of them sons-of-bitches sons.'

Clelon rolled his head.

'Had to be,' Barnes said. 'Bad stock. Lawless, shiftless. Thinks he's developed into somebody. Why I ever got to be on civil terms with him I don't know.'

James Barnes was aware who I was and where I lived, my Lowrie connections. But it almost seemed that with my comings and goings over the years he had forgotten, and only thought of me as *that child who comes around, who must be half-witted herself, to spend so much time with Clelon*. And maybe I encouraged that idea. Playing dumb, I turned into a person of no thoughts and no kin. He had never called me by name. Yet he was so extremely heedless of my presence, sometimes I felt almost as if I was a member of his family.

'My hogs are being cut and bled right now, over at Lowrie's. If I'd been thinking fast, I could have got there in time to get the marks. Mine's a swallow fork in one ear and poplar leaf in the other, his is a underslope bit and a half-moon. There's no resemblance! I could have had the evidence. But he's buried the ears in his onion patch by now, or fed them to the pack of fice dogs.'

'I came by there, and I didn't see anyone.'

It surprised him to hear me speak up with an objection, but he dismissed it.

'Then they're doing it in the swamp,' he snapped. 'They'll have hung and slit them all and got the pots boiling, drunk up on my brandy and having themselves a good old time. It don't occur to them something is *wrong* with that. It's the Indian nature to steal, it's in the blood, I don't care how long he's been a Methodist, he's *going* to do it.'

He harnessed the ox to the plow, though all she had pulled in the last ten years was an empty little cart for Clelon's games, and even then she had to be led. So Barnes called Clelon to do the leading, and they plowed two rows like that while I followed kicking clods the tongue had thrown off. I was uneasy, seeing the old ox strain so hard. I let a distance open up between me and the plow.

On the turn for a third row they headed back in my direction and when they passed I heard Barnes rambling again under his breath.

' — a thieving sneak far back as thirty years ago, got caught with somebody's ewe and claimed he thought it was his uncle's, well they lashed him for that but he must have didn't learn, thick-headed idiot, twenty-five stripes wasn't enough to teach him a lesson — '

Then the little ox quit. Clelon hummed in her ear, 'Mmm, aaahmmm,' but she wouldn't pull.

Barnes told me to go get the whip from behind the stall door. I looked but it wasn't there. Then I saw it had fallen into the dirt, lying in the corner like a dead snake. I stared at it.

'I don't see it,' I called. 'It's gone with the Yanks, Mr. Barnes.'

The howl he let out then, with his head thrown back and his teeth bared, could have been heard down to the river.

'HOW CAN I LIVE WITH NOTHING TO LIVE BY?'

Nobody answered. He let his head sink into his hands, and when he raised it again his face was blank as a dead man's.

He shrugged, and unbuckled his belt, pulled it through the loops in one slow draw, and gave it a testing snap against the air. I could hardly believe what I saw happen then. He seemed possessed, but in a dull, ponderous way, as if the fever of rage had burned him through. He looked bored, surrendered to a great tedium. Yet the blow he landed with the heel of his left hand on Clelon's shoulder, to push him out of the way, was fierce enough to send Clelon stumbling backward in surprise.

Then as if it was the only thing left to do, Barnes whipped the ox. He lifted his arm high and all the way back and then brought it down so hard he doubled over, with a grunting noise from the back of his throat. One crack then two, and more, harder every time, until her loose old flesh split, streaked red from spine to belly, and the belt was dripping every time he raised it, flecking his hair and eyeglasses.

Clelon was too shocked to cry out, and so was I, and so was the ox — at first strike she had jumped, but with the rest she only trembled, head lowered, the way they do in the rain as if they see no other choice — and I kept thinking with each blow, *That's it, he's done now, he'll quit*, because it made no sense for him to keep going, but he did.

He lashed the rump and legs and even the face, walking in a circle as you would to beat out a brush fire, around and around a dozen times or more. And then the ox bent on her knees and folded down.

Barnes took off his glasses and cleaned them with a kerchief, then wrapped the wires back around his ears.

Clelon sat on the ground between the wide-set curling horns and took the big square head in his lap.

'Leave it alone,' Barnes said, but Clelon kept on patting the bristled flat space between her eyes. A bright red gush from her nostrils spilled onto his pants. Only then did she begin that high small cry that sounded like a rat half-caught in a spring trap.

Clelon looked up with a question in his eyes. *Why?*

'I don't know . . . ,' Barnes mumbled. 'Something popped.'

Clelon's head swung wildly.

'What's he expect me to do?' Barnes said.

I swallowed and tried to get my voice back. 'Maybe put her out of her misery?'

'Okay, I'll — Oops, well, can't. No gun.'

He started yawning, one big yawn after another, and he tried to hide his mouth with his hands.

'Don't look at me like that, you,' he said to me.

The ox cried louder, and Barnes covered his ears. His eyelids closed halfway.

Clelon was unbuttoning his shirt, but when the ox snorted blood again, he snapped the buttons off in one hard rip and worked his arms out of the sleeves.

'What's he doing?' Barnes said.

'I don't know,' I said, although I thought I might.

Clelon wrapped his shirt around the animal's whole muzzle. The gray cotton quickly sopped up all the blood it could take and then began to drip.

'Clelon, that won't help,' Barnes said in a halfhearted drone, like a mother with a child she's hardly noticing. 'Get up and leave the thing alone. Go back to the house now.'

But then we saw Clelon's hands clamp down on the nose, slamming the jaw against the ground and blocking out air.

The ox fought, arched her neck, and jerked Clelon out full length onto the ground. Still he held on, his upper body twisting between the long horns.

I was too scared to scream *let go*. Clelon was a heavy man but every pitch of the horns tossed him back and forth, and if he did let go he might land gored.

Then Barnes appeared to wake up. His eyes opened, and he saw the danger. He threw himself onto the animal's back and reached between the horns from behind. She tried to rise under him with a lurch, and got her hindquarters up, but he wrapped his legs around her, riding her back down, pressing his hands over his brother's hands and the drenched shirt, pinning the head again. Trying to smother her. But from the shrieks I knew she was still getting air, until the sounds turned to something worse, of blood inhaled. She gurgled and choked, went still, shuddered once, and then died underneath the postmaster.

He rested there for a while on top of the carcass, still embracing it.

I saw a little wind run through the treetops. I saw milkweed and goldenrod nodding in the field, a cloud of barn swallows rise, the split of a hundred purple wings as the flock cut sharp and swung away. *The sun still broadly shining, the sky at noon, the lightning triple-forked.* I cast my mind into Miss McCabe's weather, to keep from crying. *The day broke clear but slowly hazed. No arc.*

'Forty-two years old and a Presbyterian since the age of seventeen,' Barnes said, laying his cheek against the dead neck, his eyeglasses hanging from one ear. 'And I've whipped and smothered an ox to death.'

Clelon began to tug at the harness.

'I'll get it,' Barnes said, but all he could do was roll himself off into the mud and close his eyes, and clasp his hands toward heaven. 'A beast of burden, a poor animal . . . Lord, forgive me. I have mingled with an ungodly world and lost the righteous way. Show me Thy mercies. Deliver me, oh Lord . . . '

I ran to the well and drew half a bucket of water. When I came back around the side of the house, I saw Barnes on his feet, staring. I followed his eyes.

Clelon had freed the fallen ox and then pulled the plow off to a distance of ten feet. He was standing by it, waiting.

He had harnessed himself.

I said, 'Mr. Barnes, don't do this.'

But Clelon smiled. It was his idea, he was willing.

Barnes said to me, 'Get on out of here. Don't you ever tell what you seen here.'

But I couldn't leave, I just hung back, and although I was still in his view, he looked right through me.

He hitched Clelon to the plow. On the first

try, Clelon lunged forward, slipped and fell. The bull-tongue bit too deep in the heavy wet dirt, it couldn't be budged. But Barnes now had it in his head that this impossible task must be done.

'Get up! Try again!'

Once more Clelon fell.

Barnes got on his knees and dug out around the tongue. He clawed off the muddy thatch of weeds that had tangled about the screw, and he set the tongue to ride higher.

'We got it now, Buddy. Let's go.'

This time Clelon threw his whole body forward, and miraculously the plow started after him.

'Haw!' Barnes yelled.

They plowed the vegetable patch, two muddy, blood-soaked men, one behind the plow streaming tears and prayers, and the other one out front, leaning into the space of air before him, head down and arms outstretched as if to reach for the end of the row, stepping so slow and hard he looked like he was climbing a hill.

When they were done, the postmaster unhitched the plow and unstrapped his brother, and forgetting me or simply not giving a damn, he tore the tail off his own shirt and started cleaning Clelon's face and shoulders with water from the bucket.

Before that day I had thought of James Barnes as an ordinary man, I mean one neither weak nor strong but beset over the years of his life by the ordinary troubles of love, anger, drudgery, envy, loneliness, disappointment, all of which have been proved bearable by the human race. Who has not known one or more of them at some time or another? Yet if they all came down on a man at once, I didn't know what might happen. His mind might fail. I was afraid for Clelon's safety. Barnes was his only protector, and who would look out for him if Barnes did not? Clelon had no one else.

But Barnes was washing Clelon now; he seemed back in control of himself. Maybe whatever had seized him had passed on by, a fit of some kind, a bad spell.

He dipped the shirttail in the bucket, wrung it out. Clelon ducked his head to get the back of his neck wiped, and then threw a clumsy arm around his brother's shoulder. The two of them stood still in that partial embrace for a minute.

Barnes said, 'Buddy, I think we'll go into Lumberton one day this week. Take a train ride. Want to? We'll see old Tab. She said if you came she would cook up all the food dishes you like the best.'

I must have let out a cry. Slowly Barnes

turned toward me, and I saw a dark, grim loathing I had never seen before. His mouth curled in disgust. For the first time it appeared to click in his head exactly who I was — a Scuffletown girl, part Lowrie myself, and the witness to his secret life. His conscience and therefore his enemy.

So I knew what I had to say.

'You do that, and you'll go to hell for it.'

His arm dropped away from Clelon.

'What did you say?'

'I know where Free Tab cooks,' I said. 'At the asylum. I know what you're planning on doing.'

'I'm planning on getting us a good meal is all. You ask Tab. She promised him a chicken and pastry.'

'Well, that better be all,' I said under my breath.

'"That *better* be all'?'

He took a step toward me. I had broken the rules, the way I talked to him. I had put myself on unfamiliar ground. Everything was shifted.

'You're a right pretty girl. Well-developed up top. I wonder if you have a fellow.'

I took three steps backward.

'Because if you do,' he said, 'probably you don't want him carried off to do some digging for a year or so. Or a brother, you got a brother? I believe you do, don't you. Well, so do I. I don't want mine sent, and you don't want yours sent, so let's just make a bargain. Your end of it is, stay away from my property and keep your little red wet mouth shut. It's dangerous to hang it open the way you like to do.'

He was smiling at me, he knew he had the upper hand. I took off, just turned and ran.

Halfway home, I walked out into the river, holding on to a willow branch to keep from getting swept away. In water to my shoulders, I let my feet swing out and my head sink under. The puzzled dog swam around me, bumping my hips. Anyone passing on the bank would have seen a girl's thin arm hanging from a tree, and might have thought I was trying to drown myself, but I was trying to do the opposite, with the silky river slipping past my ears and neck and belly and legs like a steady breeze of water, spreading my hair, pulling me slowly almost to the horizontal, reviving me — in the hum and bubble of another language, a wash of shadows silvered by light from above. We submerged, me and Girl, in that cool, clean flow as long as we could, until we had to come back.

I told my mother about the Yankee raid, and she said it must be another roving band, not likely to be attracted by a cabin like ours.

'But you are not to step foot out the door again unless I say so,' she said.

'Girl ran off. I had to go after her.'

'By water?' she said. 'You're sopping.'

'Time they both had a bath,' Andrew said.

'You ought to try one yourself someday,' I said.

'The two of you *quit*.'

All afternoon Andrew harried me, but it seemed easier just to give up and let him say his remarks. My gumption had run out. I couldn't do anything to help Clelon, or anyone else for that matter, including myself. I couldn't even say aloud what I feared, that James Barnes might try to trick his brother, with a plate of chicken, into the Lumberton asylum, and that he had run me off with a threat I didn't even want to think about. *You got a brother?* Oh, I should have kept my mouth shut like Cee said to. I should have played dumb.

I didn't tell my mother the whole story because it would have worried her too much. But if I'd had Margaret there, I'd have told her everything — the ox, the threats, and the most troubling thing of all, how the postmaster when his life went wrong settled the blame not on fate or war or his own shortcomings, but elsewhere. On the nearest one, a neighbor — a man who had once been his friend and never did him harm. But I didn't have Margaret, so I told myself what I hoped she would have said: *Forget it. It was just one pitiful man's stupid error. It can have no power or effect.*

Cee noticed something was wrong with me. That night when we were in our beds and Daddy was snoring I heard her still moving around the cabin, and I knew it was me on her mind.

But once again, I was wrong.

She said, 'Andrew, are you asleep?'

'Not anymore.'

She sat next to him.

'Don't pester Rhoda so much, son. This isn't the time for it. We might fight amongst ourselves once in a while, but when a threat comes to everyone we always pull together. You're wearing her down, and we have too much on our minds right now for that.'

'Like what? Not the fool Guard, they're never going to get me and Boss. You said so.'

'Something's fired them up.'

'Maybe the Union really is on its way,' Andrew said.

'If it was, the Home Guard would be all locked in their houses squealing,' my mother said. 'No, the Union is someplace else. I'm — I'm worried this time, Andrew.'

'There's nothing to it,' he said. 'Go on to bed.'

'I thought we might talk some, honey.'

'If you want to stew yourself sick with worry, you're welcome, but I won't help you do it. What's the use? I'm going back to sleep.'

'Well, I suppose you're right,' she said. 'There's nothing else to do.'

She chose Andrew to confide in, she told him her secret fears! It was as if she had just then, instantly, changed her whole view on him, and his hard-heartedness that had been so annoying, that she had fussed at every day including this one, was something that now she had decided to admire. But how could she? He was full of himself, cocksure and fearless, without a thought of any life other than his precious own.

I despised that in him, yet I was no better. That night I chose to put Clelon out of my mind, the way I had Jarman, the way I had Wesley and Little Allen in those weeks before they were found killed. I didn't want to save the day, all I wanted was my own life. To get my learning and my man, my little house and farm; teach a class of school, have ten sons of my own, and cook pies the rest of my cautious days. I wanted to sweep trouble and threats and dangers out of my head with a stiff hearth broom, let them die into the cold ashpile of the past and never think of them again. And so I made myself the know-nothing I had pretended to be.

⋆   ⋆   ⋆

Today the past is lively before my eyes, hot as coals. Mysteries crackle out of it and hiss through the air, and for whole stretches of days I don't eat anything real at all. I am chewing red cinders and sparks. Sometimes I am transported. Every girl becomes a woman in a different way, and maybe mine was to cast myself off, not once but again and again until the 'I' that used to be was shed like a worn-out coat. That is one way of looking at it. Or I might say maybe I let the serpent of knowledge get my leg. If you have ever seen a milk snake eat a frog, you know it's not accomplished in one swift strike but is a long, slow, miraculous business. Sometimes, if the snake comes from behind, the frog's head and eyes are free to the last, and it struggles but can't see what is happening — how the snake keeps inching on, not so much swallowing as surrounding. I am in it now, moving as it moves.

But I don't really know how it happened, the change in me. All I know is, I have been studying and pondering this story for over twenty years, feeding on it. I have lost half my life to it, two decades turning the past in my head. No toil ages the spirit faster than the toil of too much memory. And the body, too, shows wear.

Oh, I'm not yet a hag. My hair is thick and shiny and my shape not so changed from those days I'm recalling, except in ways only I might notice. On the rare occasion when I'm seen and recognized in Lumberton, the newspaper will find 'traces of her former charms still apparent'; and my girl Polly tells me I am still a beauty. But she is like me, she can't bear to see her mother distressed, and she will try to guard me from knowing I have faded, by announcing herself with a prank or a sashay so that *she* is what I see, a great big glorious girl so pretty I can't think of anything else while I'm looking at her. She is almost six feet tall — too tall to marry, she says to tease me, and claims that's why she has to stay with me. Polly keeps me alive. She does the cropping, she sells our eggs and the little bit of whiskey she makes herself — the only girl I ever heard of who runs her own shebeen. She built the still, and she tends it, and she steers clear of the law better than most, being smart and clever, more Lowrie than I am. And so she makes ends meet, and with the help of the others who bring food or sometimes even money (not for any special love of me, but only because of *him*), we are saved from the poorhouse. And if I have been silent too long or writing too late at night, or if Pol notices me glancing into the mirror, she will start to chatter away, or quibble or joke or quarrel, anything to call my thoughts away from myself and onto her.

But I know what is happening to me. One dog tooth is gone, and my monthly flow has dwindled to a spatter. I'm not as full as I used to be, my wrists are skinny, my knuckles are knobs. I'm starting to wear thin. This is the price of the years of thinking, the casting and recasting of events and the frantic pen scratching past midnight, the hoarding of paper, the loneliness, the pages accumulating while I myself shrink down.

If I thought pages were all I had gained, if this writing amounted finally to nothing but a rehearsal of bygones, I would regret my life. I'd wish I had continued unthinking, and thrown myself into the current of time and never taken up the job of reconsidering the past, never read or written a word, never learned an alphabet. I might even have thrown myself into the real current, that drowning river, and let go the branch to shortcut my profitless time on earth.

But the truth is, thinking and remembering and writing are not without profit. From all the bits and pieces stored away, a knowledge comes. It just does come, as little daily dawns collect, and months and years, until one day well past youth's hunger (that blind desire, that *fight*), and almost giving up on the brain's worth, you may see in the memories something that amounts to more than their accumulation. With luck you may find you know what was hidden in your youth.

3

The macks said Scuffletown was a floating town, that we could break down and pack on our oxcarts and haul deeper into the swamp when we wanted to, when someone was after us. That was a lie. We never moved the town. But sometimes a family might dismantle and cart their cabin a mile or two just for the sake of a change, or a young couple break off to build their own place at the head of a deserted branch where the stream fantails out into little dribbles. The town limits weren't set by geography. Wherever we were, that was Scuffletown.

There were a few mack houses scattered around or even amidst, but never *inside*. Postmaster Barnes lived halfway between Mr. Allen Lowrie and Mr. George Lowrie, and the Lowries were both in Scuffletown but the postmaster was not, because of who he was. And if you had stopped to ask him where the town lay, he could not have drawn you a good map.

What happened was that strangers looking for us often lost their way and sometimes their wits, so they preferred to say the whole place had moved rather than admit they had wandered in circles for two days. They thought a town had to be tight, laid out in blocks like a Scots plaid. But Scuffletown varied from six to eight miles wide, on both banks of the river and up and down through the swamps. If two or three houses could be seen at once, they were likely one old couple's place and the newer cabins of the married sons lined up behind. Probably we included Moss Neck and Prospect and Burnt Swamp and part of Red Banks. Maybe we even included Hogtown and Saddletree, sets that were more distant but still part of us, for all the Hammonds and Jacobses scattered through the woods.

So you can see, Scuffletown as a place was anchored but driftable, and as an idea it had the floating nature of a dream. In either form, it was hard for strangers to reach. My guess was, God had decided to let in only those who needed to come, only those on their last leg. And those He chose to lead in, we received.

Some were Rebel deserters, some were horse thieves on the run. And then toward the end of that summer the Union prisoners started trickling in, escaped out of the new Florence prison in South Carolina.

Brant Harris told Sheriff King and Deputy

McTeer that the Lowries were all homemade Yankees, guiding the escapees up from Florence; but the truth was simpler. If you had been one of those prisoners, and had scratched your way somehow out of that hellhole and still had the breath of life, what then? In the night, in the wilds of South Carolina with the treacherous Pee Dee River still to cross and miles of swamp beyond it, you could only have looked to heaven for guidance. And anyone who starts from that spot, following the North Star, will come in time to Scuffletown, direct to Allen Lowrie's house.

He was no Yankee, he loved the Southland — that is, the land itself, his home. But he leaned toward the Union for two reasons. One was because the Rebels he used to know as friends had turned on him, and the other was because he'd come up close enough to slavery to know its feel. He'd seen liberty shrink like a drying pocosin, receding from his own sons. So he took in those bluecoats who came, and gave them what hospitality he could afford, which was nothing grand, but he was proud to be able to offer a hot meal and a clean bed. I knew for a fact he never had need of another man's hogs. The opposite was true, he gave away more than he kept for his own table. And no one ever stole from Allen Lowrie. Even the Yankees seemed to recognize he was a man you'd go to hell for robbing.

Slaves found the way to Scuffletown, too. Usually they were with us only as long as it took to gather strength and move on, north to liberty, but some like Applewhite decided to stay till liberty came to them. Preacher Sinclair had offered to help him get to Ohio, but Applewhite said no. He said he was a free man already even if North Carolina didn't know it yet, and by God he might hide but he wouldn't run.

From the Oxendines', where he first hid out, he went up to Wayne County and tried it there awhile, but came back into Bear Swamp and made his home inside a tree. It was hollow to start with but he dug it out some more and rigged up a locking door, and there he lived a year without seeing another soul except Preacher Sinclair and Betsy Oxendine, Henderson's sister, who once a week took him what he needed — herself included. One of her visits lengthened out to a more permanent arrangement, and they built themselves a cabin near Red Banks, on swampland owned by Sinclair. We'd see her now and then whenever she came our way to visit her family, but for a long time Ap himself remained in hiding, and that was a pity because he was a most skillful mason. The cabin he built for Betsy was set on pretty little brick feet, and he laid a brick path patterned like a woolen weave.

But he couldn't come into public view and make a regular business of bricking. To build the new Lowrie chimney, he worked only at night. After a while he did venture out but always in disguise as a slave, and he'd walk ten paces behind Betsy. They made a game of it, and once they even went into Hardy Bell's store in Lumberton. They tricked Hardy and his mack customers all right, and over at the skin table Deputy McTeer, who had been hunting the runaway George Applewhite for three years, kept on dealing cards and cussing his luck. Betsy laughed about that for weeks. But this risky joke struck me as a measly consolation for the life they had to lead, which for Applewhite can't have been much better than his former life in the Marion District. To get any use out of freedom he had to pretend to be not free. He was still a secret man.

But then we all lived secretly, more or less. History would not recognize us or record us.

Over the years a handful of famous characters had passed through Scuffletown without knowing it. General Francis Marion, the Swamp Fox, outsmarted the British by disappearing into Ashpole Swamp, and Flora MacDonald, who had saved a royal prince, lived for a time near Cross Creek. The female academy was named for her, as were many daughters of romantic-minded mothers long after the lady herself had gone back to Scotland. Mr. John Wesley, the great Methodist, once traveled the Lumberton Road, and so did the Bunker brothers, Chang and Eng from Siam, who had been born knit at the breastbone and after a world tour settled in North Carolina. Oh yes, history trotted past our door but, as is often the case, had its mind on its own self and never took notice of the humble wayside. We saw the famous and the mighty but they did not see us. If they thought of us at all, it was with a curse for the wheel bogged, horse sunk to the pastern, luggage jostled from the coach even on the plank road. We were nothing to them and we knew it. We never expected them to pay a call.

Hestertown, where Nelly lived, was another story. That was a hidden town too — but while ours was swampbound, hers was smack in the middle of Lumberton. It had been there awhile, squatters' shacks clustered on the riverbank, but the macks couldn't see it. All they saw was a trash heap. And something strange had happened over in Hestertown. Nelly said it wasn't so strange, a town like a person will snap if pushed to the brink.

Hestertown snapped, all right. A delusion took hold. It was whispered at first and then spread like gospel. Lincoln was coming, they said. Yes, to Hestertown of all places! He would arrive at night with no fanfare, disguised and alone. He would deliver a hundred dollars to every loyal Unionist. Some of the more energetic-minded spent days clearing a path through the mud and junk, for Lincoln's tour. They built a platform for his speech. Nelly told them this was nonsense, but in spite of the respect they had for her, they continued to dream of Lincoln. I believe they prayed to him. But that was a sign of the depth of their misery, a people made desperate by despair. Losing faith in themselves, they came to expect deliverance at the hands of an outsider.

I said that would never happen to me. I had never even relied on God as a rescuer, and swore I never would as long as I had an ounce of my own power left. I did pray, and I sometimes went to church — but we weren't members anywhere, we jumped around. We tried them all, including Sinclair's Presbyterian one at Smyrna one time, where we sat upstairs among the slaves. But the only preacher my mother trusted was Patrick Lowrie, and the Methodists hadn't given him

121

a regular church. Sometimes he preached at our Scuffletown churches, New Hope and Union Chapel, or in brush arbors or somebody's yard, and I liked to hear his thundering voice when he got to exhorting. He was a fine-looking man, the son of Mr. Allen's youth by a wife who died in childbirth. Mary Cumbo called Patrick her own, but I think he always felt a deep-down sorrow for his lost young mother. I thanked God for not taking my mother that way. I thanked God for all his gifts to me, and I went so far as to make requests for more. But I wasn't relying on Him for anything. Certainly not a visit.

Not that I thought He lacked interest in us. Scuffletown was His kind of place, its people the very type He listed among those preferred to inherit the earth. But (and this is something I never said to anyone, because it is hard to explain) I wasn't sure I could be counted among them. Whenever Cee said, 'We know who we are,' or 'We live by our wits,' I wondered. Was I among the we? Was I one of us? As a body the settlement was in close touch with God, but I didn't know if I was really part of that body.

And I remember when my doubts first started, not the day of Margaret Ransom's cruel parting remarks to me but a time much earlier, when I walked into that little room in the courthouse, eight years old but proud of myself and sure-minded, and the man took down the dimensions of my limbs and features. He examined my fingernails, my teeth, my hair. With a metal instrument he determined the degree of curve in the arch of my foot.

Meanwhile I had taken my own measure of him, observing from his thin lips and little eyes that he was none too bright. I knew. Yet I stepped forward willingly. Why not? We were doing a favor for Dr. McCabe, submitting ourselves to the possum-eyed man from Philadelphia. I only thought he wanted to learn from us, I didn't know it was a *test*. But I began to feel uneasy when he looked me over, and I noticed my mother felt so too. It wasn't like her, the way she was acting — too quiet, too hangdog. She didn't say anything.

Nor did the man. He looped a measuring string around my head at the temples, and then he walked over to the closet and opened the door. Something clattered, hanging from the coat hook.

I looked, and I saw a leather strap on which were strung half a dozen skulls, the strap running through at the ear holes; and he lifted one of the smaller heads, labeled in white ink across the forehead, 'Female child,

Cheraw,' and he measured it, the same way he had measured mine. The way he held it, the holes where her eyes had been stared straight at me.

After that, I changed. I felt yanked flat. My mother laughed at the Government for its ignorance. We'd just go on with our lives, she said; we would continue.

'And honey, think about it. If they ever *had* certified us — if we'd proved ourselves to their satisfaction, with relics and bones or a language or a treaty paper — we might *not* have continued. We could be dead or in Oklahoma, and it's better, probably, to be alive in North Carolina. That's how I look at it.'

But all I could think was, I failed; and the only one I had to blame for it was Daddy. It's hard when you feel a grudge growing against someone you love, especially when it's for nothing he could help or change.

'Nobody's pure,' Cee said. But that didn't help. I kept my proud style, but inside I was beat down.

Still, I had my hopes. I set my sights on things in reach — living the life I had as best I could, holding on to the people I saw around me. I would raise a family and put together a little house-life. All I wanted was a cabin (hewed wood would do, didn't even have to be ceiled), a smokehouse and corn patch and vineyard, a honey tree or box hive, a hat with a feather, some buckle shoes, pictures on the wall, books in a glass-front case, a musical man although I didn't yet know which one, and all the babies we could manage to make. Those were the little hopes of my girlhood. Love was among them, yes. Maybe love is no small hope, but at the time I thought it not only within my reach but likely to be easier to come by than shoes or books. I thought it was something everybody could get, no matter who or where they were as long as they weren't stranded on a desert isle.

By love I meant love. Desire might figure in or not, but for love all that seemed needed was one other half-decent soul in shouting distance. Almost anyone could qualify, as long as he would shout back. Of course, I already had my loved ones — parents and brothers, Mr. Allen, Nelly, Clelon, Henderson, and Margaret, maybe even Miss McCabe. But I wanted someone for whom I'd be the only one, someone mine for life.

So at the end of that summer, I started thinking about a husband. How could I help it, with my mother's teasing plus all those stories and poems I'd read, full of love's famous delights and sorrows — and 'Time's wingèd chariot' that the poets heard rushing up on them?

I heard it too, big old wings like a heron's at my back. I had no soft, moony reveries like some girls get in those last few years before the marrying age. Maybe in other times I would have, but a leisurely dream of husbands is a peacetime thing, and mine was urgent and desperate. I held on to my girlhood hopes by telling myself the war couldn't outlast me — it fed on soldiers, and had already eaten up so many I didn't see how it could find more. It would die down like a starved mule, which was something I had seen happen four times. The mule will stand and look dead a long time before it genuinely dies, but by and by it drops. You might raise it once or twice but to no lasting avail.

And when the war died, I could start looking in earnest for someone to be my life's companion.

But it hung on. On and on. My dozen hopes seemed fated to go the way of coffee and sugar. And do you think I fell like Hestertown into surrender and dementia? No. But one day, around the middle of August, when I stood alone under the grapes in the stillness of noon, an ache washed over me, of grief without reason and longing without object. I wrapped my arms around myself and looked up through the leaves; I boiled my wishes down to one simple thing and made it into a prayer, or more than a prayer: a demand outright.

'*Give* me love,' I said to God, 'the kind fierce as fire.'

I was dying for it, itchy as a boxer waiting for the first big match or a racehorse for the run. I was young but I was ready. I would have it no matter what.

So maybe I was not so different from Hestertown, my hopes as high and unlikely as theirs.

★　★　★

The heat didn't let up. Even into September we sweated and puffed up and baked like biscuits in an oven. Andrew would spit in the chimney and look sullen no matter what we tried to say kind to him. He wanted to run off with Henderson. But Boss was more dutiful. That was the big difference between my brothers — duty never occurred to Andrew. I began to see the weight that fell on Boss. He had to be what Andrew wasn't, but he was too young for that burden of worry. He was cut out for the higher life, he needed to be sheltered from the worries of this one. I knew he might leave us someday, but until then I was determined to keep him safe.

'You ready for another lesson, Boss?' I said one night. I was using *The Golden Treasury* to teach him reading and give him a taste of poetry at the same time, and he was quick with it but not eager. Sometimes he got a troubled look that made me wonder what he was thinking. Boys won't tell their fears outright, I'd learned. Some don't even have any to tell — Andrew for instance — but Boss would now and then turn thoughtful and his brow would knit, and I knew something was dragging on him.

I saw it in his eyes. He was standing to face me, but he was looking to a spot on the wall over my left shoulder where Daddy's watch hung. And a peculiar heartache came onto me, a longing to save him from whatever the dragging thing was, combined with the certainty that I could not do it. That is why love is an anguish as it grows. Start loving someone, and the first thing you know you will be thinking of danger all the time: mumps and yellow fever, gun wounds, knife stabs, broken hearts, and smashed hopes.

'Want to do some verses?' I said.

'No,' he said. 'Not now, it's a waste of candles.'

He reached up and took down the watch,

Daddy's best treasure that he got under questionable circumstances off a man in Alamance. Every evening Boss wound it. But at the moment he only held it flat in his hand, as if it had a significance he had overlooked until just this instant. He tilted his hand so the glass face caught light from the high window and bounced a tiny flash my way. I hoped he had done it on purpose as a signal to me. But it seemed he had not.

'Rho, does Dr. McCabe have a pocket watch?'

'Not anymore,' I said. 'Miss McCabe traded it to Brant Harris for protection, along with a spyglass.'

'I heard Henry Lowrie's has a moon on it that rises and sets,' Boss said.

'Well, hurrah,' I said. 'Who'd he steal it from?'

'Henry would never steal a watch, Rho, even if he wanted it bad.' Boss spoke in a gentle, explaining voice, not knowing I'd meant my remark as a joke. Henry was his hero, and I was jealous because I wanted to be Boss's hero myself. To that end, I sometimes fell into a style that Cee called show-off sass, which was not my real nature. It was an act all for Boss, to get his attention. But it failed.

'Wish I had me one,' he said, winding the

stem. His hands were bigger than you might have expected for someone with a fine touch. His shiny hair fell down and hid his eyes from me.

'What for?' Andrew said.

'To carry.'

Andrew laughed. 'Boss, the big man. You want a chain and a fob too? You want a eagle-head cane?'

'I just want a plain old tin timepiece.'

'Oh, for your appointments at the bank? Calling on young ladies in town?'

'Shut up, Andrew,' I said. 'You're the one that knows about calling on young ladies. Maybe you need that watch, or some other boy might beat your time with Flora one of these nights you keep her waiting again.'

'Flora don't run me,' Andrew said. 'My time's my own. No girl tells me what to do when, and no watch either.'

'Fine,' Cee said in the automatic flat voice she always used to stop Andrew's needling. 'That makes things easy. Boss gets the watch. Now quit arguing.'

'But it's Daddy's,' Boss said.

'I thought so too,' Daddy said. 'My lucky watch.'

'I don't mean *now*, for goodness' sake,' she said. 'I mean after Daddy — ' Then she looked up at their two puzzled faces, Daddy's pocked ruddy one and Boss's smooth tan one, both wide-eyed.

'After Daddy what?' Boss said.

'Digs up a money pot and buys himself a brand-new, *luckier*, watch,' she said, turning back to the candle mold and mumbling, 'Lord help me. Two peas in a pod.'

Whenever something good came his way, whenever something bad was avoided, my father laid it to the watch. 'Still working for me,' he said. My mother said yes, he was a lucky man all right. I didn't know what to think. How can we know what works to deliver us? But I believe it was less the watch that helped him and more the wife.

Boss hung it back on the nail, but he kept his eye on it. After a while he said he thought he would check the latch on the gun hole, make sure it was springing right.

'You already checked it twice before,' Cee said, but he went on and did it again, as he had every day since that afternoon at the trestle bridge when he found the bodies.

The gun hole was under a floorboard before the hearth, a secret place where we kept our one old musket that Daddy brought with him from Alamance. For thirty years it had been against the law for Scuffletowners to own a gun, yet if you didn't have one you'd surely starve, so you had to hide it where the

131

law, if it paid an unexpected visit in the person of Brant Harris or Sheriff King or his deputy, Roderick McTeer, would not see it. Daddy being a digger by trade had lit on the idea of excavating. Digging was not only his profession, it was his great delight.

'I'm a born gold miner,' he said. 'I just landed in a place where no gold was.'

'Why don't we go to California?' Boss said.

Judging by Cee's cackle he might as well have suggested the planet Venus. But Boss was serious and Daddy took him seriously.

'I had that same idea,' Daddy said, 'but I done some asking around and found out it's too late. The California rush is over and its gold is in the big men's banks.'

'But don't worry, your daddy's talent won't be wasted,' Cee said. 'There's an eternal need of drainage ditching to be done in Robeson County. Everybody comes into this world with a gift, but don't all of them get a chance to put it to its highest use.'

Dr. McCabe alone could have provided Daddy with a lifetime of work, as he had embarked on an ambitious scheme to drain his swampland. For a while he was also hiring Daddy to exhume bones for purposes of research, but Cee put a stop to that. Daddy took up wells and graves and privies, too, with a sideline in safeties and stashes.

He could dig anything. Our gun hole was only one of the hollows he'd carved out for us. We had another, bigger cave under my bed in the opposite corner that would hold a full-length man, plus a hog-size hole under the smokehouse, both of them lined with pine planks and tent canvas to keep them dry, and concealed with covers that fit and matched the floorboards. All you might notice, if you got down and looked close, was one tiny prize hole into which the tip of a punchbelly file could slip and spring the catch Boss had fashioned, and the board would pop up.

That file point was so thin and stiff they said it could go into a man's belly and come out clean, the skin closing behind it without a hole, and the man would bleed to death inside without evidence of murder. I don't think this had ever been tested, but it may have happened once at any rate since every turpentiner knew the little file as a punchbelly, and there was nothing in its normal use to explain the name. It was a three-sided file for honing hacks and pulls and scrapers, small so it could file a rippled blade, with a long sharp pick at one end for opening a run through old resin. Every chopper and dipper carried a punchbelly handy in a leather sheath on his belt. This one had belonged to my grandfather Malcolm and was the only souvenir of him we had.

I sat studying the look on Boss's face while he fiddled with the springlatch. When he worked with his hands, his mouth worked too, as if he were whispering a phrase of foreign words. I tried to read his lips, thinking that if I could only make out those words I would know his secret thoughts. He would be *disclosed* to me. But he finished his tinkering, put the file away, turned his back and fell asleep.

Boredom is boring, but hot boredom is an agony. Sweat dropped from my eyebrows through my lashes and down my cheeks like tears. I would have given anything for a breeze or a newspaper.

The *Robesonian* had not yet started in Lumberton, and other papers didn't often come into our hands. When one did, from Fayetteville or Raleigh or that one from Wilmington that Nance was in, we snatched it up like food. The paper itself was what I wanted, for writing on. I'd rather have had a gilt-edged notebook, but I found that I could write sideways across the newsprint and thus cover a whole sheet with my scribbles, the little rhymes and silly stories that came like bouts of hiccups I couldn't stop. Holding a paper, my hands would start to itch. A prickling anticipation overcame me, and I couldn't wait to sneak into a corner with my slate pencil, or the pen when I had ink. But first I would read the war news to my mother, and she would say where it went wrong, based on what she had heard from the Lowries or Nelly.

We always had sources. We always knew more than we let on and more than we were supposed to know.

The main war was still somewhere else, it wouldn't come to us, we said, because our land was no good for it. There might be room for a nearby skirmish in the pine barrens, where even the lowest branches were well above the cap of a horseman, and turpentiners cleared the underbrush every winter to prevent fire. But where we were was different, still piney in the dry parts but mixed with oak and dogwood and hickory, and in the wet parts thick with cypress and gum. Armies couldn't fight on our ground, too muddy and briary, cut by the twisty river and by creeks that sometimes you couldn't tell were creeks at all because they flooded and spread to a three-inch-deep ocean, until our whole settlement, the scattered two hundred houses that we called a town, was awash and brilliant. For although the water was black where shaded by trees, in the open it could flash to green or gold or silver, or any color the heavens lent. Fields and yards and ribbony lanes shimmered, and sometimes the sky in the water was more radiant, more bluely dazzling, than the sky above. Strangest of all were the ponds at nightfall, when the sky went black but the ponds for a moment shone white as milk. Water may keep a memory of light, I thought, even when the light has died.

During the war years we'd had more rain than usual, more than was natural, because of the quantity of shooting across the South. In Virginia, smoke blocked out the sun for weeks, they say, and the boom of cannonading threw nature off. Weather everywhere went to the extremes. Nelly said those battlefields glowed green at night from a phosphor sent up by the thousands dead under their light cover of earth, the vapor borne high into the clouds and blown south to make the raging storms we had. And sometimes after the rains our waters would rise in the night and a house could be lifted, we said, so slow and easy that a family asleep might wake the next day to find themselves moved by surprise, and everything else all shifted about as well, smokehouse and wagon and yard pots, resulting in a new arrangement of life. I had never seen that happen, but it sounded good to me and I sometimes fell asleep on rainy nights hoping for a relocation.

Just a slight one, for the sake of refreshed perspective, so I could look out and see things different a little. Without traveling.

Because that's what I wanted to do. Stay in the place that was mine, and keep seeing its beauty and keep feeling alive in it and never lose heart until my dying day.

$$\star \quad \star \quad \star$$

'Daddy,' I said, 'when my time comes I want a white stone tall as a pitcher pump with a carved inscription that says *A Light from Our Household Is Gone*, and I want a special box — '

Cee said, 'You'd do better to be planning your wedding. A light has got to get lit before the household regrets it going out.' And she shot me an evil eye for bringing up the subject, a taboo in view of how it could throw both Daddy and Boss into a sinking spell.

But I was comfortable with death as a subject. It was just my own I was dwelling on, nobody else's, so I didn't see why they should mind. I had rolled it around in my head so long that it wasn't really a morbid thought, it was something I had become accustomed to, far less horrible than the thought of a loveless life. Even today, I consider my ease with the prospect of my own passing as a little gift God sent me, that has enabled me to do some things I'd not have done if I'd been scared. Other deaths, not mine, were the ones I feared. The thought of those was much more troublesome, and I tried to keep them out of my head.

I knew my own was coming, though. It always seemed right around the corner, which made every day a race. Every day was crucial. That's one reason I was reading so hard, because I didn't know how long I had. My formal education, if you can call it that, was over, and from now on I would have to read my own way to higher learning.

It was a sore topic, my education, little discussed because of the squabble it could raise between Daddy and Cee. He was for it, back when I first went to the McCabes under the arrangement Miss McCabe proposed; but Cee was torn. She had given me the will to learn, but she knew she couldn't give me the instruction. Yet she wasn't at all fond of Miss McCabe, and didn't like the idea of me in those hands. My head might get filled with lady nonsense instead of the real thing, *useful* knowledge — and she meant useful not to me but to the settlement, for she hoped I might become a teacher. 'Everything in this life is shaky,' she said, 'and education is the safest fortune. We've been crazy for it a long time here, going on thirty years. We got to get us a school.'

It was that ambition — for Scuffletown through me — that finally led to her consent, even though it meant all the work of our house fell upon her while I was off becoming learned. She would work her day at the stillery and then do her cooking and washing, make her soap and candles and molasses, all in the after hours. She had been known to plant seed corn by moonlight or hoe cabbage in the flickety light of a high bonfire flame, whereas if I'd been home like any other girl I could have cut her work in half, and she might have got a good night's sleep. As it was, I believe she had slept not more than four hours any night in the last year.

If Floral College should ever start up again after the war, Miss McCabe had promised she would write a letter to its president urging my admission, and find a way to pay my fees. The list of classes she showed me sent my heart speeding, each title a seduction: Algebra, Chemistry, Rhetoric, Moral Philosophy, Geography of the Heavens. But both of us knew a letter would not open the doors of Floral College to me, and maybe that is why she let me keep the list, as the closest I would ever get to Geography of the Heavens.

And at home I was a burden, unskilled at any of the work that needed doing. Since our cow and pigs had long since been taken off by the army, I did not have to contend with them, but I failed at the remaining chores. I could hardly hoe my way to the end of a bean row without getting a crick in my neck; I could carry an empty wash vat but not a full one. If my brain had strengthened, it was at the expense of my back.

Daddy said never mind, he preferred a daughter who could read over one who could haul, and Cee said, 'Your Miss McCabe lost interest in you, so what? We had that happen before. Don't droop. You learned enough to go the rest of the way by yourself. By the time the war's done you'll know all you need, and we'll get up a subscription class like the Bitty School that the Sampson family used to run. Even if you only can teach reading, at least it will be a start. The Bible says, 'Edify one another,' and that's what we'll do.'

'I was just thinking the same thing,' I said. 'I was going to see if Margaret and me could teach each other when she gets back. We'd have some fun of it, making up lessons and exercises.'

She raised an eyebrow.

'What's wrong with that idea?' I said.

'Margaret may have her hands full when

140

she comes back. Besides, it's a mistake to wait for someone when you're already well along the road. Don't lose your progress. You got those books, just keep going in them. And, Rhoda, whatever it is you are writing on those papers you hide under the mattress — '

I thought she was going to say, *Stop wasting your time.*

' — keep on with that, too.'

So the job they gave me was to watch the grapes in the vineyard and keep the birds out, which meant I could sit in the cool of the vines and read. Everyone knew this was no job at all, but a way for me to proceed into my future. They never complained. They loved me, were glad to have me home again, indulged my sassy spells, my impatience, my many hungers. Even Andrew, in spite of our squabbles, was willing to boil the washing and sweep the cabin so that the scarecrow in the vineyard might read and scribble the days away till grape time.

That is why I was so crazy with the confinement and hated the Guard for causing it. I longed for the green solitude, a breeze from the west, my arbor, my sunlight, but all I could do was stand at the cracked door and pine for freedom.

'Ma, am I going to turn out like Donohue McQueen?'

'A misfit lunatic nuisance? Well, I don't know. Depends on if you listen to your mother and remember your upbringing.' She cupped my chin and turned it left and right. 'But I don't see any real signs of trouble so far. I think you'll be just fine.'

The thing she didn't know was that Miss McCabe had not tired of me. She didn't send me home, I left by my own choice because I was homesick — not in the usual way but much deeper, as if every day I spent at the McCabes' was making me more and more like Donohue McQueen, just as Margaret had predicted. But I only gave my mother that joking hint of how I felt. I was afraid if I said it outright she would worry it was true.

★ ★ ★

One evening I begged to light the lamp so I could read a little longer. The pine-tar candle only spit and smoked and gave a pitiful speck of a flame.

'Can't,' Cee said. 'No more fuel. Not even a drop of turpentine.'

'Burn butter then.'

'Well, I'm sure Miss Amanda McCabe eats tubs of butter at every meal, but we've had none since June when the cow joined the Twenty-Fourth.'

'So do we sit in the dark every night the rest of our lives?'

'Honey, it's not even sunset yet.'

'Then I'm losing my eyesight. I can't see. I'm going *blind* — '

But then we heard the dogs, one howl from Jack by the river followed by Girl in the corn taking up his signal and Bluey on the porch with a low growl.

I jumped to my feet, so did the boys. Andrew reached toward the high shelf but Cee said, 'Everybody be still. It only means someone has crossed the river. They might not come our way. We won't know for a while, so hold off, Andrew.'

But he already had the punchbelly in his hand, ready to spring the floorboard and get the gun.

'Put that back,' she said.

She was listening with her left ear cupped, which she called her 'cute ear and said it could hear more than the ordinary human ear. I didn't hear anything but I could tell she did, and whatever it was was puzzling her.

She said, 'Something's off. That's not the way the dogs do for strangers. It must be somebody they know but don't like.'

She got up off the bench — Cee like all the Lowrie women was big and didn't move fast. She slid the bolt and opened a crack the

143

width of her 'cute eye, also the left. Everything on the left-hand side of her body was better than what was on the right, including the ear and the eye, the fingers, breast, leg, and foot. She could tie a knot of yarn with her left-foot toes, while the others couldn't do anything spectacular at all.

I was surprised how light it still was outside. Through the narrow slit fell a golden stripe across her eye and neck and clothes, top to bottom. That was the first moment I felt afraid, from the way it snaked down her.

But she was relieved to see who it was.

'Lowrie boy,' she said, peeping out. 'We know what he's after.' She laughed and looked at me. 'The dogs are warning you, honey.'

'What Lowrie boy?' Daddy said.

'One of Allen's. The handsome one,' she said, still peeping. 'The devilish-looking one. I know him by his hat.'

'Let me see,' I said.

'Oh, she's *interested* now,' she said. 'Didn't she claim she wasn't looking, Daddy? Don't it appear she's looking now?'

I had slid between her and the door to where I got a clear view of Steve Lowrie stomping through the soggy field in his wide-brimmed hat, out in the open as if there were no risk.

I was glad to see him, not because I was interested in him the way she meant but because I figured his coming meant the Home Guard had once more passed us by and gone back to their own houses. The men in the Guard, including the conscription officer himself — fat, vile Brant Harris — were lazy and would not ride out past the dinner hour if they could help it. Harris always got home by dark to see to his business. He ran a house on the outskirts of Scuffletown, tavern downstairs and women upstairs, where — surprise of surprises — he was willing to take Scuffletown money from Scuffletown men. I guess every night Brant Harris had a change of heart that let him line his pockets and take his pleasure from the very people he hated so bad in the daylight. Or else he liked to show he could do whatever he chose, he could keep us guessing. No one was ever sure what Brant Harris might do, whether he'd offer a fellow a handshake or a lashing.

Steve, halfway across the field now, paid no attention to Girl when she slunk to him squirming on her belly with her rump up and ears back. I rather wished she wouldn't do that. She was my dog more or less, and I didn't care to see her humbling herself. It was a groveling flirtation.

'He isn't handsome to me,' I said.

'No?' Cee said. 'Lord, if he isn't, who is? I don't know a girl in working order who wouldn't follow that boy wherever he invited.'

'Meet one,' I said.

'What boy?' Daddy said.

'Shh!' she said. She closed the door and combed her fingers through my hair and pinched my lips before I could wriggle away.

'This is the one I like best for you,' she whispered.

Did she mean it? Since she whispered, it couldn't have been for Daddy's sake.

'See what he wants,' she said.

'Tell Andrew to.'

'I said you, didn't I?'

So when we heard Steve call, 'Who's home?' I went out.

We had two worm fences, an inner one about the house and yard and truck patch, where we grew our collards and cabbage and potatoes, and an outer one enclosing us again and including also the smokehouse, the well, and the crib. Steve was standing just past the near fence, looking first over one shoulder and then the other. But he didn't come in the yard gate, and judging by his face and by his guns — a pistol on his hip and the shotgun he held across his left arm pointed at the dirt but ready to lift in a heartbeat — I could tell that

146

the danger wasn't over. He wasn't paying a social call, he was going around the settlement, house by house, the way they still were doing to check on the families and deliver information or warning.

'Is everyone in?' he said.

'Yes, and about to die of heatstroke. Are we freed now?'

'No, that's what I'm here to say. They're still riding out. Have you seen them? Have you heard anything?'

'Crows and dogs.'

'Dogs ever set up?'

'Not till you.'

'Keep the door bolted,' he said. 'Every day until you hear different.'

It wasn't like Steve to be so short with me. But I thought at least he'd have a remark to say to me, some friendly little thing with a smart-aleck edge. Instead, he told me to send out Andrew and Boss.

'I need to talk to them,' he said. 'In private.' He swung himself over the fence, not bothering with the gate.

What Daddy had said might be true, that a man with his mind on fighting has little brain space left for attention to women, and war is the enemy of love. I asked myself, *Why then do men choose it?*

'That was quick,' Cee said when I went in.

'He wants the boys.'

They went right out. Cee and I looked at each other, and then she opened the door a sliver, and we put our ears up to it, eavesdropping.

'We took a vote,' Steve was saying. 'And every man among us voted Andrew and Boss. You two. That's who we want. And we're particular, we want only the best. Andrew and Boss Strong, that's our top choices. They sent me to tell you. You'll be full-fledged from the beginning.'

'We'll be in on it?' Andrew said.

'You will, yes sir. Just like the rest of us. And we don't take just anybody. There's some that's offered us money to be let in, like Donohue McQueen. But nobody buys into the Lowrie gang.'

I knew that sooner or later Andrew would go with them. He was at the age when a boy is unhinged and thinks he must fasten upon something — love or adventure, it hardly matters — and then he is gone from home in a flash. Andrew had been noticing Flora Sampson, and sneaking out at night to notice her up close — but he was more likely to jump for what looked like adventure to him. I could have told him it was not adventure, it was only the wet and hungry Lowries bored to craziness in the swamp.

148

Well, let him go, I thought.

But Boss. A rage swoll in me.

Cee whispered in my ear, 'He don't mean it. It's his ploy, you see. To get in the door with you.'

Without thinking, I shoved past her and out onto the porch.

'Boss stays here,' I said, so mad I couldn't keep my feet still. They were all three surprised by the outburst. Scuffletown girls are raised to let men run the show. Only Mary Cumbo, as Mr. Allen's wife, and sometimes Cee, because she was so smart, were expected to speak out, but even they wouldn't interrupt serious-talking men.

Steve opened his mouth but I didn't give him a chance. 'I don't care what you say,' I told him. 'I don't care who's in your camp or what big plans you have. You can tell them that if they've come down so low as taking children, then they are a sorry excuse for men.'

'And tell them Rhoda Strong says so! Am I right?' Steve looked at me sideways with a little smile on his mouth. He took off his overshirt and came up the steps toward me. He untied the neck of his blouse. 'Say Boss's big sister wants him kept home?'

He leaned up close and I could smell the swamp on him, a cool, sharp smell. I don't mind saying I like that smell, it has a power. He stood so near I saw through his beard to the skin, and I shivered. And I saw he had more guns than I'd thought, strapped under the thin, loose blouse. A long revolver across his chest, a short under his arm, and two at his belt. Six all told. If he thought they would impress me, he was wrong. He looked silly to me, overarmed like a wild west cowboy. Steve liked to scare people, including me, but I knew it was nothing but a style. I set my hand flat against his chest and let it hang there one half of a second, long enough for him to wonder, and then I pushed as hard as I could. He stumbled back.

'Say whatever you damn please,' I said.

I believe he thought Boss would be shamed and take a stand against me. But he misjudged. Boss just sat there on the porch rail like he was watching an event at the Scots Fair.

'You plan on keeping little brother home forever?' Steve said.

'I plan to let him go forever,' I said. 'But not today and not with you. He has better things in store.'

Steve smiled and turned to the boys. 'She's got a spirit, I'll say that for her,' he said. Boss still sat there like an onlooker. Andrew was jumpy as a fice dog, but he wouldn't cross

Cee, I knew. No one would, not even Steve.

'Come if you're coming then and don't if you're not,' Steve said to them, but he kept his eye on me. He pretended to have given up, but in that eye was a look that let me know he had one more card.

'It's up to you, boys,' he said. 'But I don't have all evening, Henry's waiting in the woods. He's watching us right now, matter of fact, expecting you to join him. It was Henry who put your names in. The best two, he said.'

Andrew said, 'Henry Lowrie?'

Boss turned to look toward the end of the field where the woods started. 'Henry Berry Lowrie?' he said.

'We heard Henry was taken to Wilmington,' I said.

'Henry's never taken nowhere,' Steve said. 'He goes where he pleases. That was just a story we put out.'

Boss slipped down from the railing. When his boots touched the floor I got a sinking feeling in my stomach, but then I realized Steve would try anything. And I am a hard person to outwit.

'I don't believe it,' I said. 'If he's here, let's see him.'

'Yeah,' Andrew said. 'Call him out.'

Steve shook his head. 'He won't come into

the open, not without knowing why. He's got to be careful.'

'It's just us. Is Henry scared of us?' I said. I went and stepped into the yard and cupped my hands and yelled out, 'Henry! Henry, if you want them, come say so!'

That's how mad I was, for nobody talked to Henry Lowrie that way, commanding — not even his mother. In her youth she was called a hellcat by the macks, because when Mr. Archy Townsend tried to run her off the Cumbo farm, she surprised everyone by taking him to court, thus preventing a land grab. And Mary could be hard on her sons if they didn't toe the line. But with Henry she never raised her voice, she was sweet as pie. Everyone was.

Boss and Andrew still watched the pines, but Steve didn't even look in that direction. There was a ripple of wind in the tallest tops. A crow cawed over the field, but that was the only sound we heard. Steve fidgeted and rolled his hat brim.

'We use a signal,' he said. 'He ain't going to come without it.'

'Give it, then,' Andrew urged.

'Only the gang can know it,' Steve said.

'It's not much of a gang that its leader won't show himself just to talk to a girl and two boys,' I said.

We had a standoff. I glared, but he didn't back down. Then, thank the Lord, Cee came out.

'Steve says Henry wants us,' Andrew told her.

'Henry! Where is he then?'

Steve didn't answer.

'Get in,' she said to the boys. Then she lit into Steve, and told him to take his muddy self off the porch and go make himself useful at his mother's house instead of playing gunslinger.

'How many of you ten boys has Mary got to help her out over there?' she said.

That shamed him. 'William's still home,' he said. 'And we go around.'

'William always was the best one.' Which wasn't true, she only said it to make her point.

'No,' Steve said as if to correct a serious mistake of fact that otherwise could lead to trouble. 'Henry's the best.'

Cee gave him a curious stare and then slipped back inside. My brothers followed her but I didn't.

Steve looked at me hard but smiling, and I tried to smile back.

'You are something else,' he said. And then almost to himself, 'But I'm damned if I know what it is.'

153

What I wanted to ask him, I couldn't put into good words. It was questions I didn't have the strength for — *Where is Henry?* and *What will he do?* — and so I just stood there.

He said, 'I will figure you out though. Sooner or later.'

He walked off by the way he came, with Girl jumping to lick his fingers, and I watched him until he disappeared into the line of trees, dark now as half the sun dropped behind them, a fat red ball melting around the edges. It's bad luck to watch somebody go, but I was feeling outside luck's sway, as if something stronger had just taken charge of events and directions. A blue dusk spread over the field. Girl came loping back alone with a sorrowful face.

Second thoughts set in. *I ought to have been more courteous.* But then I thought, *No, there is a thin line between courtesy and groveling.* I didn't trust Steve. I didn't think he was as strong as he needed to be. He talked smooth and he carried the guns, but I wondered if he was the kind of man I could give my brothers to.

I had heard the danger of false prophets preached by James Sinclair at the Smyrna church when he was still in good standing there, and I remember wondering at the time, *How can you know?* Sinclair spoke of prophets but I wondered about all men. How can you tell false from true in any one of them? Prophets, heroes, suitors — do you have to be on guard against them all the time, to keep from being fooled? My mother believed so, but Sinclair said if you trust in the Lord, He will let you know who's true and who's false. I had the greatest respect for the Lord, but trust was a harder thing. He can be crafty Himself, after all. And what is to guarantee that even the man who preaches against false men is not one himself?

Maybe there comes a day when there's no question in your mind, and you just know. But with Steve, I didn't know. Although many women admire a thick-neck man, I never did. Nor was I crazy about a honey tongue. Steve talked sly, so you thought there was always something else being said without him putting it into so many words. I believed it would be hard to love a man whose talking wasn't straight, at least to you. Slyness may be a virtue in business or war but not in love. A husband should be somebody who sees true and speaks true, otherwise how can you make your way in the world? A husband is your other pair of eyes.

And then I thought I glimpsed from time to time in Steve an odd little mean streak. I thought it had something to do with Henry, the younger brother who was always outshining him. Steve worshipped Henry like everyone else did, but sometimes he did act resentful, and he would start to brag and tease and drink too much.

So he was not at all the kind of man I mentioned I'm drawn to. He was the opposite. But a woman may sometimes find herself pleased for a time by that opposite, a bad boy — I mean one that makes trouble and runs against the wind, full of strut and scorn. I was not uncomfortable in Steve's company. I never had minded sitting out on the porch those evenings he used to come by and play his banjo, and I was sorry it looked like those times were dead and gone.

★ ★ ★

Still, I was glad he had failed to lure my brothers away, and after he left, our sense of danger passed. Evening fell, a cool comfort. By the time it was full night, always our best time, we felt easy again and had no thought of the Home Guard. We sat outside in the fresh air. There were fireflies in the field and sheet lightning in the distance, maybe from a storm but maybe not, I couldn't tell.

'Sometimes it lightnings just for the hell of it,' Cee said, tamping her pipe, looking beautiful and careless, her hair down and loose around her shoulders.

Daddy lit a smudge pot to smoke away the mosquitoes. Boss sang 'And Can I Yet Delay' in a new voice, fuller than the boy-voice he'd had before. This was one of Mr. Wesley's hymns, which I liked to think he wrote while riding through Carolina, somewhere by us — a song of mystery, of complications beyond my understanding. The soul torn, the love delayed — I could not tell what it meant but I knew it blended grief and bliss together.

'I yield, I yield,' he sang. 'I can hold out no more, I sink by dying love compelled.'

With music, men will say things they would never put into plain talking. And I thought, *Well, if a husband doesn't come my way maybe I won't hardly care, this is the soul who will make everything worthwhile for me, this brother of mine.* He was so good, he could be enough. As I've said, there is a kind of love — maybe many kinds — outside the regular of man-and-wife but strong enough to live on.

Besides, what I had seen of the man-and-wife variety was a puzzle to me. Cee claimed to have fallen in love with Daddy at first sight, while he rolled on the tavern floor with the poor squire. But still, she must have known she could have had a more dashing man than Daddy. She could have had a more complicated man, one who'd have engaged her big brain more than Daddy could. The two of them were ardent enough, Lord knows, and she would follow him out to the woods in broad daylight and come back mussed and smiling, but I don't think that was the thing she loved him for. It was something else. Out there on the porch I watched her rubbing his back and playing with his hair, just as you would fondle an animal that might not be the best in the world but was the creature forever dearest to your heart.

I caught myself in a familiar dead end: *If she had married a Scuffletown man, I wouldn't be* — But that was it exactly. I wouldn't be.

'We are blessed, aren't we, Celia?'

'We are.'

'I see no trouble on the horizon. Do you?'

'Not a bit.'

She was always willing to carry more than her share of any burden. I loved her for that. Oh, she was a good one, a wonder.

To make her laugh I clowned around. 'Here's Girl with Steve Lowrie,' I said, switch-tailing across the porch. 'Pet me, pet me!'

'I saw that too,' she said. 'She changed her

mind about him. Females have the right.'

'What's Rhoda got against Steve?' Andrew said. 'Beggars can't be choosers.'

'You would know,' I said. 'Here's Andrew with Flora Sampson.' I drew myself up tall and swaggery. From watching my brothers I knew how to move like a boy, loose-jointed and wide-legged, rocking from the shoulders.

I crooned, 'Flora darlin', let me show you something you never saw before.'

'Don't do like that,' Daddy said, shocked. 'Act a lady, Rhoda.'

'She can't,' Andrew said. 'She don't know how.'

'Oh no? Here's Amanda McCabe,' I said, crimping my mouth and raising my chin and covering my chest with my hands, which wasn't fair because Miss McCabe wasn't nearly as prim as she looked, but it made Cee laugh, and I fell over on Boss and hugged his neck. It was smooth and cool, and his long hair fell across my cheek.

But he squirmed free, and went to stand by Daddy. I saw again the trouble in his eyes that I couldn't ever help.

In a voice he didn't mean the rest of us to hear, but we heard, he said, 'Daddy, have you ever discovered the cause of this world's misery?'

It was such a strange question to come

from a young boy, even a serious-minded one like Boss. We all looked at each other. I didn't think Daddy would be able to give an answer.

Cee jumped in. 'Whiskey and bad white men.'

'Land,' Andrew said. 'When there's too many people and not enough land, they'll fight it out.'

'No,' Daddy said. 'No, I don't think that's it, and I'll tell you why. The deepest hole I ever dug was McRaney's rosin pit. He wanted it twenty feet deep, so I had to witch around first, find a dry location. Well, I got my spot, started digging. Fifteen feet down I hit some pretty blue clay, prettiest you ever saw, so soft the blade slits it like a knife through headcheese. Then under that . . . a *crunch*, way down at the bottom. Well, dirt don't crunch, clay don't crunch, even sand won't make this kind of rattly-gravelly sound. So I reach down, I pull out a handful of the stuff . . . and what is it but pipe stems! Pipe bowls, arrowheads, broken pots!'

We waited.

'You see what that means,' he said.

Boss said, 'Well, I don't quite.'

'You think those things burrowed their own way down? No, all they did was lay out on the ground like you would expect, somebody's old trash. But slow and quiet over years and years the earth grew over them and folded them in. Yes. *The earth grows.* I saw it with my own eyes. So there is more people, but I believe there is more land, too. I believe there is enough to go around. About the misery, I don't know. It looks like there's enough of that to go around, too. Sometimes it just sneaks up out of nowhere, son, and the cause of it is different every time. You fight it off however you can. You might have to fight hard, and you might get set back, but it can be beat. The only mistake is if you fight alone. You need someone by your side, I've found out.'

Boss nodded.

I had heard Dr. McCabe once say, 'John Strong is addled.' But we didn't think so. His answers might not have matched the questions put to him, but then neither did the Lord's parables, did they? Yet there was truth hidden in them, which only a few could see.

Daddy hitched up his pants, unsure if he had given a good answer or not, and looked to Cee to find out. She smiled, and at that moment I believed I saw why she loved him. In spite of his personal fears and his lack of courage for daily life, he had a trust in the everlasting goodwill of the universe. She loved that, and needed it, too, because although she had plenty of daily courage, she didn't have the larger faith. She let her eyes linger on him, so gently, so gratefully.

I could almost believe the earth does grow as he said — collecting around the cypress roots and in each year's pine straw and leaf mold, the vines as they spread and bloom and die, the trees as they fall — growing and gathering over the centuries, enfolding shards, bones, treasures, and maybe lifting mankind by small degrees.

'I'll tell Dr. McCabe to go out and look in McRaney's pit for those *relics* he wants so bad,' Cee said, and we laughed.

Because that pit was a hill now. For years McRaney had been accumulating rosin, the residue in the vat after the turpentine steams off. Turned out into troughs and cooled, it hardens to a glassy honey-colored rock, for which there was little profitable use in peacetime and none at all during war. McRaney dumped his in the pit, where it rose now like the outcropping of a fabulous lode. Cee sometimes brought home little pieces for me, shiny as necklace jewels, which I would carry for luck until on a hot day they would go soft and sticky, which has ever been my kind of luck. Bright for a time and then dissolving.

★ ★ ★

So I ought to have remembered: when it seems something lucky has happened, that is when I should be most expectant of something unlucky coming. While we were sitting there, relieved to have held on to our boys, eased by Daddy's story and silenced by the darkness, suddenly with no warning at all from the dogs there was another figure among us.

He came up from the side, making no sound until his foot touched the step, and even today I am convinced he'd been waiting beyond the shadows until the time was right. I believe he stood there and heard Boss sing and watched my mother nuzzling my father and saw me playing the fool.

I lost my breath. *It's him*, my brain said — so off-kilter that for an instant I thought the man standing there was Abraham Lincoln.

Well, he did resemble Lincoln, in his frame and stance, long arms and long face, but Lincoln was an ugly man and this was the handsomest one I ever saw, or will see in my lifetime. It's no use trying to explain why, because words are weak when you try to explain handsomeness. I wish I had a photograph of him, but only one was ever taken and it was never in my possession. But he had high cheekbones. Eyes hazel gray-green, the color of spring willow bark. Black hair, black beard, and a black new-moon-shaped scar under his left eye, the size of a thumbnail. The face of someone singled out, to bear a secret burden.

He was there so quick and unexpected we didn't know what to do. We didn't say any kind of welcome, even though we hadn't seen him in months and had thought him lost.

'Yes,' he said, as if we had asked a question. I had heard that this was his common way of starting a conversation. I'd heard he was blunt and awkward but had a hidden nature, more than meets the eye. And I thought it might be true. I felt it, in my throat and belly, when he said his 'Yes.'

Some words popped from my mouth, sounding not like me but a sassy, flirtatious Floral College girl.

'Well, if it's not the great Henry.'

He didn't like that, I knew right away. I bit my tongue.

'No,' he said, 'just the Henry from down the road.'

Ashamed, I dropped back behind Boss and reached to stir the smudge pot.

'I've come to ask you to send us your boys, Ma Cee.'

We stared at him. Henry Lowrie, here in

person, saying what we ought to do. We all but leaned toward him.

'Times are hard,' he said. 'And they're going to get harder.'

Cee cleared her throat. She said, 'I heard otherwise. Nelly says Wilmington will fall, and once that happens they won't need the labor. Then it will all be over.'

He said, 'There's more to it.'

'What more? Why don't we just sit tight? Put it in God's hands? This war can't last much longer.'

'That's what we said last year,' he said.

Daddy said, 'I'm pretty familiar with Back Swamp myself, Henry. I'd consider joining you, if maybe you could use another man, and if you say that's the safe place to be — '

'Not on your life,' Cee said.

'Mr. Strong, the safe place for you is here,' Henry said. 'But they doubled the number for Fort Fisher, there's a new list out, and your boys are on it.'

'Then take them,' she said.

'Now wait a minute,' I said.

She ignored me.

'Yes,' she said. 'I see it's time.'

Andrew whooped, jumped up from the floor and went to stand by Henry like some kind of soldier with his captain. He put on a serious face — like Henry's.

'And I need to tell you,' Henry said to Cee, 'don't open your house to any soldiers. If one shows up, let us know. We'll handle it. There's going to be a number of them straggling in, not just out of Florence but from all over, and the Guard is going to come down hard on anyone caught harboring.'

Cee and Daddy both nodded.

'We can go then,' Henry said to the boys.

'Now?' I said.

'Every hour is a risk,' he said.

Cee stepped back behind Daddy with her hand over her mouth.

This was too soon, too fast. Nobody was thinking straight, only because the person before us was Henry Berry Lowrie. We stood rooted and dumb under the spell of a man who didn't even mean to cast one. That was the secret of his power: he didn't intend it.

Finally one of us proved to have a tongue and a working brain. It was Boss, our child, of all of us the one who was Henry's greatest admirer and the one you'd expect to have been most spellbound.

He looked Henry in the eye and said, 'Only one of us can go. Take Andrew.'

I almost fell to my knees in relief.

'Oh, honey,' Cee said, holding her hand out to Boss. 'Don't worry about us.'

'Who said he's worried about us?' I said.

'Maybe he doesn't *want* to go. Nobody even asked him! At least give him the choice.'

She wrapped her arm around Boss and looked down at him. 'No,' she said. 'I think it's too late for a choice. I'm telling him go, it's the right thing to do now.'

'But he just said — '

'Step back, Rhoda.'

'When it's safe, I'll bring them home,' Henry said.

It was almost impossible to doubt anything that voice said, but I tried to separate the sound of it — the steady, deep tone in which surely God's angels delivered their messages — from the gist, which could be treacherous. *He's only a man*, I told myself. *Doubt him.*

'Will you promise that?' I said.

He looked carefully at me, and I was sorry I'd spoken. I didn't think he had ever noticed me much except as yet another little silly cousin hanging around. I wondered whether he even remembered my name.

'No,' he said slowly, almost as if he were thinking it over. 'I can't promise it. All I can do is say it.'

I couldn't see much distinction between promising and saying. But then I remembered what I'd heard concerning his care with words, his reluctance to make an oath of any kind. People collected these details about Henry and passed them around like valuable news. I also knew he drank a swallow of brandy a day but kept a full flask in his knapsack to tempt himself and never yield. In one pocket he carried a chunk of rosin like I did, but not for luck; he crushed it to powder for the strings of his fiddle bow. In the other pocket was a pair of pullikens, for extracting teeth. He ran a hive of bees, had the skills of a master carpenter, and was his mother's favorite.

I knew so much, but none of it prepared me.

'All right,' I said.

In the darkness he leaned closer to me and said, 'It's Rhoda, isn't it?'

He started to put a hand on my shoulder — the way an archangel would touch a shepherd — but his fingertips brushed my bare upper arm by mistake, and suddenly he pulled back. And I thought, *Ah. No angel.* I saw the human part of him, the man part, break through, and I felt the shiver of recognition that earthly bodies know when they meet.

I remembered my recent prayer, for love like a burning fire.

Oh God, I thought. *I did pray for that, and I do want it, but don't tell me it's going to be Henry Lowrie.*

'I'm here at your invitation, I guess,' he said to me. 'So thank you for that.'

'What invitation?'

'The one you hollered. 'If you want them, come say so.' That's what you yelled, wasn't it? I believe I'd have heard it if I'd been clear across the river.'

I could not read his face. The eyebrows met to form a black straight line, severe and unrevealing, and his eyes were hooded and stern. Yet the curve of his cheekbone was beautiful as a woman's, and somehow made you think there might be a smile playing on his lips — although it was hard to know for sure because of his beard, as thick as that of a man ten years older. It hid him, which may have been no accident but something he intended. But I thought I saw the smile.

'If you heard the invitation, you took your time,' I said.

'They're young, to be out with us. I wanted to be sure it was necessary.'

'And how did you come to be so sure?'

'Watching and listening and thinking.'

That was all he said to me. But he added to Daddy, 'Better stay inside and keep locked up.'

'But if you've got our boys, what else could

the Guard want from us?'

'Your girl, Mr. Strong. If she was mine, I'd take precautions.'

He shook Daddy's hand and turned, and led my brothers away. He was nineteen years old, and we had surrendered everything to him.

* * *

Cee didn't shed a tear. But after the three of us were left alone, looking out into the solid night as if already hoping for the return he had promised — or not promised — she said, 'I don't know how we'll bear it.'

I crawled into my bed so numb-headed that at first I thought I couldn't even say a prayer. All I knew was that two things had crushed the breath out of me. One, Boss, gone. Two, Henry, come.

In the dark I heard her footstep, and then I felt the bed sag with her weight as she lay across it at the bottom and put her hand on my ankle. She said my name to herself, as if she were afraid for me. That was when I realized how hard she had been trying to keep me from knowing anything. It was like the moment when you see that the distant lightning *is* a storm after all, headed your way, even though your mother has sworn it is not; and your heart breaks in love and anger at her gruff, valiant lies.

After a while she went to her own bed.

He's not what I meant, I prayed. *He's not the one. Send someone else.*

4

Maybe every unmarried woman lives on the lookout for danger, but on the other hand the single life is safer than marriage to a dangerous man.

Ten years before I was born, a mack girl named Catherine, of the Macbeth family that lived by Patrick Lowrie in the Red Banks section, was found to be carrying a 'woodscolt child,' Cee said. When I asked what that meant she said sometimes a mack planter's blooded mare escapes to run wild with the woods herd, then later comes stumbling home fly-ridden and briar-scratched with a woodscolt at her side. The colt is worthless, a waste of feed no matter how well formed, because there's no sire on record.

But Catherine's father made her go to court and name the man.

She was barely sixteen, the baby due in weeks. Her sweetheart was a Scuffletown boy she thought her father might kill if he knew, so in court the man she chose to name was Angus McPhatter, a neighbor thirty years old. He denied the accusation, but was ordered by

172

the squire to pay his bond. When the baby was born, McPhatter came back to the court in a triumph, for the child was not white-skinned enough to be a McPhatter. He got his nine dollars refunded and went off and married old Mag Bailey. Catherine could have done like some others did — claim her baby was stolen from its cradle by Scufflers who left their dark one in its place — but she didn't, because she loved the child.

Her sweetheart removed himself to the Marion District, and she was left at home with a raging father, her baby named Chesley, and no chance in the world of ever getting a mack husband. Along came who but Brant Harris, setting up in Red Banks as a turpentine middleman, buying low-grade from the one-family stills and selling at inflated prices to country stores like Pate's and Townsend's, with other enterprises under the table.

He offered to Catherine's father to marry her and raise the child.

No one knew where Harris had come from exactly, but after only a short time in Robeson County he already had the reputation of a rough, libidinous wretch, in Miss McCabe's words; and he was widely feared by macks and Indians alike as a boot-legging, brothel-keeping woman-beater. An evil man.

Catherine's father knew that. And he accepted the offer.

That's how Harris gained a wife from a high mack family, which he could never have got under any other circumstances. We hardly ever saw her, but when we did, sitting by Harris in his buggy with her sun hat drawn close, she was always holding her shoulders stiff, her nose straight ahead, and her hands locked in her lap. She never asked anybody for help, she bore a burden we could only guess at. Harris's idea of raising Chesley was to work him hard and then send him at age twelve to the most distant turpentining wilderness anyone knew of, in Florida, the end of the earth, where men labored double because oxen couldn't stand the climate, and the mules all suffocated, their nostrils clogged with mosquitoes. Chesley's mother never saw him again.

I knew I would prefer suicide to a marriage like that. One month after her wedding, Catherine had begged her father to be allowed to come home, but he said no. He said, 'You have tied a lifetime knot.' Years later in his will he wrote a confession of remorse to her, but what good could it do then? Another example of fathers not using their brains until too late.

I'd never had a run-in with Brant Harris,

but Nelly Gibson had fought him off once, and other girls had fought but lost. Three Harris babies had been born in Scuffletown. (But they were loved, and raised to be good children, proof that the blood of bad men is not an eternal curse.)

I told Nelly I wasn't afraid, I could outrun a middle-aged two-hundred-fifty-pound fool. She said it was not a matter of running, and Harris was no fool.

'Just stay away from him,' she said. 'Never borrow money from him or drink his liquor, never take a ride in his red-wheeled buggy or cross the threshold of that house he keeps.'

★   ★   ★

Before the war, it was the settlement custom for a girl to marry at nineteen or so, after a long courtship. She'd have a big wedding feast we called an enfare, and go to a cabin the new husband had already built. But now those who married tended to just slip away and come home wed. Most didn't marry at all. Even though Betsy Oxendine and George Applewhite already had two babies, they'd had no wedding, and Cee said Betsy would do well to find herself another man.

'But she loves Ap,' I said. 'Anyone can see that.'

'Love is one thing,' Cee said, shuffling cards with an expert's vicious flip of the thumbs. To keep our minds off our lonesomeness we were playing skin, the turpentiner's game of bravado and deception, in which cheating is legal until caught and victory is gained less often by winning a pot than by steadily enduring one defeat after another, staying in for the long haul, outlasting the others. One of Cee's methods was to distract me with chatter and then deal dirty. 'Always remember what you've seen so you'll know what to look for,' she said, shooting me an ace across the table and dropping herself a nine.

'What do you mean?'

'Count the cards. You got to think. Maybe you're ahead now but don't let your mind wander.'

'No, what do you mean, 'Love is one thing'?'

'Marriage is another. We're all fond of George Applewhite, but it's best to marry a Scuffletown man.'

'You didn't,' I said back, but kept my eye on her hands, her eyes, the falling cards. 'Are you saying don't marry a black man?'

'That's *half* of what I'm saying, yes. It's been done, but the parties that did it moved over to Hestertown or down into

Marion. We don't approve it.'

'Why not?'

'Because it would only fuel the fire.'

'What fire?'

'The one against us. Applewhite is smart and kind-hearted, but Betsy would be digging her own grave to marry him. Maybe his too. As for me, who knows? I might have dug one that's lying open and waiting for me yet. So far so good, but it was a hazardous step. Being in love as I was, I lost my natural precautious habits for a while. Your old daddy swept me off my feet. But you, Rhoda — you're not the sort to get swept. That's the other half of what I'm saying. You're a level-headed girl. Remember that.'

I saw her deal the next card out of order, to herself instead of me. An ace. I got the jack of spades. But even if she had sneaked a peek at the deck, slipping the ace to herself didn't make any sense. In skin you lose a round when you get a pair, and I already had an ace on the table. The card meant for me would have set me back. If it was her mistake, it was the first I'd ever seen her make.

'Double up,' she said.

'I was going to.' I doubled my bet of corn kernels.

'No, you'll make a reasoned-out decision and choose an Indian man. At the moment I

177

don't guess none of them can afford a wife, but maybe that's just as well — gives you time to look them over and size them up. Then when the war's done and turpentine comes back, they'll get work again, and you'll have your one picked out. And I hope you're keeping your eye on Steve Lowrie like I said. They do calm down some, you know, once they've had their fling of youth. He'll see he needs a level-headed wife.'

I bent my elbow to inspect a cat scratch and said offhanded, 'What would you say to Henry?'

She stared at me. 'What would *you* say to him?'

'Nothing — just, you said size them up, and I'm wondering what you think — '

'Henry Lowrie should be your last choice on earth. He's dangerous.'

She waited for my response but I couldn't think of one quick enough to suit her.

'Rhoda? What's going on in that head of yours? What are you thinking?'

'I think what you think. He's not for me.'

'Good.'

'Because ... well, what exactly is the reason? I mean — what's wrong with him?'

'Nothing! That's the danger. You want an ordinary man with a little flaw. A hurt, a weakness somewhere. Then you can be a helpmeet, and you'll have a bond. That's a man who'll give you some security, in return for what you give him. But what could you do for a man like Henry? What does he need that only you could provide? Nothing. People have been catering to him all his life, and they always will. They'll be bowing down to him. Boys hanging on his every word, women throwing themselves at him naked.'

A flush spread over me.

'It's true,' she said. 'And a man who is offered so much develops a great hunger, but I don't mean, in this case, for women. That's a weakness. Henry is stronger, his craving will be the kind women can't satisfy.'

'What is it for then?'

'For things beyond his reach.'

'So he's no good.'

She switched her eyes from the cards up to me. 'I didn't say that.'

I sighed. 'Sometimes,' I said, 'I wish you would give me a whole story at once. Tell me a flood instead of a drip.'

'All right, I will then. I think Henry Berry Lowrie could turn out to be the best we've got. The best we've ever seen.'

'Then why — '

She set the deck down and fixed me in her line of fire.

'There's a kind of man who now and then

rises up out of nowhere — born different — and is just plain *recognized*. Maybe he's handsome, maybe he's smart, but it's more than that. It's a spirit, a magic to him. People follow him where they need to go. In good times — and if they have the vote — they might elect him to a minor post, justice of the peace or superintendent of roads, something where he helps keep life running smooth for everyone. But his fate depends on the size of their need. And if the need is great — well, he's doomed to ruin. They'll raise him up, and necessity will knock him flat.

'And,' she added, 'if he don't make the right decisions, he'll take everybody else down with him. You saw all those guns hanging off of Steve. Henry shouldn't let that happen. He ought to see, the war's going to end. We should be thinking about the schools we're going to need, and the land we're going to have to buy back, and who we're going to elect. And how we're going to have our share of the turpentine business. That's what's going to happen here. We're going to be citizens of the Union again, and we're going to be smart ones. Unless Henry ruins our chance.'

'How could he do that?'

She picked up the deck again. A deuce to

me, queen to herself. Five and seven, three and six.

'Shoot up the county. Show the Union we're nothing but what the macks always said, get himself jailed and all of us despised with him as common criminals. That would do it. You understand? Did I flood out enough for you?'

'Yes, ma'am.'

Fives to us both, and we both doubled, and I raised.

'I let him take the boys because their names were on the list. But the boys aren't going to marry him. Look at me when I'm talking. *Nobody* in this family is going to marry him. Henry Lowrie will never belong to just one person. He won't have room in his life for a wife, or if he does it will be a mighty small room. I didn't raise you to perish of loneliness. Is that understood?'

'Yes, ma'am.'

But I couldn't meet her gaze. Instead I lifted my eyes for half an instant to the wall above her head, where our one picture was tacked up — Mr. Currier's idea of feminine perfection, which I had torn from an issue of the *Illustrated News*. Its title was 'The Two Beauties, Take Your Choice' — a pair of girls almost twins except for their color. One was white. The other was dark and Indian-looking and could have been my mother in her youth, when she ran off in search of her future, still full of dreams. Before she gave up.

And although I was looking straight at the picture, I distinctly saw, at the lower range of my eyesight, Cee deal herself a card from the bottom of the deck.

'Well, hell, I'm skint,' she said. She was showing a pair of nines.

How could I call cheating? She had lost.

'In or out?' I said.

She considered whether or not to ante up. 'I'm out. That's the other thing. Count, remember what's been played, double when the prospect is good, stay in long as you can — but when you need to quit you'll know it. You feel it. I'm down too far.'

'I never skint you before.'

'Always a first time! You're getting good.'

*   *   *

When she talked about security, she didn't mean money. Nobody in the settlement had money unless you count Hardy Bell, and he got his by moving out, opening his store in Lumberton. The man who stayed faced leaner prospects, the main professions outside turpentine being ditcher and carpenter. Even in turpentine, only the woods-rider and the stiller made good money. But with luck and enterprise and a hardworking wife, in peacetime every man could get by and have what he needed. He might make a little crop of corn or sweet potatoes on the side, saw shingles or keep hives or nurse a flock of turkeys to market size and run them to Lumberton, and thus feed children as they came. Everyone farmed some, whether it was on land they owned or someone's they paid a third of the crop to. Most men were skillful and could manufacture one particular necessity like furniture or shoes or tools or keys, and trade for what they couldn't make. Before the war, a few found work on the log rolls going down to Georgetown, about the only freight the Lumbee River would carry because of its twisting course. Then, right before the war, we got the Wilmington, Charlotte, and Rutherfordton Railroad.

The WC&R was a stroke of luck for us when it opened — the longest straight run of track in America, eighty miles without a curve. When Steve Lowrie first went and asked would the company be hiring Scuffletown Indians, the man, who had been sent down from Richmond, said he didn't know anything about any Indians, what did that have to do with running a railroad? He said they would hire whoever was willing to work his tail off and stay sober and not cause trouble. Steve got the job of fireman's helper. The railroad was a godsend, everybody said.

And anyone could ride. The first train they sent through was free to all, in celebration of opening day, and it carried a ten-year-old girl who thought she'd died and gone to heaven. Me. Nelly talked Cee into a ride from Moss Neck to Shoe Heel, where we waited and caught the afternoon train straight back. On the first leg of the trip, Cee sat stiff upright with her sack on her knees, but Nelly kept elbowing her to look out the window as the pines flashed by, or a pretty pond, a farm with field hands jumping back and putting their hands over their ears — and Cee relaxed a little more each mile until by the return trip she was sitting with her forehead pressed to the windowglass, in a reverie, enjoying herself more than I ever saw before. Nelly, with her legs pulled up under her yellow skirt and her shiny black shoes peeping out over the edge of the bench into the aisle, leaned her neck on Cee's shoulder to whisper slanderous things about the other passengers. The cars were full of people riding just for fun — gloved mack ladies with their fat, fobbed planter men, Scuffletowners with picnic pails and trails of children, Floral College girls with baby-faced Lumberton boys, slaves let off for the day, old

Free Tab, and even three Hestertown toughs — Jerry Woodle and Donald Proctor and Vestor Gaskins, men who kept the Lumberton jail in business, now lounging back in their horsehair seats like they were used to such comfort. At any given moment Jerry was wanted on suspicion of whatever crimes had recently been committed, but across the aisle Reuben King, the Sheriff, merely nodded him a hello. The sheriff, thanks partly to cleverness and partly to advantages of the office, was the richest man in the county.

I have to say the train was from its first day down to now the only place in Robeson County (if a moving train can be called a place) where I ever saw all these people at once, and the odd thing was they seemed to enjoy being thrown in together. Why life in Robeson could not be run on the same principles as the railroad stumped me. The only ones who held back were Miss McCabe's Shoe Heel aunts, safely huddled behind the glass partition of the Ladies' Compartment with the windows closed to avoid contamination, while in the general section, jugs of lemonade were passed from one bench to another and everyone drank and nobody cared. I saw Ben Bethea's little coal-black boy rap on the Ladies' glass, and the Shoe Heel aunts opened their wrist-string pouches to give him a penny. And then they came out from behind the glass to stand in the aisle and watch his jig, and they started breathing the air the rest of us were breathing. Through the open top half of the windows blew in the hot Robeson County smells of pine and mud and pigs, and the Shoe Heel aunts flushed pink, their eyes sparked, and they struck up conversations with people they ordinarily disdained. Maybe this was because they were on a moving train — a ride does not last forever, and it's not likely there will be copulation of the races on a railroad bench, not in a full car anyway.

Whatever their reason for liking the train, I knew what mine was. The WC&R was a zone of freedom for our young men. Not one was ever seized there. They could be sitting right alongside Brant Harris or Deputy McTeer or Sheriff King, and nothing would happen. People said the bigwigs who owned the railroad didn't give a damn about anything but their profit, and so they let it be known they wouldn't stand for any trouble in the cars. It was said they struck a deal with Harris and King and McTeer: rich and poor, light and dark, the law and the outlaw alike would be allowed to ride as safe as ladies. There were to be no impressments or arrests or fights or gunslinging or drinking; and everyone knew it. Even George Applewhite would sometimes take the train, as it was safer than the road or the river or the swamp trail.

I loved the WC&R even when I wasn't riding it. I would go down to the Moss Neck depot and wait for the first low rumble coming up through my feet. Even after the train went through, I loved the track, how the rails shot out with nothing to stop them, and made the lonesome, empty path that was our only view of the horizon.

The railroad wasn't built for our sake, I knew. It was built to get at the inland timber and turpentine, and take them out. But it did bring things in, too. Amanda McCabe ordered her books to come by rail, and I was often sent down to wait for the newest Mrs. Southworth novel to arrive. Dr. McCabe said we might think of the WC&R as connecting us not only to Wilmington but on from there via steamer to the farthest reaches of the earth — all of creation. That was something to make you stop and think: Scuffletown linked to the world! Pondering the idea himself, Dr. McCabe came up with the scheme of importing Peruvian guano, which he said was the best fertilizer in the world and could make us all wealthy, if we didn't strike it rich off turpentine first.

Which was my mother's plan. She meant to make enough with McRaney to build a little stillery of her own, starting off humble and then growing big as any in the state. What was to stop her? She knew the business bottom to top, and the world wanted turpentine. The price of a barrel went sky-high that year the railroad opened, and it looked like the county would have its own boom like a gold-rush town. All the men were working.

But the boom had fizzled when the war broke out. At first the railroad was busier than ever, sometimes with as many as six trains a day hauling soldiers and army goods — a mad commotion that scared me, with the men eighty to a car hanging out the windows or even riding on top, yelling and drunk, and the flag hastily painted on the car along with scrawled slogans like 'Liberty and Independence,' 'Damn the thieving hordes of Lincoln,' and 'I fight for A Free white man's Free Country.' But now the trains ran only off and on — mostly off — and the painted flags and words had been faded by sun and red upland mud. The seats were ripped or busted, and all the windowglass was smashed. When a car of soldiers did come through, they stared out at us like corpses, which many soon would be. We could still ride, but Steve and the others lost those railroad jobs.

Everybody had trouble finding paid work. There was only occasional ditching or carpentering, and all the stills except McRaney's were shut down. Turpentine had no market, as the Yankees had been our best customers, and the barrels were too heavy to ship out on blockade runners to foreign ports. McRaney Junior sold some to the Rebel army but was seldom paid. He hung on because it was his only hope, to keep going until the war ended and commerce was restored. He piled his barrels of turpentine and pitch along the riverbank, and set a guard to watch them, counting on the day when a starved world market would open up again, and all those barrels bring a handsome price. But he had to cut production, lacking cash for labor. Cee still worked a few days a week, and McRaney kept small crews in the camps, but it wasn't a big operation, only thirteen crops, ten thousand trees per crop. Five years earlier he had been running more than a hundred crops.

We were at a standstill. Our men were souring. Where once they'd been full of feisty charm and clever schemes for getting ahead, now there was a surly kind of recklessness growing among them, and none were obvious candidates for the position of bridegroom.

Cee kept pushing the idea of Steve. He was

known in Scuffletown as high-strung, cheeky, and wild — but smart, very smart, and she said that was the thing to look for first. She managed to leave us alone together when he came around, which at one time he used to do with the frequency of a courting man, although he never professed to be one. I didn't know for a fact whether he was interested in me or not. He left it open to interpretation. But I doubted that my mother really favored him. I thought she only said so because she had so often heard me fume against him, and she assumed I would not favor him myself.

★ ★ ★

At noon on the first day of September, the dogs signaled someone harmless had come, and I was sent to stick my head out.

'A bent-up old slave uncle,' I said.

The old man wore a black Sunday shirt and a crushed Nassau hat on his gray head. He was slow coming up the yard and had trouble with the gate, crippled as he was, but he ratcheted along the path to us and called out when he saw me.

'Can you give me a drink of sweet water?'

'Gourd's at the well,' I called back, and I closed the door.

'What did he say?'

'He wants water.'

'But did he say 'a drink of sweet water'?'

'Yes — '

'Let him in.'

'But it could be a trick. He's not from Mackenzie's.'

The Mackenzie place was the closest big plantation, and although I didn't know the field hands, I did know the old ones who were past the age of usefulness and came sometimes to fish on the river. This one was a stranger to me.

'It is a trick, you're right,' Cee said. 'But don't forget to ask *on who*.' She opened the door.

Not until he was inside did he unfold to full height — six feet at least — and take off his hat, from which there fell a sprinkling of white flour. He was barrel-chested like a boxer but slim-hipped, and no older than twenty-five.

'George Applewhite,' he said to me with a quick bow, hat in hand.

'Ap, this is my daughter, Rhoda,' Cee said.

I'd seen him before but never so close. And I could understand why Betsy risked her neck for him. The reason was, he had the same countenance of ease she did, and the same eyes, large and keen, although Betsy's skin was the gold of river sand, and Applewhite's was hickory brown. It was said his father was a white man whose name was well known, but of course Ap didn't use that name, he let Betsy pick one for him.

'I chose the name Applewhite just to confuse things,' she used to say, 'to throw in some more colors.' I always loved the sound of Betsy's laugh. It was the sort of confident true laugh that tells you the laugher is someone staunch-hearted, who sees the world's foibles as an entertainment. I was struck to think those two found each other by accident of fate, when he came one night for shelter and happened to choose her door to knock on. I'm not sure whether or not any love matches are made in heaven, but some do suggest heaven had a hand in the introductions.

Applewhite wiped his face with a handkerchief and took a cup of water from Cee. The message he brought was 'The order stands.'

'Order? Are we now taking orders from the Lowrie boys?' I said.

'I know I am,' he said. 'Have you seen anybody else coming forward to offer us any better? Harris is on a rampage. Shot the Sampson chickens, busted into Mr. Jack's to look for Henderson or Calvin or stolen goods or anything at all he might could use against someone. Looked inside the coffins at Mr. Jesse's! He's been driven mad. Can't find the labor they told him he had to come up with, and he knows it's there, just hiding from him. So he's tearing up the county. They think he won't quit until he has to, and that might be when he goes to jury duty in the October session. So we will hold till then.'

'October!' I wailed out. 'I can't stay caged another month, it's a torture. My leg is knotted up from sitting still. This place stinks of sweat and the night bucket, bad enough to choke a vulture.'

Applewhite laughed, Betsy's laugh. 'There's worse things in the world than stink,' he said. 'You'll survive it I believe.' He crunched himself down into an old man again and went his way.

★ ★ ★

And we did survive, he was right. We followed the orders, and the days went by, and finally Henderson came to say our confinement had ended. Brant Harris would leave the next day to serve in Lumberton as a grand juror — for which I pitied the suspects, but their plight was our relief. The Guard had taken nine Scuffletown boys — Chavises and Brayboys and one Locklear — and more out of

Hestertown. They were chained up and carried by train to the mouth of the Cape Fear River, where the earthworks had grown to rolling hills across the tongue of land guarding the inlet, and so many diggers had died the army kept no count or list of names, just buried them under the hills they had made.

Henderson said, 'Harris wanted Lowries. He didn't get any, and he's still in a fit, but he's off the roads for the time being. I wanted to let you know. You can go about freely now.'

'Thank you, Henderson,' I said, feeling so tired I could not rejoice in the news of freedom but only mumble and sigh.

He lingered.

'You want to walk down to the fish traps?' he said to me.

'Go on and go,' Cee said. 'Walk that knot out of your poor old leg.' She winked at me.

It was half a mile to the McNeill dam and the fish traps, a spot where I had spent a lot of time with Henderson when we used to run our trap together, splitting each day's catch of redbreasts and bream. So when we got down there I went straight to where that old trap used to be near the spillway, but it was gone. All the traps were McNeill's now, and he swore to shoot anyone who put theirs in. I threw myself down in the wiregrass on the slant of the dam, not troubling to be proper. I always could be myself with Henderson, and at the moment I wanted to lie flat on my back and look up at the open sky. Henderson, the way he always used to do, sat on the ground next to me.

The thing I loved best about Henderson was his outlook. He was in a state of wonder most of the time, the way a young boy is — engaged by the most ordinary things as if they were great miracles.

'Look here, Rho,' he said. He reached into his blouse and drew something out and dropped it into my hand. A white tooth with long roots, and a crack running through it.

'That's all it was,' he said. 'Not the mumps. Henry pulled it. The doctor was wrong. It was a tooth the whole time.'

'Well, Henderson, I'm glad to hear that.'

'Yes,' he said. 'You can keep it.' He picked up a little pine cone, the kind that's green and hard and closed tight. 'So see, my wife when I get one, she'll have children. We'll have a whole bunch of children, her and me.'

I sat up in the grass. 'All right,' I said.

'I thought that might make you see me in a brighter light.' He laughed and threw the cone into the pond.

'Oh, Henderson, I always saw you in a bright light.'

'We did get along, didn't we? We didn't talk much but we were always together. Paired up.'

'That's true,' I said.

'Childhood sweethearts. And that's why I come to talk to you. I never did forget you, Rho, even after you went to Miss McCabe's. It's like we grew up so close, you got stuck in my heart for good. But probably you forgot all about me.'

'I didn't, Henderson.'

I was thinking fast, and even though I'd been caught off guard without time to weigh the consequences, I came to a snap decision. I would say yes.

Henderson was more than a good man. He came near to being a holy man. And I was so tired of longing for love. Maybe I should have thought it over more carefully — maybe I should have asked myself, was it *fair* to marry someone for those reasons — but as soon as I made the decision, I felt a burden lifted. A kind of comfort settled around me like feathers.

'I used to think we might get together for life,' he said. 'Did you ever think it? But we went separate ways, I guess. Still, I kept the feeling of a close brother to you, so I wanted to let you know, I think I'm a man in love. It's Virginia Cummings.'

He picked up another cone. I drew in a long breath.

'She's the girl for me, Rho. Kind of quiet, real pretty. About your size. Her daddy's Isaac Cummings in Burnt Swamp — '

'I know Virge.'

'That's her. Duff's sister. What's the matter, don't you like her?'

'No, I do. I do like her. She's a sweet girl, Henderson. No, I was just thinking — she's young, isn't she? Younger than me.'

'Well, I know that. I'm not saying anything is set between us. Maybe someday. But nobody can predict a destiny, and mine right now is up in the air. I been wrong before, back when I had the thought I'd be a preacher. I hoped to be . . . well, called to a higher purpose. Even if it meant I'd never rise much above the poverty line. I didn't hope for a church or a circuit, or even a brush arbor; I only wanted to get caught and lifted — by something, I didn't really know what it would turn out to be. I would just be called to it, and then I would know. I would see a beacon. Well, that's all over and done with. That was just a dream. I'm in with Henry now. How long I can't tell. Until he says go, I'm with him. I won't quit him. And that's what I need your advice on — is it fair to ask a girl to wait?'

I said, 'I think it's fair to ask. She can always say no.'

'She already said yes.'

'Then that's your answer.'

He nodded and looked pleased. 'She's a good Christian girl. The Lord will keep her until I'm free. Daddy worries what will come of it, though,' he said. 'He says I ought to get married and settle down right now. He don't want me and Calvin lying out, he says we ought to be on the farm. Without us he can't get in the winter patch. He couldn't find all his hogs out of the woods to start ripening off. And Betsy don't want Ap out either. But if they could see, they'd know better. Henry gives us something. It's him who sees the beacon, and we follow. I can't help but think it's to the good in the long run. I told Virge that.'

In the silence that followed, I ran through the necessary thoughts to shore myself back up. Virginia Cummings was just right for Henderson. She was as good-hearted as he was, and she could sing, too. They would have a house full of musical children and make their own choir. I hadn't really wanted to marry Henderson. I didn't need a man. I would give my life over to my present family.

'Henderson, is Boss all right, and Andrew? Are they fed healthy?'

'They're good.'

'Why haven't we seen them?'

'Well, only thing on Andrew's mind is the Sampson girl. He sneaks off about every other night to see her. Boss, I don't know, but he did say he didn't like to think about home too much. And he's made himself useful, he's getting to be Henry's right hand. He's put on weight, too — filled out. In camp our food's not so good but we have some houses we go to, people cook us meals. You don't have to worry, both those boys are well fed and doing their part.'

'What is their part? What goes on out there?'

'That I can't tell you. You now I can't, Rho. But I'll tell you one thing, Boss is a fine shot.'

'He never fired a gun before!'

'You wouldn't know it. He's a natural.'

That news made me sad and fidgety, and after a while I said I would walk back home by myself because I had work to do, and I left him sitting on the dam, with a mist coming up from the water and the ruckus of herons flying in for the night, the flap of their wings beating the mist into swirls.

I couldn't think of Boss shooting, I couldn't imagine him with that narrow-eyed look men get when they lift a gun to aim, as if an outside force has taken over their brain.

But that was not what sent me running. Something else Henderson said had clanged a bell of alarm, and it was not the announcement of his love for Virge either. It was something that I couldn't shake out of my head, and by the time I got home I was out of breath, and had to lean against the fence to calm myself before going in.

'Well, what did Henderson have to say so important?' Cee wanted to know.

'Not much. He never had the mumps, it was a bad tooth.'

I didn't mention to her about the boys, or Virginia Cummings, or even the remark that had made me so uneasy, his description of the man who is called, who is caught and lifted and follows a light — because it appealed to me. It appealed to me very much. When he said it, a terrible thrill had run through me. 'The one who sees the beacon.' I couldn't help thinking of that man, and I kept on thinking of him through the night and another long hard crashing rainstorm.

*   *   *

In the morning, we found two big pines fallen into the cornfield, where our puny crop had long since lain down flat and rotted to a mush. Now we would have a hard time

200

planting anything for winter, with almost half the field blocked by the two sixty-foot-long trunks and their spreading branches. The purple bark was plated like a turtle's back, in scales as big as loaf pans. Where the trunks had cracked open, the gold of the pine's heart splintered out, wet and jagged. No other trees were down but these, one lying across the other.

I said, 'Sign of warning.'

Cee shook her head no. 'Sign a storm came through and wrecked our field.'

But we sloshed through the standing water and she walked the length of both trees, climbing across the limbs and pushing the needles aside to examine the trunks, hunting a lightning scar. She didn't think the rainstorm could have knocked them down on its own power. But she didn't find a burn. She came back to one of the stumps and stooped down for a close look at it. Taking hold of a long splinter that was standing four or five inches high, she broke it off to the side.

'Damnation.'

'What is it?'

'Pine beetles.'

She showed me where they were crawling, and the tunnels they had made.

I said, 'Those little things? They couldn't

gnaw down a whole tree.'

'I don't know how they do, it might be poison, but they'll kill the heart of the tree in secret, before it even has time to turn brown. And by and by the windflow will knock it over. These two were already dead and ready to go. The storm just polished them off.'

And left us sopping wet again. It must have dumped four inches of rain in five hours. The yard was one big bullfrog pond, and they were croaking and hopping, and the crows came down to get some. Our woodpile was floating in pieces like a river logjam. Daddy went to collect and stack it on dry ground behind the smokehouse.

'Maybe it was a hurricane,' I said. Sometimes a big storm from the coast could spin inland to us, bringing sea birds on its winds, peeling off shingles and cracking trees.

She looked worried, but she shook her head. 'Scuffletown shower,' she said in her usual scoffing way.

The town had not been named Scuffletown by us. That was the mack name for it, a joke name, a nothing name. Who cared? We answered to it, and used it the way Cee did, to make a little fun of ourselves. The days we had good food, Andrew used to stuff himself and belch out loud, and Cee would scold but Andrew would say, 'Scuffletown seal of approval.' Cee herself called a shovel a Scuffletown spoon.

And I didn't mind the name, I liked it — because I thought of it as signifying our fiber and nerve. Among ourselves, however, we more often called our place the settlement. Why name it if you already live there and don't need to ask directions? The names are invented by outsiders, for their own purposes. The reason behind the name Scuffletown isn't hard to fathom, scuffles and fisticuffs being what the macks often encountered when they came in. But not because we were more primed for a fight than they were. There's nobody more hard-fighting and grudge-bearing than a Scotsman. In fact it was a coincidence I had observed, but not so surprising, that in many customs and habits we were a lot like them — clannish, pennypinching, hard-drinking, churchgoing, holding to family honor and hard work and cleanliness, quick to take offense and ready to fight — but they didn't notice the similarity.

5

Although the official battlegrounds were still far away, I saw the war getting closer and closer to us. And I wished we had some pitched battles with armies and bugle boys and drums and all the ranks in their lines with their flags rather than the kind we did have.

It was a sneaking, no-rules war now. Uniforms meant nothing, except if you saw a gray or butternut you guessed Union, and if blue then Reb, for the soldiers slinking around were ones who didn't want to be identified — beats and skulkers, malingerers, bummers, deserters, escapees.

A Pennsylvania paper Nelly got hold of said that North Carolina held more Union sympathizers than any other Confederate state, and more Rebel deserters — and I believe it but I don't know how the paper made its head count. What people said publicly didn't always match what they thought privately.

The best method I could figure out for judging sympathies was by altitude. The high and dry would most likely be Reb. That would include Lumberton and Shoe Heel, the two mack towns connected by twenty straight miles of track or thirty curly miles of river, depending on your method of travel. And wherever along the way the land was high enough to stay unflooded, there were Rebel mack plantations — Mackenzies, McQueens, McNairs, all those. But where it sank, the politics turned Union. On the little soggy farms you'd find the other kind of Scots, Daddy's kind, broke buckskins like McLaughlin and McLean; on even littler and soggier farms were the Indians and a few free blacks like Ben Bethea, and Tab and Jack; and then, on the muddy back sides of the plantations, all the unfree.

Tucked right inside die-hard Rebel Lumberton was the Unionist hotbed, in the shanty neck of Hestertown, home of the down-and-out — a nest of peddlers and vagabonds and castaways, some of them wicked but most only luckless — where the Lumbee River regularly shortcut its own bend and collapsed the shacks, which were soon propped up again in optimism or stupidity, I don't know which, maybe both. Hestertown never truly dried out even between floods. Old mud crusted everything including the residents. You could hardly tell what skin color they were.

And there was at least one of every color in Hestertown, white and black and Indian side by side, plus other shades you surely never heard of — claybank, sandlander, smiling, laster, brass ankle, redbone, tarheel, copperneck, blackleg, and some they called the strawberry people. All strayed in by ones and twos, looking for a refuge, a place where they would not have to declare themselves in one of the categories the world had been narrowed down to by bishops and legislatures, who I doubt had any idea how many there were that didn't fit — how many different kinds roamed an inland backroads belt from Carolina to Tennessee. Hestertown was a way station, and it was also home for a lot of unmatched pairs, if love had crossed the color lines. In Hestertown, those lines weren't even drawn. They couldn't be. In Hestertown there was so much color it was only color, it didn't mean anything.

★ ★ ★

The day after the storm, Cee took the morning train to find out what Nelly knew. She made me go with her, even though I wasn't fond of Hestertown. I disdained it. Maybe Scuffletown was 'destitute and low,' as the papers said, but believe me, Hestertown

206

was worse off than we were and, as far as I could see, didn't have our mettle. I wondered why those people couldn't just shape up, work hard, and pull themselves out of the muck. In our worst times, we never failed to clean our yards and lanes. And we kept our wits; you almost never heard of an Indian gone raving mad. We always put our children first, we honored our old people, of whom we had many, and we cared for the sick, who were few. 'Sometimes broke but never poor' was our old saying, and when I heard preachers talk about the poor, it was Hestertown I thought of, not us.

Nelly's shelter was more substantial than the rest, but it was makeshift, rigged of wagon parts and planks she'd hauled out of the river. Around back I saw two children she was trying to catch to feed, their mother having been taken to the asylum. They were white-haired little things, both girls but wild as cats and not a stitch on them. Nelly cornered them and held out a crust, and you could tell they wanted it, one of them took a step forward with her hand outstretched — but when they saw me and Cee, they darted. Nelly went after them but they were quicker, and she was left standing alone, staring at the brambles they'd slipped into, her hair half unknotted, curses spewing. Nelly did have a mouth.

'God damn you then, little shitballs,' she yelled after them. 'Rot in hell for all I care.' But the tears were rolling down her cheeks. 'I found them eating grasshoppers,' she said.

Cee said don't worry, they'll come back, and Nelly said no, she was sure they could not live much longer, as she had seen maggots in their noses.

I had never heard of such a thing. I thought maybe that wasn't what she really meant. She and Cee sometimes spoke in cut sentences that left out a main part or had a significance I couldn't catch. They liked code words and double meanings, especially when I was around. But it could have been true about the maggots. This was Hestertown, and children had died here from maladies I never heard of anywhere else. Nelly tried to care for them the best she could, and in this work she was helped by Preacher Sinclair, who brought medicines and poultices sent by the northern Presbyterian mission board. But now she was down to one bottle of camphor and a little turpentine for worms.

Standing there in the sunlight, Cee pinned up Nelly's hair.

'Stay much longer and you'll be crazy with the rest of them,' Cee told her. 'You're the only one here still knows up from down.'

'That's why,' Nelly said.

'It's hopeless! Half the time running who knows where, risking your neck and other parts just to scrape up a few dollars to come back here and give it away? To people who're killing themselves off?'

'You're talking to yourself.'

'Hardly. I don't go to any lengths. I like having one old bedfellow and a real roof over my head, which you might find you like too. My offer stands. The roof, I mean.'

Nelly shook her head. 'I've gone past that,' she said. 'I thought you knew.'

'Too far if you ask me.'

'Did I?'

'I'm just afraid that one of these days — '

'Spare me.'

We went inside. Men didn't come to Nelly here, she always went out to them in tents or hotels, sometimes a general's plantation headquarters. This was her private place. The room was no bigger than our smokehouse, and Cee had to bend to get in — but Nelly had made a cozy place of it, with a rickety table and cloth, a bench, a cupboard built from sugar boxes, and her bedding rolled in a corner. There was a peach on the table. I could smell it the minute we came in. I hadn't seen one in two years. I remembered when they were so plentiful we fed them to our hogs, but they went for Lee's great hog trough now.

'Yankee peach,' Nelly said and tossed it to me. Then she rooted in the cupboard and dug out a tin and two pipes, filled and lit them both, and passed one to Cee. It wasn't tobacco but Life Everlasting that she picked in the woods, good for the lungs and spirit.

We sat on the bench, Cee sucking on the pipe and me on the peach, while Nelly lounged in the open doorway, gazing across a low stretch of green fern and ground vines that ran to the river, which was high after the rain but slower and lighter-colored than usual, the shade of a deerskin, and so sleek that dragonflies could light and ride. Thin trails of steam rose from three or four untended boilpots on the bank — though there really was no bank, only a line where ground stopped and river began. I could hear voices laughing and growling . . . someone chopping wood . . . tin pans clinking . . . and parakeets in the willows. Something was in the air, a last bright summery shine before the snap that was due any day.

'You know he took them,' Cee said, exhaling.

'Heard it from Sinclair,' Nelly said. Her dark eyes looked even more sunken than they usually did, and her hair wilder. One lock still fell across the back of her long neck. I thought her not as beautiful as Cee, but she drew men like corn draws crows, so I studied to see how.

It was not just one thing. She made a lure of her whole self with every movement and gesture, even when no men were in sight. I preferred Cee's direct and almost mannish way, which let her talk with anyone on a level footing. But I thought it could be useful to take a style like Nelly's from time to time. It was magic what she did. Lowered her chin and raised her lashy eyes, lifted one eyebrow the littlest bit, ran a finger across her lower lip or behind her ear. Her smock was open and loose at the throat but tucked tight into the waist of her thin cotton skirt, and she held herself in such a way that the top curve of breast was always in view, part of a leg always flashing from the skirt.

I could do that, I thought. But I could never keep it up the way she did. Sooner or later I'd have to relax and my guise would fall apart. But it was second nature to Nelly, effortless.

'When he took them, he said times are going to get rougher,' Cee said. 'What does that mean? Is something going on I haven't been told?'

'My old girl, I tell you all I hear,' Nelly said.

'That, we both know, is a bald lie.'

Nelly took three tiny puffs on the pipe and leaned back against the doorway, blowing smoke into the green outdoors. 'It's probably Barnes and Harris he meant,' she said. 'They were at Townsend's store, crowing. Drunk talk.'

'About what?'

'The Lowrie War, they're calling it. Said round all of them up and ship them west.'

'Barnes said it too?'

'Missing some hogs.'

'I don't like it. I shouldn't have let the boys go.'

'Listen,' Nelly said. 'Whatever happens, Henry's a match for it. If it had been me, I'd have gone with him.'

'I don't doubt it,' Cee said, 'but for different reasons.'

'Maybe, maybe not. Not sure he's my type of man. Too stiff.'

'Thought that was your type.'

'Ah. Well, I can't comment on that aspect of him. Never had the pleasure, and never heard anything. Believe he keeps to himself.'

Cee glanced at me, and I realized I was eating so fast and furious that juice was trickling from my mouth. I dabbed it with my hem.

She reached over and took my peach — I tried to grab it but she bit out a chunk before I could get it back. Still chewing, she said, 'Johnny wants to know, Nelly, what have you heard about the Petersburg blowup. Some of the Twenty-Fourth are back. He's asking for details on the tunnel.'

'Five hundred feet long. I wish I'd seen it. Irish miners from Pennsylvania dug it. Ran straight under the line into the Rebel camp and blew a crater sixty feet wide by thirty feet deep. There was nothing in the hole but Rebel legs and brains. It was so bad it shocked the Yanks to tears when they saw it, and they stopped to try and help those they'd blown to bits. Then the Rebel reinforcements fell on them in a rage. So the Yanks lost, after all that digging. The McFee boy was there with the Twenty-Fourth, said his company paid the Yanks back double. Took all the black prisoners and tied them up, then set about cutting them to pieces with bayonets, 'Because Yanks love their niggers,' McFee said. 'We stuck and jagged 'em for twenty minutes,' he tells me, and then he wonders why he's all of a sudden kicked from bed and locked out, wandering the hotel corridor without his pants.'

'Nelly, your hair's fallen again.'

Nelly sighed. 'You know,' she said at length, 'you can't hope to keep truth hidden from someone who's right intelligent in the first place, and plus it isn't fair — '

'I'll decide.'

'All right, all right.'

Nelly took time to study the pipe bowl and then stare down through the sunlight and the ferns, until with a shake of her head she clicked her attention back to us.

'Well, it was a good tunnel, tell Johnny. Brilliantly dug. We should reduce this war to a digging match, those Yank miners against the Fort Fisher diggers, and let the winners run their flag up over the nation.'

Wilmington held, Nelly said, but she still thought Fisher could be taken if the Union set its mind to it, which would be a mixed blessing for us — no more need for forced labor, but also no more supplies coming through Wilmington on the blockade runners. Atlanta was doomed, she said. She had recently met a Massachusetts boy on his way to run a telegraph operation for Sherman himself, so the general could know what was happening in his own battles.

'I wouldn't mind seeing that young sergeant again,' she said. 'That little lightning slinger. I love a man who knows something. Who can *do* something. He thought it was other things he was doing that I liked, but really the whole time I was thinking about that tapping machine they use. He said after Atlanta falls, he'll call on me when he comes back through with Sherman.'

Cee threw up her hands. 'All right, I give up. You might as well just let loose with every foul thought in your head.'

Nelly's eyes flashed. 'You haven't heard the least of my foul thoughts yet today. I'm full of them.'

I tried to make Cee think Nelly's remarks had gone over my head.

'But how could Sherman come through here?' I asked. 'Before he even made the North Carolina line he'd hit the Pee Dee River. It's too wide. How could an army cross? And then get through the swamps?'

'Pontoons. Corduroy. The Pee Dee wouldn't even slow them down. But Sherman, the ragamuffin — don't put your hopes in him. He doesn't give a damn for us, he's only thinking now of our sister state, and if he can have his way with her he just might go home satisfied. But he's too wrought up. Can't sleep at night. Hears someone mention South Carolina and becomes incapacitated. I mean *completely* — no matter how eager and

215

previously capable.'

Cee choked on a bit of peach. And then all of a sudden she was laughing.

'See?' Nelly said to me. 'I can always make her laugh. Celia, listen. Big brass don't mean big anything else, let me tell you. For instance, the recent hero. I wasn't such a hit with him but he did enjoy my *clothes*.'

'I don't believe a word.' Cee tried to look stern again.

'Shoes too,' Nelly said.

'You're talking about *the* recent hero? In Raleigh?'

'None other than.'

'But clothes — what for?'

'Celia Ann, you are so ignorant! To prance around in, of course. Kind of like — *this*.' She twisted her shoulders and tossed her chin. 'Sometimes it works when nothing else will. When the usual thing won't do the trick. Don't ask me why because I don't have the faintest idea, but I've seen it with my own eyes.'

My mother doubled over. She cackled, and I loved hearing it.

We stayed in Hestertown until late afternoon, just lazing and talking and laughing, and Nelly and my mother were very happy. So I was too.

And I changed my mind about Hestertown,

I started thinking maybe you don't have to look down on a place just because it is low. Or on children because they're wild, and men because they've lost their reason by dreaming of the impossible.

Nelly walked with us back to the station, and I thought I'd try to see the good side of Lumberton, too, but I couldn't find it. The shabby houses and shops were black with soot and mildew. Some were still burned out from a fire the year before. The boardwalks had rotted through in parts, and the other parts were slippery with tobacco from chewers who couldn't take the trouble of aiming for any number of spitting pails that stood just inside the doorways of the shops. On Front Street we thought it safer to walk in the muddy thoroughfare, but I was charged by a mad goat and we had to get back on the walk. Goats have a frightening look in their eyes, and I was already a little scared by Lumberton.

A few mill owners and distillers had built pleasant-looking houses with rounded porches, and a row of oak trees had just been planted along Front Street in hopes of beautification, but the town was still the rough-and-tumble sawmill crossroads it had started up as. The courthouse and the jail were its grandest structures. On Fourth

Street every other door seemed to belong to a rowdy tavern.

Cee looked at her feet as she walked past those doors.

'I thought this town's mayor had outlawed drunk-houses.'

'They pay a fine now and then. What's outlawed is circuses and wire dancers. *Immoral curiosities.* But soon as one thing is forbidden, something else comes in. Now we get veil dancers and dog pits. Soldiers need their entertainment.'

'I see your friend Peg Faulk is here to provide them her kind.'

Camped at the Mud Market near the river were two old canvas-covered wagons, with lettering in red and yellow: *Madame Faulk's Caravan of Doves.* And at first I had a pleasant vision of a stage act, a lady tossing armfuls of fluttering white birds into the air, until I realized it was something else.

'Peg's all right,' Nelly said.

'In your book maybe. But I don't see any difference between her and Harris. Sin is sin.'

'There's a big difference, Celia Ann, between women in business for themselves, and a man who misuses them for his own profit. And where do you put me? I suppose I'm bound for hell.'

'I have more to say on the subject but not right now.'

The streets were crowded with men, a few Rebel soldiers on leave or on crutches, but mostly loungers of the typical Lumberton type — idlers, drones — and an occasional settlement man who had fallen in with the ways of the town. Half the loungers looked well fed and half looked dirt poor, but none were seeking any kind of work to do aside from the job of drinking themselves into a stupor.

At the depot the stationmaster told us the train was late and might not come till after dark.

'I don't want to be stranded here at night,' I told Cee.

'You don't want to be stranded here in the daytime,' Nelly said.

It wasn't the dirt and goats and sins that worried me, but the men. A crowd of a dozen had congregated across from the depot, where the roofs of the ramshackle shops and liveries projected over the sidewalk to make a gallery. They were drinking tanglefoot brandy and buying meat pies from the vendors. On the corner a sluggish organ-grinder cranked away. His thin, sad music rose and fell with each turn of the crank, with a pause at the bottom that made it uncertain for an instant whether the tune would continue or not, and his monkey went scavenging as far the chain would allow in all directions, picking up peanut shells and bits of tobacco with his careful bald fingers. The men baited him with pie crumbs, then kicked him away. When they lost interest in that, they started watching us.

We decided not to wait for the train. The walk home was long, three hours at a steady stride, but we had done it often. We always were good walkers.

We had just taken our leave of Nelly — which meant taking also her kisses and whatever food she insisted on slipping into our bag, this time a jar of figs — when she said, 'Before you go, you might ought to know one more thing. In regards to Margaret Ransom.'

'What happened?' Cee said.

'Nothing yet. But they have a plan.'

'Dear God.'

Nelly took her by the shoulders and looked her in the eye. 'Now don't fly off the handle. I can't tell you the details, but there won't be anything to worry about. I'm only telling you because you'll hear about it soon enough anyway. But don't say anything to Johnny, understand? Cee?' Nelly gave her a shake.

'Is Andrew and Boss part of it?'

'I said it will turn out all right. You can't

ask me any more about it. You better go now.'
She had her eye on the knot of drinkers.

'But where *is* Margaret?' I said.

'She don't know?' Nell said to Cee, who
shook her head.

Nelly smoothed my hair back from my face
and straightened my collar. 'Well, Margaret
had a loan come due,' she said, 'and couldn't
pay it. She had to hire out as a kitchen girl.
But the debt's paid off and she ought to have
been home by now. So her brothers asked
Henry Lowrie to go after her.'

I was overjoyed at the thought of seeing
Margaret again, but I was mad my mother
had hidden the truth from me.

'Henry's bringing her back?' I said.

'Someone has to,' Nelly said.

A man staggered across the street in our
direction while the others watched him, as if
he was on a dare. He put his hands in his
pockets for a casual effect, but then he
couldn't balance so well and had to pull them
back out again.

'Go,' Nelly whispered to us. 'Don't worry, I
know this one. It's McTeer.'

So we headed to cut across the tracks
toward the river, but we looked back to make
sure Nelly was all right. I had never seen
Deputy McTeer before. He was a dark-haired
shouldery man with a wide mouth, and he

was trying to snap his fingers to get our attention.

'Come on, Rhoda,' Cee said.

'Hey, where you off to?' he yelled after us. 'I got a dollar riding on which one of you was going to come over with us and have some fun. I said the li'l one.'

'You're sure going to lose that dollar, Rod,' Nelly said.

'Oh, it's you, Nelly.' His head bobbed back an inch.

'It's me, all right.'

'Well, damn. I didn't know, the sun must have was in my eyes.'

'I'd say so. Go back to the monkey, you got a better chance there.'

'Who's the gal?'

'No idea. Somebody refugeeing from Richmond.'

'Why's she going with a Scuffler woman?'

'Rod, you got something . . . right *here*.' She curled back her top lip and tapped her front tooth. 'Piece of meat pie or something, spoiling your handsome looks.'

She waved us on.

★ ★ ★

I waited for Cee to talk first. She knew I was mad she had deceived me about Margaret.

222

We walked at least an hour in silence, to the turnoff onto Chicken Road, before she gave in and spoke.

'I only didn't want you to worry,' she said flatly.

'Yes, well, you knew I wanted to see her. I've been lonesome and wanting to talk to her, and all this time you could have told me where she was. You didn't tell me. You don't ever tell me anything important until after it's over.'

'I happen to suspect there's plenty you don't tell me, and the reason is the same. We don't like to get each other downhearted. And you couldn't have seen her anyway.'

'Why not?'

'Because she's at Harris's.'

My heart stopped cold. My feet stopped. 'Not Margaret,' I said. 'She had a young man.'

'It wasn't her choice, honey, she was forced.'

'Not Margaret. You're wrong about that. Nothing could force her there, she would die first.'

'He got a court paper and she had to work off the debt.'

'And nobody helped her? Nobody tried to prevent it?'

'The boy tried to get her back, but he

couldn't. It was Wes Lowrie.'

'Wes is dead.'

'That's why he is. Harris wanted to
. . . *keep* Margaret, see. So he killed Wes. And
I don't want Andrew and Boss busting into
Harris's place and getting shot for — '

'For saving a girl's life and honor?'

'Her honor is long gone, and her life isn't
worth much.'

I sat down in the road.

'Rhoda, let's get home and I'll fix you some
pine-top tea.'

'How could you have let her go there? It
was *Margaret*.'

'Me? What did I have to do with it?'

I closed my eyes. 'Well,' I said. 'You go on
ahead. I don't feel good, I'm going to rest
here a minute. I'll catch up with you.'

'I won't leave you collapsing in the middle
of the road.'

She held out her hand, and I slapped it
away.

'I don't want to walk with you, Ma.'

She stepped back from me.

'You don't mean that,' she said.

'I mean it,' I said. 'Just go, please.'

'Well, I don't see how you can blame me
for something I had nothing to do with.'

'That's right, you had nothing to do with it
— by choice. You looked the other way. And

224

you *knew* her, you *loved* her. Just as much as I did. You should have helped her.'

'How?'

'I never heard you ask how on anything before.'

'We are up against some hard troubles, Rhoda. Harder than I ever saw before.'

'You could have thought of something. Margaret was on her own. Who else did she have but us?'

She was standing over me, and I thought she might pull me up by the arm and force me along with her. I was small-boned, and she was big and much stronger than I would ever be. But she walked away.

For a while I could see her, tramping black-booted down the road until it curved, but then I saw only the white sandy ruts divided by a thatch of red pine straw, and on either side of the road the dark green pines, so close they left only a string of sky showing overhead.

I wanted to think but I couldn't. I only sat, faint inside, failing in a deep way as if the body I lived in had lost its pump and verve, and I could only wait and hope it revived.

No one came by. I lay down in the soft sand of the rut. The thing I could not get out of my mind was how much time I had passed in ignorance, not knowing. Margaret must

225

have been there, at Harris's, since December. How could I have lived so carelessly all those months, why didn't a hint come to me, a shiver I couldn't explain or a dream to alert me she was in trouble? But even if I had known, I couldn't have thought how to help, any more than my mother did. There is a kind of evil that maybe you could stop, but you think you can't, and so it continues, and it grows, until it really is beyond you, and only something extraordinary can destroy it.

A sweetness from the pines drifted down, the fragrance they say is healthful to inhale. The earth was cool in my arms, and gradually my breathing grew more regular.

After a while I got up and started walking.

We had two kinds of roads, the straight kind for travelers to get through the county as fast as possible, and the meandering ones like Chicken Road, for those who stayed. Ordinarily it was my favorite road, passing through all our variety, but I walked now without my usual attention, through the pines to the open fields, a long arm of swamp, then field again, and into more pinewoods, a steady solid green except for the occasional stand of dead trees, dry and white and cocked at angles like pipe stems in a jar.

I saw all that, but it was nothing to me. It was there, but it had no force. I was just cut off. I didn't see a soul.

But one could have seen me. In these pine barrens a little army neither Grant's nor Lee's but Walter McRaney's was at work, spread so wide that one man might not meet up with another for days on end. Armed with weapons that would make a stranger shudder — broadax, iron paddle, knives with teeth — they followed separate courses through the pines, lone as bees hunting bloom.

Sometimes one might emerge, a dark man with a blank, haunted eye and ax in hand, standing still as a deer and staring out from the pines, but then he would fade back into the woods as if the sight of the road, and of you, reminded him of something he didn't want to remember. Probably home, if he had one, and home even more if he didn't have one. He slunk back to his work in the deserted pine tract.

With that toothed knife he scraped a wing-shaped wound in the face of his tree, and with the ax he chopped a box into the trunk under the scrape, guttered deep enough to catch what would bleed but not so deep as to kill — although the patches of dead trees proved how hard it is to wound without killing. Even if the cutting was careful, if the scrapes never girdled the tree and the box never went too deep, the tree still could not last more than six years; but by then new ones would have grown to size, or else the camp would move a mile and start over fresh. And the chopper didn't always have time to be careful. Five thousand trees were his duty to scrape and box, and tend as the boxes slowly filled with gum, silver-gray and sticky; then the dippers came around to scoop it into buckets and dump it into barrels at the bunching ground for the mule wagon to pick up and haul to the still.

I can't explain what came over me then. I was alone in the barrens, and I should have been afraid. Turpentiners can be rough sorts, who might not have seen a woman in a year. But I was not afraid. Instead, I got strength from the company of those unseen men. Their work came to me, the idea of it, and bore me up, because it seemed like the only continuing thing. My grandfather had done it all his life, and these were the men who had followed in his steps, still working the woods in spite of war and despair all around. Some people might think it no great achievement in life, simply to continue. But I saw it as a feat of courage.

When I got to McRaney's, the last wagon was just in with gum for the next day's charge, and in the sunset light two men prepared to load it off. So I lingered. Even at this time of day, when the run was over, I liked the look of the place, the round wooden tank, brick chimney still smoking a wisp, shed roofs blanketed in pine straw, and the idle machinery all connected by looping pipes. It was quiet except for the wagoner's low commands to his team, and the rest of the mules corralled nearby, shifting and snorting with evening apprehension. Compared to town, the stillery always struck me as a place of purpose. No organ-grinder, no loiterers or lazy troublemakers. There was nothing but the work of turpentine.

Some men liked it, for the smell of the gum and for the solitude, but for the most part anyone with enough love and food in his life wouldn't choose turpentining as a career, if he was free to choose, which most men were not. It was a hard and dirty line of work to follow, said to be the hardest and dirtiest in the world, and the men, no matter what color (some were slaves, some were us, and some were others), were called turpentine niggers, partly because the job was so low-ranking and partly because after a month in the woods boxing and hacking and pulling, all were dusky, all were woolly-headed from resin and dirt. Those who fired the stills were further darkened by smoke, and the kiln-men, piling and burning lightwood for pitch and tar, were blacker than any man was ever born. Slowly, I thought, all those men might be dimming and bending toward the grave, but they sent the gum, that gluey mess, in the other direction — skyward, seeking lightness, seeking a form all unlike its original.

I watched the mules back their wagon to the dock, which they did on their own, just by being told to. Turpentine mules are smart, unlike the slow-witted oxen that used to do the job, and compared to horses they are more level-headed, not likely to spook and bolt. I've heard of men killed by horses but never by mules. They can work without a driver, and treated right they will work their heart out. I watched them back that wagon within an inch of the dock. Then the men unloaded the barrels and rolled them up the skid pole to the top deck to wait for daybreak, when the still would be charged.

Nine barrels made a single charge, poured into the great copper kettle, mixed with water piped from the pond and heated by a wood furnace underneath, tended by a stiller swearing from both heat and worry. Too much water or too little would ruin the charge; too much heat would overboil the gum, and then it would foam up and stiffen and clog the works in an instant. McRaney had been trained by my grandfather, and as a result was one of those few who could gauge the mix by listening, resting his ear against the wooden tank surrounding the condensing worm, alert for the ominous rumble of a high boil. If he heard it, hell broke loose. The call for water would go out, a particular yell that could be heard ringing through the woods, and as fast as could be, more water was pumped in.

There remained a danger of explosion, the still-bang. Even though at my grandfather's suggestion the spirit room had been removed a greater distance from the furnace, occasionally the pipes might back up or a spark fly out from the fire. And there was also the danger of men pushed too hard. But McRaney seldom overworked his crews because he understood the one most important fact of the business: that a single match could put a quick loud end to it. No need to rile the men. For woods-rider he liked to hire an Indian man who knew the work and the workers both, could move among all colors and keep them going. And McRaney would give his woods-rider a gun, despite the law.

But at last, if everything went without a hitch from tree to still, a magical cooking began. The gum simmered almost five hours, sending its pungent steam rising through the overhanging cap and down through the worm. It cooled in the coils of the worm, and changed to liquid, and ran by pipe to the spirit room.

There the part that was water sank to the bottom of the catch vat and the lighter part was siphoned off the top, so purely refined it would seep through the staves of any ordinary water barrel and needed special barrels of its own, coopered and glued right at the still. From here turpentine went out to the world — or did once, and would again when peace came — to be put to the variety of uses men had discovered it was good for. But none of them noble, none worthy of the gift. Paint and varnish, polish and wax, lamp fuel, rubber coats, putty, inks, soap, liniment. Potions to keep fleas off dogs, cure bowel spasm in mules, or stop a baby in the womb. These were the products that had made a few big men rich and kept middling men like McRaney hoping.

I might have judged the whole effort a grand waste, considering who bore the cost and who reaped the reward, and how lowly the uses. But turpentine was a secret treasure to me. Not as an emblem of future prosperity — not as an emblem at all — but as a real elixir, made from this particular spot of God's earth. Each clean yellow barrel stamped *Spirits of Turpentine, Robeson County,*

N.C., held thirty-two gallons of our sun and soil and rain, our trees and men, distilled. Our spirits indeed. Our essence.

I took heart from that transformation, the forest full of hidden men who were becoming spirits. I loved those men! They were despised as low — as nothing — and their secret worth was known only to me.

★ ★ ★

Halfway home, the white ruts of Chicken Road grew hard to see and then disappeared altogether in the darkness, and the road became a narrow lane I followed by memory and stars. Little owls whistled and big ones barked, and the whippoorwills signaled one to the next in an unbroken relay, to sound as if only one was following me all the way. After a few miles I began to see the first lights of Scuffletown. At night is when it most resembles a town, when some of the wide-spaced houses all hidden about in the woods show their flickering candles and lanterns, and seem to the eye to have drawn closer together — but still, God's is the only eye that will ever see Scuffletown entire at a glance.

The first house I came to, set back from the lane but well lit by two porch lanterns, was Brant Harris's. Not the one where he lived with his wife, but the other one.

There was no crop, as Harris had never planted here, and the oldfield had sprouted its own pine saplings and thin, ragged pin oaks. But I could see through to the lights of the house, where on the porch four or five men stood drinking. I don't know if I expected to see Margaret or not. It was the house I studied.

There was a well, a chimney, a path to the step. A blue rocking chair. In the upper story, two windows glowed.

I stepped off the lane into the grove, and I shivered as if there was something creeping up on me. One of the men on the porch opened his trousers and relieved himself into the bushes. Another laughed. They were scroungy, lickerish men, more Lumberton drunks. They were weaklings.

I didn't see a fence around that house. I didn't see armed guards. And all of a sudden I said out loud to Margaret, 'Damn you then. Rot in hell.'

On the other side of the trees, someone called my name.

'Rhoda, is it you?'

From the shadows Cee came out to me, folded me up in her arms and rocked me.

'It's all right,' she said. 'You don't have to

curse that man, he's already damned. He'll rot without a word from us. I didn't know you were so lonesome for her, I forgot you are such a loving-hearted girl.'

'I'm not, I'm mean! I'm blaming Margaret. She knew her life was a pattern for mine, that I would follow. She wasn't supposed to let this happen.'

'She fell into a trap you're too smart for.'

'She was smart.'

'Not *was* yet. I regret I said her life isn't worth anything. I was wrong. There's always a chance to get free of trouble, take yourself a new direction. Your daddy did it, George Applewhite did it. If I remember, Margaret was a right tough girl.'

'Was.'

Cee sighed. 'Harris is the worst I ever saw.'

'She could get away. He sleeps at night, doesn't he?' And I answered the question myself: 'But she needs help.'

'She'll get it,' Cee said.

I knew what it took for her to say that. She meant she would risk her sons if the cause was good enough, and she had decided it was.

We couldn't help looking back at the lighted porch again, and the upper windows, until I had to turn away.

'I hate the sight of it,' I said. 'It looks so like a regular house.'

We walked the rest of the road together. She tried to shorten her steps to match mine, and she put her arm around me, my shoulder against the side of her breast.

Our walking had a rhythm sometimes hobbled — when my steps were an instant behind hers, and we jostled each other — and sometimes smooth, our feet going together. 'Waterwhite, Windowglass, Nancy, Betsy,' was the beat of our steps, repeating through the woods, through the cornfields and the parts of Chicken Road that are closed over like a tunnel, around the pond where Margaret Ransom's young man and his brother had died, and down to the path toward home.

★ ★ ★

Two men in ragged Rebel coats came to Brant Harris's late that night, after the last of the regular customers had left. Harris poured two brandies and overcharged the soldiers. In his puffed face his eyes were small as acorns. Because of his fat, no one could read him or guess his meanings.

'What's your regiment, gentlemen?'

'Twenty-Fourth,' said one.

They paid and drank, called for more, and

asked to know where this Margaret was that they'd heard so much about.

Harris smiled. 'Has news of Margaret spread through the Twenty-Fourth then?'

'They say she's the one to ask for.'

'She is,' said Harris. 'That's why it's six dollars. In advance in greenbacks.'

'Six! I thought it was two.'

'Not for Margaret. You heard she's a pretty thing, didn't you? The one to ask for? But if you aren't convinced, I'll do this for you. I'll make it a money-back guarantee.'

'We don't have it. All we got is four dollars and fifty cents.'

'I can't take four, even from a fighting soldier who was at Petersburg. For four, all you get is a look.'

'What do you mean by that?'

'You pay me four dollars, and Margaret will come down and sit at your table and you can lay eyes on her and buy her a drink with your other fifty cents.'

'That's it?'

'That's it.'

The red-headed one laughed and pushed his chair back. 'I never heard of a four-dollar peep show. For that I can get a whole girl in town, or hell, two or three of them.'

'In that case I suggest you do so. And this is no peep show. All I'm offering you is a chance

237

to brag you had a drink with the famous Margaret.'

The dark-haired one said to Harris, 'We'll pay.' He put four dollars on the table.

'All right, then,' said Harris. He took the bills up one by one and rolled them. 'I'll inform her of your visit,' he said.

He climbed the stairway at the back of the room. After a few minutes he reappeared and nodded to the soldiers, and raised his hand toward the top of the stairs.

'Miss Margaret Ransom,' he said.

She came halfway down and hesitated, a thin figure in a dirty nightdress. Her hair had been cut off above her ears, a purple bruise circled her neck, and her left eye was swollen shut. She held one arm in a sling of rags.

The soldiers stared.

'Come all the way down now, Margaret,' Harris said. He moved aside to let her pass, but then stopped her with a hand on the back of her neck, and whispered something in her ear.

Margaret shook her head.

Harris sighed and fumbled in his pockets and drew out a small pistol. He wiped it off with his handkerchief, taking his time, then cocked it, and aiming toward the three-legged table where the soldiers sat, he closed one eye and sighted down the barrel.

'One more chance, my dear,' he said. 'You can tell me, or you can watch them both die slow.'

She closed her eyes.

Then she said, 'One of them's named Zack.'

'But that's not enough for me to go on, is it?' Harris said. He fired a shot and the table fell, one leg shattered, and Margaret started trembling like someone with a fever chill.

'You understand what I need. The full names of both these brave young soldiers.'

'Zack McLaughlin,' she said. 'And Andrew Strong.'

'Well, well. What a surprise. Berry's boys out on their own.'

Zack made a move to draw his gun, but Andrew stopped him, because Harris's aim had shifted to Margaret.

He smiled. 'As you can see, Zack and Andrew, it is unlikely that anyone ever recommended you ask for Margaret Ransom. I must say I'm impressed by this effort at a rescue, if that's what it is. Or did you really hope to pump her?'

They didn't answer.

'Slide me those guns, boys,' Harris said.

Not once did she let her eyes meet theirs.

★   ★   ★

239

I heard a knocking and yelling on the porch and then a thump of something hitting the floor. Cee sat up in her bed and shook Daddy awake.

'Johnny, someone's out there.'

She stumbled across the room in her nightdress and raised the bolt, but the door was blocked. The cries from the other side dropped down to a low groan and then a silence.

'Andrew, is it you? Move off the door so I can open it. Do you hear me? Can you move?'

He crawled to the steps, and we were able to come out to him. Daddy held a candle while Cee looked for a wound. She tore open his shirt to see his chest and back, felt through his hair, bent his arms and legs. But there was no blood.

She took his face in her hands.

'Are you hurt, son?'

When I saw his eyes, I knew he was. They were emptied out, with no spark of himself showing. He turned his head away from me.

'Andrew, where's Boss? Were you at Harris's place? What happened?'

'It went bad,' he said. 'And I ran. Boss is with them somewhere, I don't know, we all ran.'

'Start at the beginning,' she said. 'Henry

went in and then what?'

'He didn't. He sent Zack and me in because Harris wouldn't know us. We were supposed to make sure she was there and then give the signal for Henry and Boss and the rest — but it's not my fault! Harris kept the gun on her. There was nothing we could do but sit there.'

He slammed his fist into the step.

'Is she dead?' I said.

'No.' He rolled his head back and closed his eyes.

So it was something worse.

'Boss got hurt?' I said.

'No, no. Leave me alone.' His shoulders started shaking.

Cee knew then what it was. 'All right, son. Just come inside.'

I grabbed his sleeve. 'Tell me.'

'I can't.'

'You have to. What happened?'

Cee shook her head at me, and then all of a sudden Andrew broke down sobbing. I never had seen that, and it scared me worse than if he'd had a bloody gunshot wound. She sat beside him on the step and pulled his head onto her shoulder, and she smoothed his hair. I could barely understand what he was saying.

'I couldn't stop him, I couldn't think of

anything — and it *was* my fault, Ma, my fault, I didn't save her and I only made things worse — '

She shook him so hard his head hit the post. 'Stop it! Listen to me! You done what you could.'

He stared at her.

'You said yourself, Andrew, there was nothing you could do, so how can it be your fault? The Lord doesn't require of us more than what is possible.'

But Andrew knew things now that she did not know.

'Yes,' he said. 'What's possible is, you put up a fight. What's required is, you don't turn tail and run.'

'But you might have got killed.'

'If you fight to win, you got to be ready to die. I saved my own hide, that's all, and so I lost.'

She had no answer to make. In the still dawn air a funnel of gnats hovered, and new cobwebs glistened on the vines. We didn't know how to go forward, everything seemed stopped dead.

'I have to think,' he mumbled. 'Have to decide what I'm going to do.'

Cee nodded. 'Daddy, can you please get us some kindling, thank you. Rhoda, sit here with your brother while I boil him an egg.'

'I don't want anything,' he said. 'Let me be.'

But she nodded me toward him. When I sat down, I felt him draw a few inches back from me, and he would not look me in the eye.

'I was trying to get her out,' he said. 'I wanted to save her.'

'I know.'

A layer of fog three feet thick floated over the field, not touching the ground. Daddy coming back was only a bobbing hat above and a pair of boots below, until he stepped all the way out with his armload of lightwood. He went around us without a word, not knowing how to help except to start the fire.

Andrew stared at the white cloud, which slowly began to rise. I laid my hand flat in the middle of his back. I don't think I had touched him once over the last five years but to fight or annoy, and I could feel a sudden surprise of muscles tightening under my fingers, and then a give, an easing, and his shoulders fell as his head dropped back. He stared straight up at the part of the sky that was not yet bright.

'Rho, when she came down the stairs — I couldn't even tell it was her. She was so beat up.'

I kept my hand on his back, to steady myself.

'That's when we should have made a move, when she was on the stairs. But I wasn't thinking fast enough. After he made her tell our names, he pulled her down and he put the gun inside her mouth. There wasn't nothing we could do after that, he said if we tried to stop him he would shoot. He said we had to stay — to see what happens when you meddle with someone else's women — and then at the end he kicked us out and said anyone who comes back and tries to be a hero only gets her hurt worse.'

'You can tell me.'

'No,' he said. 'A girl shouldn't hear it. I don't want you to know, or Ma. I don't want Flora to ever find out. That's what Harris planned we would do, run spread the whole story. The rest might, but I won't. I'm done with them. He made us look like fools trying to play a game we didn't know the rules of. Not even Henry. He wasn't ready for it, he didn't expect it. They all ran, but I couldn't, my legs wouldn't hold. I jumped in a ditch to hide, and Zack came back for me. But I said I wouldn't ever go with them again. I need to think what to do now, but I know one thing: I'm on my own. I'm not in with them.'

'Henry ran?'

'It was him that gave the order. He didn't have any choice, I guess.'

Andrew sat on that step almost two hours. He peeled the eggs Cee brought out, but didn't eat them, just stared off and let the shells fall onto his boots. We came and went from him, to let him know we were close by and ready to help, but we didn't know how.

At last with a shudder he seemed to resolve himself. He buttoned his shirt and tucked his shirt tail in. We were afraid to ask what he was going to do.

Daddy stood up. 'Andrew, stay with us. Stay home.'

'I can't. As long as Harris is alive it can happen again. Every girl's in danger.'

Daddy said, 'But you can't do nothing about him, no one can. You have to think of something else. Don't go back there.'

'I hope I never lay eyes on him again. I told you, I'm through with that, through with Henry and the gang, all of it.'

I said, 'Where are you going then?'

'The Sampsons.'

'What for?'

'Flora! I have to make sure nothing bad happens to her. I'm going to marry her.'

I waited for Cee to say he was crazy and Daddy to forbid it. I waited to hear my own voice cry out he couldn't mean it. But none of us spoke. We all understood what the

245

reasons were that could have brought him to that wild leap.

'The Sampsons might not go along with it,' Daddy said.

'So we'll come with you,' my mother said. 'We'll help.'

★ ★ ★

The Sampsons were eating breakfast when we got there, and it surprised them to see us all come in together.

Right away Andrew said, 'I come to ask you, Mr. Sampson, to let Flora marry me.'

Flora dropped her cup, spilling coffee across the table, but no one moved to sop it up. Mrs. Sampson and Mariah both looked at Mr. Sampson.

He was a big square-jawed man who ruled his family hard, and he was a Baptist. He sat there with his fork in midair, not saying a word. A kettle boiled on the fire. I could see Flora's little chest moving with each breath she took. A fly walked along the back of her chair.

'I'm not eighteen yet, but Flora is,' Andrew went on. 'We love each other and I can't stand to be apart from her any longer, not even for an hour, so I hope you and Mrs. Sampson will give us your blessing.'

'No,' Mr. Sampson said. 'I will not.'

Flora made a small noise, and Mariah put one arm around her sister's shoulder. Andrew shifted on his feet but didn't have anything else ready to say. Mr. Sampson went back to eating.

'Now, Samp,' his wife said. 'Don't be so quick.'

'On second thought, then — hell no.'

'Oh for goodness' sake. You might at least talk it over some and give the boy a reason.'

'The reason is I'm not ready to lose my baby girl.'

'Did you lose Mariah when she married Cal?'

Mariah had her own house now that she was married to Cal Lowrie, but she came early to the Sampsons' every morning to help her mother, whose eyes were bad.

'He's given his answer,' Andrew said. 'And I won't argue against you, Mr. Sampson, but I have to tell you it only means I will have to run off with her behind your back. I rather not do that because I know how she loves her family, but you leave me no choice. Nothing will stop me.'

Mr. Sampson pointed his fork at Andrew. 'I believe a rifle gun could hesitate you some.'

'Don't pay him no attention,' Mrs. Sampson said to Cee, folding and refolding her hands. 'He can't take in yet what exactly is going on. It's a shock to us. But Samp, let's try to talk civilized. You know you like this boy, you said so many a time.'

'I liked him for a yard child, not a son-in-law! If she runs off with him, she needn't think she'll be setting foot on this place again in her lifetime. I don't hold his age against him, I guess I wasn't much older when I married you, Nancy, but I was saved, I was farming, and I had built the first room of this house. My head was full of plans. I already had my idea for the Bitty School, and I got it going not two years later.'

'That's true,' Mrs. Sampson said. 'But these young people, all they have known is wartime. They never seen the inside of a schoolhouse. The Bitty School didn't last long enough for them.'

Andrew said, 'I'm ready to work, Mr. Sampson, and I can work hard enough to make up for time I wasted up to now. You won't be disappointed in me for that. But you're right, I'm not saved. I don't know if I ever will be, and to be honest I have to say there's not much chance of it. I can only tell you, I wish I was.'

Mr. Sampson leaned forward. 'You wish you was?'

'Yes, sir.'

'That's a step,' he said. 'Can you say you hope to be?'

'Yes, sir, I can say that.'

Cee spoke up then.

'It's my fault he isn't saved. But I know he is good. And I have an idea that might work for him and Flora. If he could come live here with you — sleep in the smokehouse, help you out with the farm — but not marry Flora, not even talk about it, we could try it and see how that goes. Then when he's eighteen, the whole question can come up again new. Your boys are gone, Nancy, you could use another hand.'

'It would suit *me*,' she said. 'I liked him from the start.'

'He runs with Henry Berry,' Mr. Sampson said, and everyone went quiet as if we'd come to a dead end in the road. 'Deny it all you want, I know it's so,' Mr. Sampson said. 'I been informed.'

'Well, you told me you were behind Henry all the way,' his wife said.

'I am. I given him the little money I could to help out, and two guns, but my daughter's another question. I don't want that life for her.'

'I don't either,' Andrew said. 'So I quit Henry, Mr. Sampson.'

'Nobody ever quit Henry except his brother William.'

'And me.'

But Mr. Sampson was unconvinced.

My father saw what must be done.

'Look here, Sampson,' he said. 'Last night at Harris's place the Ransom girl was hurt bad. She was raped and beat up and she might not live.'

Mrs. Sampson gasped. 'I knew it. I told my girls, I said he will kill her one day.'

'She was alive the last we know of,' Cee said.

'You don't mean she's still *there* with him, do you? It's still going on?'

Cee couldn't answer.

Mr. Sampson's mouth was shut in a tight line. He got up and then sat back down and looked hard at Andrew.

'And your idea is, maybe you can keep my girl safe?'

'Not maybe, sir. I guarantee, I *will*.'

Mr. Sampson turned to Cee. 'If it's just board and no pay . . . and if he keeps to himself at night . . . well, I couldn't object to that. But they're too young to marry. And he'll have to swear they won't run off.'

'Flora?' said Cee.

Flora was a quiet girl raised the settlement way, to obey her father. But to my surprise she said, 'I'll do what Andrew says do. I'll let him decide. If he wants to wait, I will. But, Daddy, I love him, and if he decides on running off, that's what I will do.'

Before Mr. Sampson could get mad again, Cee said, 'Then Andrew, it's up to you. Will you wait a year?'

'I can't.' His face was twisted up with worry, and he could hardly stand still in one spot. He was walking back and forth across the room. 'I made myself a vow. Flora's going to be my wife, married to me no matter what. So we'll have to go live somewhere else.'

'And how will you get her a house? Life is harder outside the settlement, Andrew. Strangers don't know you or help you.'

'We'll go to the Georgia camps.'

Cee stared at him. 'A girl like Flora — ' She seemed to lose her voice, then cleared her throat and started again, her hands folded on the table. 'Andrew, if you take her away, it'll be just the two of you, and you'll have to leave her alone in the daytime. There's men like Harris all over the camps, it's no place for a young girl. I been there, I know. You want her cared for and safe, Andrew? Then the best way is to stay home in Scuffletown. Stay in the families. We are all together here and that's how we make it. But you take that girl to the Georgia camps and I won't ever call

251

you my son again.'

She was on the edge of tears. Only her hands, laced tight and white-knuckled, held her together.

'All right,' he said. 'We'll stay. I'll move in here and work for the Sampsons until we can get married.'

It took a minute to settle into everybody's head, and then a celebration broke out as if a wedding had already occurred. Mariah went singing around the room, and Mrs. Sampson patted Mr. Sampson's arm, and Flora — little house-mouse Flora — kissed her father and took Andrew's hand. She looked as solemn and brave as a real bride.

He didn't even plan to come back home a single night. He told us if Zack McLaughlin or anyone else showed up looking for him, we were to say he was gone we didn't know where. We left him there in the Sampson dooryard, still holding on to Flora.

★　★　★

I guess Zack did come, after I was in bed that night. Voices rumbled in and out of my dreams, and even half-sleeping I knew there were people on the porch. Around midnight someone opened the door, and I saw Nelly and a crowd of others — Mr. Allen and Mary

252

Cumbo, Henderson and Henry and Steve, their figures lit by lightwood torches — and I heard the words 'our wives and daughters,' and Margaret's name, and Harris's.

Someone leaned into the room and looked, then pulled the door shut.

He wanted to know I'm safe, I thought, and my skin came alive, my throat tightened.

But I knew better. I buried my face in the mattress and pulled the quilts over my head. To keep him out of my mind, I turned my thoughts to the happiness of Flora. I tried to see her good fortune as a tiny bright ray, a little hopeful scrap — but I failed. What had Flora Sampson done to deserve love more than Margaret, or any other girl? Was it only a man's love that could keep girls safe?

6

Nothing happened the next day, or the next week. But in November we heard that the postmaster had filed a complaint against Allen Lowrie, and had been seen leading Harris on a search through Back Swamp near the Lowrie farm, Barnes looking for stolen hogs, Harris for diggers. December was a month of nothing, a cold wet dead empty time, until five days before Christmas when Free Tab reported to us that the postmaster had delivered his brother, Clelon, to the Lumberton asylum and signed him into permanent custody.

When I heard it, I filled up with hate.

Maybe he had reasons he told himself were honorable. It was true Harris had threatened to send Clelon to Fort Fisher, but whether he ever would have done so was another matter. However afflicted Clelon might be, he was still a mack, and it was hard to believe that Harris meant to send him. But Barnes was convinced of it. Tab, who watched from the kitchen when Clelon was brought in, said the postmaster only signed the papers and left as quickly as he could.

If he thought his life would improve by that act, he was wrong. It fell apart the very next day, and I was there to see the sight.

And maybe I had a hand in it.

The morning was overcast and cold. I was headed to Pate's for cornmeal that was rumored to have come into his hands somehow. We had heard no news of Boss, no word from Henry or Steve or Henderson. Margaret had not been rescued, and now Clelon, the only man who loved me, was removed from me as well. Yet we still had winter to go, a season in which we could always expect whatever trials we already had to worsen.

The whole county appeared edgy and desperate. Hestertown was on starvation, putting children out in droves. There was a report Big Swamp now held five hundred runaway Maroons who would swoop out on Christmas Day to cut the throats of all the white people. Harris arrested couriers he said were sent to arm McNair's slaves, and the next night McNair's gin house burned to the ground. The Townsend farm was raided in the middle of the night by men in disguise, who might have been black or might have had their faces blacked with soot, no one could tell — and no one recognized their voices. Deputy McTeer said they were Scufflers, but that couldn't be. We were always recognized by our talk, a sound to our words that marked us more clearly than skin or names. The Townsends would have known straight off if those raiders were settlement men.

All we had left in our cupboard was sweet potatoes and parched corn. The molasses barrel was empty, and even the salt was gone. Cee's instructions were to ask Pate for the meal and have him bag it, then pretend to discover I had lost my money along the way.

'I won't beg.' I said to her.

'It's not begging.'

'Or lie.'

'Look at it this way. You're providing Pate a chance to do a deed of Christian kindness.' She gave me the empty sack.

'He won't.'

'Talk nice to him,' she said. 'Like Nelly does.'

'I can't'

'You have a choice,' she said. 'It's that or woodpecker soup.'

So I went.

I had just reached the road when I saw the figure of James Barnes coming toward me with a fast irregular step, on his way to the Clay Valley Post Office. He was talking to himself. His clothes were in disarray, one trouser leg hitched up on the top of his boot, and he wasn't wearing his spectacles. His naked eyes were as vacated as a goat's.

He saw me and stumbled, hesitated, then lowered his head and would have rushed past without a word. But I was not going to let him do that.

'Mr. Barnes, where is Clelon?'

He halted. Stared at the ground.

'What have you done with him?'

He tried to dodge me but I darted to block his way and made him look at me.

'Why did you get rid of him?'

'It's not my doing.'

'Oh. I guess Allen Lowrie's behind it, then. Like everything else that's gone wrong for you. Allen Lowrie is the reason Clelon got locked up!'

'You know?' he said in surprise and with some joy to think that someone else saw the truth, someone else understood. But then he narrowed his eyes. 'How did *you* hear what Lowrie's done to me?'

'It's plain. He stole you out, didn't he? He ditched his land so it would drain onto yours. He butchered your hogs and buried the ears so no one could prove it against him, and — '

'The fences . . . ,' he prompted.

'Cross the line? Onto your land?'

'Exactly!' he said, hunching his shoulders. 'They're all in on it. Him and his ten sons.'

'Not so loud,' I whispered. 'They might be following you. Watching at this moment.'

'Do they watch you too? But they slip around like swamp devils, and you can't see them or catch them. I told Harris where to look, but he couldn't ever get them. Allen Lowrie shirked his duty. He ought to have sent his sons to do their part for the war, but he wouldn't. And so Harris was going to take Clelon in their place.' His lip quivered, and anguish wound across his face.

'You don't have any sons, do you, nor a wife. All you had in the world was your brother.'

'It was my duty to save him.'

'Yes, because you promised your mama on her dying bed you wouldn't let harm come to him. Does chains on his legs count as harm? Well, no! Not to mention that saving him the way you did will make things easier for you, won't it? You being a free man now, and still young, maybe you can have a new life. Maybe a bride. I doubt old lady Prevatte will reconsider, but you might get Fat Bridget back.'

He recoiled from me. But I came at him.

'Was it Allen Lowrie who sent his nephews to their death and all those others to the breastworks? Who made the list and put my brothers on it? You'll pay for that, Mr. Barnes.

258

You are worse than Brant Harris.'

He drew himself up and lifted his chin into the air. 'Move out of my path, young woman. Harris is an animal and an idiot. I am a Christian postmaster.'

'I'd prefer a thousand Harrises to a single one like you. You started off a good man — you were Mr. Allen's good friend and Clelon's good brother — and you could have beaten Harris back. You had the power of goodness behind you. But that was a long time ago. You got weaker and weaker. You melted down into a puddle.'

Sorrow and regret, two signs of human sanity, flickered in his eyes. He said, 'I had burdens.'

It occurred to me that James Barnes might be yet salvageable. If he got a shoulder to lean on, someone to share those burdens, another pair of eyes . . . he might recover himself.

And I despised that thought, the idea of Barnes recovered. I wanted him to fall into the darkest hole of lunacy. I wanted to see him bound in chains and hauled to the asylum and pecked to death by buzzards.

On an inspiration I flung my elbows out like a snakebird's wings and pointed my fingers at him and hissed.

'Curses on your soul, James Barnes! Rot in hell for your misdeeds! You'll never be free of

Lowrie. He's on your back, he's got his beak into your neck and will never let you rest.'

Shoving me aside, he bolted. If I had not hated him so, I might have laughed at the figure he made in flight, running full speed, his coattails flapping and his hair lifted in all directions from his head like a wig afire, until he was out of sight altogether. But I did hate him, for the very reason I had given: he could have acted a different part in life, a noble part. Instead, he let his personal lot, which he ought to have borne, drag him down to the level of a brute.

I walked on as slowly as I could, not wanting to catch up with him.

The ground was dry. Under a gray sky, the grasses and brush, the branches and bark of the trees were all of a color, brown. By the almanac it was winter's first day.

And I was winter's witch, powered with icy spite. Barnes was a lost and troubled man, but something possessed me to bedevil him, and if it happened to drive him over the edge I wouldn't care. I *meant* to spook the wits out of him. And having done it I felt zesty, alive and energized. Everything around me shifted to a brighter liveliness: in the thin brown woods I saw a sudden lift toward purple, in the gray sky a silver wink. There came a squawking of crows, jays, squirrels all at once, and the sound of hunters far off, a couple of distant gunshots and the yelp of dogs. But I didn't even care who I might happen to meet up with now. Let it be Harris, let it be McTeer. I would bedevil them all.

Let it be, in fact, Henry Lowrie, who had become in my mind the man responsible for my plight of loneliness and privation. All I could see in him now was haughty pride and bluster. Like Barnes, he was given the chance to stand up against Harris, but he had weakened and let the chance slip by. All his secret signals and hideouts were nothing but a game. He had called off the rescue of Margaret. He had failed to notice me. All he could do was hide in the swamps. If he was going to waste himself like that, I would rather have almost anyone in the world, Clelon or Donohue McQueen or Zack McLaughlin, they were all the same to me. I made up in my head a fantasy scene in which Henry appeared to me on the road and I told him off.

But no one appeared. No hunters came. After a while I picked up my pace in the direction of the rumored cornmeal, which I knew I would get. I was filled with new power. If I could be a witch, I could also be Nelly, or any number of other figures of magical endowment. I could take forms I never even thought of before. I could get the cornmeal and anything else including Henry, if I wanted him — but I didn't.

Spirited along by thoughts of my great capacities, almost floating, I crossed the plank bridge over Little Turkey Branch just beyond the cutoff to the Ransoms, and noticed a dark mound a few yards into the woods ahead on my right, which appeared to be a pile of clothing tossed or fallen from a cart. I thought it might be something we could use, so I ventured a few steps off the road before I saw that the clothes had a man inside.

There were the soles of two boots, then the legs, and a body on its back with its hands near the head.

For a minute I stood frozen, still a good thirty feet distant. Corpses weren't unheard of on the roads of Robeson County, but I had never seen one. I had never been the discoverer. Every child was warned, 'Never touch one; go your way and swear you never saw a thing.' But some old people said that to leave a corpse alone by itself was to invite death into your own family. I walked a wide circle around it, and then a closer one. I felt a kind of expectation, as if I was about to learn a big secret no one else knew yet. See something no one else had noticed.

'Hey!' I called out. No answer, no twitch of

motion. Yet the body had a presence, a kind of privateness that seemed not to want disturbance.

I picked up a pine cone and tossed it. It landed on the belly and bounced off.

I walked slowly toward the head or what I thought was the head, but it was not all there. Part of its face was gone, the nose and eyes nothing but a pulp. Another blast had opened a hole in the man's chest. I looked closer at the clothing, and saw the pants cuff caught at the boot top.

It was Barnes's cuff and boot. Barnes's coat, watch fob, and pocketbook half slipping from his pocket. But I couldn't believe it was him. The difference was too great between this man and the Barnes I knew.

I tried to recall if I had prayed for his death or included it in my curse. If so, I never meant it to come like *this*. The face was bad, terrible, but even without looking at it, which I tried not to do, the rest of him, laid flat and stopped cold, struck me as an awful mistake. His arms seemed raised up in surprise, as if death had caught him off guard and he tried to brush it away, and I noticed that his hands, too, had been shot through. He had stared down the barrel and covered his face in vain against what he saw coming.

In tears I said to the dead man, 'Well, who

killed you, you old damn lunatic?'

'Lowrie!'

I jumped like a sheep. The lips had moved, the voice creaked out a word.

Whether he heard my question and gave his answer, or whether his last word as he lay dying was merely the one that had been haunting his thoughts in life, I had no way of knowing. But he said it a second time, that name he hated.

'Lowrie!'

'Which one?' I said.

There was no answer. A pair of squirrels spiraled up a pine trunk, with a loud grating skitter of claws on bark.

I slipped the pocketbook out of his coat and lifted the watch chain from his belly, pulling from the vest pocket an old round watch. I snapped it open, but there was no face or works under the scratched glass, only a lock of hair. Not gray like the widow Prevatte's or auburn like Bridget's, but the dull coarse brown of Clelon's.

I did sit by him awhile, since he was not yet dead. I thought, *I am his final living witness*, and therefore it seemed I had a duty to stay. What if the name he called was not an accusation but a cry for the forgiveness of his old neighbor, whom he had wronged? If Barnes had more to say, I wanted to hear it.

And I don't know why, but I cried over that man as if he'd been a loved one. Yet I didn't go for help, he was beyond it; and he said no more to me.

A dying man, unlike the dead, is hard to tell about in words. The only part to be described is the wound, an incidental detail in view of what is *happening*, looming wordless, an enormity and a nothing. I felt I understood it at the time, but all I can relate now is that in the throes of death a man looks innocent and wronged, no matter what he did in life.

When I heard the sound of voices nearing, I scrambled up to cut through the swamp towards Pate's. But before I left, I looked into that hole in his breast. I didn't want to, but I couldn't help it. And I saw the glistening, pumping heart.

I wished I hadn't seen it. All the way to Pate's it stayed with me, even when I shook my head and rubbed my eyes. There are some things you shouldn't see, because they are too strong to fade. I knew I would never forget that wet dark struggling thing. It was only a heart the same as you would see if you could look into any man. But you should not.

Buying my sack of meal with the postmaster's money, I felt weak and short of breath. I said nothing to old Pate while he scooped out the last five pounds from the bin. There was no one else in the store, and its dark oaken shelves were cleared of merchandise. Pate himself seemed drained and pale, a spent storekeeper in a dying store in a starved country.

He handed me the sack with a slow, tired arm, and I heard the door behind me open, and I saw Pate blink, and slip his hand under the counter where he kept a rifle.

Henry and Steve came in. The door banged shut.

'Miss Rhody,' Steve said. 'How do you do?'

He was grinning and slick-eyed, and I thought he smelled of tanglefoot. I wanted to touch the shotgun he was carrying over his shoulder, to see if it was warm, if it had made the holes in James Barnes's chest and face.

Henry took off his hat to me. Steve sauntered up to the counter and said, 'Cornmeal. Ten pounds.'

Pate said, 'I'm out.'

'What kind of a store are you running then?'

'An empty one. As you can see.'

'We heard grits and meal came in by the uptrain this morning.'

'She got the last of it,' Pate said.

'But maybe you would hold some back. You're saying you don't have another barrel hid, for your own pantry?' Steve shifted the shotgun from his right shoulder to his left, swinging it wide so the muzzle passed over the counter.

'Don't mouth off to me, Steve, and don't go waving a gun under my nose. I know you boys too well, and I done you a lot of favors, but I'm not going to put up with any bullying. You're starting to think you're something.'

'Y'know, could be you're right. Maybe I am starting to think that way. And maybe you're going to find out it's true.'

'Steve,' Henry said. He nodded his head toward the door, to say go on out.

Steve was wound so tight, he didn't seem to hear. But I could see that it wasn't anger that had him coiled. It was something I used to see on my father's face when his knee had been hurting so long and hard that pain was the only thing he felt. All Daddy knew to do for it was get drunk, but he couldn't do that so he would go out in the yard and yell. Just yell and howl.

'Steve, wait outside,' Henry said.

Steve looked at Henry and then at me, still all tight in the face. Suddenly he shrugged and smiled. He tipped his hat as he passed me, and I saw him go sit on the railroad track, where he started picking gravel rocks from the bed and tossing them down the bank.

'Mr. Pate,' Henry said, 'We do need a sack of meal — and sugar, some coffee, and whatever meat you can give us. We could use blankets, too.'

'Everybody needs what you need, Henry. It's not to be had. Nothing coming in.'

'I can pay what you're asking and a little more.'

'I don't have it at any price. That fifty pounds I got this morning is all I've seen in a week. I can't even buy off the farmers close around — anybody who's still got grain or meat ain't selling. And not only that, they don't want to admit they have it. Don't want their neighbors to know. I heard Mackenzie's hoarding a thousand pounds of cured pork, and put a armed guard over it.'

'All right. If you get anything, I'd appreciate if you'd send word. Just let Daddy know.'

'Henry, I won't sell to benefit the Yankee army, you know that. I'm your daddy's old friend, I never met a finer man, but you can't expect me to aid the enemy. Allen has tooken a side, and maybe I understand why he did, but it's not my side. Anyway, I heard your daddy has a full smokehouse himself and plenty of Union coffee.'

'Mr. Pate, I won't lie to you, he takes what they give. But he has a reason. He is feeding about half of Scuffletown right now, keeping the ones alive who have flat run out. And that's why I won't go to him. I have to take care of my own boys myself. People around Back Swamp have been giving us what they can, but that's not right either. It's food from their own babies' mouths.'

'All I can suggest is, it's no wonder babies go hungry when all the fit young men is lying out instead of working. It's your own damn fault.'

'If there was work for us we'd take it.'

'Didn't you tell me you had money in your pocket?'

'Yes, sir, cash.'

'Well, that makes me wonder. It's a coincidence you should be flush the very day after the courthouse safe was robbed. You wouldn't have a dozen new Spencer rifles, too, would you?'

'Are you accusing me, Mr. Pate?'

Pate sighed. 'I'm run into the ground, Henry. I feel like the world's tiredest man. Sometimes I can't hardly tell what I think. But you ought to know, that's what I heard in Lumberton. People believe it's you that raided the courthouse last night, took the guns and money of the militia. But if it was you, don't tell me so, Henry. I'm too old to be knowing that kind of knowledge. If King and McTeer ask me when they come in for their card game, I want to honestly say I got no idea.'

I decided to slip on out, and I was almost to the door when Henry called my name.

I didn't want to talk to him or face him straight on, afraid I would see some mark upon him, a sign, a look in his eye, a stain of blood on his hands. Like Pate, I didn't want to know. But I couldn't help it. I looked him over for bloodstains. Saw none. I turned to go.

'Don't run off,' he said.

'Cee's waiting.'

'You all have enough to eat?'

'We're low. Like everyone.'

'I'll send you something.'

'I thought you were low yourself.'

'We're all right for the time being. I'm just thinking ahead some. I like to know what's going to happen, in advance, try to be ready.'

'You weren't so ready that night at Harris's,' I said. And I regretted saying it, seeing the flash in his eyes. But it was not directed at me, or even at Harris.

'I should have gone in,' he said. 'I blame myself. It's the worst mistake I ever made.'

'But you will right it?'

That surprised him, I could tell.

'I'm doing what I can.'

I wondered if that included murder.

'Henry, I want Boss back. He's not cut out for this.'

'Well, when you see him you might change your mind. You'll know he's treated well and taken care of.' Henry smiled.

For an instant I thought, *He didn't do it. Couldn't have killed Barnes and then smile it off so easy an hour later.* But I had seen the wounds on that body in the woods. It was not a simple killing done as an ordinary robber or rogue would think to do it, with a ball to the brain. It was deep murder. Whoever opened that breast and shot that face away — straight through the upraised hands — was a kind of man I didn't understand. He might smile or he might not, I couldn't know. I had no way to recognize a killer so brutal.

The only way I would find out was if he told me himself.

So I said, 'I saw the postmaster. On my way here, by the Ransom cutoff.'

I gave him the chance to let me in on it, to take me into his confidence as he'd taken my brothers. I was offering myself. But he said not one word. He was blank-faced.

'I have to go,' I said at last. 'Don't send us anything. We're getting by.'

I went out and heard the door swing shut behind me. And heard it open again — knew he must be standing there — and I took a deep breath and said loud and clear, 'Steve, where have you been keeping yourself?'

Steve jumped to his feet.

I took his hand to cross the rail and stand in the bed. 'We haven't had a visit from you lately,' I said, lowering my chin and looking up at him. 'I believe you must have forgotten all about us.'

'Not me. I'll pay you a visit anytime you say.'

'That would be nice.'

Henry said, 'Steve, let's get going.'

Steve ignored him. 'A girl shouldn't be walking out these days,' he said to me: 'There's men on the loose you don't want to meet up with. I can see you home.'

I was about to say no when Henry said it. 'No, I need you with me, Steve.'

'Hell, Henry, just to make sure she — '

'I said no. She doesn't want your company.'

'Maybe she does,' I said.

'Tell her,' Henry said.

'Tell me what?'

'He won't be walking you home, or paying a visit either. Isn't that right, Steve?'

Steve glared at him. 'I don't know what's

272

wrong in seeing a young lady safely to her own mama's house.'

'Because it's not right,' Henry said.

I said, 'Well, thank you, but I'm sure I don't need you to say what's right and wrong for me.'

Henry looked uncomfortable. I didn't understand what was going on.

Finally he said, 'He ought to tell you himself, but since he won't, I will. He's not going to walk you home because a married man can't. I think that's a good enough reason.'

I laughed. 'Steve isn't married.'

'Ask him.'

Steve frowned and rubbed his mouth and cast his eyes to the end of the railroad track. 'It don't really amount to anything,' he said. 'It's nothing.'

'Who are you married to?'

'Cath Oxendine, but — '

'Since when?'

'I guess about a year and a half ago, but see, she says we don't count as married because I'm lying out, and she won't have me until I promise I'll come in for good and settle down . . . '

My face and ears burned. I couldn't come up with a word, just stood staring until I could gather myself and start down the track, so hot with shame I imagined the ties igniting under my feet, flames snarling up to punish me for pride, stupidity, flirting.

Cath Oxendine. I hardly knew her. She was one of the Prospect Oxendines, older than me — a plain-looking, big girl most people predicted would live out her life a spinster. Married to Steve Lowrie, the lady's man, the charmer! I ought to have been glad to hear it; Cath Oxendine would surely be good for him, a steadying force. But all I could think of was my humiliation.

At Three Brides Bridge I threw away the dollar I still had of the postmaster's money. An hour before, I'd been bold enough to steal from a dead man, but now I was down a peg and getting scared. I watched the dollar fall into the river, and then I threw in the pocketbook and watch case. But I kept the cornmeal, and for myself the curling lock of hair.

Barnes's body was found that day by Ben Bethea, who ran for the nearest white men, Arch McNair and Willis Moore. They said that with his closing wheeze of air Barnes named his killer — but gave no account of what had happened, only that single name.

★ ★ ★

On the day before Christmas Eve, the Yankees attacked Fort Fisher. They disguised one of their own boats as a blockade runner, packed it solid with two hundred tons of powder and slipped it up against the fort in the middle of the night. When the fuse was lit, the whole thing blew sky-high in a blast ten times bigger than they'd even hoped, throwing fiery timbers back onto the watching Yankee fleet. Eighty of their own men died. Inside the fort, some of the Rebels noticed a rumbly sound like distant thunder or a train, but forgot all about it till morning, when they learned they had won, in their sleep, a brilliant victory.

We had no Christmas celebration other than the little birds Cee had made from blue paper one long-gone year of my childhood. She strung them from the rafters so they would swing and turn. But I thought I was sad to see them now, without the boys home, and without any food but the potatoes and flat pone Henry sent. No one in the settlement had much of a Christmas. Usually it was a big noisy day of drinking and gun-shooting, but we didn't hear or see anything like that. Everyone was lying low, wondering who Harris would pick out to blame for the murder.

Sheriff King and Deputy McTeer went asking around, but no one came forward as a witness or informer, and the name on the dying man's lips only narrowed down the list of suspects to twenty-nine men. The rumor was that robbery was the motive, as the watch and pocketbook Barnes was known to carry had not been found. And would not be found, I knew, as both were gone the way of all incriminating evidence, downriver.

Whether Henry shot James Barnes, I didn't know. I feared it one minute and hoped it the next.

★ ★ ★

Two weeks into January there came a freezing rain, not a storm but a careful, quiet sleet that coated everything and froze hard, and by morning we had turned to glass. Twigs and branches of the bare trees glittered, and every separate leaf in the water oaks was cased in its own clear brittle shell, molded to the shape and veins of the leaf. Now and then plates of ice slid from a roof and clattered to the ground, but mostly there was no sound at all. No whisper of pines, no crows or dogs. Everything was frozen stiff and silent. It was a day set like a stage for something to happen. And something did. It took a while before I heard the whole story, but Cee was the one who finally told it.

Through the woods at noon a one-horse buggy carried Brant Harris and his woman companion along Chicken Road a mile west of Harris's Scuffletown house. Later, Walter McRaney saw them go past the stillery; he didn't get a good enough look to recognize the woman, although she waved and called him by name. She was bundled up in a black woolen head scarf and a black coat.

Past the stillery the horse went along slow, setting each hoof with care on the skim that covered the road. Under the red wheels the ice cracked and splintered but the buggy didn't slip, weighted by Harris.

The woman at his side acted playful and teasing in a way she'd never been with him before. Every so often she laughed out loud. There was color in her cheeks and a flirtatious flutter in the way she cut her eyes at him. She could tell that he'd never had any woman behave so in his presence; and that it seemed to throw him off.

'Brant, I got to tell you, I am *happy* to be riding along with you on this beautiful morning.'

'It's raw and ugly.'

'Brant, Brant.' She was breathless with excitement. 'This might be the finest morning of my life.'

The night before, she'd said she would

forgive the past because the time had come. She didn't want to bear any ill will in her heart. And to prove it she stayed in his bed all night, all smiles. Probably he never saw any woman smile underneath him before.

In the morning she swept the tavern floor and boiled his egg and made him a cup of rye coffee, and looking out the window she remarked on the horse and buggy he had brought over from Red Banks. She said she wouldn't mind a ride. Wouldn't he take her out?

He said hell no, the road was dangerous.

'Now, don't tell me you're scared of a little ice.'

'Where you want to ride to?' he said.

'Up by McRaney's, or to the river, I don't care. I just feel the need of an outing. I want to take the air. Maybe we should go to church, Brant. It's Sunday.'

He laughed. 'And you think I could get saved?'

'There's always that chance, honey. No time like the present.'

Probably no woman had ever called him honey or anything like that. Certainly she never had. She noticed it seemed to have a shock effect on him. But he was hard to read.

'I'm not going to no church,' he said.

'Well, I don't s'pose we have time for it

anyway. Let's just take a short ride, see if McNeill's mill pond is frozen.'

He proposed another plan, but she laughed and pretended to pout and said he had a one-track mind, and he might at least find the manners to grant her the only little request she had made of him, and he said all right, he would take her for a ride to McNeill's.

'Now keep your eyes skinned,' she said when they got out on the road. 'I want you to *notice* how pretty it is.'

She sat close to him on his right-hand side, now and then patting his thigh. She pointed out the pine needles tipped with water drops now that the sun was full and the clouds had burned off. She waved to McRaney as they passed him. She remarked on the ditch frozen white, the wiregrass sparkling, the six hawks spiraling upward without a single wingbeat. She was in high spirits, but a kind of pondering mood, too.

'Look at those birds. It seems against the laws of nature. You'd think they would fall right out of the sky. What lifts them?'

'How should I know?'

She smiled.

'Do you regret, Brant,' she said in a musing voice, 'anything you've done in your life?'

'I never think about it.'

'What do you think about then? What's on

your mind right this minute?'

'Nothing but you and your charms,' he said. 'Last night.'

She laughed. 'Are you really still thinking about that, on a day like this?'

'I said I was, didn't I?'

'All right then, what particular charms of mine did you like the best? Tell me.'

She'd done this kind of teasing last night, too. She showed she wasn't scared of him. But she didn't tease about his girth or the difficulties he had in bed. She helped him along.

'I bet you don't know the right words,' she said. 'You only know the words men use with men. Oh, it's too bad. You've missed a great deal, Brant, the life you've lived. But that's all right. Slow down some now, I'm scared of slipping off the dam.'

They had come to McNeill's pond, and started onto the south end of the dam. 'Oh, good, it's frozen. Almost all the way across! I've only seen that happen twice before. Stop a minute so I can look.'

'I never knew you to be so interested in the wonders of nature,' he said.

'I wish we had some Yankee ice skates. I bet you never ice-skated. Or swum in the ocean or danced the waltz? Don't you regret you missed all the fun? I just can't help thinking if someone had come along and showed you how, you might have learned to take a delight in the world. You might have turned out a different man, Brant. Maybe you might have. But on the other hand — it's interesting that you got no regrets. Nothing you done or left undone. So who cares, I guess. But you ought to have a thought now and then to the condition of your soul.'

'Seems to be another new interest of yours, my soul.'

'I was just giving you the chance to unburden it a little, if you needed to.'

A pair of wild geese jumped from the one spot of open water in the center of the pond and flew east.

'I do regret one thing,' he said.

'What's that? I'm dying to know your human side.'

He hesitated. 'Well, I'm sorry I got so big I can't wear a pair of store pants.'

'That's all? Good Lord. But how in the world did you come to this pass? Didn't you see what was happening to you? I don't guess we have time to go into it. I'm so curious to find out how you got to be the way you are, but I can see it's something I'll never understand.'

'I *et*, that's how, goddammit.'

'Oh, I don't mean how did you get so fat.'

That word made him frown. 'What'd you mean then, how'd I get to be the way I am?'

She was squinting her eyes in the direction of the pines ahead to the left. The horse whinnied, ready to move on. Wind blew across the dam and ice slipped from the trees.

'How I got to be *what way?*' he said, but he was distracted because she was lifting her skirts above her knees, gathering the folds in a bunch, and he could see the curve of her thigh, the black stockings.

'Well, so very, very *stupid,*' she said.

And before he could understand or reach for her she had flung herself out the right-hand side of the buggy, and he stared flabbergasted at the shoes and legs kicking from the black skirts that wrapped her up like a cocoon as she whirled down the embankment.

The wiregrass bent to leave a trail where she had rolled, to the edge of the ice; and she lay still, furled and black against the white pond.

He was shot from the woods. The bullet entered his skull at the left temple and did not come out. The reins dropped out of his hand, and the horse leaped forward. More shots rang out, but Brant Harris had disappeared, toppled under the bench and wedged tight. The horse went flying through the woods, buggy careening, past Heck Oxendine's empty turkey blind, past the Chavis cabins near the river, the McNair plantation and Mackenzie's, all quiet and deserted-looking because everyone was staying inside by fires or under featherbeds; across two bridges, onto the Upper Road, and past Moss Neck before the horse slowed to an easy trot, headed west toward Shoe Heel.

Ben Bethea was the first to stop it. But when he saw the dead body, and knew from its size who it had to be, he slapped the horse's rump and sent it going again, and he ran. He didn't want to be the one who discovered this particular corpse, especially since he'd found the first one.

The next man to grab the horse was Andrew, who jumped away the same as Ben, and left the buggy standing still in the middle of the road in front of Pate's. Some Chavises on their way to church recognized the familiar red wheels before they were even close; they wouldn't walk any nearer than thirty feet, just stood peering. McTeer saw them through Pate's window. He got up from his seat at the skin table, came out and inspected the buggy, saw the body and knew that his future had just taken a turn for the better.

But when he shouted for the sheriff, the

horse spooked and was off again, faster than ever. By the time King had roused the skin players and organized them into pursuit, the buggy and its cargo were long gone, and they did not know where. They rode all the way to Shoe Heel. Meanwhile Harris's horse had taken the cutoff to Red Banks and was barreling down the last mile toward Catherine Harris's house. It took the turn into the yard at full speed. The buggy tipped, and the dead man shook loose and tumbled out into the road.

From a window his wife saw it happen. Saw him rolling, saw him come to rest on his side with his ear against the frozen dirt. The horse streaked toward the barn, but a pine caught the front corner of the buggy and flipped it sideways in a heap, with the horse tangled in the wreckage. One red wheel ran on alone. Catherine Harris leaned forward against the windowpane to see how far the wheel would go: fast across the grass, losing speed as it bumped past the house toward the canebrake, then slower and slower until it came to rest against a clump and stood erect a second, then fell. She sighed.

She took off her shoes and put on an extra pair of stockings, and noticing that a shoelace was broken, she strung in a new one. At the mirror she braided her hair tight and coiled it behind her neck. Then she put on a coat and walked out to edge of the road and stood in the cold for ten minutes, looking at her husband. When she was satisfied there were no signs of life, she freed the horse, watered and saddled it, and rode to her lawyer's house in Shoe Heel.

An hour later, stepping out into the street where the sun was shining and eaves were dripping, she saw the sheriff wandering up and down asking everyone if they'd seen a runaway buggy, and she told him where he could find it.

★ ★ ★

The day Scuffletown froze over, everyone saw at least one strange and unexplained thing. Cee found minnows caught in ice at the pond. But under the warming sun the ice melted and the minnows swam, no worse for the freeze.

'But was it Margaret who jumped from the buggy?' I asked her.

'No one knows.'

'No one says, you mean.'

'Think again.'

'Catherine Harris?'

'Couldn't have managed it.'

There was only one other possibility, only

one other woman who hated Harris enough to endure a night with him, who would so enjoy witnessing and abetting his murder, who would tell Cee all the details. And the Fayetteville paper did mention later the unnamed woman who'd been seen riding with him, who they began calling the 'Hester-town Wh — re.'

In Red Banks, Sheriff King and Deputy McTeer enlisted Floyd and Heck Oxendine to help them. Harris lay as he had fallen, huge stomach up and head lolled back.

'She wants him brought inside. Everybody get a arm or leg,' the sheriff said, and they all did, but they couldn't hoist the bulk up more than a few inches clear of the ground. They staggered with him into the yard and toward the porch, halting along the way several times when the body swung too low and hit ground.

'Jesus Christ,' said Sheriff King. 'The widow's watching, boys. Try to keep his ass up out of the mud.'

She stood in the doorway while they struggled up the steps, and she showed them into the parlor, watching while they dragged her husband across the floor by his arms, with his chin on his chest and his hair fallen over his eyes like a drunk's. They set him in the central flower of the blue-and-red Turkey carpet, boots pointing up in a wide V. The clock on the mantelpiece had a loud tick. There was not much heat coming from the fire, and she sat on the sofa with her hands inside her sweater sleeves.

'My condolences, ma'am,' the sheriff said. When he saw she seemed unable to speak, he signaled his men to bow their heads. An uncomfortable silence followed. He figured she was expecting something from him, so he cleared his throat and started a prayer.

'Heavenly Father, in our hour of grief — ' he began, but she interrupted.

'Floyd; you want his boots?'

'No'm.'

'They might fit you. They're new, he paid forty dollars for them in Lumberton.' She nodded her own head yes, to encourage Floyd.

Floyd and Heck were cousins of Catherine Harris's dead son, which explained her interest in them over the years. Probably she'd noticed that Floyd's old boots had shrunk in the wet cold, and he'd had to slit them across the instep to get his feet in, which meant they now took on even more water and chilled his feet to ice blocks. But Floyd said no, thank you. No one wanted to wear anything Harris had worn.

'Is that a bug on him?' She pointed at the

round black spot between his eye and the top of the ear.

'That's the bullet hole,' said McTeer.

'Not much of a wound, to kill so big of a man.'

'Straight to the brain,' the sheriff said. 'I can assure you he didn't feel a thing.'

'Nothing at all? I hate to think he died completely unawares. Don't you think there was a little buzz of some kind? One little moment of utter horror?'

'No way to tell, ma'am.'

She nodded.

'He certainly looks undignified, spread out like that. Not the way we all hope to be seen by our loved ones when we depart. He often thought about his death, you know, and left written instructions for a mahogany coffin and a proper wake. He'd be quite unhappy to be seen this way, Sheriff. Look at that. He's *muddy*.'

'I'm sorry, Mrs. Harris,' the sheriff said. 'I can order a box for you from old Jesse Oxendine, but it has to be oversized, and I doubt you can get it before tomorrow. We don't have nothing suitable to put him into for you. I guess I ought to of wrapped him up in something.'

'Well, I don't see a reason to go to any lengths. Getting a special coffin built and all

... it seems unnecessary. I was thinking it might be nice — in spite of his instructions — to have final rites of a humble plain nature. Something like a burial at sea. They don't use a coffin for that, do they? I don't mean cart him all the way to Wilmington or Georgetown — the river would do fine. There's a good place at Gilchrist's Bridge where you could dump him directly off into the deep part. I thought about a pyre, too, but that might be problemsome ... and a waste of firewood. Either way, there's no need for a coffin. I'm very grateful for your help. Sheriff. I wanted to see him laid out right in the middle of his own parlor, and I'm satisfied. I've seen enough. You can carry him back out now.'

'Beg your pardon?'

'Yes, find somewhere to store him until you can make the necessary arrangements, whether it's in the dirt or the river or a grand big fire. I'll just leave it up to you.'

'Excuse me, Mrs. Harris, I think you got to take him,' said McTeer. 'Being next of kin.'

'I don't believe I do, Mr. McTeer. I spoke with my lawyer, Hamilton Macmillan. Brant had a sizable business, you probably know. Evidently everyone knew except me. Hamilton says there's a shebeen in the woods which he understands was very profitable, and a roadhouse in Scuffletown. I have all the papers. Hamilton received them this afternoon from an anonymous person.' She pointed to a desk covered with four or five open ledgers. 'Brant kept thorough records. Accounts, debts, loans. He was owed a great deal of money. Of course, it is the devil's money, and I'm not interested in collecting. Or reading other people's secrets either, from the notebook Brant wrote them in. My husband was a man of base interests. He took pleasure in knowing things Satan himself would have put out of mind.'

McTeer's eyes sprang to the desk.

Sheriff King said, 'I don't see what that has to do with disposal of a body. The next of kin's responsible.'

'I don't know, Sheriff,' McTeer said. 'She might have a point there.'

'What are you talking about?' King said.

'This might be a case where exceptions can be made,' McTeer said.

The sheriff eyed him. 'Jesus, Rod.'

'I've instructed Hamilton to destroy the shebeen and burn the roadhouse,' Mrs. Harris said. 'And I thought you would do me the favor of taking these papers off my hands. I leafed through them, and although they might be of interest to someone, nothing of Brant's interests me now. I was so hoping you would dispose of everything for me, including the carcass.'

'Sheriff, that's a *real* good idea,' McTeer said.

King threw up his hands. 'All right, Heck, Floyd — haul him on out.'

'Thank you, Reuben,' Catherine Harris said. 'You understand, I want to make sure Brant's death is — well, *complete*. After you leave this room, I intend to forget he died. Or lived. So I must not be reminded of him. For example, if there's an inquest, you'll understand that I can't be called to it. If you bury him, I don't want to know where. Is that possible?'

King hesitated, thrown off balance when she called him Reuben. Everyone called him Sheriff, even his own wife and daughter.

Deputy McTeer said, 'Yes, ma'am. I'll see to it personally.'

'There was cash in the safe. Hamilton handed it over to me, but he said it won't be legally mine until a probate judge approves. Is that true? I don't see why it's not mine right now. I want your approval on that, Reuben, and then I want you to take half the money and give it to the girl Hamilton said is lying upstairs at that house with a broken arm. The other half will be divided among however many children my husband left in

Scuffletown. All I want is this house. My father paid for it and I raised my son here, and I want my name on the title now.'

Sheriff King nodded. Now he knew what it meant, her calling him by his first name. Death had set her free. She had no fears, no desires, and nothing to lose — a dangerous woman. For the first time he was dealing with someone who didn't care if he was sheriff or not.

She passed him a thick envelope.

'I know the amount,' she added. 'Seven hundred and forty-six dollars. In greenbacks. Be sure she gets it all. And try to find someone who will take the boots. Maybe a soldier who never heard of him.'

McTeer gathered the ledgers and papers from the desk.

They dragged Harris back into the yard, where it took the four of them several minutes to load him onto McTeer's horse, and all the while the sheriff was lighting into McTeer.

'What'd you owe him for, the liquor or the women? Or was it bribes? Or was it just a record of how many times a week you went down to poke something?'

'Let's just say he had me,' McTeer said. 'Every which way.'

'Well, damn it all, Rod, did you shoot him?'

'Not me. But when we string up the Lowrie who did, I'll be saying my silent thank-yous to him, and to the widow Harris too.'

'I doubt anyone will hang for this crime, or even be charged.'

'But we could get the Lowries for it. We could get Henry Berry if we put our minds to it — '

'Forget that. Listen here, Rod, you might better slow down some. The situation's slipping, and you can't tell who might be for you or against you anymore. Every man on the grand jury would have done this murder himself if he had the guts, and they'll all be happy as you are to learn the fat man's gone. You don't see me shedding any tears. In fact sometimes I feel ready for the whole damn thing to be over. The war included.'

McTeer said, 'Well, I sure don't. I'll fight till I die.'

'I believe you will. But I'll tell you. If Henry Lowrie killed Harris, I would pin a medal on him in the public square if he was a white man, and even so I'm going to go home and drink his health in private. How about you, Heck? Floyd? There'll be a juba in Scuffletown tonight, wouldn't you say?'

★ ★ ★

There was, but it was to celebrate news more welcome than the death of Harris. During that quiet ice storm, while Nelly was spending her one and only night in the roadhouse and Margaret her last, the Federals attacked Fort Fisher again, this time with doubled fury and a smarter man in charge.

From sixty ships at sea they sent twenty thousand bombshells slamming into the earthworks. Nothing like it had ever been seen. Hour after hour the shells ripped holes in the mounds, blowing dirt like geysers and smashing Rebel cannons till none were shooting back, and five hundred bodies lay in the ruins. Then the fort was overrun with Union soldiers from the inland side. The Indian diggers, when they saw those blue-coats swarming on the mounds, broke loose and started home. One, Weldon Brooks, rode a Rebel horse to Wilmington and caught the last train for Scuffletown. Behind it, the Yanks began to tear up the track and bend the rails in loops.

So we got word of the victory long before the macks did, before the newspapers and even the garrison captain in Lumberton. The fort that could not fall had fallen. The South had lost its lifeline, its only open port. A full hundred miles from the coast we smelled the sulphurous smoke of the bombs, and danced to think it meant the war was over — just as we thought the death of Brant Harris meant the end of our troubles.

But soldiers know, you may knock down the enemy coming at your throat and win your little victory of the moment, only to look up and see the line of his fellows advancing to fill his place. There was drinking and shooting and juba dancing that night, the fifteenth of January, like a late Christmas outburst; but the next day began a time of havoc and misery.

Food stopped coming altogether. Flour went up to two hundred dollars a barrel, but it didn't matter. We had no dollars and Pate had no flour. Within a week there were so many Union bummers about, it seemed their generals had let them out for picnic time, to fill their wagons with goods from mack houses and Indian cabins and slave huts alike. There was nothing they didn't want. I saw a Yankee wagon piled with turnips and fodder, sewing boxes, two oil portraits of Mrs. McNair, a pea hen, some rotted lumber, old gunny sacks, and an Italian pianoforte, with an Arab gelding and a blind goat tied behind. Meanwhile those hundreds of loose slaves in Big Swamp failed to come forth in the predicted swoop, but they snuck out and picked clean what fields and smokehouses the Yanks had overlooked. I could understand the motives behind these depredations. The Yankees were on the eve of victory, and the way I understood war, all those turnips and peacocks would be rightfully theirs anyway, pretty soon. The Maroons were about to be free, and to have starved to death in advance of emancipation would not have done them any good.

But parts of this last spurt of war had a hidden politics, property and lives being lost without a reason I could see. Three macks shot a Locklear they said stole a mule, but it was a subterfuge mule that they tethered outside the cabin only minutes before they went in. The tied-mule method was their old way to get a farm hand — but to shoot the man foiled that purpose. Then there was a mack lady, old Mrs. Witherspoon, who I always knew as kindly, poisoned at her breakfast by a dose of arsenic in her hominy grits, and two of her house hands gone missing, one found the next day beat to death under a pile of leaves on Chicken Road. An Indian in jail for fornication with a white woman was garroted in his cell. There were two unarmed McQueens shot and wounded from a blind, and a slave burnt to cinders in Raft Swamp. This was a turbulence of motives and parties that even the newspapers could not explain, a free-for-all.

'When there's no food and no law, war don't stay where it's meant to stay but spreads wilder and meaner out on the fringes.' Cee said. 'Nobody in command, and everybody scrambling for advantage.'

By February, thirteen more plantations had been raided, four of them near us — Townsend's by those unidentified men, McCallum's by Union escapees, Martha Ashley's by more men in disguise, Bullock's by Confederate deserters. Mack ladies robbed down to their petticoats stood in doorways screaming curses at the retreating marauders and even firing pistols from their bedroom windows. There was gunfire every night, everywhere, and just about every farmer's watchdog was shot. Some were eaten.

Mr. Allen was plagued with Yankees who came to drink up his brandy and devour his food, demanding guides to take them to the big plantations. He was seventy years old. Mary Cumbo was much younger than her husband, but she was ailing. With only William home to help, the job of caring for the Union Army had become an ordeal for them. The swarm was out of control. One night there were twelve in his house, and a drunken captain patted him on the head and said, 'We'll see to it, old man, that you're made Big Chief of North Carolina when this war's over, and that's a promise straight from Uncle Abe. He told me so himself.'

The Yanks were crazy, Mr. Allen concluded, and his wife was worn out nursing them. He started turning them away. The last one was a Florence escapee found dying in Ashpole Swamp and brought to Mary looking lifeless, but no sooner was he laid on her kitchen table than he sprang alive and ran out the door raving. Night-blind from his prison diet of parched corn, he wandered onto the McNair plantation, where Mrs. McNair fired a shot at him, and he almost drowned in a ditch before William found him again and brought him to us, to ask if Cee could take this one because he didn't think his mother had a thread of strength left. Her heart was going weak, and Dr. McCabe had prescribed two weeks of bed rest.

I told William no. Cee and Daddy were leaving to cook for a new crew of choppers. McRaney had heard a rumor that General Lee now meant to arm the slaves and send them into battle, a last-minute idea to turn the tide. Desperate with hope, McRaney opened a new camp deep in the barrens to start chopping virgin boxes, but the woods-rider he sent with provisions absconded, and for a week the men had been living on a single daily ration of dooby, cold cornmeal cakes flavored with wild onions and a few shreds of tinned pickled beef. It was raining, too, and the camp had flooded; there were no cabins, the choppers were sleeping in treetops. They were getting restless, and so McRaney offered Cee two hundred dollars in scrip if she would take supplies out to the crew, cook them a week of meals, and have Daddy ditch the camp. The money paper might be worth nothing, but there was the food to consider. So she agreed.

The night before they were to leave, McRaney's meat was delivered and stashed under our floorboards. Six big hams and two little ones. It was not the best meat in the world, but it was all he could find. His ox and cart were hidden in the woods behind our house, with pine boughs covering all the cabbages and army raincoats he had managed to bribe out of the Twenty-Fourth, plus three canvas tents. Cee and Daddy were ready to go. But she told William he could leave the soldier at our house anyway.

'Rhoda can nurse him,' she said.

'I can't,' I said. 'What if he dies on me?'

I was sick to death of dead men. I didn't want to hear of any more, or see one.

But William set the unconscious soldier on

our floor and gave Cee a Rebel jacket and britches to put him in if he survived. Cee shoved the bundle at me.

'Don't you *let* him die,' she said, tying potatoes in sacks around her waist and a ham over each shoulder. All night long I'd been smelling that smell from under the bed, and I almost got up in the dark to nibble on it, but I thought of the choppers out there, the ones I secretly loved, with nothing to eat but dooby. So I didn't filch even a sliver, and in the morning my hunger pangs had gone.

'Just keep him breathing until I get back. Try to get water down him even if he don't wake up.'

I started to object again when I accidentally looked into our piece of mirror by the door, and was so surprised I forgot what I meant to say. I saw big mournful eyes that seemed almost to shine, hair glossy as an otter's pelt, a sharpened face with bright teeth showing and skin with a sheen like new tallow. I saw that I was starved to a brilliance.

'Rhoda?'

'I can't do it.'

'Can't means don't want to. I advise you to change your mind.'

I was still looking in the glass, I couldn't take my eyes off myself.

'Because if you do let him die,' she went

on, 'he'll have to set here moldering. I doubt you could bury him. If he revives, send him away. Unless, of course, something develops. He might turn out to be a pretty man, once you get him cleaned.'

'Ma! He's a Yankee corpse! Let me come with you. The man is going to die, I know he is. Don't leave me alone with him. Suppose he wakes up hungry? There's enough potatoes here for one person for one week. What am I going to feed him?'

She thought for a second, then unshouldered one of the smaller hams.

'Rhoda,' she said, 'listen to me. Your Daddy has had me raise you odd. He wanted you to have liberties, and to speak your mind. He always said there was no reason that you shouldn't turn out a lady, so he sent you to Miss McCabe. I thought, well that won't last long, but then she told him you're smart as a whip, working through the lessons at twice the expected rate, and that got him all fired up with hopes. So he don't want you cracking your hands with soap or candles, and he keeps you apart from the true things of our life. You might not know that, but it's so. We have guarded you. I went along because it was his dream, and he has precious few of those. It comforts him, the thought of his daughter as a lady. I'll keep up with it for his

301

sake, but I don't mean for you to be dreaming along those lines. It's just for him. We have work to do. That's our life, as you will find out, that's what we are put here for, and most of it is hard. Sometimes Daddy still don't see, after all his time here, what we are and what we mean. But you can. You have Lowrie blood, not much but enough to help you through life — '

'Life?' I almost laughed. 'What life? We are wasting, Ma.'

She refused to hear. She charged on.

' — but if you rise or if you don't, I don't give a damn. What matters is who you are, and in case you don't know the answer to that, let me explain it. Who you are depends on what you *do*. When someone needs help, and it's someone who never hurt us before and don't seem likely to, we give it. Not only because we're better-hearted or more Christian than the rest, which I do think we are, but also because it's smart business. We need who we can get right now. We save a life where we can, we share our food. So you clean that boy. Feed him, care for him, get him back on his feet. It can be done, and you can do it. I've seen them worse off than him. This is a harsh time. If we get through it, we'll see the glory days of our lives. Everything will change. If we don't get through, well, you are right. We will waste away. The lucky ones of us will be looking just like that fellow on the floor, and the rest will be planted in the side yard among the onions. Now, it will help if you pitch in. You think you can do that?'

'Yes, ma'am.'

'Well, then?' she said. 'Get started.'

'Right now?'

'Yes now!'

So she watched me while I got down on my knees by the soldier, pushed the matted greasy hair back, and looked.

His face was a death's head, ridged browbone and knobbed cheek, eye sockets that could have held hickory nuts.

'He's dead,' I said. 'Nobody alive looks like that.'

'They all look like that, those that come up from Florence,' she said. 'Most of them don't even get this far. They give the last piece of strength they have to their escape, then drown crossing the Pee Dee. I'd say if he got here, he'll make it to wherever he's bound.'

'What did they *do* to him?' I said.

'Nothing. That's what does the damage. The human body will kill its own self after a while, given nothing.'

Her voice was steady, but she was staring shocked just as I was, and delayed leaving to help me hoist him onto the bed. I took his feet (bare, sliced so raw I knew he never felt the pain but ran like a Hindu over coals), she took his shoulders, and we easily swung him up. He was light as a straw-stuffed suit of clothes.

On her way out the door, she turned and looked at me and said. 'What counts is now. You may learn something by this, or you may not, but do your best to keep your mind on what's around you. Keep the door locked, keep your mouth shut.' Then she was gone.

Too much locked-up silence and watchfulness takes a toll — and I felt like I'd had years of it, I'd had centuries. Caution becomes a habit that you fall into even when you don't need it, until by and by you distrust the world and your own self, and wonder if someone is watching, and always feel you are doing something wrong.

At the same time, there are advantages. You are alerted. And if you have by coincidence just passed through to the other side of hunger, suddenly the unexpected may happen: everything you see is tinged with possibility. Have all modest hopes been dashed? In that case a wild grand one can spring up.

Daddy lingered after Cee had gone out the door. He was wearing a strange thing, a white rubber raincoat of the Rebel army — and I could have laughed and cried together at the sight. It came up over his head from behind and down over his eyes.

'What is it, Daddy? You're not worrying about me, are you?'

'I have a feeling something is going to happen,' he said.

'Don't start fretting, now.'

'I mean something good.'

'And maybe you'll come home to find I have grown overnight into a fine lady?'

'You already are one! That's what I wanted to say. She was wrong about me. I got no desires for you to rise in the world, because that would take you in the direction straight away from me.'

'I'm going nowhere, don't you worry.'

Down by the gate Cee was calling, and I saw her throw one of those rubber coats over her head. He fumbled with the door, then looked back at me.

'Your mother,' he said, 'sometimes she paints me out to be somewhat of a idiot, but don't get the wrong idea. That is not her true opinion. It's her play-acting, and I go along. That's just the way we do. The fact is, we have depended on one another since the day we met. I stuck to Celia Ann and she stuck to me. She's been a loving wife, I'm proud to say, and if she wasn't in the habit of hiding her sentiments, you'd hear her say I've been a loving man to her.'

'I know that.'

'All right. You be careful. I'll dig us up a money pot out there.'

'We'll be rich!'

'We'll all of us rise,' he said, and kissed the inside of my hand.

It was almost a comedy, like many tragic things in life. We were on starvation. They were leaving me alone with a corpse, with war raging across the countryside, a cold, hard rain falling; and still we believed we were on the verge of discovery. Freedom, true love, a pot of gold!

7

The dying fire log hissed and fell in half. Sparks flowered where it broke, but no flame. On the white bed that soldier was a shock to the eye, like a root doll someone slips you for a hex, grimed and twisted and man-shaped enough to give your heart a chop when you see it.

But I went to him because she said it was a duty.

When I opened the shirt, it fell apart in my hands and a folded note of paper dropped out.

'Whoever finds my dead bodie please notify mrs Martha Wright of Greenville Illinois on the sawyer's stream that her son Owen is met his end, and give her this from me. Mama, thank you for all you done for me. It is sad I must die so young, Ma, and was never married. Tell Milly the promise she made me dont count. Tell her, she is free.'

After I read that, he looked different to me. More solid and not so filthy.

I poked the log and got up a little flame to warm a pan of water, and I ripped away the rest of the boy's rotted clothes. Cee didn't tell me he would be crawling with graybacks. He was a chinch banquet top to toe, their pearly shells fat on his blood. I picked off all I could find and cracked them, and because when smashed they gave off a terrible odor, I burnt them with the shirt and pants. Then I washed him.

And she had been right, I discovered, in her prediction about his looks. He was worn to the edge of life, starved and blood-sucked and mud-caked, but as I washed, he turned beautiful. Better than the medical drawings I had seen, because no ink line can tell the grace of flesh, the light it gives and the spell it casts. I cut off his tangled yellow hair and washed his head, all gently as I could so he might keep on sleeping or dying or whatever it was he was doing. I dried him, and spooned a little water between his lips. My mother had told me that when she tended the sick, even those times when death was certain and no medicine would help, she always had a secret selfish reason for continuing: because the one who gives comfort is comforted. And it seemed so to me.

I paid special attention to his feet, that had brought him so far at so great cost, and I bound them in lint. The feet, plus the note he'd written, made me cry for him — not in pity but more in honor. And I ran my hands over his skin.

It was hot but silky, no sign of camp itch or any wounds except the bug bites. I could feel that his thin legs and arms had once been muscled. Rubbing his calves, I began to think of him as my own — only for the time being, because he would either die or live and go home to his Milly. But till then, he was in my care and power. And who else did I have? Every other one was gone. I rolled my fingertips over him, so that even unconscious he might feel a comfort, through his skin and in his blood. I thought of his Illinois home, his loved ones, his valor in the field, his courage in the prison, his faithful heart. Milly wouldn't begrudge the caress I gave her man, if she knew about it — which she would never. And feverish as he was, he wouldn't know of it himself if he revived, would only maybe have some dim, dreamy recollection of a soothing.

He didn't move or make a sound. And he was so noble-looking, so *sacrificed*-looking. I could tell he was a quiet boy, but one with a deep spirit. He had lived a farm life, before he joined the war. Had fished the stream and played the fiddle, and maybe kept a hive of bees. In years to come — if he survived — he might sometimes have to stop in the middle of his plowing, and the Florence prison would burn across his thoughts like wildfire on a dry field, and he would have to sit down between the rows. Milly would come onto the porch and shade her eyes to see what was wrong and he'd wave to show it was nothing but one of his spells, nothing bad. In the night her sweet stroke down his belly would strike a chord of memory, but he wouldn't know it came from me, my hand, my touch.

In short, I got carried away.

All of a sudden he responded, as I had not known was possible.

I snatched back my hand and scrambled into the corner. To be honest, I was surprised that a man so close to death might rouse in that fashion — a rare marvel. Well, I still think it a marvel but not rare. It does not take much. They can do it under the most unlikely conditions.

If that part of him could wake and rise, I thought the whole man might. But he didn't. After a minute I crept out of the shadows. He was back to the way he was before, subsided.

And then I began to hope I could become more to him than a bell of memory. He might be the man that was *due* me, sent to me, meant for me. I fell in love.

It is easy to love a man who is unconscious. Anything seems possible. Yes, I had the thought of marriage.

I kept on touching him, but only the shoulders and ribs, neck and arms. By now he was gorgeous to me, a noble soul and a hero. He was *America*. I saw him taking leave of Mrs. Martha and pretty Milly, marching off toward the unknown ... and what could drive a boy to do that, except some dream he had? Not for liberty — he left his own at home — but for Liberty. The word and the idea, the cause.

I lay down next to him and slept the night with my arm across his chest. I never felt him move. There was only the tap of his heart underneath my arm, and several times when I lost it I had to set my ear against him to find out he was still alive.

In the morning he looked improved, pinker in the face. I went to pump a bucket of water, and when I came back I sat in a chair by the bed. I sat hours, giving him water and watching over him, but the time did not seem long. I found a kind of faithful patience I'd never had before, as if I'd learned a way to let go my own troubles, to loosen and detach myself. And I sent my strength into him.

Thinking I ought to make a thin soup to have ready for him. I sliced a chunk of

311

McRaney's meat. But I shuddered when I discovered the whole ham was full of skippers. I took it out by the well and set it in the sun to run them out, but had little hope of success, they were burrowed in so deep. So the soup was nothing but water and dandelion greens.

★ ★ ★

By late afternoon his breathing was deeper and his skin had cooled down some. I leaned over his face to have a close look, and he woke up.

Something was wrong. His eyes were pale as a thin sky on a dull day.

'What's this place?' he said.

I started to tell him all — how he'd been found, how I'd nursed him — but the blank blue stare stopped me.

He tried to put things together. 'Dug out of the prison, swum the river . . . crawled days in swamps but I was night blind from bad food . . . I smelled a pond but couldn't find it so I sucked up water out of the mud, and that's the last I remember until I woke up on someone's kitchen table. I guess I took off, but then someone else started shooting at me and I fainted in a ditch. And I'd have been dead by now if the nigger with a torch hadn't found me. He was a nigger, wasn't he? I couldn't tell but I am glad he brought me here. I'd hate to have lied dying in a nigger house.'

My heart drained out. A curtain fell. Love went up in smoke.

He raised his head and looked toward the sunset orange seeping in around the door.

He said, 'Can you tell me how far I come?'

When I didn't answer, he pulled himself up by the bedpost and slid his feet to the floor. On his white bandages he shuffled to the door and opened it and studied what he saw.

'Hell, it's Carolina still, isn't it?' he said, wrapping his arms around himself, disappointed to tears.

I gave him the uniform and watched him struggle with it. He was weak. Getting the britches on wore him out, and he could only throw the jacket over his shoulders as a cape. I never offered to help.

'What's wrong with you, miss, can't you talk? Are you a dumb mute?'

I nodded, with a rolling head.

He nodded back with only a slight look of interest. He was hungry, sniffing around the shelves and cupboard in vain. He asked did I have any animals and I shook my head no, but he went out to look for a pen or coop anyway, and he stumbled upon McRaney's ham. With a triumphing grin he brought it inside and proceeded to eat a hole in it then and there, propping his shoulder sideways against the wall and holding the haunch at both ends like it was an ear of corn, never thinking to inspect it first.

If he was night-blind, what he needed was vegetable food. And I did show him the dandelion soup. But he didn't want it, he wanted the meat, so why should I stop him? It was his choice. He ate like a dog until his teeth hit bone. His mouth was rimmed with grease. He wiped it with his hand and looked up at me.

'I wonder how you get by. Can you write down words when you need to say them to someone?'

I shook my head, thinking skippers must squirm on the way down.

'Well, can you holler?'

Our gun was under the floor, but even if I could have got to it, I didn't know how to shoot. The pig knife was gone with Daddy, but Cee's punchbelly was still in the cupboard. I made out to be searching the shelf for food, and slipped the file into my pocket.

'I heard there is a Chinaman with two heads living in North Carolina,' he said, staring at me but not really seeing. 'Freak of nature. But better to be two-headed than deaf or dumb, I guess.'

He was a witless clod. All I wanted him to do was leave. But having got myself into the impersonation of a mute, I couldn't order him out. I wasn't afraid of him, he was too simple to be a real danger; but I was careful anyway to keep the table between me and him.

'Can you show me the railroad track?' he said. 'There was a whistle. Whoo-whoo? Choocah-choocha-choocha? Me want you' — he pointed at himself and then at me — 'show *train*.' He made the noise again and chugged his arms. 'Are you a idiot? Don't you understand I got to get out of here?'

I didn't want to help him or cooperate in even the smallest way, because he had failed me. I held it against him, that he was not the man I'd made him out to be. But finally I nodded, seeing it was the only way I could be rid of him.

Outside he said, 'Whew, this is mighty poor country,' looking around, shaking his head.

What did you fight for, then? I wanted to say. *If not for this poor country, if not for the niggers?* Even if I could have asked, I doubt he could have said an answer. I doubt he knew.

I kept gesturing to him the direction of

Moss Neck and how to flag down the engineer, but he was unsteady on his feet. His knees buckled and he caught himself on the fence rail.

Oh, go, I thought. *Please go.*

'I need to lie back down,' he said.

He turned toward the house, and I blocked him.

'What in hell is the trouble with you?' he said. 'You're starting to rattle me.'

I knew I couldn't let him inside again, no matter what. So I pulled the file out and held it pointed at his stomach.

'Jeezer,' he said, backing away. 'You got me wrong.'

'I know,' I said.

He tripped and caught himself. 'You said you couldn't talk.'

'Well, I can, and I'm saying get out of here.'

He started backing again. 'I don't know what I done to make you mad. Is it I'm a Yankee? But I don't mean harm. I only came here by accident. I don't even know where I'm at or who you are, and all I want to do is get home.'

'Good, because that's what I want you to do. Start now. Go on back to your stupid Milly.'

He squinted and his mouth opened, and he pitched backward, flat on the ground.

'Now what!' I said. 'Get up, you slacker. If you can eat a ham, you can walk.

But he had fainted away.

I dropped the file and knelt and grabbed his shoulders and shook him as hard as I could, but his eyelids only fluttered a little. I slapped his face, and when my hand touched his skin I knew the fever was back on him with a fury.

It was the low point of my life. I knew I had lost my senses. Had fallen in love with a common fool, believed him sent to me by fate. I had slept by his side! Worst of all, I had imagined he stood for something, when the truth was he was in the dark. He was ignorant.

And now I was stuck with him. He was my destiny of nothing, my loneliness, my error and my sacrifice. He was what the war had done to me.

I beat on his chest and then shook him some more. I wished he had died so that I could bury him and not have to think of him ever again, and when I picked up the file I regret to say I had the thought that one quick stab might solve my problems. Straight to the heart, I thought — not the soldier's but my own. When you see your fate, and it is a sorry one, what can be the purpose in going on to meet it?

But I knew. You meet it so that you can see what the next one will be. No fate is sealed, there is another on the way as long as life continues. And so I couldn't kill myself, and I couldn't kill him.

He moaned.

'Damnation,' I cried. 'I'll never get rid of you.'

'Yes,' I heard a voice above me say. 'Keep on slugging and you'll get rid of him in nothing flat. If he's not gone already.'

It was Henry, standing between me and the sunset.

All I could see was a dark man with a fire behind him. But I knew the voice was his, that deep, smooth, level sound that never shook or broke.

A wrath boiled up in me.

'You again,' I said.

He shifted, and the sun hit my eyes.

'What do you want now?' I said.

'Well, nothing in particular.'

I don't think there was another answer he could have given that would have made me angrier.

'Nothing?'

'I heard they brought you a Yank, and I thought I ought to come take him off your hands. I gave orders no soldiers were to be brought here. William knew that.'

He moved around me, looking down at the fainted man. His boots crushed the grass. I couldn't see his face.

'Have you come to give more orders?' I said.

He sat on his heels next to me and lifted my chin. 'Rhoda, are you feeling all right?'

'Who cares?'

'Let me take you inside. You're cold.'

'I guess you're right. They say you're always right, they say you know everything.'

'Sounds like you're ready to give me a piece of your mind.'

'I could.'

'Go on ahead. But I'd feel easier if you did it without that punch-belly in your hand.' He took the file. Then he stood up and looked off toward the pines.

He isn't even listening to me, I thought. He is still playing a desperado captain.

I shook that soldier one last time, so hard his head flopped back and forth like a doll's, and I hated him more than ever.

'I hope when you get home you'll find your mother won't know you and your sweetheart has married another man.'

Henry did look at me than.

'I was talking to him,' I said.

'Maybe you should talk to me. Say what's got you so angry.'

'I was about to. I was going to give you the piece of my mind that's the maddest of all, so you could take it and ponder it, just think it over the way you think everything over, go out in the woods alone and meditate it — and then come back and let me know if in your plans and schemes for the future, you thought there was a chance, just a little possible chance you might ever see your way clear to someday maybe loving me, because I am about at the end of my rope.'

I couldn't believe I had said it. But I felt a relief. At least it would jolt him, and he would regret not having seen his effect on me. He would be shocked to realize how cruel and mean it was to ignore me as he'd done.

There was a long silence, and then he said, 'Another invitation.'

He wasn't surprised. He had known all along.

'No,' I said. 'Not really. You know, it was just something that — didn't mean anything. I don't know what possessed me, I think I lost my senses there for a while, I've been a little shaky — '

'Stop. Catch your breath.'

'But I couldn't talk for a long time, so now I don't recognize my voice, it feels like someone else is talking out of my mouth. I

was pretending to be a mute. The soldier —
I thought he was one thing and he turned
out to be another, and he drove me half
crazy.'

'The answer's yes,' he said.

I was still kneeling on the ground, tired to
the bone, and I had a great desire to close my
eyes and go to sleep there.

'I'm sorry,' I said. 'I'm about dead.'

He touched my forehead. 'You'll live,' he
said. 'What I meant was, yes to your
invitation.'

My fingers were still digging into Owen
Wright's arms. I couldn't think or move, even
when Henry reached down to undo my grip
and drag the soldier away.

He laid him out on the porch and then
came back for me, lifted me to my feet and
led me inside.

Closed the door and slid the bolt.

'Where's your mama and daddy?'

'They went off to McRaney's new camp.
McRaney's starting early, and he needed a
cook, so they both went — '

I saw his face but it was dark around the
edges and a cloud was closing in. His palms
went under my arms, thumbs on my
collarbone.

'How long before they get back?'

'Two days.'

I closed my eyes and felt his arms go around me, felt his beard brush on my neck as he leaned down, felt his breath at my ear. He didn't draw back, and neither did I, for I had been so starved so long I could not help myself. The sour musty smell of his coat went to my head and filled me with longing. Everywhere along the length of where we touched there was a sweet pull. His mouth touched my ear, then my neck and chin — and although I had never kissed a man before, I planted my mouth on his and fell into him as if I were long familiar with love, its turns and progress and outcome, as if it were the river where I was always meant to swim. I was caught and swept and carried along, and it seemed to me that if I could kiss forever I could live forever. We didn't move from the middle of the room. He held me up.

But at the same time I knew some spectacular kind of hunger in him was being fed by me, and I could tell he was surprised by that, as if he had asked a question he expected no answer to, but got one.

And when the kiss ended, I was shaking because I knew it wasn't enough. I knew I would need another, another, again and again the rest of my living days.

'I love you to death,' I said.

I call that night my wedding night, since I never had a real one.

*　*　*

The same night, miles to the south, a bridge was built across the Pee Dee River. By torchlight the pontoons were lashed and the planks were laid. A storm broke, and the rain blew in sheets, but the bridge held, under the weight of a thousand men with horses, wagons, cannons, cattle, and a thousand more men after that, and a multitude of ragged rearward followers blind to their destination but surging ahead as if they somehow knew the bridge would hold. When the torches were extinguished by rain and the way was thrown into darkness, pines on the other side were set afire. They crackled and burned as if the rain were fuel, flames leaping one tree to the next and next until the whole bridge end to end would be seen as if by daylight, and the crossing was made, and the column of marchers passed under the bursting trees.

Then the planks were taken up, the pontoons drawn ashore and loaded on wagons at the tail of the march. In the morning the pines were still booming and burning, towers of smoke climbing with the sunrise, but the bridge had vanished, gone on with those who crossed.

★　★　★

I woke alone in my bed. Henry was outside, gathering Owen Wright into a blanket sling.

'How is he?' I said from the doorway. Not what I meant to say.

'He's failing. I'm going to carry him over to McCabe's, maybe the doctor can do something.'

I didn't know what to say to him. I was talking like someone nothing had happened to.

'Miss McCabe won't hide a Yankee,' I said. Thinking, *His legs, belly, mouth, his voice when he cried out* . . . 'She won't let him past the front door.'

'I don't know. Last week we stopped there to get water and she fed us all a supper. She gave us blankets too, and a map.'

'Amanda McCabe?'

'She said it was because of you. Her affection for you.'

'That might get you a free supper but not much else.' *The way he lifted me.*

'We'll find out.' He hoisted the sling onto his back, with the soldier curled inside it.

My mouth was dry as flour. I took in a deep breath and said, 'And . . . you think you'll be coming back by here?'

'I hope I may,' he said.

After he left I sat down and closed my eyes. *Let him come back. Send him, and this will be my last prayer. I'll never ask for anything more. I'll shoulder burdens the rest of my life without complaint, if he returns.*

I said it out loud, over and over. I meant every word, I raised my hand while I spoke. I couldn't help myself. Maybe I shouldn't have made that kind of bargain, maybe Henry would have come back anyway, but I had no guarantees. What was to keep him from disappearing out of my life? 'Henry Berry Lowrie goes where he pleases.' Everyone knew that.

But at sunset when I saw him crossing the field I knew I had to keep my vow even though I couldn't be sure whether God was behind it or not. Why would a promise like that — never to pray again — tempt God, after all? It sounded more like a pact with the devil. But either way, I could never pray for anything else in my life.

I didn't care. If I got Henry, I wouldn't need anything else in my life.

'She said yes,' he said.

'You talked Miss McCabe into nursing a Yankee soldier?'

'Nelly was there, she did the talking. And we can use the house for a meeting place, Miss McCabe said.'

'But why would she agree to that?'

'I told you, it's for you. After I gave your name she said yes to everything we wanted.'

★   ★   ★

We had a second night together, the same as the first. And I didn't mind that we didn't speak much, didn't tell our secrets. Henry Berry was not a man to give himself away, and I could get used to that. Even if he wasn't all mine (for I was sure he would always be looking off into the distance, not fully hearing me, his mind on everything beyond his reach), I did believe I'd be able to keep him as close as anyone could, and ward off his cares.

We were lying still, and the rain had stopped for a while. He sat up and took my hands in his.

'Rhoda, I hope you'll be my wife.'

I could have hollered yes and jumped for joy, and I almost did, but then I saw his eyes. Some women are pleased to discover a man can be moved to tears, but it scared me. I didn't know what to do. I pretended I didn't notice.

'Yes,' I said.

'Then tomorrow we'll tell the world,' he said, and pulled me close like something he meant to hold on to.

8

A wind woke me the next morning — Friday, March 3, the day of my life I most regret and would give my soul to undo. First came that sighing wind like a creature come from afar to die at my door. The gate banged and a low branch scraped the roof. Then a gust licked down the chimney, stirring soot, raising a cloud of dry ashes that sifted across the hearthstone. I heard one faraway crow, bird of trickery. But after a while everything hushed, and there was no sound but Henry's breathing.

I lay still, to keep him asleep as long as I could. Not because he looked peaceful — no, his face was pinched with a dream of trouble, his eyes rolling under their lids — but because some secret of my own self was now fastened in him. While he slept, I studied his face.

But he caught me, opened his eyes and saw the kind of longing a woman is supposed to hide.

I kissed his wide, cool palms and square-nailed fingers. In the middle of his chest there was a hollow like a ground dove's nest, where I lay my head.

'We didn't eat yesterday,' he said. 'Or the day before.'

'I can go weeks.'

'But today's the day,' he said, stretching himself out. I never had seen anything so fine, the beauty of a perfect man, even his feet perfect, and his legs long and muscled, belly flat as wood. 'Rhoda Strong and Henry Lowrie announce their engagement,' he said. 'For that, we need a breakfast. I don't suppose you know how to cook, being a girl of high education.'

That was what I wanted, the easy way he spoke, the smile he almost smiled. My mother had said I could give Henry nothing he needed, but she forgot that love is a mystery, not a bargain. It springs up, not to answer a need but to make one.

I said, 'There's no food here but what's left of a wormy ham.'

'Mama will feed us. When she hears the news, first thing she'll do is fix us something. She'll say, 'Look at these little old scrawny arms. We'll have to put some meat on the girl's bones if she's to be a Lowrie.''

'I don't want anyone to know yet,' I said. 'I want to keep it a secret.'

I meant that. He was restless to go, but I held him back, twined my legs with his and made him lie still.

'We'll go to the house and tell Mama and Daddy and William,' he said, 'then go over to Sink's and then Cal's. Might have time in the afternoon to get up to Patrick's too, and tonight we'll come back here when your parents are home, and tell them.'

'Henry —'

'Mama always praised you to me,' he said. 'And you know you're Daddy's favorite. He'll dance you around the room when he hears you said yes.'

'But let's stay here a little longer,' I said. 'We don't have to go right away.'

I knew Mr. Allen would be glad to know I was marrying Henry, but I didn't know what Mary Cumbo would say. She might wish her son had picked an Oxendine or a Kersey for a bride, a girl whose family owned land and had a settlement name, a nice quiet girl who was a hard worker and a good cook. I was worried what Daddy would say too. But what scared me most was Cee, and how she would take the news that I meant to marry the one man she had warned me against.

'Please not yet,' I said.

So he stayed for my sake, at my begging, for my pleasure. I kept him until the sun was in the high window, surprised I could hold him with so little effort. All I did was let love

330

come. But I know he felt pulled to his parents' house, and if it hadn't been for my pleading we would have gotten an earlier start. I take the blame. It was only because I wanted to lengthen out the time we had alone, and pretend there was no one else alive.

He laid his open hand against my cheek. 'I fell in love with you at a funeral,' he said 'Wes and Allen's.'

'I knew I saw you there.'

'I was watching Mr. George, and Boss, and then I looked across and my eye landed on you. Since that day you've been the only girl I could think of. I wanted to ask you right then if you would consider me, but I knew I didn't stand a chance. A girl like you could have a rich man, one who could give you everything you want.'

'But you never said a word of it to me.'

'I'm no good at talking. The more important a thing is, the harder it is for me to say. And then, after the funeral everything changed. I knew I'd be a wanted man with a price on my head, and I couldn't ask you to promise yourself to that. And still I want you to think hard about it. Barnes and Harris — '

I put my hand over his mouth. 'All I want to know is if you love me.'

He nodded.

'Do you swear?' I said.

He pulled back from me, and my heart tripped.

'Never sworn to anything before in my life,' he said.

'I didn't mean you have to make a Bible oath.'

He got up and walked around the room — to the fireplace, the table, the shelf.

'It's all right,' I said. 'It doesn't matter.'

'Don't your family have a Bible?'

'No.'

'Have I got myself a heathen girl?'

He came back and pulled me to him and said, 'Well, if you did have one, I'd swear on it I love you and always will, with a love as true as any on the earth's face. I'll be the best husband to you that I can, if you want to take a chance on me.'

The vow was flawed. But I accepted it. He gave me what he could.

What I wanted from him wasn't his soul, but my own. I thought I saw myself in him. But that is a kind of thing you should never reveal to the man you love. Never confess, 'I can't live without you.' It's too much burden for him. Yet I knew, from now on the only life I had was with Henry Lowrie. I didn't care what people might say, how I should have known better, how I should have realized he was going to be trouble. All I knew was, that beauty of his and that heart could become mine.

I hoped he didn't notice how close I watched as he dressed. You can see the whole man in any little bit of him — the way he lifts his arm to chop a log of wood, or how he holds his reins, how he sings or plows, or dresses in the morning. If you find that you love each move and gesture, for no reason you can explain, then you are in love for life. He was so careful, step by step, as if preparing for a ceremony: trousers, shirt, belt, boots, coat, handled with a motion slow and exact. The homespun could have been fine tailor's linen, the cowhide a finished English leather. He smoothed his hair and beard, then ducked his head for a glance into our broken mirror on the wall. None of this was for show. It was soldierly, a duty, the way of a man who is proud of being a man but has no pretensions. Still, the quick look he stole of himself was almost boyish, so shy and fast I had to smile.

'What's so funny?' he said.

'Well, you're all buttoned up and looking like a proper man now. I saw you sneak a look in the mirror to admire your own handsomeness.'

'Grandad Cumbo carried a hand glass with

him all the time, on a string over one shoulder. I never saw him without it. He said he kept it so he would know who he was. I guess that's what I was looking for in the mirror.'

'And who did you see? Who are you?'

'If you just met me for the first time, what would you think?'

'A cold-blooded villain,' I said.

'That's how I look?'

'To some, but not to me, because I know your other side, your warm-blooded night-time side.'

'Brought out by a temptress.'

I held up my arms to him.

'No, I want to go on home and get this settled. I want to set a date, and I want it to be soon. I'm worried some handsome fellow will come along and you'll fall for him.'

'I already did that, and I don't plan on doing it more than once in my lifetime.'

He came and sat down next to me on the bed and took my hands in his.

'You know who I saw in the mirror?' he said. 'A man who's ready to quit lying out, ready to settle and make a life. There's a chance for it now — for us all to work and raise up families and prosper. Maybe we'll have some hard years first, but we'll use them. We'll *build*. I want to see a school here, and the children reading books — I know once we get a school there won't be no stopping us. Why are you smiling at that now?'

'It's what my mother always told me. She said after the war, we'd get schools and land and the vote and our share of the turpentine business.' I didn't add what she had added — 'unless Henry ruins our chance.'

'We will. It's coming, and you and me will see it happen, Rho. But do you know how when you get right up close to something you've always hoped for, sometimes a shadow falls? I had a dream last night, I was on the road to church and I saw a funeral coming, a long line of people and a wagon carrying a box, and I said, 'Who has died?' and it was answered, 'Henry Lowrie.' I called out to say it wasn't true, I ran from one to another, but no one believed me.'

'That's foolishness. Put it out of your mind. You said you want to work and make a life. Well, you know you're going to have to work double hard since you picked a lazy girl for a wife. You see how I like to lounge in bed all morning. That's what I plan for the rest of my life. I'll give the orders and you'll be a hen-husband, and everybody will whisper when we walk by, 'There goes bossy Mrs. Lowrie and her old Henry. She runs him hard, poor fellow, while she just lolls.''

I lay back flat, still holding on to his hand. 'And you'll have to get to work right away — building a house. That's *my* dream.'

'So,' he said, 'if you could have one wish, it would be a house?'

'No, a house is my second wish.'

'What's the first?'

'To see Boss.'

'Then I'll have to give you two. Suppose I take you to Boss tomorrow and then to the spot where your new house will be. Suppose I already cleared it, across Back Swamp way out from everybody else, and already set the posts — maybe already framed it up — maybe raised the roof — '

'But you didn't. Don't tease.'

'I wonder who did, then. Because it's there big as life, on land Daddy's giving me. Won't be but two rooms, shingle roof, little porch — but it will be solid. It will hold us. I started the first day of February.'

'I don't believe it. You didn't even know I was thinking of you then.'

'I hoped.'

'But you can't have been so sure of me you went and built a house!'

'Well, it's only half built. I wasn't but fifty percent sure. We could have lived with Mama and Daddy, but we'll want room for children. Won't we?'

I closed my eyes. 'Are you telling me the truth?'

'I don't know how to tell you anything else. That's why I want you with me. You're the only person I trust besides Boss, but I can't tell him all the truth. He thinks I'm better than I really am. I can't tell him my doubts; I wouldn't ever tell him something like that dream of the funeral line. But with you I won't hide anything because — well, I don't think you need it hidden. You're strong. And that's what I want. Our house — yes, it's true. You'll see it tomorrow, or you'll see the half that's done.'

'Tell me the doubts.'

'At this moment I don't have a one.'

We made another delay, after which he had to get dressed and proper all over again.

So it was long past noon when we left. I was filled up with love. It seemed too much luck, more luck than I had earned, to have that man as mine. That's why I couldn't put out of my own mind the dream I had told him to forget. A dream may not reveal the exact future, but it can haunt and weigh down the dreamer nevertheless, and I wasn't going to let that happen. I was starting my job as a helpmeet.

While we walked, I understood I was not to break his concentration, which was on the trail, the birds, the river. He might as well have been alone, for all the notice he paid me, but I didn't mind. I liked walking beside him without his attention, as if he considered I was his natural companion. I watched him, and he watched everything. Nothing escaped his eye. Once, he stopped and stared at a patch of leaves beside the trail. Just leaves. But when he kicked them away, there was a burnt circle.

He wasn't concerned by it. 'Donohue McQueen,' he said.

'How can you tell?'

'Seen his fires before. I should tell him he's getting better. I almost didn't notice that one.'

'It seems pitiful to me, the way he lurks around hoping to gain favor.'

'Donohue's trouble is he thinks he needs a stamp of approval.'

'Did I ever remind you of him, I mean in a kind of way?'

He laughed at me. 'I can't think of a single likeness between you and him.'

At the river we turned east, and had gone a short way along when there was a sudden commotion in the brush. Before I could even see what it was, Henry had swept me behind him with one hand and with the other had drawn and cocked a pistol. But it was only a doe we'd scared up, who had sprung to her feet and leapt backward in one quick sweep, then stopped to turn and face us.

Her coat was oily and bright, more green than brown, her eyes black and wet and her belly fat, and I knew she was carrying a fawn that would be born in late spring. I hated to scare her, to send fear rushing down through her blood to the heart of her unborn.

'Stay,' I whispered, and held out my hand. 'Oh, stay.'

She looked at me, but in the next instant she tossed her head back, and flew.

Henry slipped the gun back inside his shirt, the barrel under his belt.

'I didn't know you had that,' I said.

'I always do, now,' he said.

'You said you wouldn't hide anything from me.'

'Everyone knows how Cee hates guns. I didn't know what you'd say. Do you mind it?'

'No.' I didn't tell the truth, which was that I loved it.

Maybe a year earlier, I'd have said I hate it, don't carry it. Maybe I'd have said I don't want a man who is always armed, a life in which death is always in the pocket, under the pillow, tucked in the boot. But now I thought about it a different way. Henry was known to be the best shot in the settlement and maybe in the county. For the first time in my life I felt safe — with him, with that gun.

And to my surprise there was a kind of thrill in safety. I never had felt it before. The shiver of liberty.

A gun, I know, does not mean real liberty. But it will give the sensation. Nothing could touch us, no one could stop us. That was the feeling I had. As a result, the woods and the river had never looked so beautiful or so much *ours* — mine and his, and everyone's who had lived and died along these banks. I thought of Sally America Kersey when she married James Lowrie and set up with him to run the ferry, and I couldn't imagine a better scheme of life than to be a partner with your husband, working alongside him in the place of your history, feeling safe.

But the truth is, Sally America would have known it was a false feeling. All who ever lived here knew deep down the same truth that doe's fawn learned long before its first breath of life. *Stay watchful. Stay ready to run.*

★ ★ ★

When we got to the Lowrie landing, Henry stopped me with a hand on my arm.

'Doesn't look right,' he said.

To me the place was the same as the last time I'd passed, quiet and peaceful — except for one thing.

'Dogs ran off somewhere,' I said.

We crossed the field, and the closer we got the more odd things I saw. The sheep had drifted to the edge of the woods. Mr. Allen's hoe was lying in the dirt with a bag of seed. The mule and cart were gone. Behind the house there was a jimmyjohn broken in pieces, and the smell of brandy. A trunk lay busted open by the back door, with clothing strewn about, and I remembered how the postmaster's farm looked after the Yankees tore through it.

'They got raided!' I said.

'I was promised they'd be left alone.'

'Who could promise you that?'

'Preacher Sinclair. He said he could fix it with the Yanks and the Home Guard too, to keep them off this place.'

'Then maybe it was robbers out for themselves.'

He called but there was no answer. Inside, the table was set for three, with a round flat cornbread cake on each one, and three full cups of cold coffee.

'It must have happened just when they sat down to breakfast,' I said. 'And then maybe they went over to Sink's house or Cal's.'

'I don't know,' he said. 'See if anything's missing in here. I'll check the other rooms and the sheds.'

All the cupboards stood open, but nothing had been taken from the shelves. Jars of plums and peaches were lined up in rows without a gap, the fat globes of purple and red and gold pushing against the glass. A basket of brown eggs, full sugar box, tin of ginger cakes. My mouth watered. Our cupboards at home were filled with nothing but cobwebs, and I had forgotten what a house could be like when it was packed with food and furnishings and keepsakes, all the signs of a good life — framed pictures of art on the wall, a shelf of books, a blue glass vase. The family Bible lay open next to Mr. Allen's plate on the table. In the window a string of brass hawk's bells turned, and Mary Cumbo's yellow curtains waved.

I confess I had a shameful thought just then: some of those bright pretty things might be mine someday. I'd be Rhoda Lowrie and my new house would be as bright as this one. I sat at the table and ate a piece of cornbread. Even cold, Mary's cornbread was better than any I'd ever made. Sugar instead of molasses,

342

I thought, and butter instead of lard. I had a lot to learn if I was going to be a good Lowrie wife. All those girls the older boys had married were fine cooks. Patrick's Cate won a prize at the Scots Fair for peaches-and-snow cake made with eleven eggs, and Cal's Mariah won for scuppernong wine.

Thinking of Cee at the stillery every day all those years, chopping wood and hauling water at night, using her last bit of strength to mix up a cornmeal mush, I saw that even a little prosperity changed the kind of life a woman had, and the kind of food she could eat.

'It doesn't make sense,' Henry said, coming back inside. 'I can't find William's gun. He always kept the stock hidden in the peas crib, and the barrel behind the smokehouse wall. Some bedclothes are gone off the bed, and Daddy's old Sunday coat and pants are missing from the trunk. But that's all. Why would Yankees pick and choose? They didn't want food, just the brandy . . . '

He frowned, eyeing the table in front of me.

'Did you touch anything there?'

'I only ate the cornbread — '

'Then Daddy left the sign of distress. The Bible open.'

A dog barked, far away, and then another.

Nothing in Henry's expression changed, except a quick squinting of his eyes.

'Listen to me,' he said in a steady voice. 'I want you to follow me now, and not make a single noise. Not a sound. Not even a cough, and stay as close to me as you can. Go where I go. If I say the word, I want you to run, no matter what. Go to Dr. McCabe's, by way of Turkey Branch, not the river, and I'll come find you there.'

'But what do you think is — '

'I said *not a sound*. We don't have time.' Then he was out the door without a backward glance.

I followed through the yard to the edge of the field, where he fell to the ground and crawled into a thicket of bull briar, and I was behind him, thorns ripping my skirt and sleeves as I went, until we were in the center of the thicket where the canes sprang in a low arch making a sort of den, and I crawled up next to him. From there we had a view of the front porch.

Within seconds I heard the sound of men's voices, and Mr. Allen's four dogs came trotting up the road, followed by his mule and wagon. We lay flat, looking out through the briars and leaves.

Ben Bethea was holding the reins, and behind him sat William and Mr. Allen. There was a crowd of men walking by the wheels, eight or nine on either side.

'Draw up close to the woods,' Rod McTeer said to Ben. They passed right by us and came to a stop. Mr. Allen climbed out and helped William down.

'I want those ears, Lowrie,' McTeer said. 'I'll find them if we have to dig every inch of dirt off the place.'

'You said you already got what you needed,' Mr. Allen said.

'You know well as I do it's not hard evidence. The gun was broke down and you done filed off the mark. John Parsley identified the head of his cane, and McCallum might swear the suit of clothes was his, but I'm going to need more. I want the ears of somebody's hogs you stole, with the marks.'

William said, 'The gun is mine. The first we saw of that gold-head cane was when Taylor pulled it out of our corn crib. And we can get witnesses who'll tell you Daddy wore that old black suit to New Hope every Sunday for eleven years. If we was going to steal a suit of clothes, we'd find something better than that. And you'll find no hog's ears here, McTeer, dig all you want.'

While he spoke he was bending at the waist, one hand pressed against his side. Mr.

Allen took his arm, and Daniel McNeill led them both toward the house. Daniel was about William's age, and they sometimes hunted together. His father had kept him out of the war, and when Sheriff King took him into custody to ship to the army, old McNeill grabbed him right back home and told the sheriff if he knew what was good for him he'd keep his hands off Daniel. So Daniel was not a die-hard Rebel, and I thought he would watch out for William, his old friend.

'I want a word with you, McTeer,' said a man I recognized as a justice of the peace, Hector McLean. The two stepped apart from the rest, on the side of the wagon near us.

'A hog's ear buried any length of time won't show you much,' said McLean in a low voice.

'Christ's sake, I know that, McLean. I don't expect to find anything but it would help if we do. It would be better evidence than what we got.'

'But what difference can it make?' McLean said. 'We had the vote. It's done.'

'You aren't thinking straight today, are you? You nearly messed up everything at Mackenzie's, arguing to let them off. Lucky for you, I'm doing the thinking now. We got a guilty verdict from a crowd of eighty drunks in a cornfield back there, on bad evidence without witnesses except two whose word is worthless. It won't hold up. The sheriff wasn't even there, he's cowed now and good for nothing. I'm the one that has to do what has to be done, and you can believe I will.'

'Stealing isn't the charge. It's harboring. It's aid to the enemy, and those eighty men are a duly constituted company under Captain McCrimmon. He ordered us here, and he's the one I'll answer to, not some renegade deputy.'

'Listen,' McTeer said. 'Don't ever let me hear you say that again. The charge is larceny. That's how I'm going to report it. You think we're going to win the war, McLean? If you do, you lost your brains entirely. No, we're going to have a Yankee government on us in no time. When that happens, harboring Union soldiers is not going to be looked at as no crime, it'll be called a act of heroics. Patriotism. While a thief is a thief, under any flag. You see what I mean?'

'But we had the trial. It's over. It won't go back to court.'

'Everything will go back to court. Yankee court. And *this* case will be the first they'll look at.'

'You want them inside, Rod?' Taylor called.

'No. Start 'em digging.' McTeer brushed McLean aside and joined the rest.

'Where at?'

'Hell, I don't care. They're going to shovel up the yard inch by inch until they decide it's easier to show us the right place.'

'My son can't dig,' Mr. Allen said. 'He's too hurt.'

'Christ,' said McTeer. 'Who popped that cap at him anyway? What idiot?'

'I did,' Taylor said. 'Because you said to, when he broke and ran back there at Mackenzie's. You hollered get him, so I did. But it just winged him, Rod. He can dig all right.'

'He needs a doctor,' Mr. Allen said.

'We get the ears, he gets a doctor,' McTeer said.

Ben and William and Allen took up shovels and started turning the dirt. I saw a dark round blot on William's shirt the size of a dollar. Now and then he had to stop and lean on the shovel handle.

McTeer swung up on the porch railing and sat astride it like a horseman, snapping his fingers. The others leaned against the wagon wheels or stood around watching, and some went inside and brought out jars of peaches to eat. Some sat on the ground and cleaned their muskets or stretched out to sleep. From time to time McTeer directed the diggers to work faster. He never walked over to look at any of the dirt piling up outside the hole.

Henry didn't move a muscle except to pull out the gun and slowly cock it and turn his head just slightly, to look along the tree line, then back to the men. I could see him counting. Then he aimed the barrel directly at McTeer and held it steady. I felt sick.

I don't know how much time passed, with only the sound of shovels slicing into the ground and the thumping of the dirt tossed aside, until Ben Bethea stopped digging.

'What's wrong, Ben?' McTeer said.

'I'm through here, Mr. McTeer. I won't be part of it no more.'

'Oh you won't?'

'No, sir. You know there's nothing here. And while we're digging, William's bleeding blood.'

'Is that right.'

'I didn't hear what was said at Mr. Mackenzie's,' Ben said. 'You put me to guard the ones in the smokehouse, and I couldn't tell what was happening. But I see now, you're going to horsewhip these men. I don't want nothing to do with it.'

'You're a free man, you're saying.'

'Yes, sir, I am. So is Mr. Lowrie and William, and you all can't do them like this. One is too hurt and one is too old. A whipping could kill them.'

'I believe in the nigger vote, you know, Ben. I'm willing for you to vote with your feet right now. Go on home. You done your part to help us out.'

'I didn't do nothing to help you out. I didn't know what you was up to. You told me it was a regular court.'

'Didn't we have a justice of the peace, Mr. Hector McLean, Esquire, and two preachers? Didn't we find some of the accused innocent? You better trust it was a court, because if you don't you'll be held in contempt. That means held in jail. You got a gal and four head of children at home, and with you locked up who's going to feed them?'

'I can't let you do it, Mr. McTeer. You might lock me up if you want to, but I got to stop you from what's wrong.'

'Well, I'm curious to know just what it might be, that you're planning to do to stop us.' Macmillan picked up his musket.

Henry was barely breathing. He switched his aim from McTeer to one and another of the other men scattered about the yard, then back to McTeer.

'Ben,' said Mr. Allen, 'don't make trouble.'

'All they told me was they had a gun-stealing charge against William. That's all I knew, Mr. Allen. I didn't know they would up and shoot him. And then to whip him on top of that? No, it ain't right. And now I'm thinking they mean to whip you, too, Mr. Allen. I couldn't stand to see it.' Ben's voice shook. 'I believe they're going to plant some ears when our back is turned and whip us all.'

McTeer laughed.

William said, 'No, Ben, they won't. I told McTeer, there's a crowd of Yanks on their way here now, forty of them who are friends to us. McTeer knows it's true. Anything happens to us, and there'll be hell to pay.'

'Oh, I don't doubt your Yanks are out there,' McTeer said. 'But my guess is, the Union Army don't give a damn about what happens to you, William. That's you all's whole trouble, you been taken in by sweet promises from your pretty Yankee soldiers. Still and all, I'm a cautious man, and that's why I don't want to hang around here too much longer. Tell us now where to find what we want.'

Allen Lowrie laid down his shovel and stood up straight. 'We took no hogs that weren't our own,' he said. 'I said I have had Union soldiers in my house, and I said why. They came to me starved and dying. But I never stole a single thing in all my life, Mr. McTeer.

'You were whipped once already for sheep-stealing, I recall.'

'Twenty-five years ago. I was tending my uncle Jim's flock, and I pulled a ewe out of the mud. The sheriff rode up and found Townsend's mark on it. But I didn't know anything about it. It wasn't my flock.'

'How many times have we heard that story from a thief caught red-handed?' McTeer said to his audience, and they all laughed. 'But you know what done you in, Lowrie? Your own boys. They ought to have put in their time on the forts instead of running. You let them turn to a life of crime, and they drawed you in.'

'My sons are grown men on their own. I don't rule them. And if you want any of us for a crime, then give us a trial in the courthouse and let us testify.'

'See, we can't do that, Lowrie. The court don't recognize you as a man the same as me. If it's my word against yours, you got no say.'

William said, 'I know I ain't the man you are, McTeer, but maybe you'll tell me where you think the difference lies.'

'I'll boil it down for you. It's not your fault, no more than a mongrel fice is to blame for sucking eggs or a mule for balking. It's their nature. Your kind don't have and never will have a capability for the higher reasoning. The noble morals is bred out. Your makeup is what they call bestial, and if you don't know what that means, it means I fight for honor and you fight for something to fill your belly.'

'I guess I can make out the sense of that. You mean we both fight for what we got none of?' William laughed even though it hurt him to, and some of the company laughed as well.

McTeer's shoulders stiffened and he drew his hand back in a fist, but then he smiled. 'I'm not going to waste my time with this scum no more.' He turned toward the rest and said, 'Who is going to do it?'

'You go on home, Ben,' Mr. Allen said. 'They'll let you walk away. I see four or five good men here, who won't let harm come to you. Go on and go.'

Ben climbed out of the hole, but he didn't run. He stood looking at Mr. Allen.

'I'll find Henry and send him,' Ben said.

Mr. Allen shook his head. 'That's what they want,' he said. 'No, just tell him — '

'I can't wait to hear this,' McTeer said. 'A message for the great Henry Berry Lowrie.'

Mr. Allen ignored him. 'Ben, tell Henry, and tell my wife, I'll see them when we all come home. Those words.'

Ben started walking toward the road. Slowly, McTeer raised his gun.

McLean said, 'Let him go.'

'Damned if I will,' McTeer said.

McLean reached out and knocked the

barrel down, and a load discharged into the porch floor. Ben made it to the treeline and cut into the woods. McTeer cursed.

'That's going to be a step you regret, Hector,' McTeer said. 'He's seen you. He knows your name, and your part.'

'I'm not ashamed of my part,' said McLean. 'This company is a legitimate arm of the law, authorized by the county. I'm an officer of the Confederacy here, and I'm doing my duty. I don't like it, but these men were found guilty of harboring the enemy, no matter what you say. I favored acquittal, but I will uphold the verdict. I have no choice. It was fair and square for time of war. So don't threaten me, McTeer.'

'All right, fine. Let's get on with the upholding, then. We're wasting time. You can come on out of there, Lowrie, and get your smart-mouth boy out too.'

Mr. Allen pulled William onto the little hill and got down on one knee next to him to open the shirt, to see the wound.

'Billy,' he said. 'Why didn't you say it was bad?'

'Is it?'

'Pray with me, Preacher Coble,' Mr. Allen said, with one arm holding William around the shoulders and the other stretched toward the Shoe Heel preacher. 'This boy's dying.'

Henry got up in a crouch, both hands on his gun.

'Rhoda, go.'

But one of the company was walking straight toward us, and before I could back myself out of the thicket, Henry jerked me forward again. The one coming in our direction was armed, but he was looking scared and his skin was a sickly gray color. He came right up to where we were, and could have seen us if he'd looked down, but his eyes were lifted to the sky, and he was praying the Lord's Prayer out loud, and blubbering. It was the McNeill boy, Daniel, William's friend. He walked off into the woods, and we heard him break into a run in the cane behind us.

Someone shouted from the wagon, 'Rod, you ain't really going through with it, are you? I thought it was a sham, to scare 'em.'

'Some of you men make me sick. You think we're playing games here? Or you running scared like the sheriff? Step out of the way, Coble, that's enough praying.'

Henry closed his eyes. Alone, he would have shot McTeer; even if it cost him his life. But I was there. He couldn't endanger me.

'All right, you two,' McTeer said.

Mr. Allen helped William to his feet and tried to hold him upright. William started to crumple, and Mr. Allen had to catch him with both arms.

'I got you, son. Lean here.'

Eight men were standing in front of the house. 'Who are the other four?' McTeer said. No one else came forward. 'Hell with it. Eight will do. Four left and four right, on the kerchief.'

Then I saw nothing. Henry slammed me down and fell onto me, his left hand over my mouth and his right arm across the back of my neck, grinding my cheek into the dirt and thorns. My neck was wrenched sideways so hard I cried out, but his hand muffled me, and even the noise I made in my throat went unheard.

A deafening sound like lumber clattering from a height drowned me out.

For a few seconds the air seemed to ring, followed by a great silence. There was a sharp, oily dusty smell.

'Are we waiting for Jesus Christ?' McTeer said. 'Fill the hole.'

It started to rain, a sprinkle as fine as a waterfall spray blown off; and a rain crow called in the woods. Sound of shoveling, shoveling, shoveling, broken now and then by a faint high wail from somewhere, like a hawk or the crying wind. And at the last, the clank of shovels tossed into the wagon.

'What now, Rod?'

'We go back to the company. They're still holding Cal and Sink in Mackenzie's smokehouse, and the old lady. I think I can convince her now it's in her interest to tell me where Henry's at. She won't be feeling so high and mighty and stubborn this time.'

John Taylor said, 'But what did you make of it, Rod, the way they took it? They didn't even flinch or blink an eye, and the way the old man held his boy up . . . '

'It don't mean nothing.'

'I always thought — I was told — only a man of honor will take it like they did, but a rogue goes a-sniveling and begging.'

'Will you shut up? You can forget how they took it. I want an oath from every man here. We call no names and tell no tales, from now on. Let's move out.'

They walked by us, and faded down the road. Minutes passed, with the light rain dripping in the leaves, the dogs whining. No voices.

★   ★   ★

'Henry.'

He tightened his grip on me; wrapping both his arms around my head and holding it against his chest.

357

'Henry, are they *shot?*'

He wouldn't let go of me. I had to kick to get away, and I hurled myself through the briars into the yard.

It was so empty.

I saw only the mule and wagon, the vacant porch, and the place where there was no grass, a bed-sized mound of bare earth, pitted by raindrops.

He came walking like a ghost toward me. I shouted, 'Get a shovel,' and I ran past him toward the wagon, but he grabbed my arm and spun me back.

'They could be still alive,' I said.

'No. I saw. They were torn to pieces.'

His face looked ruined. He was staring at the mound.

'But we can't be sure — '

'I thought . . . I thought he would let them go,' he said.

I put both hands over my mouth, and I started to tremble all over. Circling the grave — three, four times, with that wrecked stare of surprise in his eyes, he kept shaking his head as if to clear it but it would not clear, and then he stopped in his tracks, and his face began to change. It hardened and darkened. His eyes narrowed. He turned away from the mound and away from me.

'Henry — '

He raised his hand to cut me off.

I closed my eyes. I lost sensation, aware of nothing except the one thought: *Torn to pieces.* But then I heard an unmistakable sound, a cry of someone calling for help from a far distance.

And I was on my knees, digging with my hands. I was calling out, 'They're alive, I know it, I heard it,' and then my arms were in to the elbows, lifting as much of the loose damp dirt as I could and tossing it off to the side.

He seized me by the shoulder and threw me back on my heels.

'Stop it,' he said.

'I heard crying. I heard it.'

'No, you didn't.'

'Yes, I did, it was from underneath, it was your daddy — '

He tried to pull me up, but I was gone wild. I thrashed and struck out at him until he let go and I fell back panting, my wet hair stringing over my eyes.

'Listen to me,' he said. 'They were shot through the heart, both of them. They're dead.'

'I won't believe it. I'm going to dig — '

'Stand up.'

'I know what I heard!'

With one hand he grabbed me by the hair

and lifted me high enough to slap me across the face with his other hand.

I lay down and put my cheek against the ground. There were still a few raindrops falling, or blowing from the trees. I didn't feel them but I saw them hitting the ground. One of Mr. Allen's dogs came up and sat by me.

I broke down then and cried my heart out — or tried to.

Henry's back was to me, his shoulders hunched and his head low. He was like a boulder of stone.

I remember looking at the cabin windows and wondering why those curtains were still there. How could such things remain — curtains, table, dishes, bells, plums, Bible? How could there still be trees and crows, and me myself? But it was so.

He raised his head and looked into the distance, toward Mackenzie's.

In that instant I understood I must do as he said or he would go off down that road without me, and he would get himself killed. I rose to my feet, my skirts heavy with mud, and I calmed myself. I went and stood behind him.

'Tell me what to do,' I said.

He didn't even turn.

'Go home,' he said.

'Henry, no. I'll be all right now, don't send me away.'

'It's best. You're no help to me,' he said, so cold and hard I choked, struck dumb.

I picked up my skirts and stumbled toward the path. But I stopped and managed to say, 'You can't go against them alone.'

He swung around. 'Don't tell me what I can and can't!'

But he must have seen my cuts and scratches, the mud and blood on me, the mark of his hand on my skin. And he remembered: he had traded his brother and father for me. He had chosen and was bound to me, no matter how weak I was, how little help to him. He had sworn to marry me. Maybe he remembered he had loved me an hour before.

He stood still. 'I let them die,' he said. 'I let them be shot down before my eyes.' He meant because of me. I was the reason. 'I have to find the rest,' he said. 'My mother. They said they got her. I have to find Sink and Cal, and by God, Rhoda, *by God* I don't have time for a woman who's screaming crazy. The only way you can help is by leaving me alone. So do it.'

I couldn't breathe.

'Didn't you hear me?' he said.

'Do you mean — leave for good?'

'How can I know? I don't know.'

Some more time must have gone by. I remember he went into the house and came back out carrying six rifles. I was still standing by the mound of earth. One look at his face told me that every single bit of the love I'd seen there the night before was gone. In his heart there was no room for anything now but rage.

I didn't even see a sign of recognition. The dead were his only thought.

I had to force something from him, even if it was only pity or duty. Any little thing to keep me alive. And so I begged for it.

'Please let me stay with you. Please keep me. You swore you would, Henry, you promised.'

'I'll keep my word.'

'I'll help you. Any way you say, only don't send me away.'

'You'll have to hold up better.'

'Oh, I will — '

'You'll have to be strong. Stay out of the way. Don't give me any trouble, don't try to tell me what to do. Never question me.'

'I won't.'

'Or tell me what's right and wrong to do,' he said.

'I promise. I never meant to. I was only hoping you wouldn't act alone. I was just saying get the law.'

'There isn't any law for us.'

'What about Sheriff King? He'll have to see it was murder, and they'll be made to pay.'

'No,' he said. 'They will *be* paid. I swear it before heaven, they will all be paid.' And in a low iron tone he started listing the names. 'McTeer, Taylor, McCallum, McKay, Coble, McNeill . . . ' He was saying those names to God. He called them all except Hector McLean, the justice of the peace — and I knew then that I could not stop him from whatever he meant to do.

'Can I come with you?'

'You go to your mother's house.'

He turned and started away, and my arms flew out against my will as if to try and catch him back, but he was past my reach.

I called after him, 'What about your mother, Henry?'

He stopped.

'She'll need someone,' I said. 'I can take care of her.'

I tried to clear my face of grief, to appear brave and sturdy.

'She's never spent a night without Mr. Allen, the last thirty years,' I said.

He put his head in his hands and he cried like a sighing wind, that sound I knew I had heard.

When he recovered, all he said was 'I'll take her to the doctor's house. Meet me there.'

* * *

After he left, I stood in the drizzling rain and the smell of turned earth rose up to me. Then all across the farm a pretty afternoon sunlight broke, and the clouds fell into thin separate strands like flax with a yellow sheen, and I wished I was dead.

Mr. Allen used to call me Rhody or Girl Cousin or Cee Junior, funny little names he made up for me. People loved him because he was generous and fair in his dealings, and because he worked so hard, but I loved him for all the times he noticed me, and called out to me. Whether he was plowing or hoeing or sawing, he'd stop from his work and look up at me and smile, and say the same things he always said.

'Are you roaming loose? Are you here to visit my old wife, or have you got your eye on one of my boys again?' And then he'd wink at me. 'Your mother was a great beauty,' he said. 'You'll never make her size, but I bet you're just as *nervous*.' He used the word our old way, to mean brave and tough.

'Yes I am,' I always lied.

At home Cee was waiting for me. She snatched me through the door.

'Something's happened bad,' she said. 'We saw Mariah on our way past the Sampsons, she said the Guard got new men, a whole company, with orders to go out in the settlement and collect the Lowries. They arrested Cal at his farm and Sink on the road, and Allen and Mary and William at the homestead, carried them all to Mackenzie's and had some kind of trial, then carted Allen and William off but no one knows where, no one knows what happened — '

'They are killed, Ma. Mr. Allen and William are shot through the heart.'

I told her how. She fell into a chair and cried, and I could not comfort her.

I packed up some clothes in a bundle and sat next to her at the table. Daddy was standing by the chimney. I saw that for the first time they were both afraid, but I could do nothing for them.

I said, 'I'm going to Dr. McCabe's. And after that, I don't know where I'll be. I might be at the Lowrie place.'

She raised her head. Her eyes were red and tired.

'Why?' she said. 'Rhoda, what happened

here while we were gone? Where is that Union soldier?'

'Henry came and took him. Ma, Henry and me — '

Her stare was a cold fire, and I couldn't finish.

Daddy said, 'Rhoda, what have you gone and done?'

'I have tied a lifetime knot.'

I saw it sink in, what I meant. She rose up. She came toward me. Never once in my life had she hit me a real blow, but I could tell she was about to, and I braced myself. She did it with words.

'Go on after him, then,' she said. 'Go on, run to him. And don't plan on running back to me when you find out everything I said is true. Because I won't take you in. I will turn you away as a whore.'

'Celia, what are you saying? You can't mean that.'

'I warned her. She went against me.'

'Celia, she's our *daughter*.'

'Not if she's to be Henry Lowrie's woman. Not now.'

It wrenched my heart to see the stubborn set of her mouth, the hurt in her eyes, and I almost fell crying into her lap because I already knew that what she'd said was true. But it was too late.

Hold up better, I thought. *Steel yourself*. I tied my bundle, and I left the house where she had raised me, the house I had always loved so. She didn't say goodbye, and neither did I. When Daddy called after me, he got no answer, but that was not because I had any sort of new strength. It was because I couldn't face his sadness and his terror, caused by me.

'Rhoda, wait, come back,' he said, but I ran hard.

I was obliged now in another direction, and I could not undo what had been done. Girl followed me awhile, but I didn't speak to her, and when I passed the deserted Barnes place, she gave up and let me go on alone.

9

The McCabe house stood on a half acre of high ground in Back Swamp. In all my time there I never saw anyone pay a visit except the two aunts — and Allen Lowrie, who had built the house and kept it in good repair over the years. More than once I saw him standing hat in hand in the doctor's study, suggesting some improvement which Dr. McCabe, bent over his books, would half hear and then authorize with a wave of the hand.

But no one else came there. The McCabes were cut off from the world.

At one time there had been a kind of road to the house, a causeway of logs, but it had sunk. All that remained was a rotting plank path through swamp muck wetter and wetter until suddenly the ground rose and the path hit a dead end of brambles — but I pushed through and broke into the clearing, and saw the house. Wide gray porch, four dormer windows above, a chimney at either end.

At first, I thought it was deserted. The shutters were closed and latched across the lower windows, and everything was quiet. But I knew Henry would have set out a guard, who would already have seen and heard me coming. I climbed the front steps, knowing that someone was watching me.

And there he was, a young man stepping out of the shadows at the far end of the porch. I didn't know him. He had a bandit's thin mustache, a Kentucky hat low on his head, and a long gun in his arms.

'Hullo, Rho.'

I didn't even know the voice. But he pulled off the hat and set the gun at his side like a hoe, hand on the barrel, and I saw who it was.

He was so different.

'Oh, Boss.'

I hugged him and kissed him. But in my arms he did not feel like my slim, sweet brother. His chest was broader and solid, his hair cut short. The mustache gave him a hardened look that didn't suit him. Still, he sidled out of my hug the way he always used to.

'I thought I wouldn't ever see you again,' I said.

'Here I am.'

'Rhoda, come inside,' Nelly said from the door.

I hadn't expected to see her at McCabe's. 'I can't,' I said, starting to cry. 'I need Boss — '

'Later on,' she said, pulling me into the

369

hallway. 'We have work to do. Now listen. What's happened is terrible but there's no time for weeping. We'll do all that later.'

I was in a daze. I had thought only Henry would be there, waiting for me, but the house seemed full of people. Mary Cumbo was lying on the parlor sofa.

'They blindfolded her,' Nelly said, 'and tied her to a tree behind Sink Lowrie's cabin and said they would shoot her if she didn't tell where Henry was. She wouldn't, and they fired. They only meant to scare her — they fired over her head and all their bullets ripped the tree to pieces — and she slumped over, and they ran off. Just left her there. She was still unconscious and tied up when Henry found her. The doctor said her heart seized with fright. But now she's doing better — better than Dr. McCabe himself. He's taken to bed, he doesn't look good.'

'How did you get here, Nelly? How did you know to come?'

'James Sinclair sent for me.'

She led me down the hall past the dining room where the men all were: Steve, Boss, Henderson, Applewhite, and Zack McLaughlin, with Preacher Sinclair at one end of the table, Henry at the other, and the Union soldier underneath. Henry looked up at me but said nothing. I started to go in, but Nelly stopped me.

'Can't I see him?'

'You'll have to wait. There's someone back here anxious to see you.'

Miss McCabe was sitting on a chair in the pantry hallway, looking bewildered.

'Rhoda! Please tell me what's going on. Father is frightened to death, and — and no one will tell me anything. They've made me stay back here — Henry promised he would just use the dining room for an hour, to talk with James Sinclair — but then they all came in, and they wanted food, they wanted my scuppernong wine — I knew I shouldn't have fed them those other times, now they'll think they can show up here for a handout whenever they please. Rhoda, listen.' She took my hand and whispered. 'These men . . . I know they're your people, and I wanted to help — but they frighten me. They can't use my house for a headquarters, for God's sake. They've *commandeered* me! Put a Yankee soldier in my dining room! It's too much to expect of me. And who is the woman they brought in and laid on the sofa? Who are the other two they carried upstairs? No one will tell me anything. One of them — Steve — he shoved me down and ordered me to sit here and keep my mouth shut.'

Nelly said, 'Miss McCabe, that's Mary

Cumbo Lowrie in the parlor — '

'Well, get Allen over here then. He'll know what to do. Send for Allen — '

'Mr. Allen's dead,' I said. 'McTeer and his men shot him.'

'Rod shot Allen Lowrie?'

'And William his son.'

'But that would be . . . insane. It would start something — it would turn the county upside down.' She glanced from me to Nelly. 'Allen Lowrie? What has Allen ever done against anyone?'

Nelly took my hands. Behind her down the dark hallway I saw someone else, a woman I almost recognized, although she was facing the kitchen window.

'Who is that?' I said, my eyes on the tall, familiar shape.

'Why, it's your friend you used to tell me about,' Miss McCabe said.

'Yes, it's Margaret,' Nelly said. 'She's been asking for you.'

The worst kind of dread filled me.

'I don't want to see her,' I said. 'I can't.'

I was afraid of how she would look, afraid I would see not just bruises and scars but also the deeper damage that I had done nothing to prevent. And I didn't want her to see me, and what had become of me. Because I knew she would understand, the instant she saw me.

Margaret Ransom knew me better than anyone in the world did. She would know I had cast my future to the winds, and there was no hope for me.

But Miss McCabe and Nelly both stood back to let me pass, and I had to go. I walked the long hall to the kitchen.

She was rolling pastry and didn't hear me come in. All I could see was her back, her clean blue dress of cotton sacking dotted with yellow flowers, the same colors she used to like. Her hair was still short but it covered the back of her neck as she bent over the dough board. I could not bring myself to call her name, I could only reach for her.

When my fingers touched her elbow she turned; and she was beautiful. She was herself, unruined. The prettiest soft round face, the spray of little freckles, the easy smile.

'Margaret, oh, thank God.'

'I do,' she said. She seemed pleased but not surprised to see me. There was not much in the world that could surprise her now, but I don't mean she was deadened. Instead she had an air of knowing, as if she could see a far distance. She had a grace.

'I have to talk to you,' I said. 'Can we go upstairs to my room?' I still called it mine, the little upstairs room with the dormer window and slanted walls.

'Not now,' she said. 'The bodies are there.'

'The bodies?'

'Henry sent Steve and Henderson back to the Lowrie cabin to dig them up, to give them a decent burial. But first they need to be washed. And in a while that's what you and I will do, after we tend to Mary. Then, Henry said, he'll take his mother home. He said you'll go with him.' She didn't ask why, but the question was in her eyes.

'He asked me to marry him, Margaret.'

'I was afraid so.'

'But it doesn't mean anything now.'

'I know.'

That was all she said, and all I said. She turned me toward the light and looked me over, and kissed me. Margaret didn't need love and death explained to her, or anything else.

Nelly asked me to sit by Henry's mother in case she woke up not knowing where she was or who we all were. She was flat on her back on the sofa, and I couldn't tell if she was asleep or unconscious or both. Her mouth was open, her shoes unbuckled. I put a laprobe over her feet, and she opened her eyes.

'I know who you are,' she said.

'I'm Rhoda.'

'The one that was there when they shot my

husband and boy.'

I knelt by her.

'The one that loves Henry,' she said. 'Bless your heart, poor thing.'

She took my hand and we just stayed that way for a long time. Her fingertips were cool and tough as horn.

'I never told them nothing, I never broke down,' she said. 'They got so mad they shot me dead. Don't tell anyone.'

'No, Ma Mary, you're all right. The shots went over your head into the tree.'

'Sugar, if I was alive I wouldn't be able to bear it. If I was alive, do you think I could sit still one minute, knowing my dear ones was killed, the way they was killed? Do you think I would put up with it? No, I would have gone for blood, I would have slit the throats of every one of those that done it. Don't you know that? But what happened was, the end came for me. I crossed the river.' She closed her eyes.

Nelly eased me out of the parlor and sent me into the dining room with more rye coffee, and I poured their cups around the table one by one.

'Before the Lord delivers us, he first puts us to the test,' Preacher Sinclair was saying. 'And the trial is harder as the end nears, Henry. That's why I'm urging you to wait. Be calm, call on Him for the strength to endure.'

Henry said, 'Steve, how many rifles have we still got, how many shotguns?'

Sinclair said, 'I thought all your guns were seized.'

'Applewhite builds a good chimney, Mr. Sinclair. My father and brother died rather than tell just how good it was, but if McTeer had looked he might have noticed there's never been a fire laid in it, and the outside measures twice as big as the inside. McTeer got William's rifle, but he missed a bigger find. That chimney's our arsenal.'

'How many?' said the preacher.

Applewhite gave the count, leaning forward and speaking out with a sure voice. Forty guns all together. Henderson said more were hidden on other farms, and could be gathered up pretty quick, and Steve mentioned a barrel of powder that their older brother Sink was keeping for them even though Sink wasn't really in on their plans.

'Let us hope there will be no need for any of it,' the preacher said. 'And it would be far better if you were to turn your weapons over to me for safekeeping.'

'We can't do that, Mr. Sinclair,' Henry said.

'The Lord would prefer it.'

'I'm not sure that's true.'

'Do you know His will?'

'I don't claim to. I'll give Him a chance to deliver us, but He might decide to leave it up to us like He always has before, and in that case we'll want our guns.'

Because none of them looked my way or seemed to even notice I was there, I knew Henry had told them about me. Each one had known me in a different way, but now I was the same thing to them all: a girl in the background, almost invisible, Henry's. It didn't matter whether we married or not. This was my part now, to fade behind him.

In the garret bedroom, on the bed where I had once slept, the dead men lay side by side. We huddled in the doorway, looking in.

'I don't think I can help with this,' Miss McCabe said.

'No,' Nelly said. 'You and me will wait downstairs. Henry wants Rhoda and Margaret to do it.'

She gave us four candles, the rags and the basin. Miss McCabe handed us sheets. Through the window I saw the moon like a small high stone, casting a silvery path across the floor and onto the bed. I lit the candles, then fell to work beside Margaret. Her thin hands moved with a slow deliberate elegance, and I let mine follow her lead. For a long time we didn't speak, but as we worked our eyes now and then met. Certain memories came back to me, of times when we were girls together — the plans we made to go to school and marry brothers — not knowing then how things would change. Yet regret for those lost days was not what filled me. I wouldn't have restored them if I'd had the power to. Something else was filling me, coming, it seemed, through my hands.

Like a calming, a soothing, a trust, *settling* me; from those bodies through my hands to my heart. It is possible to love the dead, and possible that the dead love back.

Looking at William, Margaret said, 'I never saw Wesley's body.'

'Neither did I. I went to the funeral, but the coffin was closed.'

'I mean his living body. I wish I had. But we held back, we said we would wait until we married. I went to borrow that loan from Brant Harris so we could start a house.'

'Margaret, I'm sorry I didn't help you.'

She smiled. 'You did though. I thought of you when I needed to. I remembered our plans, and tried to keep thinking of them, just as I tried to keep seeing Wesley's face. And still do.' Her hands cradled Williams chin. 'He looked like this a little, don't you think? His chin was the same, and his eyes.'

'Because they were cousins.'

She washed the stains from William's face and neck, the dirt from his hair. Outside, clouds rolled over the moon, and it disappeared. A heavy rain broke, roaring down on the roof like an endless thunder.

'Are you in love then?' she said.

'Do you think it's a mistake?'

'If so it's one that can't be helped, like getting born. Nothing stops it, I can tell you. I still love Wes.'

'But Margaret — Wes is dead.'

'You think I don't know that, every instant every hour? I love him just the same.'

'But he can't love you back.'

'It never was a business trade.'

All the while, we were washing the bodies. We left the wounds for last, fearing the sight, but as we washed them they grew less horrid to see. The flesh was torn like Henry had said, but I found each separate bullet wound and touched it. The places where death had entered were small and black, the size of my finger, just holes.

'It's easy to die,' I said.

'No,' she said. 'It's easy to kill.'

That was all we did — washed two dead men and wrapped them in sheets. But afterward we stood by the bed for a while in a kind of wonder, knowing something more had happened, and when we left the room I thought to myself: *We were cleansed.*

* * *

We had started down the stairs when the front door was flung wide and Boss burst in, dripping wet.

'They're crossing the swamp.' He bolted the door and put out the lamp on the table. 'McTeer and ten more.'

All the men snatched up their guns. Chairs were knocked over, and Miss McCabe moaned out loud.

'I can't be seen here,' I heard James Sinclair say to Nelly in the hallway. He was a small elfish-looking man whose eyes were usually keen and determined, but now he seemed to panic. 'I can't be found here!'

'Go out the kitchen door,' she said, leading him toward the back of the hall.

'Come with me,' he said.

'No, I'll stay. I'm the only one that can handle McTeer.'

There was such confusion and rushing about in the front rooms, what I saw next almost failed to register in my mind: Nelly's hand gently laid against the preacher's sharp little face just before he hurried from the house.

380

Our Nelly. With James Sinclair, a married preacher who drank to excess and wept from the pulpit, a man Henry said did not know his own mind but bent with the wind. She said nothing as she passed me. She didn't even care if I had seen.

We all crowded into the parlor. Henry cornered Miss McCabe, holding her by her upper arms.

'I trust you to think of something. Don't let them in.'

She was shaking her head. 'I can't manage it.'

'You can,' he said. 'If you want to.'

We heard horses, then footsteps on the porch and McTeer's voice.

'Amanda, open the door,' he yelled.

Nelly whispered, 'Don't send her out there, Henry, she'll fall apart. Let me talk to him.'

'What do you think, Rhoda?' he said.

Miss McCabe was shrinking against the bookcase, her hands clasped over her chest.

'She can do it,' I said.

'She's a mack, Henry.'

'She'll do it for me,' I said.

Henry pushed Miss McCabe into the hall and closed the parlor door. McTeer was knocking and yelling, and finally we heard Miss McCabe slide the bolt and walk onto the porch. She closed the door behind her.

We strained to hear, and I made out the sound of a key in the lock.

Smart, I thought. She's thinking.

'Amanda, don't do that,' McTeer said. 'You're only going to have to unlock it again.'

'Father is ill, Roderick.'

'I'm sorry to hear that.'

'And your yelling has waked him. I don't appreciate this intrusion.'

'We won't bother you for long. We'll be on our way, soon as you give us the fugitive we want, that we know you've got inside the house.'

'He's not here,' she said. 'I haven't seen him.'

'How do you know who we want?'

'Well, it doesn't matter. Whoever he is, he's not here.'

'Look, we tracked him halfway here before it started raining again. There's nowhere else he could be.'

'Maybe he came and went without my knowledge, then. Now that you mention it, I do remember hearing something — a commotion outside — but I was busy with Father. Yes, I had quite forgotten that noise I heard. Footsteps, the door rattling — but he's gone now.'

'There's no use in lying. It don't befit you. We know someone's here, and we have reason to believe it's Henry Lowrie.'

'Henry Lowrie! Why would I let a man like that in my house? You insult me. I demand an apology.'

'I'll tell you one more time. If you don't give me that key, I can promise I won't hesitate to shoot you.'

'Shoot *me*? You must be drunker than usual.'

'You're obstructing justice.'

'What are you talking about? I had an agreement with Brant Harris, he promised to keep his low-life posse off my property, and I expect you to honor that promise. I remind you, your uncle Pierce MacBryde's wife is my father's cousin. I am a McCabe.'

'A McCabe that harbors and abets Lowries. We know they've been here before, and you've done them favors.'

'Maybe you can explain to me, exactly what are the Lowries wanted for?'

'Hog-stealing.'

'Until today I never heard of hog-stealers being executed. I know what happened to Allen Lowrie, Rod. That was out-and-out lynching. I wouldn't have expected you to understand the injustice of it, but I'd have thought you might see the idiocy. Didn't you understand what you might be unleashing?'

'I don't want a lecture. I want the man

you've got in there. You took someone in, and if it's not Lowrie it's someone else we can use. If you don't cooperate — '

'I'll take in whoever I want, and it's not going to be you. Get off my place.'

A shot was fired, and Miss McCabe screamed. We heard a shower of glass fall into the hallway from the fanlight over the door. My heart sank. Miss McCabe was going to panic now.

'That was just so you know we mean business,' McTeer said. 'Now calm yourself down and give me the key.'

'For God's sake, don't you think if there *were* a soldier here I would tell you?'

'A soldier?'

'Maybe she's got a Yank, Rod,' Taylor called out.

'Well, that would be a nice catch for us,' McTeer said. 'Is that right, Amanda? Are you hiding a Yankee boy? A Southern lady like you ought to be ashamed of doing such a thing. It's treason to your flag, and to the cause our boys are dying for.'

Miss McCabe started crying. 'But he was about dead,' she sobbed. 'I couldn't just turn him away.'

'We'll take care of him for you.'

'I can't let you have him. You'll kill him, and it will be all my fault.'

'You have my word we won't hurt him. Now where's he at?'

'He's — he's under my dining-room table. Wait, Rod, don't you see I was in a quandary . . . '

'Let go of me.'

'I didn't mean to do wrong. Do you really think it was treason, to take him in? I only thought it was Christian.'

'I wouldn't know — '

'I thought maybe he was just a boy like our own, that went to war planning on glory and adventure. That's what we all planned on, but it came to be this long nightmare, this *horror*. I am so tired of it, Rod. That's all. Just tired. I didn't intend an act of treason. I hope you believe that.'

'Dammit, you're tearing my coat.'

'I have to know you believe me. Am I to be arrested? I don't think Father could bear that. For his sake, please believe that I meant no harm. It was just a silly woman's impulse, I wasn't thinking — '

'Taylor, get her off me.'

There was a scuffle, and then the door opened. Sounds of boots stomping in. I held Margaret's hand in the dark and saw Henderson and Steve raise their guns.

'The other room,' Miss McCabe called. 'To the left.'

'Here he is, boys,' McTeer said. 'Little weasel. Makes my blood boil to see him in our grays. Soon as we get him outside, strip off that uniform, Taylor, then you and McQueen carry him off and get some information out of him. Find out what he knows. Ask him was he helped by Allen Lowrie. If he was, keep him alive.'

'And if he wasn't?'

'Then you can do whatever the hell you want with him.'

They left with Owen Wright slung over the back of a mule, and I tried not to think of his fate.

★　★　★

'Miss McCabe, next time I need someone for a performance of acting, I will call on you,' Henry said.

'Most of what I said was true,' she said. 'I can't have you in my house, Henry. Take all of your gang out of here. I'm sorry. I understand it's dreadful what's happened — it's the damn war.'

'There might be a war, but we aren't the enemy, Miss McCabe.'

'People say you are. They say you killed Harris and Barnes because they were Confederate officials, and you're a spy, and your gang is behind all the looting. How do I know it's not true?'

I stepped forward, and everyone looked at me.

'From me,' I said. 'I can tell you. He didn't kill anyone. If he had, I wouldn't be in love with him and I wouldn't be engaged to marry him.'

Miss McCabe was speechless. She shook her head, and then she managed to say, 'You don't mean you're going to marry Henry Lowrie.'

'Yes, I mean that.'

'But that would be the end of everything we planned — your schooling — Floral College . . . Your chances will be ruined. Rhoda, don't throw your life away. You have a *future*.'

'I know I do,' I said.

'Henry, I appeal to you,' she said. 'Don't do this to her. Nelly? Margaret, *you* know — tell her it's a mistake.'

No one said a word.

'Rhoda, I promise you,' she said, 'when the war's over I'll send you off to school. You can get out of North Carolina, become a teacher, you can marry well and no one will ever know — '

'Where I came from, and who I am?'

To her credit, she shut up then. She yielded

to me, in a way she had not ever done before. That moment for me was the true end of the war, the moment when Amanda McCabe learned that I did not owe her any love.

And I never saw the McCabe house again after that.

Allen and William Lowrie were buried in a place where they would not be found or disturbed. Across a little creek at the head of Turkey Branch a log was laid, and another was set to lead the stream aside. The bodies were buried in the bed, the logs removed, and the stream restored to its course.

★ ★ ★

It took the Guard an hour to go three miles after leaving McCabe's, with water washing over their stirrups and rain blowing into their eyes. McTeer led, trusting his horse to find the way through the darkness to Lumberton. The rain finally let up enough so that he could make out the thick straight trunks of giant cypresses all around, and knew he was in the deepest part of Back Swamp, called Devilsden, where those trees had grown two centuries untouched. Cold water rose around his legs and then his thighs, and numbed him. He felt almost loosed from the earth in a kind of slow, rolling, dream-like motion, and realized his horse was swimming, and the other horses too.

Finally they came to a hummock, and saw higher ground beyond.

'You got us all turned around, Rod. This ain't the way we come in. We're riding east instead of north. You ain't even found the road yet.'

'Yeah? Then what's this? Looks like Chicken Road to me.'

The horses slipped and slid on the muddy embankment but made it up, and McTeer turned left down the winding lane.

'Still don't look right,' Taylor said.

McTeer reined in, face to the wind.

Taylor said, 'See? We're lost as hell.'

'Shut up. I smell something.'

'Don't tell me you're going to smell your way home.'

'Wait here,' McTeer said.

He rode on a little way alone until suddenly his horse whinnied, and he looked up to see a pink haze like a sunset reflected by low clouds. But it was after midnight. *Barn burning*, he thought. *Bummers and mulattos*.

No, that couldn't be it. If he was where he thought he was, there should be no barn or house beyond that curve in the road, only the river. He kicked the horse onward, and when he rounded the curve he saw the most amazing sight of his life.

The Lumbee River, flowing fire.

It burned as it rolled, licking the shore and singeing reeds and willows, hissing.

'What the devil — '

Near the bank a twisted ribbon of iron had fallen into the sand. The hoop of a barrel. He looked at it, then turned his horse and raced back down the road.

'They've torched McRaney's pitch and turpentine. Ride for your life, it's going to spread, the river's afire. They burnt the river!'

'Who, the Lowries?'

McTeer swung around in his saddle toward the glow. But there were more flames now in other parts of the sky, and he heard a distant sound he recognized from his days fighting fire in the barrens, the sucking blast of a sixty-foot pitch pine when the running sap heats to boiling and the whole tree blows apart like a bomb.

'The whole barrens is going up. No, it ain't the Lowries. It's the goddamn Union.'

★　★　★

After crossing the Pee Dee and all its swamps, W. T. Sherman had entered North Carolina with an army ten miles wide, slogging through rains so heavy and mud so deep, all his twenty thousand men were cursing North Carolina as a pit of filth. Rain saved some houses from fire, but only the two chimneys remained at McCabe's. In Lumberton the whole courthouse and half of the jail were burned. The asylum house was unlocked and the inmates set loose before it too was torched, and nobody knew until later that Clelon had stayed hidden inside. He was found where he died, curled under a bed.

On the river where McRaney had stored his four hundred barrels of turpentine and three hundred of pitch, there was a great hole blown into the bank, where the water pooled like a dull mirror hatched by the reflected trunks of charred and leaning pines.

Owen Wright was questioned by the Guard and then dumped on the side of the road and picked up by his own army, and was already rattling along in an ambulance wagon by the time Sherman woke up in the morning. Having slept two hours stretched out on a wooden pew in Bethel Church, the general was in poor spirits. With rain still drumming on the roof and echoing through the empty church, he took out a pocketknife and cleaned the North Carolina mud from his fingernails. Then, gouging the hymnbook rack with a quick knicking motion, he carved his name.

The next day he moved on, leaving behind a detachment to hold Robeson County. Two months later, the war ended.

* * *

'Union. It's a real pretty word,' Henry's mother, Mary Cumbo, said to me. 'I don't know why, it just sounds good.'

But when it came, there was not much more to it than the sound of the word. R. E. Lee surrendered and so did I, and the season of spring did not touch me. I had gone too far under to be reached, I was dead to the world. Not even grief could move me, and I never cried a tear for Clelon. I said to myself I couldn't, yet.

On the little farms there was some planting started, but the big places all sat idle, for the freed slaves didn't want to make a contract until they heard if they would get the forty acres Preacher Sinclair told them the Union would provide. A few hired out at five dollars a month but with no guarantee they would stay on, and most only worked their own small plots behind their cabins. Some of the once wealthy planters got out in their shirtsleeves to struggle with a plow for the first time in their lives.

I stayed with Mary Cumbo, and although

Henry was still lying out at night, James Sinclair said everything was quiet, and pretty soon all the boys could safely sleep at home again. By day, Henry came to work his mother's fields, and I worked with him. But we said little to each other. The work was the only thing connecting us.

Boss was always with him. We might not see him, but we knew he was there, in the crook of a tree or in a blind he'd made at the edge of the field. Guarding Henry had become his only purpose.

While Henry plowed, I kicked clods and sowed seed. I thinned the first green shoots of corn, and kept the furrows hoed, trying to make way for the future, but I did not think it would come.

McRaney would not be rebuilding the stillery. When he went out to see how many trees survived Sherman's fires, he found thousands burnt — but hundreds of thousands more dying, far from Sherman's path, destroyed by pine beetles. The turpentine business would soon be over for good in North Carolina, McRaney said, and he packed up and moved to Georgia, predicting the other stilleries would follow. Sherman scarred the county, but the bugs chewed out its heart.

So Cee lost her job and needed Andrew

back home to help put in a crop. Mr. Sampson agreed to let Flora marry. They lost no time; it was a clap-hat wedding, Flora's mother said — quick as grabbing a hat on your way out the door — and Andrew and Flora moved in with Cee and Daddy. Cee talked Dr. McCabe into giving her a piece of swamp land where Andrew could start building a cabin. 'Rhoda's got herself a new mother,' Cee said. 'So I figure Flora's my only daughter now, and I'll see to it she gets everything she needs.'

But Mary wasn't my mother. Henry wanted me to watch over her and keep her happy, ease her load, and run off the newspapermen who had started coming around in hopes we would tell where Henry was. As if we knew. He had not given us a hint of where he spent his nights. All he told me was to do what I could for Mary. She had not really recovered after being tortured by the Guard, and seemed not to know exactly why I was living in her house. She seldom spoke the names of her dead husband and son, but sometimes she looked at me and said, 'You were there, weren't you? You saw it?'

I just said yes.

'You washed them?'

Yes, I said, and she thanked me.

But her thoughts roamed. Sometimes she was bewildered, and she spent her time doing the old things she used to do when Allen was alive. She washed and ironed all his clothes, and spent whole days cooking the dishes he had liked, even though there were only two of us eating. Whatever was left over she had me carry down to the Chavises and the Betheas, so their children would not have to go out hunting dandelions and sheep sorrel for a weed-soup supper.

'We have too much food, Henry,' she said when he showed up for supper. 'Your daddy always said keep enough on hand for times of need, but if it's going to be just me and this girl, we don't need much. I declare a pullet eats more than she does, and talks more, too. Is something wrong with her? Why did you bring her here?'

'To help you out,' he said.

'Well, she does that, she's handy, but who is she?'

'Cee's girl.'

'Oh. The one you are going to marry?'

'Ma, she's here to help you now. Don't try to do everything your own self.'

'She watches me too close, Henry.'

'I told her to. She's not to let you out of her sight.'

'You mean for her to be a servant girl? But I don't want one.'

★ ★ ★

One afternoon I missed her and went out to the yard, where I found her holding one of the new lambs, bleating and kicking, on the top of a stump.

Her eyes met mine.

'Spying on me.'

'No, ma'am, I'm — '

'Come on over here. I'll show you how to do this. Pick up that hammer.'

So I did it. It was my job, to do her bidding. I killed that lamb, and the next day I killed a chicken. She showed me how to hold it by the head, its eyes and beak enclosed in my hand, and then swing it in one fast, hard circle like a lariat.

'I'm going to teach you chicken and pastry,' she said.

'Ma Mary, I don't have any appetite.'

It seemed crazy to spend hours making a big supper when a corn cake would have fed us both. I would even have preferred more slaughtering and neck-wringing to a day of cooking, for I had found an odd kind of thrill in the swift blow of the hammer and the killing twist, as if the action satisfied a need I never knew I had. I did not look forward to a day of slow, hot cooking to no purpose.

'Suit yourself. But Henry likes it. If we cook up, he might stay for supper.'

So I agreed.

'Nobody fixes it the way I do,' she said, 'because I take out almost every bone before I cook it. And I don't cut the meat or skin, except around the feet. Here's how.'

She had me make a slit around the base of each drumstick. She leaned over my shoulder and directed me to run the point of the knife close along the bone on all sides, turning the leg back like a stocking as I went, snipping the joint, pulling out the ropy tendons, continuing into the thigh and around to the breast, sliding along wishbone and ribs. It was slow work. I proceeded through the chicken inch by inch, severing and lifting every bone from its place except in the spine and wingtips, until an hour later I was left with a limpy meaty mess all inside out. It looked massacred and hopeless. But then she showed me how you turn it back. You restore its shape, arrange the legs and wings as if nothing had happened, stuff it with onions to plump it up again, tie a crisscrossing of string all around it and lower it into a barely simmering pot for two hours with the ends of the string hanging out. You roll a thin dough and cut it into wide strips to drop in the pot for the last six minutes. The string is to lift out the chicken, because it is now a delicate thing and will fall apart if handled carelessly.

And all that work is for the sake of artifice, not taste — so that on its platter with its ribbons of pastry floating in a yellow gravy, the chicken will look ordinary. So that a man will sit down to eat, suspecting nothing, but when he begins to carve, his knife will slip easy down through the whole bird as if through a loaf of bread, and he'll look up surprised. So that he'll be impressed, and even if he's seen it once a week for twenty years and knows its coming, will say, 'How do you do that?'

By the time it was cooked and ready, I was so anxious I couldn't sit down at the table with them. I put the platter in front of him and went to scrubbing pots.

'I'll never understand how you do this, Ma.'

'But how does it taste?' she said. 'Is it good? Good as usual?'

'Better than ever.'

'Thank her, then,' Mary said, satisfied. 'She did it. I decided I'm not going to bone another chicken in my lifetime. I'm teaching her all my secrets.'

I kept on scouring, and he kept chewing.

'Well,' she said, 'I see I'm going to have to speak up. Because this just isn't right.'

'What's that?'

'The way you are to her. You treat her kind of ugly, Henry. She is your darling, ain't she? Yet I don't see you ever give her a peck or a hug, a sweet word. I thought you said you meant to marry her.'

'I do,' he said, his head down over the plate. He had eaten three helpings, so I knew I had cooked it right.

'When?' she said.

'Just as soon as I can get a stake. When this crop comes in.'

'I hope you don't put it off no later than that, because I want to be still alive and kicking for the wedding.'

'I thought we'd just go down to Marion,' he said. 'Save you from all that work.'

'Oh, no,' she said. 'None in our family ever run off.'

'We'll save money that way.'

'But it will shame him.'

'Who?'

She fiddled with her fork. 'He won't like it. He told me, make sure that little girl has a big old-timey wedding enfare. She's going to be a Lowrie wife, she needs a celebration.'

Henry stopped chewing, elbows on the table, knife and fork touching his plate. He swallowed and cleared his throat.

'Are you talking about Daddy?'

'He says a man should be proud enough of his wife to marry her right in the settlement, with all the wedding guests looking on. Not sneaking off like it's something you rather hide.'

'And when did he say that?'

'Last night.'

Henry got up from his chair and went to stand beside her. He kissed her on the top of her head, where there was a little bald spot.

'We'll have whatever kind of wedding you want,' he said.

'Good. Now open up that thing for me,' she said, directing him to the trunk in the corner. 'I tried to lift the lid today but it was stuck. Now, see if you see a coverlet down at the bottom. You'll have to dig down. That's it, that white one. Unfold it here over my knees.'

'Be careful with it, Ma.'

'Just because something's old, Henry, don't mean it's about to fall apart. The quilt is fine and so am I. Yes, I'll be careful. Carefulness is my best quality, more than you even know.'

The spread of quilted satin spilled across her lap and onto the floor in a shiny white pool. She tapped it with her fingertips in an absentminded way, and said, 'We called it

America's quilt, but it's too thin to keep a bed warm — even though it's big enough to fold double. I don't think it was ever used. Still bright and pretty.' She looked at me. 'You know who Sally America was — Sally America Kersey? This was her bedcover, a wedding gift from her husband's father. She married James Lowrie, and their son was Bill who married Ma Bet, and their son was my old husband. You remember him. You were there, weren't you?'

'Yes, I was,' I said.

'We were a good match. Allen and me. He was the teasingest man. Always something to say funny. It's good in a marriage to have laughing times whenever you can. Allen, he would be joking and eye-twinkling even in the middle of our most serious business. When we were making all those children together. The last of them was Henry, and I always said the quilt goes to the girl he marries. But I imagine you'll want to hide it away just like everybody has always done, pass it down to the ages as they say. So I'm going to be careful to make sure you don't. I'm going to have Sally America's old quilt serve a purpose now instead of sitting useless another hundred years.'

She reached into her basket and drew out a pair of long sharp scissors.

Henry said, 'Ma, what are you doing?'

But already she had cut into the satin, and quickly sliced straight through the middle of the coverlet, which slipped away from the blades in two pieces at her feet.

She winked at me.

'Now what?' she said.

Henry lost his patience. 'What did you go and do that for?'

'Ask her. She knows. I see it in her eyes, she understands what I mean. What comes next, Rhody? She knows. Tell him, Little Cee.'

'Now, we — '

'Yes?' Mary leaned forward, eyes bright and wide, eyebrows up in delight. 'Yes?'

'We make a wedding gown.'

She sat back. Her sly smile reminded me of Mr. Allen's.

'Smart girl. Skinny arms and legs, but smart. Sally America would be right pleased to see what comes of her quilt at last. It'll make a pretty dress, and a warm one, and pad out those arms a little. Feel it, Rhody, how smooth it is! Will it suit you?'

'Yes, but — it's a shame to cut up something you saved so long.'

'Unless.'

Henry said, 'Unless what?'

'Unless this is what we were saving it for!'

402

I kept up my work in the fields and saw the corn inch higher every day. In the woods the charred earth broke out in fiddle-back ferns, cinnamon, and maidenhair, and pine saplings that had looked burnt to death sprouted a brush of green needles at the top, clownish but alive. In the late afternoons I cooked for Mary and washed her things, and at night I learned to sew.

I was clumsy with the needle at first, too impatient, and I left at least one droplet of blood on the white satin. A stitch is so tiny, and when you think ahead to how many it will take to sew a whole dress, you lose faith and start to rush, and maybe even give up. But Mary taught me to keep my mind off the dress. 'The stitch is all you have to think of,' she said. 'Make each one fine and straight, and trust it. You can do that, can't you? One little stitch? And then, you see, you can go on.'

★ ★ ★

By autumn the dress was done. We had made two good crops, pulled all the fodder, and put the hogs out to feed themselves in the woods. But Henry had still not set a date for the

403

wedding. In fact I hardly saw him twice a week, for there was no more cropping to be done other than the little winter patch already showing its rows of collards and cabbage. I had no idea how he spent his days or when he was likely to show up. One afternoon when Mary had fallen asleep for a nap, I heard footsteps on the porch and jumped to open the door, but it wasn't Henry.

It was Donohue McQueen, the skulker.

'Hello, Donohue,' I said. 'Were you going to knock or just eavesdrop some?'

He was a red-headed boy. I didn't like him, maybe because he was like me, with a buckskin Scot for a father. But Donohue was raised by his father's people.

'I come to leave a message,' he said.

'For Henry?'

He nodded.

I said, 'I haven't seen him in a long time. I wouldn't be surprised if I never saw him again. I am past all surprise, Donohue. And here's my advice to you. Give up on him. He's a phantom you're following, while your own fate waits.'

'Yes, ma'am,' he said.

'Listen, Donohue. It's hopeless. Do you know what I'm saying?'

'Yes, ma'am. But could you give him my message?'

'Oh, all right, what is it?'

'Tell him I will do whatever it takes.'

'You didn't even hear me. What do you hope to get from him, anyway? What are you after?'

'Heart and soul,' he said.

I stood there with my hand at the back of my neck trying to think how to get through to him, but finally I just said, 'I wish you luck.'

He nodded.

'Was there something else?' I said.

'Heck Oxendine,' he said. 'He went missing. His wife was told to go dig near the plank bridge, and she found him buried. Beat to death.'

Donohue saw I was trying to ask why.

'For aiding the Union. Heck was Sherman's guide when the Yanks came through.'

We looked at each other. There wasn't anything to say, but we stared into each other's eyes for a long time before he turned and left.

I closed the door and went to sit with the sleeping old lady. She was curled on the bed like a child, and her white hair had fallen loose. I covered her feet with a light blanket.

★ ★ ★

The first part of my life was over, and the second had not begun. I was drifting and waiting, and even though I had kept myself busy, inside the carcass of a chicken or rolling dough or running out a line of stitches so tiny I couldn't even see them, I felt deeply idle, stopped cold in the middle of my life. Even working outside with a view of the sun's progress across the sky, I felt that no time at all was passing. I longed to be possessed by hope, holding on for life; I wished I was a preacher or soldier caught in his calling, or a singer lost to her song, a love-wrecked woman, or anyone at all who followed a voice. But I was dull and leaden and unmoved.

Eventually the one who came to my rescue was not someone I would have expected. It was Boss. He showed up one afternoon and sat me down for a talking-to.

'It's time to put aside your childhood,' he said. 'You have responsibilities.'

He sounded like an old man. And his words might have been comical, if they had not been true.

'You have a duty,' he said.

'What is my duty?'

'To live,' he said. 'That's all.'

He might have been thinking of our grandmother, who had dwindled and taken her own life.

I said, 'I don't know what will keep me going.'

'Children, I guess.'

I was surprised by that answer.

'And you,' I said. 'What is your future?'

'I'll take what comes along.'

10

Our famous wedding took place the winter after the war — December 7, at the Lowrie homestead. It would have been famous for its food alone. Mary planned for two hundred guests, but more came. On foot and mule, by oxcart and wagon, from all parts of the settlement and even beyond. Cousins I didn't know we had, old people who hadn't ventured off their own porches in years, and babies wrapped against the cold with only their tiny eyes and noses showing — all because it was Henry Berry Lowrie's wedding. He had come to stand for everybody's dreams; his name was whispered everywhere as 'another Allen,' the hope of the future.

And the future was starting to look good. Preacher Sinclair had gotten himself appointed agent of the Freedman's Bureau, and Squire McLean was high in the Republican Party. Ben Bethea was in it, too, and got elected to the convention. '*Conventio scalawagorum niggerorumque*,' the newspaper said. I didn't need to know Latin to get the drift of that — but I wasn't paying attention to the newspapers anymore. What they said was not the same as what was really happening in Robeson County. Reuben King still held the office of sheriff, but the Republicans ordered him to drop all cases that had been brought against 'Union sympathizers.' The same party promised to put up some Scuffletown men for jurors, and one of the new magistrates was a Union soldier, Charles Barton, who had married into the settlement; his wife was Bess Cumbo, Mary's niece.

We were sending out our vines into the world.

But the best thing, the thing that had once seemed impossible and now was promised, was an investigation into the killing of Allen and William Lowrie. A judge had ordered it.

So Henry Lowrie's wedding meant more than just another marriage ceremony. It was a victory celebration. A display of hope, energy, high spirits — and food.

In this long-starved place where larders and smokehouses had been empty nearly two years straight, a banquet appeared. With money she got by selling to Ben Bethea the ten acres he'd been cropping, Mary bought everything she needed to put on an enfare like those of the old days. Pate delivered the wagonload of meat and sugar and white flour, crates of oranges and dates, potatoes and cabbages in bushel baskets, barrels of brandy, and tins of oysters from Wilmington. Mary and I cooked four days straight, and then the guests brought more. Those who had nothing found something — a fat rabbit, a string of river redbreasts, a basket of shelled hickory nuts — because the war was over, our future had begun, and Henry Lowrie was getting married.

Set on the winter grass where the yard sloped down to the river was a table of planks over sawhorses, so long that it required twenty cloths, borrowed from every house Mary knew that had one. And when we put out the food, there wasn't room for it all. Hams, turkeys, mutton legs, haunches of venison, and a boar roasted whole; barbecued peaches, potato pies, grape wine, cornbread, rice — more food than anyone had ever seen at the same time in one spot. People lined up just to look at the cake Mary had baked.

'North Carolina's tallest wedding cake,' my mother said when she saw it — and that was as close as she came to giving me her blessing. I hadn't thought she would come to the wedding, but she did, and walked the length of the table inspecting each dish. I followed, telling her who brought what, and which things Mary had cooked, and how I'd made my dress from the Lowrie quilt. But all she said was that remark about the cake, and then she went to stand at the edge of the crowd with her arms folded and her mouth grim, Daddy at her side. They never moved from that spot, stiff and awkward in their Sunday clothes. I tried not to look at them, but once when my eye fell on them by accident, I saw how firm she still was in her opinion, that I was digging my own grave. Daddy didn't agree, but he went along with her. They were almost leaning against each other, as if they couldn't have stood upright otherwise, and they spoke to no one else.

Nelly and Miss McCabe came up to admire my dress. Margaret swooped down on me from behind and flung her arms around my neck. 'I'm glad you're getting married, Rho, because I'm hungry. I'm going to eat myself crazy. Just look at that table.' She turned me around and pointed.

'Who brought all this? How did they do it?' I had never seen potato pies so red, or so many different shades of green all in one bowl of cabbage slaw.

Nelly said, 'Why cry now, silly? When everything has worked out as you hoped? You got your man!' She put her arm around my waist. In my other ear Miss McCabe whispered, 'You don't have to go through with it, you know. You can back out right now.' And Margaret told them both to give me breathing room. 'She's tired is all.' She pulled me aside and said I ought to sit down.

But I explained while she dabbed a handkerchief to my eyes, 'It's just the sweet potato pie and the cabbage — '

'Boohooing over pie and cabbage?'

'Because it's the food we used to dream of, but better and more.'

'It seems to me you ought to be hopping with joy and eating as much as you can.'

But I didn't want to taste anything, not even when she offered me a piece of peeled orange, our favorite thing when we were little.

'Eat something or you'll faint,' she said.

I shook my head. Hunger had become my driving force, and I didn't want to lose it. It strengthened me to look at that pie and that orange, and then to walk away.

I was put on the porch so the families could come up in waves to take a look at Henry's bride. Two bonfires roared in the yard while juba dancers whirled, and a dozen fiddlers played side by side — settlement music, the high mournful tunes known only in Scuffletown, that never did have words. People danced until they gave out and dropped back, and new ones took their places, and all the while a steady stream

412

moved up one side of the table and down the other, eating everything. I felt a little dizzy, and when I thought no one was looking I ducked into the house.

But I was not frail or fainting. Under my quilted and historic dress I was hard as a lightwood knot. My arms were muscled from chopping and hoeing, and my back could carry any load. In Mary's kitchen I sat in the rocking chair and closed my eyes and rocked myself. I could hear the fiddlers and the cries of children chasing each other in circles around the house, dogs yapping at their heels. Night was falling. Popping with resin, the bonfires blazed so tall and furious they lit the sky and field and sent a glow into the kitchen.

I had a sharp little sting of memory, of two nights of love so long ago it seemed like an earlier life. But I was steeled now, and that was all it could do to me. A little barb, a spike, and then it was gone — just as Henry came to find me.

That first desire had left us. But we had another of a different sort — not for each other but for something off in the distance. I hoped it was for justice, but sometimes I thought it might have been for blood revenge. Between us there was an understanding not to spell it out, but we both knew something was destined. So we weren't like any sweethearts I ever heard of. We were more like partners in a plot yet unrevealed to us, bent to the same unknown purpose, yoked blind.

'It's almost time,' he said.

I kept rocking. 'I still wish Patrick could have married us.'

'I told you, Hector McLean's a friend to the settlement.'

'How can that be? He was *there*.'

'You can't ask too much of a man. He did for us what he could.'

'Still, Patrick's your brother.'

'Let's just say, we don't see eye to eye. Patrick's a godly man. He asked me was I planning on drenching the county in blood like the macks say. I told him no, I was planning to farm and live my life. I promised him there'd be no guns brought to this wedding. But then he asked me to swear an oath. I couldn't, so we parted ways.'

'He ought to stand with you.'

'Well, he has his wife and children to think of.'

It didn't surprise me that he made that distinction between Patrick and himself, as if he'd forgotten he would soon have a wife, too. He didn't think of me that way. And neither of us had spoken again of children. We were marrying for other reasons.

'Are you ready?' he said.

I knew it was strange, this marriage. I didn't understand it, but I knew it was important, and I knew it would be hard.

'All right.'

★ ★ ★

When we stood in front of Squire McLean on the porch, I might have looked pale and fragile but my energy was coiled to spring. Nothing in the world scared me. I saw everyone I loved. Henderson and Virge, Applewhite and Betsy with their children, Steve and Cath, and Andrew with Flora, who was already expecting a baby. Boss stood alone, holding his hat and looking forlorn.

I said to myself, *I am being married to Scuffletown.*

'I now pronounce you . . . '

Mr. McLean stopped there. His eye had been caught by something in the distance. Under his breath he muttered, 'Hellfire.'

Henry heard it, I heard it, but no one else did, and McLean hurried on.

'Man and wife.'

A cheer went up, a toast to the bride and groom, a roar of yells and whistles. McLean leaned close to us and said, 'Edge of the woods. Past the well.'

I looked, and saw nine horses tied to the pines. There weren't more than four horses in all of Scuffletown.

The fiddlers struck up and the wedding guests spilled onto the field again for the last dance. We were swallowed into a group of well-wishers — Margaret and Nelly kissing me, Boss shaking Henry's hand over and over again — but Henry's eye was on the horses. And I knew why they were there.

I ran to where I'd last seen my mother and father. When she saw me coming, Cee turned away. She thought I was going to throw myself into her arms. But I said to them, 'There's trouble. Get Andrew and Flora and walk over to the fence and follow it down. As soon as you're in the cover of the woods, run for home.'

They did it without a question.

I thought Henry would slip away, too. But I felt his hand on my elbow.

'We're supposed to dance,' he said.

'Didn't you see who's here?'

'I won't be run off from my own wedding and my own bride.'

He took my hand and led me to the middle of the field.

I had never danced with him before. He was surefooted and smooth, his arm around my waist. He held me close, and we whirled, and everyone fell back to make room for us. He was steady, and so calm.

'I hope you'll understand this even if I put it wrong,' he said. 'I'm grateful you held me to my word. I'm glad to be a married man.'

I just said, 'All right,' but I felt his arm tighten around me.

People called out and reached to touch us as we went by.

'They love you,' he said. 'They'll take care of you.'

As we went spinning they smiled to see us whispering to each other, although it wasn't what they guessed. But my skin tingled, my heart raced, and I'm sure the look on my face was the same it would have been on a real bride's.

'Tell me what to do,' I said.

'Boss takes over. Not Steve. But no one's to follow me or try anything. Send Ma to Patrick's.'

'All right.'

'You can go there, too, they won't bother him or anyone with him. But if you want to, you can move into the new place. Boss is the only one who can find it. McTeer doesn't even know it's built.'

'Yes, I'd rather do that.'

'I am sorry the wedding has to be ruined — but no one ever saw a prettier bride.'

'Nothing can ruin it.'

'It won't be more than a week. That's all I'll give them. If it's more, Boss knows what to do.'

The other dancers closed in around us, and we were carried along in the circle. The field was packed full. I almost thought we could lose ourselves in the crowd. But we came to a standstill against the sheriff and the deputy, and the circle of dancers went on without us.

'Why, it's the bridegroom hisself,' said McTeer.

In the darkness, with the hubbub and the music, no one else saw what was happening.

'You don't want anyone here to get hurt, Henry,' the sheriff said, 'so just cross your hands behind your back.' He was holding a short piece of rope.

Hector McLean appeared out of the shadows and stepped between Henry and the sheriff.

'You can't make an arrest without a warrant.'

'Watch us,' said McTeer.

'You don't even have a charge. Give up this madness, Reuben — the war's finished. Are you going to claim he stole a pig? Fed a Yankee? That won't work anymore. You can't run things the way you used to.'

The sheriff said, 'I got no choice.'

'The Confederacy's dead, Reuben. This man has his rights.'

McTeer said, 'You might think it's dead, but some of us know better. We have a good charge. And I'll have a warrant by the time we get him locked up. It ain't stealing this time, and it ain't harboring. It's murdering James Barnes.'

'There's not a shred of evidence for it. As justice of the peace, I'm telling you this is an illegal arrest, and I see three hundred people here that will agree with me. Let's ask them. Let's see how they feel about you taking a man at his own wedding. I don't believe you'll walk out of here in one piece.'

Henry said, 'No, that's not what we'll do. Mr. McLean, I'm going with the sheriff. McTeer's to walk behind us. We'll go slow so none of the old ones or the children here gets scared, and the sheriff will tell his men there's to be no guns in sight. And I go on my own steam. No man ties me.'

'I'll take those terms,' King said.

At first only those standing near us saw Henry walk off with them, and even they weren't sure what it meant. But Margaret was watching. She saw them move off together.

'Who are those two?'

'Margaret, don't say anything.'

But Margaret remembered something. The

last time she saw Wes Lowrie alive, he was walking with those same two men close on either side of him.

'Stop them!'

She started running after them. A buzz of confusion rippled across the field. The sheriff and the deputy hurried Henry along, and they were joined by seven other white men who had been hanging back on the dark edges of the crowd. The nine of them formed into a knot around Henry, and I couldn't see him.

A deep ditch ran between them and the horses, with a narrow bridge of planks. They crossed it and threw Henry onto a horse before anyone else could get to him, and the first man who tried to cross the bridge after them was knocked into the ditch with the stock of a rifle. Two more came on, and they were knocked off too. The next wave might have made it if we had not seen six barrels rise, leveled at our heads. We had no guns.

Squire McLean stepped onto the bridge. 'Will you knock me down, too?'

'No, but we'll arrest you,' McTeer said. Three of them took the old man and tied him.

Henry signaled with his hand to halt the crowd and to silence Margaret. He said something to Sheriff King, and the sheriff snapped at McTeer, and the guns were lowered. Then they rode away, and we had no horses to follow. Steve got someone's mule and said he would catch them or die trying, but Boss stopped him.

Maybe it was McTeer's idea of a joke to wait until we were married, until we were dancing — to snatch the groom from the arms of his bride, and snicker later how the Queen of Scuffletown got wedded but not bedded.

Boss went quickly out among the families all milling around the fires.

'Cousins and neighbors,' he said, 'maybe some of us are thinking it's time to take things into our own hands no matter what the cost. But Henry wants us to go home peaceably. He said he'll be back inside a week, and we know he keeps his word.' Then Boss took Steve aside, and sent him to pack Mary's things for a move to Patrick's house.

The wedding guests trailed off into the night. All that remained of the wedding feast was scraps and bones, the jugs and pans scattered across the trampled grass, a bride holding back tears.

* * *

Near midnight, while Henry was being locked in the Lumberton jail, Boss and I fled into the cypress wilds without a lantern or a torch but only starlight to see by. He knew the way. By dawn we found the house Henry had built for me, and when I saw it, I knew it would suit me better than any house I could have imagined. It had everything from pots to salt. It was ready for me.

'You don't have to stay,' I said after Boss had finished lighting a fire. I drew my chair to the hearth and sat. 'I'll be all right alone.'

'He said don't leave you. It's miles to anyone, and there's nothing for you to do here, you'll go crazy.'

'I'll occupy myself.'

'Doing what?'

'Just waiting, I guess. Keeping house.'

But he stayed. He sat on the floor by the fire like he always used to do at home, leaning back on his elbows. The firelight feathered in his eyes, and he seemed at ease in spite of the arrest and our flight through the swamp and the uncertain days ahead. He pulled a mouth harp out of his pocket.

'Aren't you afraid for him, Boss?'

'He'll be back. He said so.'

'I wish I was sure of that as you are.' I stared into the fire. 'There's some that want him dead.'

'No one can touch him,' Boss said. 'No one. And he can walk out of that jail whenever he wants to.'

'You talk like he has a magic power.'

'I don't know if he does or doesn't. What I mean is, the Lumberton jail never got fixed after the Yankees burned it. There's only one cell standing, and the wall of that is charred so deep you could kick a hole straight through it. He'll only be there as long as he wants to.'

'Boss, did he kill James Barnes and Brant Harris?'

'I don't know.'

He stretched out flat, head on the new pine floor. He cupped his hands and played 'Johnny Come Fill Up the Bowl.' I closed my eyes. *In eighteen hundred and sixty-five, the soldiers all at home with their wives.*

'You've changed so, Boss. You seem like you know what you want in life.'

He kept on playing.

'When you were little,' I said, 'you were wondering so much. Always asking questions. We thought you'd go off into the world to find your answers.'

'No need to,' he said, stopping in the middle of the song. 'If there's answers anywhere, it's here.'

'So you found them?'

'Some.'

'What are they?'

'I expect you know as well as I do. I found the same ones you did.' He put the harp to his mouth again.

And we'll all drink stone blind. Johnny come fill up the bowl.

11

The house my husband built was all pine, yellow as the sun and still smelling like trees. The chimney was lined and floored with clay, and opposite its wide hearth stood the bed. Overhead ran two poles to hang clothes on. People don't think a man on the run cares for the future — but you could look at that house and see, Henry Berry had a plan for life. Starting with the first board, and the heel of his palm on the knob of the plane, the shaved curls brushed slowly away as his hand lingered on the pine to test it, to learn its possibilities and what it needed. I knew that touch.

And I missed it so bad I hurt.

So I leaned against what he had made, in the same way someone cut off from God may rely on the created world. I rested my face against the wall, and ran my hands over the boards. I don't mean I thought Henry was God. I knew his faults, and I never thought he had more than human powers — unless it may be said, and I do think it may, that everyone has more than human powers.

What I mean is, anything he made, he put

himself into. I could almost always see his design. I knew why he had chosen a spot so hard to get to, between Back Swamp to the north and the wider, shallower Ashpole to the south. I knew the reason for two doors, double latches and heavy bolts, plank floor instead of puncheon, and no windows. Because windows show who's home. A single door means nowhere to run when danger knocks, and a puncheon floor, of half logs resting on the ground, can't have trapdoors.

'Didn't he make a hidey-hole?' I asked Boss. I was on my knees, feeling along the floor.

'If he did, no one will ever find it.'

'Show me.'

'Maybe you're not supposed to know.'

I sat up. 'But this is my house.'

'He didn't say to tell you.'

'Boss, he'll tell me everything, now I'm his wife.'

'I'm the only one he tells everything,' he said, cleaning his gun, wiping the barrel with an oily rag.

I couldn't find the trapdoor. But I did find the lady's glass hung on a nail, the bookshelf built into one corner, the date of our wedding carved on the bedstead. When I opened the table drawer there was a tablet of paper, a new pen, a little glass bottle of ink.

It seemed years since I'd had a pen in my hand. But when I set it to the fresh paper, words flowed like a logjam breaking. Sentences streamed as fast as I could move my hand, and for the next few days I wrote and wrote. What for and who to, I didn't know.

A week passed, and Henry did not come, so Boss went to Lumberton and learned the prisoner had been moved to the Whiteville jail for better safekeeping. Whiteville was thirty-five miles distant by road but closer through the swamps.

'We'll go tomorrow,' Boss said, 'Leave before the sun's up, to get there by dark.'

'Both of us?'

'I'll need you. You'll keep the jailer busy while I get Henry out.'

'How?'

'With a punchbelly inside a cake.'

'Boss, they'll think of that. Everyone's heard of a file in a cake.'

'He left me in charge. It's up to me.' Boss handed me the little three-inch file. 'Just bake it.'

'How can I with no sugar or flour? No eggs?'

'The taste don't matter. We won't be eating any of it.'

I had a better idea, but I didn't think he would take it from me. I had to plant it.

'It's too bad we can't come up with something else,' I said, 'something the file would fit into, like it was meant to — so it wouldn't raise suspicion. But I can't think of anything unless maybe a chicken. But then, we don't have a chicken.'

He picked up his mouth harp and tossed it from one hand to another.

'Put a pot on to boil. I'll be back after a while.'

I don't know where he went, but he was home in an hour — and in the morning somebody's coop in Back Swamp would be missing a scrawny rooster. By then it would be well on the way to Whiteville in Boss's rucksack, plucked and boiled, packed in a tin dish wrapped in newspaper, with a punch-belly file where one of its leg bones used to be.

'They'll never look there,' I said. 'I knew you'd think up a clever idea.'

'It was yours.'

'No, you — '

'Don't try tricks on me. Save them for somebody they'll work on.'

★   ★   ★

Before dawn I put on all the winter clothes I owned, a flannel shift and two shirts, woolen

428

skirt with jeans britches underneath, an old long Rebel coat and scarf.

'Bring a dress,' he said.

'What for?'

'To look good so they'll let us inside the jail.'

I showed him my two dresses, and he was disappointed they were so plain, but he chose the green muslin.

We headed down through the Ashpole, taking the deer path. He didn't want to be seen by anyone who might recognize us. Where the path crossed the road, we stopped a minute and then darted like turkeys, even though I'm sure there was no one to see us, and we went on through the dark toward Asbury Church.

When we got there, the sun had risen pure and open, without a veil of haze, and I knew we would have a good day for walking. Skirting the churchyard and its tall white Presbyterian gravestones, we dipped back down into swamp, moving east with the sun in our eyes whenever it got a chance through the winter trees. I thought it would warm us up, but I felt colder and colder as the hours passed. Boss never stopped to rest.

We crossed Oldfield Swamp and Hog Branch, and at noon we came to the river. From here it was only a mile to the Whiteville

Road, and the going would be easy from then on.

Boss walked upstream and I walked down, looking for a crossing — but the river was wider here than it was near home, and we didn't see anyone's boat along the bank. When we met back at the first spot he said, 'This is as good a place as any.' We tied our coats in a bundle, and he waded in holding them high in one hand, rucksack and gun in the other. I watched till he was waist deep, halfway across and then rising toward the other side, and I went in after him.

When the water closed around my hips, I thought, *No river was ever this cold*, and all of a sudden I had no breath. My legs gave out. I was swallowed to the neck, and even though the toes of my shoes bumped along the bottom I couldn't stand up, the current had me. I saw Boss already on the other bank, but I couldn't even call to him, there was no air in my lungs.

'Swim!' he yelled as I was borne past him.

My muscles had frozen. I remembered something from the Union soldier's letter: 'It is sad I must die so young, Ma, and was never married.'

But I am married, I thought. *I'm not free to die*. I forced one arm out and pulled it through the water, and then the other, and I kept going until I was past the midstream flow. Gentler water floated me in circles toward the shore until my knees ran aground, and Boss pulled me out. We didn't have time to build a fire and warm ourselves, he said. We started again.

My coat was dry but the wet britches and shirts clinging to my skin began to freeze stiff as pasteboard. Boss got so far ahead of me that sometimes when the trail turned I lost sight of him. *Maybe I could just lie down for a little while, just for a minute*, I kept thinking. But still it was marriage that prevented me. I wasn't free to die or even to take a nap. I was drawn along, thinking of Henry, and pretty soon my body had warmed itself back to life, and a steady thumping of the heart. When we came to the public road, Boss said we could take it because we were now so far from home no one who saw us would know us.

We walked all day. I don't remember anything I saw or thought on the road, I was only moving ahead, with the kind of steady effort that drains the thoughts from your head and puts you in a trance. I didn't even think about the walking — I only walked.

At dusk we came to the edge of Whiteville, where Boss told me to step off into a thicket grove and put on the green dress. When I came out, his face fell.

Shivering in the muslin, bedraggled and dog-tired, I was no use. I pulled out my hairpins to let my hair fall. Still he wasn't pleased. It wasn't enough.

'Give me your knife,' I said. I cut my collar out and turned the edge to make a lower neckline. 'Will that do?'

'It's just to get us in the door.'

We hid my other clothes and his gun in the brush by the side of the road and walked on into Whiteville.

It was a cramped little town of dirt streets and low houses, the kind of place that makes you wonder what could have lured people to it, and what kept them. I got a bad feeling as we crept along its shadows, dodging the light of porch lanterns and tavern doors — as if the whole town was a creature lying in wait to gulp me. Boss was uneasy too, and he kept his hand on my elbow as if to steer me clear of a danger we both sensed. But then we found the jail, a two-story wooden building with a heavy oak door and barred windows above. Boss took it in with a glance, and saw a complication.

'Cell's upstairs.'

'We'll talk our way up, or we'll just leave off the dish and hope they take it to him.'

He stood behind me and said, 'You knock,'

but he was jittery. 'If anything goes wrong, we just walk out. All right? If it doesn't work or if it looks bad, if you get scared — '

'Don't worry.'

The man who opened the door was unshaven, big-eared, with a lantern in his hand and a revolver holstered on his hip.

'We've come to see the Scuffletown prisoner,' I said.

'No one sees him.'

'I'm his wife, this is my brother. We've brought him some food. With the permission of Sheriff King.' I showed him the wrapped dish.

'You're Rhoda Lowrie?'

He raised his lantern. When the light fell on me, his eyes dulled over.

And in that light I rose into a new part, as if I had just stepped onto a stage. My real self dropped away, and all my fear; and I answered, 'That's me.'

He looked us up and down.

I said, 'And you must be the Columbus County sheriff.'

'I'm the jailer.'

'Well, mister jailer, it's a cold night out here. Am I going to freeze to death before I can make your acquaintance, or are you going to invite me in?'

He opened the door and stood aside, still

gawking. Around the table sat three hollow-cheeked children and a gaunt wife much younger than himself. The room was mean and moldy smelling, but someone had tried to make it into a little parlor, with a busted-down sofa and a picture on the wall, showing a cottage with a grass roof and flowery path. I thought how terrible it must be to live in a jailhouse, having that man your husband and three children for whose sake you are stuck there forever. But the woman glared at me, and spat tobacco onto the floor.

I set the dish on the edge of the table.

'How do you know my name?' I said to the man, backing up to the little coal fire they had, rubbing my bare arms.

'The newspaper.' He almost couldn't talk, his eyes were working me over so hard.

'And do they call me a scoundrel like they do my husband?'

'They call you worse than that,' the wife said.

'Clear out,' her husband growled, and she took her children into the other room and closed the door, so quick it showed she had learned the hard way. He slid the thumb bolt.

I smiled at him. Boss stayed in the corner.

'Well, well. Who'll believe I seen the beauty belle in person,' the man said, recovering himself. 'When word gets out, the whole town will be over for the story.'

'And I'm sure you'll report I was plain and homely.'

'If I do, may I be whipped for a goddamn liar.'

Behind him Boss edged toward the narrow staircase.

'No one goes up there, boy,' the jailer said without even turning. He was wilier than I'd guessed.

I said, 'You mean I can't see my own husband?'

'Miss him, do you?'

'I hardly even know him. We only got married a week ago.'

'The paper said so. Had your bridegroom stole right out of your arms.'

'That's why Sheriff King said it would be all right.'

'Did he now? But you didn't bring no letter or nothing, did you. No authorization of a written nature.'

'He said his word would be enough.'

'In his own county maybe. I don't answer to him. Only way someone gets upstairs is if I say so, and my rule is law. Course I have my leeways. Nights, I might could let a person up if I thought they'd be grateful for the favor. I'd expect to be owed a little gratitude.'

'Well of course you would.' I lifted my skirt

a few inches to warm the backs of my legs. 'The trouble is,' I said, 'I don't have a penny.'

'We got a problem then, don't we?'

There was a silence. He poured himself a cup of coffee.

'What I'm going to suggest here is that your brother goes on down the street and occupies himself while you and me work out the terms of this agreement. If we hit on something satisfactory, then I'll give you ten minutes with your husband. That ought to do it I guess.'

Boss said, 'I'm not going to wait in the cold.'

'Too bad then. You can leave your supper food with me but I won't promise he'll have a nibble if my children get their hands on it, they're hungry as rats.'

'Forget it,' Boss said. 'Let's go, Rhoda.'

I laughed at him. 'He's a young boy,' I said to the jailer. 'And kind of slow-minded. Thinks he has to watch over his sister like a hawk, I swear it about drives me crazy. Maybe you can send him upstairs with the food while we have our talk down here. I don't want him wandering around outside. Who knows what trouble he could find to get into. I rather have him where I know where he is. Go ahead, you can search him, he hasn't got anything on him. If it makes you happier, you can lock him in your other cell, I don't care.'

'Let's see what you plan on feeding your man.'

'Rhoda, I said come on,' Boss said. 'Now.'

I turned on him. 'Will you shut up? This nice man is trying to help us out and you got no manners at all and I'm getting real tired of it. You see he has a loaded gun on him, don't you? And if you don't watch your tongue I'm going to have him use it on you.' I winked at the jailer, and carefully I unwrapped the rooster.

It was a poor specimen with no breast to speak of at all, and its skin had shriveled, but it looked all right. Nothing was showing.

'I sure hope that ain't the quality of what you give him every night.'

'Scuffletown turkey,' I said, and he laughed.

Boss looked at me with anger boiling over, and he reached for my arm but the jailer pulled out his gun.

'I don't like your little brother,' he said. 'I got a short temper.'

I locked my eyes onto his. 'Put him in the other cell,' I said. 'Then you come on back down here.'

It was like commanding a dog. He didn't hesitate, he picked his ring of keys from a nail on the low mantel. 'I'll do that.'

'And I'll make myself at home. You got a nice place here, considering. I never knew a jail would have a little parlor like this with a sofa and all.'

'Get upstairs,' he said to Boss.

Boss didn't move. 'I don't like it,' he said straight at me.

'I don't care if you don't like it. I didn't come all this way to turn around and go home. It's warm in here, and my feet hurt. I need to rest up. Don't you understand a word? You heard the man. Do like he says.'

What had he expected? If you set a bait, you expect to deal with what you trap. My anger was real and Boss knew it, but still he wouldn't go.

The jailer shoved the dish into his hands and pushed him up the steps.

'Don't try anything. I'm right behind you. And I don't want to hear a peep out of you or the prisoner either till I come back and get you, understand?'

There never was a lock Boss could not pick. But I had no idea how long it would take him. From above I heard the rattle of keys, the clank of iron, but no voices. The jailer came back down the staircase, slow, and I said a little prayer not to God but to Nelly, Cee, Margaret, and Mary. *Help me.*

He was a vile-looking man. His hair was a

stringy gray, his teeth when he smiled showed a life of brawling and tobacco and poor food.

Charm him. Outwit and outlast him. Fight. I knew I didn't have their powers — Nelly's wiles and Cee's brain, Margaret's endurance, Mary's will — all I had was a husband locked upstairs. But he was mine and I wanted him back. Pure and simple. Like a blinding beam.

'I wouldn't mind a cup of coffee. I'm sitting here just smelling it.'

'You need something hot I bet,' he said.

'You hit the nail on the head.'

And when the jailer in reaching for the pot let his arm brush my breast, I hardly felt it. It was no worse than gnats, a bother, the annoyance of a worm.

'You gals know how to treat a man right I heard.'

'Depends on the man.'

He was looking at me different now. Instead of a dull leer there was a sharp cold slice in his eyes.

'You pick and choose, you mean?'

'Doesn't every girl if she can?'

I took a sip of coffee, raising my eyes to him over the rim. I could banter him as long as it took, with back-and-forth hints and glances.

'Not you,' he said, 'not you with me,' and he jumped me.

The cup fell. I was knocked back against the wall, his hand over my mouth.

He whispered, 'Did you think you could just tease me along? Did you think I was to be your fool?'

He locked his mouth to mine.

I knew not to fight. I let him do it. I put myself in another place — with Margaret, in the yard, an afternoon chasing chickens, brown eggs she took from the hen boxes, and one she cupped in her hand and held out to me, perfect except for a white tuft stuck on the top — and then I bit. Bit hard, a dog's death-jaw clench, clamped on his tongue.

Howling, he sprang back from me, blood dripping from his mouth. I heard Henry call my name from upstairs, and a banging of iron. The jailer's gun was on the desk. I jumped for it but he kicked my leg out from under me and I went sprawling backward, and he dove onto me so hard we slid together across the floor. He was jabbering but I couldn't understand, it was just slippery sounds. His hands closed around my neck and blood trickled from his mouth into my eyes. But I would not close them. I wanted to see his face, to watch for my chance even though I couldn't move or breathe. And then

I saw it. His grip on me didn't loosen but his eyes shifted. His head lifted as if he'd heard something — and I clawed my fingernails into his neck. Then the face disappeared. I saw the whole jailer flying across the room, and Henry standing over me.

Sweet air rushed into my lungs. I tried to reach for him but then I sank somewhere else, back with Margaret and her hens and the pretty eggs in the yard. I had a collapse.

He carried me home from Whiteville, and then for days he sat by the bed and watched me. I said I was all right and Boss said so too, but Henry wouldn't listen. All he could see was my purple neck and all my bruises.

'It's crazy to stay here. We ought to go down into the Pee Dee,' Boss said.

'No,' Henry said. 'I'm not running. If I hide out anywhere, it'll be right here in this county.'

The jailer never told the whole story of that jailbreak. Missing the tip of his tongue, he didn't like to talk much after that. All he said was a man he didn't know had knocked him in the jaw and stolen his keys, and when he came to he found the prisoner had escaped.

The governor announced that Henry was now an outlaw, with a reward of two thousand dollars offered for him dead or alive — and if dead, the corpse was required as proof before the reward could be collected. There was a reward for Boss, too, and the others — a thousand dollars a man. This was in a time and place where you might never see more than twenty dollars cash together at once, and wages ran eight dollars a month.

An outlaw is not the same as a criminal. He has been disowned by the state and officially abandoned. In spirit, he is an exile. He can be legally murdered. It is as if war had been declared — against one man.

He came home, he lived with me in the house he had built. But strangers started nosing around, and after a while he had to go lie out again in the old swamp shelter at Devilsden, where Boss and Henderson and Steve and Ap still were.

Everyone in the settlement knew where he was, but no one turned him in or gave a hint to the sheriff. So he was not much of an outlaw, this side of the river between Shoe Heel and Lumberton. Scuffletown would not disown him or abandon him.

★ ★ ★

When I was a girl with Margaret, we named all our unborn children. Knew their ages and their looks, what their best school subjects were, and which of hers would marry which

442

of mine. Now those play-pretend children had slipped my mind, and I was thinking about real ones. But I found out they were harder to come by. My husband wasn't often with me.

Flora didn't have any trouble. Andrew was home. Day and night they were lovebirds. She'd had her first baby not long after my wedding, a girl named Ida, whose round face and fat knees made me sick with envy. I tried to tell myself not to have those mean feelings. Flora got married first, it was right she should have the first baby.

Three months later Flora was expecting again.

'You need a baby yourself, Rhoda,' she said, 'Maybe then Henry would stay around home more.'

I laughed out loud.

'Sometimes I don't understand you,' she said, pouting.

If God was punishing me, He was clever at it. For when I had finally steeled myself to the prospect of a second bundle of joy in Flora's arms, she took to bed and was delivered of twins. Della and Liza, two little matching darlings.

I was ushered in to see them, both suckling while Flora sat propped by quilts. Her breasts were swollen bigger than the babies' heads. In the closed cabin, the odors of birth and milk were too rich and strong for me.

'Child, are you all right?' Mrs. Sampson said.

'Just tired,' I said.

But I swooned. The next thing I knew I was flat on the floor, looking up at Mrs. Sampson.

'I'm sorry,' I said, getting to my feet.

'If you're squeamish just coming in the room, wait till you have you yours,' Flora said.

Mrs. Sampson handed me a cup of pine-top tea and said, 'I guess it won't be a long wait, either.'

'Who, me?' I said.

'My lord, she don't even know it,' Mrs. Sampson said. 'Honey, I'll bet a dollar and a half you've got one on the way. It's snuck up on you.'

And she was right.

* * *

I asked Nelly if she would help me when the time came. If I couldn't have my own mother, Nelly was the next closest thing. She had delivered plenty of Hestertown babies without a hitch. But when my time did come, something went wrong that Nelly wasn't prepared for.

My pains started on a Thursday morning and continued through Friday night. I was so tired I was in and out of consciousness, and I hardly knew what was happening.

'Go for Cee,' Nelly told Henry. 'Say I said I'll kill her if she doesn't come.'

I managed to find my voice. 'No,' I said. 'Get Dr. McCabe.'

'I don't want him,' Henry said. 'He's gone addled. The medical board took away his doctoring license.'

I lifted up on one elbow. 'It's not for you, is it?' And I fell back.

So he went.

When the doctor got there, I was shocked to see him, and somewhat frightened. His white hair was long and thin, and his hands were mottled with dark spots.

'How is she?' he said to Nelly.

'Slow,' she said. 'I don't know why.'

He sat down in the rocking chair, and within a few minutes he was asleep.

'Nelly?' I whispered.

'Don't worry now.'

I drifted off again, into clouds of weariness, but a while later I woke to hear Nelly's frightened voice.

She and the doctor were both standing at the bedside.

'Why would it just *stop*?' she said.

'Always a chance there's no baby,' the doctor said, opening his bag.

My eyes flew open. 'What did he say?' I asked.

'Could be an anomaly,' said Dr. McCabe. 'Could be a hairball. Whatever it is, we will soon find out.' He reached into the bag and pulled out a metal helmet. 'McCabe's Cap,' he said. 'Works wonders.'

Nelly stared. 'Doc, listen,' she said. 'You're probably right. I'm sorry we brought you all the way out here for nothing. I'll call Henry in and have him take you back home now.'

'Oh, Henry's gone. He left me at the gate and went off alone in the wagon. The husbands do that, go on a binge till it's over.'

Nelly tried to stop him but he came toward me with the helmet in his hands.

Behind them both I saw the door swing open.

'What is that contraption, Dr. McCabe?'

'Why, Celia!' he said, his arms still stretched toward me, McCabe's Cap hovering over my head. But he drew back and turned his attention to her.

'I want to see that thing up close,' Cee said. 'But I need a word with my daughter first. Give us a minute.'

'Ma, are you here?'

'I'm here.' She nudged him back into the

corner and took his place next to me.

'Celia, I have good news to report,' he said.

'Just stay right where you are and tell me from there.'

She was laying her cheek against my belly, listening, when I was seized by an enormous pain that shuddered through and left me barely breathing.

'I've found evidence,' the doctor said. 'Proof your people trace back to an early tribe. And not only that. I've something even better, a discovery altering the history of North Carolina. Extraordinary findings.' He droned on, a comforting sound familiar to me from childhood.

Nelly climbed onto the bed between my knees. Cee held my head in her hands.

'Easy,' Cee said. 'Easy.'

Another pain hit, twice the power of the one before.

'The English would have starved, you see,' Dr. McCabe was saying. 'After all, they were shoemakers and tinkers.'

I felt one last push, the slippery baby squeezing forth, and then a most glorious release, an instant of joy past description. Nelly was sobbing. My mother took the baby from her.

'There can be no doubt,' said the doctor. 'The names coincide to a degree not explainable by happenstance. There was even a Henry Berry among them.'

'What's that?' Cee said.

'The ship's list. The first colonists. Celia don't you see? I've discovered that Scuffletown is Raleigh's lost colony! The settlers were never found because they had taken refuge with a friendly tribe — migrated inland, steering clear of enemies, coming at last to rest — here!'

She gasped. 'Oh, Doctor McCabe, just look. Look at my beautiful granddaughter.'

★ ★ ★

I named her Celia — for my mother, who had come back to me, but also for other Celias, starting with the sister of the first James Lowrie. It was a name so stately and dignified it needed a nickname.

'Sally,' I said, looking down at her little face.

'That's good,' Cee said. 'High-spirited and carefree.'

For a week, my mother stayed with me. But there was still a distance between us, and things we didn't talk about — Henry, for one. I knew he had gone to fetch her the night Sally was born, but she didn't say anything about that to me. She never even said his name. But I didn't try to force anything on her. I found other things to talk about.

'Was it true what Dr. McCabe said?' I asked her.

'Could be,' she said. 'I have heard it before. Aunt Bet said the old ones came from Roanoke.'

'Dr. McCabe said it's an important discovery.'

'To him, yes. He'll think more highly of us now.'

'But do you think it's true?'

'Well, *someone* English converted us. And, to put it nice, married us. Are we the leftovers of Sir Raleigh? I don't know. I do know *I* wouldn't think any more highly of us for it, if it was true. Looks to me like it would only matter to someone who didn't think much of us to start with. See what I mean?'

'Yes'm,' I said, hiding my smile. I was so happy with my Celias.

★ ★ ★

There were babies born right and left in Scuffletown that year, and more the next, a new generation getting off to a long-delayed start. The babies were bigger than usual, it was said, and hungrier and noisier, because this was the generation that would make itself known.

12

Then came our hardest trial. With Sally to feed, and to my surprise another on the way, Henry and I needed more than our neighbors could lend or give. We were tempted to do things we knew weren't wise.

In January I made up my mind to find help. Henry had been in the swamps three weeks and couldn't get to us. Nelly came to stay with my children.

'This is a mistake,' she said.

'We'll see,' I said.

I took the Lumberton train and walked through that town once again, much as I hated it. I walked directly up the Courthouse steps, and into the little courtroom where I'd once been scientifically measured — to be measured again in a somewhat different way.

Nobody noticed me. I sat at the back of the room while three men at the front heard stories from people hard up and desperate one way or another. After each case, the judges talked amongst themselves a bit, and then one said, 'Granted.' Papers were shuffled and stamped, and the next case was called.

'Name?'

'Rhoda Lowrie.'

When they heard the name, their attention got a little sharper.

'Situation?'

'I have a baby girl, and I'll have another one by summertime.'

'Where's your husband at?' said one of the men.

'I haven't seen him in a while. I don't know when he'll come back.'

The man sucked his teeth and reared back in his chair.

'Are you starving?' said another one.

'Not starving, but in need, sir. It's my children I ask for, not my own self.'

They bent their heads together. There was no argument that I could see, only a joke of some kind being told, for they laughed. And then called me forward again.

'Mrs. Lowrie, don't you know your husband is held responsible for half a dozen robberies in this county? Plus the theft of six wagons of corn, and so many cases of petty larceny they ain't been totalled up yet? There's not a silver teapot or a gold watch left between Lumberton and Shoe Heel. Are you telling this court he don't share his loot with you?'

'I don't know about any robberies, your honor. I know six wagons of corn were found in Scuffletown but nobody knew where they came from. The corn was given out to the neediest families. That's all I know.'

'Maybe he ought to have kept a wagonload for his own family. This court isn't in the business of feeding a murdering outlaw's urchin children. Application for county assistance is denied. Please sign here.'

I stood still and quiet for so long they started to worry I was going to cause a ruckus, but I was just trying to think of something clever, some other way to get what I wanted from them. I tried to think what Cee might say. But my mind was blank. I hadn't ever heard with my own ears Henry called a murdering outlaw. Cleverness failed me, and when I saw the bailiff coming my way, I turned to leave.

He held out a pen and showed me the paper to sign.

The main judge said, 'It's nothing but acknowledgment your case was duly heard. You were given your day in court.'

I realized he assumed I couldn't read.

I shuddered. So they thought they knew me.

You will never know me, I said silently.

'Mrs. Lowrie?'

My eyes glazed over in disguise, and I took the pen, and I wrote a wavery, splotchy X where they wanted my name to be, and I walked away.

On the street a wagon had pulled up in front of the courthouse.

'Get in,' I heard, and saw Henry.

People would say later that he flew into a rage and struck me for begging county help. The truth is, it was worse than that. He said nothing. We drove without a word passing between us. He took me home but he didn't stay.

But the worst was yet to come. My mother found out. She was on my porch the next day.

'Did I ever once lead you to believe it was anything less than sinful to shame your family like that? A daughter of mine putting herself forward in public as a common pauper?'

'What was I supposed to do?'

'Starve like we always have! Didn't I raise you on potato skins and parched corn?'

'I don't want that for my children.'

'Oh, so you think you can do a better job than I did.'

'Ma, I'm not going to fight you.'

'Good. I want you to get your children and pack up and come home now.'

'What?'

'Leave him, Rhoda.'

'No.'

'He can't even feed you! What kind of man

lets his wife throw herself before the poor board?'

'Don't say another word.'

'Again? Are you choosing him over me again? After all this?'

'Yes, I am. I chose him then and I will always choose him, he's my whole life — '

She cut me off. 'I've heard enough.'

And we were back to where we'd been before Sally came.

★   ★   ★

When our son was born, his first cry was a hawk's single keer, and I sensed he was fated for sorrow. Henry named him. He named him Henry. I didn't object, but it wasn't the name I'd have chosen. I feared it would weigh him down. I called him by his middle name instead, which was Delaware.

And since most of the time it was me the baby heard, calling or singing his name or cooing it into his ear, Delaware's the name that stuck. Del for short, a long, slim baby, quiet in his cradle and as sharp-eyed as they come.

Henry and I managed somehow to live on a little dribble of money we got from a peddler who gave cash for stolen watches and jewelry. But it was true, there was little of value left now in those farmhouses along the river road. Only the sheriff's house had gone untouched. Most had been raided six or seven times, sometimes by Henry but sometimes by the dozen other parties who would terrorize and then ride off yelling, 'Lowrie strikes again.' One of those was Reuben King's own son-in-law, and King knew it. He also knew that any raid in which there was a fire set or a woman insulted was not the work of Henry Berry Lowrie.

But Lowrie was the name on every victim's lips. He was given credit for more crimes than one man could handle in a lifetime, some in other states. He robbed a bank in Indiana, the paper said, and the next day he stole horses in Georgia. It was as if a ghost had sprung up, a double of Henry with a life and energy of its own, and it was growing.

While the ghost grew, there were signs the real Henry was losing something of himself. He and Boss were sometimes at home weeks at a time, but even then he was careworn. I don't know when he slept. I would wake in the morning to find him still sitting at the table where he'd been when I fell asleep. He might stay all day playing with the children, but other times he went out to his bees at dawn and didn't come back until after Sally and Del were asleep, as if he didn't want them to see him. As usual, he never told me his plans, but on those hiving days I could be almost sure of a lonesome bed. After supper he and Boss would clean their guns; Steve would come by, or Applewhite, and they would all go off together. I might not see him for a while then, depending on who was robbed that night and how long the law would try to track him.

I had always been willing to give up certain wifely expectations because of what we were fighting for. But one day I realized that I no longer knew what that was.

One night I heard him talking to Boss and Steve about Reuben King's house. How many dogs were there, which windows might be left unlocked. King had lost the election and wasn't really sheriff any more — but he was still called sheriff, and he meant to run again and win his office back. The best way to get the mack votes would be to bring in the Lowries — and King had made a public vow to do that.

Steve said, 'He bragged he's the only one can do it.'

Henry said, 'He's old now. I don't like to bother a old man, but he's rich too.'

Unlike most others, Reuben King had not lost his fortune. He was rich before, and during, and after the war.

Henry went out to his hives the next morning. Boss simmered all day in a bad temper because he didn't know where the hives were and he never liked for Henry to go anywhere unprotected. Finally he settled down on the porch and started taking his gun apart.

Around dusk he went down to the fence to wait for Henry.

I tore up a sheet and wrapped the strips around me to bind myself, tied up my hair and put on some of Boss's clothes.

When Henry came through the door, he stopped cold.

'What is this?'

'I'm going along.'

'No. It's not something for a woman.'

'You thought I was Boss at first, didn't you?'

'Get dressed proper.'

I took a breath. 'Either I go with you or you stay with me.'

'A man has a man's part, and a woman has hers.'

'That's true for some but not for us. I can do more.'

Boss was listening, but I didn't care. Boss was always listening. It was a two-room house.

Henry rubbed the back of his neck and sat

down at the table. 'It's all winding down to nothing anyway,' he said. 'Sooner or later it will end.'

'They offered him a deal,' Boss said in an off-hand way.

'What deal?' I asked.

'He gives himself up, signs a promise he won't disturb the peace, gets a pardon.'

'Who believes that?' I said.

'Nobody,' Henry said. 'But I did tell them I would think it over. It'll keep them busy, and meanwhile I might can think of something else. There's other possibilities.'

'Like what?' Boss said.

'I can't say yet.'

'You don't say a lot, these days.' Boss lay down on the floor before the fire, propped on an elbow.

I didn't give up. 'I'll stay out of sight, Henry. I can keep watch for you. Otherwise, don't you see, I'm left in the dark. And it's starting to seem like I'm kept out on purpose, like you don't want me to know anything.'

'I'm trying to keep you safe.' He looked so tired at that moment, my old feelings rushed up in me, the sweetness of desire.

I put my arms around him, and he held me for a minute, his hands on the sides of my head, and kissed me.

'If she's going along, I'm not,' Boss said.

I drew away and went to the stove. There was a long silence in the room, which I thought would make me scream if it continued, so I broke it by a clattering of tin pans and forks.

Henry closed his eyes and rubbed his forehead. When he opened his eyes again, I knew he had decided — and there would be no more use in trying to sway him.

He took out his watch and wound it. 'You used to like this watch, Boss. Do you still?'

'You can't buy me off.'

'We're shorthanded. Henderson's in Fairmont, and we need a lookout.'

'A woman?'

'Your sister. My wife.'

'Suit yourself. But I won't be there.'

'Come on, Boss,' I said. 'It's me.' I went and sat by him. 'I can help. And I need to. I want to go along, just this one time.'

'Like it's a church outing?'

'I know what it is.'

'I doubt you do.'

'Then let me find out. Say yes.'

'But I'm not the one who says. Henry's the one. So which is it going to be, Henry, her or me?'

'Both. And I don't want to hear any more about it.'

I made the supper and tried to smooth

things over between them the way I knew how to do — smiling, joking. But they ate without looking at each other.

When Henry blacked his face with soot from the ash can, I did mine, too.

'You coming, Boss?' he said.

'You forgot something,' Boss said.

'What?'

'The watch.'

Boss held out his hand, and Henry laid in his palm the watch with the moving moon. Boss dropped it into his pocket.

★   ★   ★

We had to wait a long time in the thickets behind the sheriff's house, until the upstairs lights went off, and then another hour to make sure he was asleep. Applewhite got talking about his children. Boss lay alert and still as a snake watching a wren. Steve acted jittery and drank from a bottle of rum until Henry reached over and took it.

Henry said, 'Remember what I said. Don't touch the old man.'

It was after midnight when they climbed in through a back window, Henry and Boss followed by Steve and Applewhite. I was supposed to watch the road, but there was a light in the parlor window, and when I looked in, I saw the Sheriff enter the room, wearing his pajamas. He couldn't sleep, I guess, and had decided to come downstairs. He stirred the fire and sat down in his chair close to the hearth, reading a paper by the firelight.

Then something caught his attention. He glanced up from his paper, peering over the rim of his glasses.

Across the room stood Henry with a revolver drawn.

'Keep your seat,' Henry said. He came closer. 'We just stopped by for a little visit. Do me the favor of lighting your oil lamp, Sheriff.'

Sheriff King lit the lamp and leaned back in his chair again. He had an almost kindly look on his face. I thought he might be one of those men who admired Henry but couldn't say so. I liked to imagine that under other circumstances Henry would have been the kind of young man that the sheriff would take under his wing, in memory of his own promising youth. He might have chosen Henry as a deputy.

That's what I was thinking, when Sheriff King lunged from his chair and grabbed the barrel of Henry's gun with both hands.

'Mr. King, don't do that. Sit back down,' Henry said.

But the sheriff wouldn't let go. He was

461

making a growl in his throat, and holding on to the gun like a madman.

'Just — sit down, Sheriff. Everything will be all right — '

There was a struggling dance between them. They turned together. The gun discharged at a slant across the floorboards, and cut a smoking furrow in the pine. King let go, and another shot rang out. But it had come from the dining room. The bullet hit the back of King's head and drove him forward into Henry's arms, and they landed together on the floor.

I ran to the back window and climbed through into the dark hallway.

Applewhite saw me first, 'Get out of here,' he said.

I moved past him into the parlor where I saw Henry still cradling the sheriff.

He wasn't dead. His eyes were open and puzzled. He looked up and asked for a drink of water.

'Damn you, why did you have to go and fight me?' Henry said. 'What did you do that for?'

'I'm parched.' Reuben King's face was like a child's when it calls in the middle of the night, round-eyed and blank. 'I'm afire.'

'Boss, get some water,' Henry yelled.

Boss, in the doorway with a painted jewelry

box in his hands, said, 'That's a fire no water will quench.' He kept working on the little lock, trying to jigger it open with a pin.

'Just bring it,' Henry said. 'I don't want to hear him crying.'

'Kill him then. I warned you we'd have to if he put up a fight.'

'Why the hell did he? He knew it was useless.'

'Maybe that's why he fought. Nothing to lose. That's the way I've come to look at it myself. Goddamn this box, he's hid the key.'

A thread of blood came from the sheriff's mouth. He said, 'I am begging you. Send to the spring for a bucket.'

I said, 'Henry, someone might have heard the shots.'

Boss shoved me back. 'Sit down and keep your mouth shut.'

'Henry — '

Boss pushed me so hard I fell sideways and across the arm of the chair.

But Henry didn't notice. He was seeing only the dying man.

'Did you shoot him?' he asked Boss.

'It was Ap, but I'll do it now. Move off and I'll cap him for you. Isn't that what we really came for?'

'What are you talking about? We came to get his watch and valuables.'

'Pilfering has never been my aim.'

'You have been eating off pilfered watches a long time, Boss. Now do what I said.'

'I'm not your water boy.'

There was a look in Boss's eyes at that moment that had never been there before — a frenzy. Or maybe we just hadn't noticed it till now.

'Move off,' Boss said. 'I'm going to shoot him.'

Henry held the sheriff's bleeding head. He didn't let go of it, he held it closer. If Boss took a shot, the bullet would kill two men.

'Something's gone evil in you, Boss,' Henry said.

'All my evil I learned from you.'

'Boss, how can you say that?' I cried.

'He taught me. I got my blood thirst from him, my murdering know-how. Tell me, Rho, how many men has Henry Lowrie killed?'

'Not one.'

'You forgot Barnes and Harris. And — let's see — about nine others after that. Maybe ten. Henry, is it a dozen even? Didn't you tell her?'

I felt sick. There was hatred in his voice. He was holding the gun with his arm stretched full length, pointed like an accuser.

Henry didn't flinch. A sadness greater than I could ever cure filled his eyes. Some message passed from him to Boss.

Boss wavered.

'Wait,' Boss said.

But Henry picked up his own gun from the floor, and the two of them were aiming directly at each other when Applewhite came in.

'What in hell?'

Henry slipped his gun inside his shirt. Boss steadied himself.

'He thinks I put that ball in the old man,' Boss said.

'It was me,' Ap said to Henry. 'I heard the shot, and all I could see was you and him tussling.'

'You thought I couldn't handle him? Look at this!' Henry lifted the sheriff's pale skinny arm. 'It's a dry old stick. He's nothing.'

'I didn't know, Henry. I couldn't see what was happening. I only did it to save you, which don't seem to make you feel grateful.'

'He's going soft,' Boss said. 'He wants to retire home now and play with his wife.'

Ap said, 'Whyn't you just put the gun down?'

'Whyn't you mind your own business?'

'That's what I'm doing, Little Boss. He, Henry, is my business, and so are you. We're all each other's business. You have some other occupation? You have a life of your own maybe?'

Henry said, 'Ap, just leave him alone.'

'After I set him straight. You know what, Boss, I ain't slept at home once in thirty-seven days. But you wouldn't understand that. What's happened to you is you got to liking it too much, because you never known any other life. Never had no woman, no young ones coming up. Everything you got is going into — this.' He pointed at the sheriff, and the blood pooling under Henry's thigh. 'This here is what you love.'

'You did that, Applewhite, and you didn't do it very good, either. Left him maimed and suffering, and now poor Henry can't bear to see it.'

Boss tossed the little jewelry box straight up to the ceiling. Before it even began to fall he fired a shot, and the box blew apart. Across his boots fell rings and lockets and silver earbobs, and a pendant of amethyst on a gold chain.

'For you,' Boss said, kicking the chain across the floor. 'Sell it to the gypsy peddler or give it to my sister for her pretty neck.'

Henry said, 'Pitch your fit later, Boss. This is the damn sheriff of Robeson County dying on our hands. They'll be hunting us to hell and back.'

466

'So let's get going,' Ap said.

'We'll split up and meet at the camp,' Henry said.

'Ap,' Boss said, 'ask him if he doesn't plan on giving himself up. He's going to cut a deal. Ask him.'

'I'm not asking him a goddamn thing,' Applewhite said, pulling the sheriff's watch from his vest.

I went down to the well and drew a bucket of water, and in the shadows cast by the trees under moonlight I looked back at the sheriff's house. How had we come to this? We'd begun by wanting fair play, but now a man of the law lay murdered in his night clothes.

The well gave off the smell of water from a deep place.

'You see now,' Ap said when I brought in the bucket. 'It don't help Henry, you being around when he needs to be thinking. Where's your babies?'

'Home.' I watched him pour a trickle of water across the sheriff's lips, which no longer moved.

'If you want my advice, that's who you need to be watching over.'

I was crying. I said, 'Ap, what will happen?'

'Time goes on. Everybody dies. I don't know no more than that.'

'We fight for nothing?'
'We fight for everything.'

★ ★ ★

The sheriff died.

Warrants were put out for all the Lowrie gang, but the only ones caught were Henderson and Calvin Oxendine. The night of the crime, they had been in Fairmont, where a whiskey caravan was camped. When they came home to their sister's house, Betsy warned them to go into hiding — but they were tired and worn out, and besides, they were innocent. So they went to bed. When they were arrested and taken into custody the next day, the moonshiners who could prove their alibi had disappeared, moved on to some other whiskey crossroads in some other county.

13

Under the swamps and barrens of Robeson County there is no bedrock, and in Drowning Creek no stones. Our fences are wood, our chimneys clay, and a man may plow his whole life without turning up so much as a pebble. So it's not known why, maybe once or twice a year, a peculiar-looking stone is found lying in a field or ditch when there was nothing the day before, as if delivered in the night by a laboring of the earth. Pitted and golden brown like sand turned to iron, these rocks have no name. I call them luckstones or night lemons or dead man's pillows. Most are the size of a hen's egg, but the rarest — most sought, most prized — can be big as a saddle, and whoever finds one saves it, for a tombstone.

Everyone else must settle for a wooden cross, and hope the family's grief will last until someone down the line can afford a granite slab. But who knows if those who come after us will have any money — or memory? It's not wise to count on them. We're at their service, not they at ours; and any scheme we make to bind them is a manacle of thread. Still we go about it, conniving one way or another to cast our will across the ages.

When I was little, I worried my cross would rot, and by and by nobody would know where I lay or that I ever lived. So I was always watching for a luckstone. And then one day Henderson and I found one — a big one, giant beyond our dreams — in a ditch on the Oxendine farm. He spotted it first and told me to keep watch over it while he ran to get his father. I never took my eye off that stone. Not that I really believed it was going anywhere — but luckstones are a mystery, and I thought, well, something that suddenly *appears* might suddenly *disappear*. I stood guard against I didn't know what, watching the stone until Henderson came hurrying back with his father.

But when Mr. Jack looked, he shook his head and said better to leave the thing alone, it was too much to handle — because to own it Henderson would have to bring it home by himself. That was the only way to prove it was rightfully his, meant for him. No other hands could help. And Henderson was a scrawny fourteen-year-old. The luckstone, three feet across and three times the weight of the boy it might be meant for, sat in the bottom of the ditch like a giant old turtle.

Henderson jumped down in there with it anyway. He dug out around it, he shoved and pushed, but he couldn't budge it. After a while Mr. Jack said there were some things you maybe shouldn't try so hard to win, and he went back to the field.

Henderson climbed out and sat by me, disappointed. He'd been sure that stone was meant for him, and I had thought so, too. Even though I saw it at almost the same moment he did, I was weaker. If he had failed, I didn't stand a chance.

All of a sudden he opened his mouth, and out came 'Shall We Gather.' I thought, *He aims to sing it loose!* I half expected the rock to break free and fly up to him, for his voice seemed able to raise any earthbound thing. But after three verses, nothing had happened. The luckstone was unmoved.

He sat there quiet and thinking, and I didn't say anything. Then he got up and headed off toward the end of the cornfield, where the ditch had its shallow starting point.

'You give up, Henderson?' I called, but he paid no attention, and when I was sure he wasn't going to look back, I lowered myself into the sharp, cool smell of dirt and roots, and knelt to put my arms around the stone. I only tried it once, just to find out, just in case it would yield, ready to come with me — and when it didn't, I got out and brushed myself off so he wouldn't know.

Pretty soon I saw Mr. Jack's turpentine mule backing down the ditch. Henderson followed, rubbing the mule's neck and gentling it along until it stopped, belly deep, in front of me. He crawled under the mule, and with a long iron gumscrape he pried up the stone enough to get a survey chain around it, and he dragged it out behind the mule to the Oxendine shed, where it would remain until the time came.

We used to go check on it sometimes, in the musty corner where it lay behind the rabbit traps, waiting. At first he was proud of it. But as time went on he had less to say, and sometimes at the sight of it he plunged into a mood — as anyone might, I guess, to gaze in advance on his own fate like that.

I was like my mother, who hated to see a man troubled in mind, and felt she had to be the cure. That luckstone was weighing too heavy on Henderson. So I made light of it. I told him it just looked like a rough old rock to me, and you could never carve letters in it, and for myself I would prefer a smooth marble shaft with my name and a line of inscription to remember me by, so my mourners would be wrecked by sorrow for years to come and never forget me. I told him

I was thinking also of a winged angel or a lamb on folded feet, or maybe a pyramid of Egypt. He laughed at me, as I had hoped. But we both knew the luckstone was better than any boughten stone.

That was the trouble. Its value was high, and its cost was likely to be the same. Especially for a boy like Henderson. He brooded over the stone as if its pocks and scratches were some lost alphabet with meanings beyond him.

I said maybe he wasn't supposed to have gotten help from a mule, and we should have left the stone where we found it. I suggested he should give it to someone older, who could use it sooner. Henderson said no. I offered to buy it from him — with pennies, with cakes, with everything I owned or a debt to pay him when I grew up. I even begged him to drag it to Three Brides Bridge and drop it over. But he said he couldn't do any of those things because the stone was his.

Years it lay there in the dark, collecting mouse droppings and locust husks. Henderson and I grew up and went our separate ways, until fate threw us together again on the same road following the same man. By then I had forgotten the luckstone, and the marble shaft too. Tombstones, like other things that once seemed so important, had faded out of my mind. I no longer felt the need to be remembered.

If I was to have any memorial at all, it would be my children, bouncy and elastic as trapballs in mind as well as body; and I did not want them ever to grieve on my account. They would find enough to mourn elsewhere, in what Boss used to call the misery of this world.

At the same time, I swore I would never hide that misery from them or give them false hopes. I wanted them to see the world as it was.

* * *

That's why, on the seventeenth of March in 1871, when Sal was four and Del was three and my third had just quickened in me the day before, I woke the children early. They were sleepy and slow, not knowing why we were getting up in the dark.

'Because we're taking a ride on the train this morning,' I said. 'This is a day that will be written in history, and we will be eyewitnesses.'

'Oh, I know what it's going to be,' Sally said.

'Picnic,' said Del. 'Lemonades.'

Sally said, 'No, it's a *hanging*. Johnny

474

Cummings's daddy is going to get hanged today in the jailyard.'

'Where did you hear that?' I said.

'Ida and Liza and Della. Aunt Flora won't let them go see it but I said I knew our ma would let us. Because we ain't noisy like them, we don't behave so ugly.'

'Sal, Del, listen to me. Johnny's daddy was my little best friend when I was a girl. Mr. Oxendine. That's why you're going with me today. Because I loved him.'

They both trusted me. They had no reason to think I would take them anywhere bad. And I was determined they must go, and see this event in case history failed to write it. You can sometimes save what history neglects, if you make sure it's known to children. I wanted this story passed down to someone in years to come, a singer or a poet not born yet, Henderson's heir, who'd know what to do with it.

'Why does he have to get hanged?' Sal said.

'Because there was a crime committed, and he is the one blamed. But he didn't do it.'

'Who did?' Del said.

'Well, they don't know. But Henderson is the one getting punished.'

'No fair,' Del said.

'That's why we're going to Lumberton,' I said. 'We'll be with him, when he dies for someone else's mistake.'

'He'll *die*?' Sally said.

I began to worry that maybe I was wrong, maybe they wouldn't understand anything of it.

'Well, yes, Sal — when a man is hanged, he dies.'

I decided it was all right if they didn't understand. All I wanted was for them to see, and they could understand later.

★　★　★

We started out toward Moss Neck just after dawn. Others joined us along the way, coming out from their hidden houses to meet on the lane just as if it was Sunday. Everybody wore church clothes and some carried Bibles. There were no children except mine. Henderson's sister and mother walked separate from the rest, Betsy holding Ma Christie's elbow.

'Is everybody going?' Sally asked.

'It looks so, doesn't it.'

'We'll see our daddy,' Del said.

'No. We won't see him.'

An extra car had been added to the train for this day. It was packed full, but not like any load of passengers I had ever ridden with before. So quiet. Sal and Del saw the drawn faces, and they sank low in their seats, staring straight ahead. Just before the train started up, Flora got on and made her way back to me, not noticing my children until she was standing by us. We slid over to make room.

'You're *taking* them?' she whispered. 'You could have left them with mine at Mama's. They shouldn't see something like this, it could have a lifetime effect.'

'I hope it will.'

'Where's Henry?'

I took a deep breath. I didn't want to argue with Flora. In the past year I had come to appreciate her and almost to love her. She was just a girl wanting what every girl wants. And even though there was a rebuke in her question — 'Where's Henry?' — I started to love her right then, at that instant, because we were on that train together. I had to love her.

Besides, I felt sorry for her. She was worried her cozy home life might come to an end. Andrew had seen it was not so easy to be a law-abiding citizen when everyone else was in trouble and need. He couldn't turn his back and pretend to be above it all. So he had started sending food to Henry, and sometimes going out to the camp at night. He swore to Flora he wasn't in with the gang, but she saw him losing respect for himself. And she didn't really know whether she wanted to keep him home or let him go.

'Henry went to the bee yards yesterday,' I said. 'If Andrew sees him, ask him to give Henry a message. Say I have important news.'

But I knew it might be weeks before he would come to me. 'Or no, just tell him — by the end of summer he'll have another mouth to feed.'

'Oh, Rho.' Flora wasn't so crazy about having babies any more.

'I'm glad of it.'

'But — well, have you heard anything? I mean, some people are saying Henry's trying to get out of the state. Maybe out of the country.'

'People say a lot of things. That doesn't mean we have to listen.'

'If he goes' — she was staring out the window — 'you know he'll go alone. And then what? Without him what happens to Scuffletown?'

'Flora, if I knew the future you'd be the first I'd tell it to.'

She bit her lip. 'Maybe the two of you are going to take your children and sneak off from the rest of us.'

'I won't do that. I'm raising my children here where they belong. There's no other place I want to be.'

'It's not right to take little ones to a

hanging. And you know a baby in the womb will strangle on its cord when the trap drops.'

'I don't believe that.'

'Let me take your girls to Nelly's until it's over. I don't mind. I don't really want to see it.'

'You have to,' I said. 'We all have to.'

Tears filled her eyes.

'Lean your head on me,' I said. 'You're tired out.'

'Is anybody not? Look around.'

I remembered my first train ride, when the car was full of merriment, a picture of how I thought the world should be.

'The macks look the worst of all,' Flora whispered.

There were only a few of them sitting in our car, the ones who knew Henderson. Catherine Harris sat alone at the front with her head lowered, and I thought she was praying. Six rows back Squire McLean slumped against the window with his hands limp on his knees, palms up, like a beggar without the energy to beg anymore. He saw me, but all he did was nod. I got the same from Miss McCabe and her father in the Ladies' Compartment. But that was all right. It meant something that they were in this car at all, instead of the one ahead of us, where a rowdy crowd was already half drunk.

Through the glass doors I could see men laughing and celebrating.

One of them came back toward us. Between the cars he swayed for a moment, grabbing his hat against the sudden wind. When he opened the door to our car, a whoosh of air blew in, and he stumbled forward — a stranger wearing a Yankee hat and carrying a notepad in one hand. Steadying himself with the other hand, he walked the aisle like an inspector of some kind, and when he neared us, I leaned down to untie Sally's shoe and tie it back again. He passed on by. At the squire's seat he stopped and tapped the old man's shoulder with his notepad.

'Anything to say, sir, to the people of New York City?'

'Who the devil are you?' Mr. McLean said.

'Correspondent of the *Herald*, your honor. Thought you might have a comment to make upon the occasion.'

'I've got no comment on any subject for the *New York Herald* or any other newspaper.'

'But you'll agree with the rest of the respectable citizens of Robeson County that this is a great day of victory. After six years of terror and rampage, justice at last?'

McLean sighed. 'Either you're deaf or

you're a jackass. I repeat, I have nothing to say. Kindly leave me alone.'

'Sure thing,' the newsman said, as if he had heard worse before and didn't really care. Scanning the car, he said, 'You can't tell me if Rhody Lowrie's on this train, I don't guess. The outlaw's wife? The Queen of Scuffletown?'

'Yes, I can tell you.'

'Yeah?'

'She's not.'

'I hear she don't go out in public because half the time she's sporting a black eye. How do you figure it, a beautiful woman putting up with a man who does her like that? I hear he's the Don Juan of the swamps, with women hanging all over him. Fellow in the forward car told me if the wife makes a stink he pops her one. Any truth to that?'

Mr. McLean said, 'Do you carry a gun, sir?'

'A gun? No — '

'I suggest you arm yourself. Someone might think you made up those lies yourself. Henry Berry Lowrie loves his wife. Why do you think he's still here, you fool? He could have gone and started a whole new life by now, somewhere where no one knows his past. He'll never leave her.'

A weasely look came into the eyes of the

reporter, and he jotted a note on his pad. 'So you're saying he's still in Robeson County?'

Squire McLean snatched the pencil and broke it in two. 'Get out of my sight.'

'I guess it's a free country and a free railroad.'

'Look around you, sir, and rethink your position.'

The reporter saw sixty Scuffletown faces turned his way, and half a dozen men already on their feet. He raised both his hands.

'Just inquiring,' he said, and he went back to the other car.

I sat still, with my hands folded on my knees. The train rocked easy, full speed now, flying toward Lumberton.

'Flora, do people really say those things of me and him?'

'Henry never thought of any girl but you, no matter what's said in town.'

'Is he staying here for my sake?'

'Well, I hope so. To leave you here would be to throw you down in a snake run.'

★ ★ ★

In Lumberton we moved as a crowd down the middle of the street from the station to the jailyard. We walked the way some soldiers had come home after the surrender: slow, beaten, with nothing to say. Ahead of us the rowdies ran and sang.

Henderson, Henderson Oxendine,
Send him home in a box of pine.

I held my children's hands tight. The air was chilly, but there were signs of an early spring. Some of the plum trees had just put out buds, white wads with a pink frill at the tip. The oaks were shedding pollen, covering Fourth Street with a fine yellow powder that swirled when a wagon rolled through. Like gold dust, like a blessing, it stuck to our shoes. I buttoned my old coat and pulled my shawl up over my head so no one would know me.

Just when we got to the jail, a guard yelled no more spectators could come into the yard, and he closed the gate. It was flimsy, only two pine rails — it wouldn't have held up under a rush — but no one rushed it. There were young men who might have, but the mood of the whole Indian crowd was set by the old people in it, the grandmothers and grand-fathers who had never caused any trouble or made any complaint, but had lived their lives by the only pattern they knew — farming, working, holding on. In the war they had been neither Union nor Reb, and now were neither Republican nor Democrat — just Baptist and Methodist. But they had come out for Henderson. Nothing could have stopped them from it. In their silence and their sharp old faces there was a power that quieted our young men and seemed to agitate the guard, who was one of the Townsend boys from Back Swamp. He didn't know what to make of it, or what to expect.

People took up stands along the sidewalk, to peer through the gate and fence. Others began climbing onto the roof of the livery stable next door and into the treetops leaning over the yard. Flora hung back, hoping she would not find a place at all. I saw that a number of black people had come, although how they got there I couldn't guess. They hadn't been on the train, they must have walked. Ben Bethea was the only one whose name I knew. He was a Republican now, and the freedmen looked up to him; maybe he had brought them. But why? Henderson was no one to them. They had come for more than that.

An old aunty stopped me and whispered, 'Ain't you her?'

'Who?'

'His wife.'

'He isn't married — '

'Berry's wife I mean.' Others heard her and

turned to look at me with a flash of excitement in their eyes. A younger woman curled two black fingers around Sally's wrist.

I said, 'No, no, I'm not — '

'He'll pay 'em back for this, won't he? He surely will. Henry Berry will make it right. The trump will sound, yes, Lord.'

'I don't know what you mean.'

I dragged the children away. Ahead of me I saw Henderson's mother, Ma Christie, moving straight toward the gate as if she hadn't noticed it was closed. The guard laid a rough hand on her shoulder and held her, but she didn't seem to feel it; her feet kept on walking in place, shuffling, and her eyes were fixed on the platform in the yard and the contraption it held.

She was alone. I don't know what had happened to Betsy, I couldn't see her anywhere, though she'd been with her mother on the train. Mr. Jack hadn't come, he said his heart was hurt, and he wouldn't move out of his porch chair. Virginia Cummings, who was like a daughter to them now, had started out with us but fainted on the road and was carried back.

So I marched forward. I carried Del and pulled Sally along, and I could feel her bumping into people's legs. When I got to the gate I was out of breath and starting to be scared.

'Let go of the old lady,' I said to the guard, that boy younger than me. 'It's her son that's to hang. You needn't fear she'll start a riot. Let her pass through.'

Her hands swatted at his arm as if she couldn't see what was holding her back. She saw nothing but the scaffold.

'Nobody else gets in,' he said.

'You *know* her,' I said. 'She's Christianne Cumbo Oxendine. She bought a nickel of snuff from your daddy's store every Wednesday for thirty years. You can't keep her out, she's come to see her own son die.'

'I don't know her, and I don't know you. Now just back off from the gate.'

'Frank,' I said. 'That's your name. Ma Christie, it's Frank Townsend. Don't you remember him?'

Without even looking at him or at me she mumbled, 'No, Frank's a bitty thing, Mrs. Hannah Townsend's babiest boy.'

That moved him a little, but not enough.

I said, 'What if it was you hanging today, Frank, and your mother scrambled to lay eyes on you one last time?'

But I guess he couldn't imagine himself as Henderson, his mother as Christianne.

'Even if I wanted to let her in,' he said, 'I

486

couldn't. I'm under orders.'

'Can we just stand here, then?'

'Well — '

'Thank you, Frank. I knew you were a good-hearted man. And I appreciate that you don't act afraid of me.'

'Why should I?'

'No reason at all. Sometimes people think I have some kind of power over my husband. They think I tell him what to do — what houses to go to at night, to get me rings and bracelets. But the truth is, Henry Berry's his own boss. These rings are just Gypsy trinkets. But he does like for people to treat me nice. He gets mad if he hears I've been slighted.'

All it took was Henry's name — the *cutthroat demon*. Frank Townsend let go of Christianne, and he opened the gate just wide enough so we could slip through. I hadn't told him a single lie.

Christianne marched a straight line through the several dozen men who had been let in, mostly the upper element of Lumberton, the bank men, the newspaper editor, preachers and merchants — the kind of citizens whose duty it was to witness hangings while their wives sipped tea at home and waited for the report. It wasn't proper for a lady to go to a hanging — much less bring children. But the men in the jailyard ignored

487

the big slow Indian woman in her heavy black shoes and rusty black skirt, and the smaller one in an army coat with a shawl over her head, and those two little urchins. Scuffle-town women would go where ladies did not. The men paid no notice.

And Christianne didn't pay them any. She plowed on toward the front row, elbowing her way into a spot between the mayor and the newspaper editor. I thought her the bravest woman I'd ever known, even when I saw she was breathing as fast and shallow as a bird in a net.

'Ma Christie,' I said, coming up behind her. 'Let me stand with you.'

She looked at me in alarm, as if she'd never seen me before, and I realized how frightened she was. But that didn't make her any less courageous.

'It's Rhody,' I said.

'I know who you are,' she snapped.

Maybe she blamed me for what was happening to Henderson. Some did, especially among the Oxendines. I didn't care, they had to blame someone. It was a burden I could bear.

'And your little grand-niece and grand-nephew,' I added.

'Sally and Delaware?' she said, looking down at them in surprise.

I was afraid she would add, *Are you crazy, take them away from this place.*

She touched the tops of their heads, and her mind seemed to wander.

'Virge Cummings had two boys for Henderson,' she said.

'Yes, James and John.'

She was not wandering. In her green eyes there was a hard need and a clear purpose — and she wagged her finger in my face.

'You tell yours to tell Henderson's someday, what they saw here. And to tell their children too. Do you understand me? You *do* that.'

'Yes, ma'am,' I said.

She turned back toward the scaffold, frowning. It had been put up the day before in the center of the yard, with a high platform and a tall pole with a crossbeam, and a rope so new I could smell it, a summer smell like fresh fodder. Under the platform a small dray stood, ready to haul away.

Guards were yelling, 'Get the Scufflers off the roofs.' But what did they think we could have done? They had guns and we did not.

Henderson's mother, still looking straight ahead, said to me, 'Well, is your husband going to show up or not? Is he going to do something, or is he just going to let Henderson die?'

I was afraid the mayor and the editor had heard her, and would take a closer look at me. But they were drifting away from us, and no one was listening.

I had to tell her the truth. 'The reward on Henry is up to twenty thousand dollars,' I said. 'There are too many people here — any drunkard with a gun could collect it. Even a friend would be tempted. That's more money than a man could earn in two hundred years. And, Ma Christie, there is just nothing, anyway, that Henry — or anyone — could do now.'

She nodded and turned back toward the scaffold. After a minute, she took Sally's other hand, and we stood lined up like that, the four of us, staring at it.

'Ma, what is that thing?'

'It is the gibbet, Sal.'

'What for?' Del said.

'She already told you,' Sally said.

'You be brave, now,' I said, 'and keep your eyes open, for James could not come today, and you're the ones who will see it for him and tell him later on when you are bigger.'

Sal said, 'I'm brave all the time.'

But Del whimpered. 'Bellyache,' he said. His skin was cool and clammy. 'Pick up me,' he said, raising his free arm, so I lifted him to my hip.

I heard Ma Christie gasp, and I knew they had brought Henderson out. Everyone was looking in the same direction. But when I looked, I hardly recognized him, because he appeared to be so healthy. In prison he had gotten better food than he ever had in his years of lying out.

It would have been easier if he had been thin and sickly. But there he was, a handsome young man twenty-six years old, no hat, hair blowing across his eyes. I heard a catcall from someone in the yard, but after that there was no sound but the train pulling out for Wilmington, on schedule.

He saw his mother, and he broke out in a smile. A peculiar joy crept over me. Henderson was at his best. He had come into his full strength, his spirit was strong, and I knew I had been right to come, to bring my children to see him. He had the dignity he'd been growing toward all his life.

I thought there would be some speeches or something of a ceremony. But there was only the prisoner, and the hangman, who wore a hood showing his eyes through two slits; and the new sheriff, Roderick McTeer.

'Say your piece,' McTeer said, but his voiced sounded a little thick.

Oh yes, they were starting to see now. Even

McTeer. And if Henderson made the right speech, no one could fail to see it — innocence bright as the shining angels. Not just Henderson's innocence but everyone's, if they would only choose it. Even McTeer. It seemed so simple to me. Henderson had it in his power to lift a veil and show the way. He could turn aside a coming storm.

He stepped forward on the platform. My heart beat in my throat. His eyes were full of knowing.

'My last words are, goodbye and God bless you.'

But that wasn't enough. I started to cry out to him, *Reveal all!* This was his chance. I didn't care whether he called for peace or for fighting, I only wanted a message. He was like a man who reaches a hilltop while the rest are still mired below; he should tell us what he could see from there. He should tell us where we'd been, where we stood, and what might lie ahead.

'And I'll sing two hymns.'

The first was 'Amazing Grace,' the slave-trader's salvation. At the first note, those childhood days came back to me, the boy I fished with, his dreams of preaching, his longing to be called.

His amen was no more than a whisper.

Then he raised both arms and spoke to the sky.

'The second one is 'And Can I Yet Delay.''

That was Boss's favorite.

> *Though late, I all forsake;*
> *my friends, my all resign;*
> *Gracious Redeemer, take, oh,*
> *take and seal me ever thine!*

But I could hear him saying he didn't want to go. Saying how hard it was to tear away, saying it hurt, to go to God.

Del started to moan, and twined his arm around my neck.

'Sleepy,' he said.

'All right,' I said to him. He hooked his chin over my shoulder, with his face buried behind my ear, under my shawl; and he wrapped his legs around my waist.

McTeer left the platform. I doubted he'd heard anything at all. Some of the men in the yard turned away, but in the trees and on the rooftops and all along the fence, no one moved a muscle. The hangman tied a blindfold over Henderson's face, but Henderson pulled it away just before the noose was put around his neck. I was afraid he was hoping against hope, looking around for Henry and Boss. But his eyes fell on my son and me, and stayed.

And I was the one who started hoping then, searching the trees and the rooftops, looking for my husband. He might be there in disguise or hidden behind a cart, ready to leap to the platform. Wasn't he there, wasn't he coming? But I couldn't find him.

I turned back to the scaffold. I saw the second rope, the one that ran taut from a ring in the trap up to the gibbet, passing over the short beam and down along the upright to a clamp, which held it against the wood on a level with the slits in the executioner's black mask. I saw the hatchet rise, glint in the sun, then swing sharp, slice the rope, bite deep and lodge in the pine. The trap fell, and Henderson dropped down.

I thought something had gone wrong, because it seemed to me that nothing much had happened. It wasn't a far distance to fall. There was no crash of noise and no outcry. The New York man scribbled on his paper. A wasp settled on his hat and bobbed along the brim. The mayor crossed his arms. Del traced with his finger the curl of my ear.

Christianne shifted from one foot to the other but never took her eyes from her son, and after a while Dr. McCabe climbed the steps and looked at him, and they cut him down. When he hit the dray, there was only a thudding sound, because he was barefooted.

The eastbound train came in.

They gave his mother his boots and clothes and the contents of his pockets: a tiny Baptist hymnbook and a piece of bone tied together with some dry leaves and twigs. The dray was hauled to the station where the coffin waited, made by Henderson's uncle Jesse; and the coffin was loaded onto the car with us. I sat with Ma Christie next to it for a while, but then I went back to our seats.

'You didn't even look, Del, like you were supposed to,' Sally was saying. 'You hid your head like a baby.'

Del's eyes were the color of little luckstones.

Sally would always have sharp memories of that day — the people in the trees, the white bone from Henderson's pocket, and the yellow dust on her shoes. She would tell herself the story over and over again until it was like a printed page, unchangeable, and then tell it to the Cummings boys. But Del said he only remembered me, the smell of my wool collar and the curtain my shawl made falling around his face. He forgot almost everything else; I think it was too much for him. In order to be brave, a boy learns to forget what might otherwise break his heart. Even as we rode the train toward home, Del was forgetting.

'Mr. Oxendine didn't cry,' Sally said. 'He went down through the hole and the rope choked him.'

'Ma cried,' said Del.

'No she didn't either. You were the only one.'

'She cried inside her neck.'

I sat down. Just then there was a rolling under my ribs, like a river log making a quarter turn, slow and deliberate. My next child, my Polly.

★ ★ ★

Some weeks later the caravan man appeared before a judge, swore he had been with Henderson and Calvin Oxendine in Fairmont the night of Reuben King's death. And Calvin was released.

Henderson's sons would go on to start big families of their own, and even if they never bore his name (for he had not lived long enough to marry, and the boys would always be Johnny and James Cummings, and all their boys would be named Cummings) — still, they all knew they were *Henderson Oxendine's line*. Johnny and James stood by their mother when the luckstone was rolled onto the grave at the Sand Cut burying

496

ground, to be Henderson's own and only marker until years later when another Cummings might have a granite headstone set there, and inscribed.

But as long as the old stone stays, I will take my children to that burying ground every year, and then I'll take my grand-children. We'll stand under the trees and I'll tell them, 'The old ones are all around us. They were a quiet people. A man had a man's place and a woman had a woman's place, and they worked themselves to death for a crop of puny corn. But they were strong: I can't tell you where they came from. They were just here.'

It is important to tell children everything you know, even if it's not the whole story. Someday someone will put it all together.

'This is the grave of Henderson Oxendine, last man hanged by the state of North Carolina. He was loyal to Henry Berry and never betrayed him, not even to get rich and save his own life. These trees are saddletree poplars. This rock is like no other, but grows in the earth for a thousand years and then when the time is right it rises, and is found.'

★   ★   ★

North Carolina thought the Lowrie war would be over after Henderson was hanged. Public sentiment would turn against the outlaws. Citizens would no longer help or hide them, and Henry would surrender to save his neck. But North Carolina forgot one thing. Citizens sometimes don't like the hanging of an innocent man.

Even some of the planters were hoping that the militia captains riding every night would lose their way in the swamps and go home empty-handed.

For Andrew, the hanging was a last straw. He packed a rucksack, kissed his wife and daughters goodbye, and became the full-fledged member he had once so longed to be. What surprised us all was that when Andrew went out to the camp, Henry put him in charge. And Henry came home. No one would think of looking for him in his own house, he said, and he wanted to be with me when the baby came.

We named her Nell, and called her Polly.

14

Now, Henry wanted me close to him all the time.

He carried himself like a man who's been hurt but won't say so. If I was out of sight too long, he came looking for me, and at night his hold on me never loosened. But nothing could refresh him — not sleep, not food, not me. And least of all the new baby. Every time he held Polly in his arms, new worries occurred to him. It got so bad I tried to keep her out of Henry's sight.

Some days he hardly spoke a word but sat and watched me work, as if all the fire was gone out of him. But other days he was so stirred up he couldn't be still. He would go out behind the house to shoot at trees, wearing guns the way Steve used to, five at a time.

I said, 'It wasn't your fault, you know. They were going to hang somebody no matter what.'

He brushed me off.

'It's over and done. No need to talk about it,' he said.

I felt over and done myself. The children

sometimes got no kind word from me for days on end, and I could see them learning to do for themselves without even thinking to ask me. Every night I dreamed about Henderson.

We lived on.

Men were elected who favored us, but others who hated us were elected too. And all of them were trying to figure out what to do about Henry Berry Lowrie. The Democratic Party men wanted him arrested and hanged, but they feared that would cause rioting among those in the swamps and backwoods who loved him. A rumor rose in Hestertown that the Republicans would run him for Congress, and when Margaret told me I laughed out loud. The truth was, that party had broken its promises to us and to the freed people, and wanted to be rid of Henry any way possible. The more he was loved, the more he was hated.

And all the news was lies. Henry had been pardoned, Henry had been poisoned. He was in Washington meeting the president and in Missouri robbing banks.

We couldn't trust anyone. We were on the watch at all hours, with a lookout in the woods and dogs to warn us. A dozen times we woke and had to run from our own house — and once, when the alarm came too late and someone was already coming up the step, we used our trapdoor to crawl out the back and into the woods. We heard a spy would be sent in to win our confidence by pretending to be a schoolteacher, but that could have been another lie to discourage us, like the report we heard of Applewhite's death. They said he had been shot and killed, and we didn't learn for months that it wasn't so.

Sally grew shy and Del sullen. The baby had trouble sleeping. They had never known the kind of life where home is safe; instead they were used to being snatched up and carted off in the middle of the night. They knew not to ask questions when we said to come quick.

'I declare your children are the best behaved I ever saw,' said a mack lady on the train to Lumberton one day. 'They don't raise a ruckus like some do.'

I nodded to her, and I pulled them all close to me. Fear will go a long way to making children meek and shut-mouthed. I promised myself that someday I'd teach them to act up, to make their presence known. I couldn't do it yet because it was dangerous, but that was my goal for a future date. I would teach them to speak out.

Meanwhile I tried to make light of the danger when I could, for their sake and

Henry's too; but children know when you are pretending, and so do men.

★ ★ ★

One night he was so restless, he was running in his sleep. His legs would shoot straight out and then draw up again. I tried to wake him, just to pull him back into whatever comfort I could give.

'Oh, please, Henry, wake up. Don't torture yourself so.'

He sat up, but I didn't think he was all the way awake. He got out of bed and lit a candle, then went to the peg where his clothing hung, fumbling with his shirt.

'What are you looking for?'

I am sure he didn't hear me. From his shirt pocket he pulled out a knotted handkerchief and untied it, spreading it open on the table. By the light of the candle, I saw bobbing in the middle of that white square a living bee. Henry picked it up and, holding it pinched between two fingers, he stretched out his bare left arm and applied the bee to the inside crook of his elbow. The stinger arched and sprang and went in, and Henry's head dropped back.

'Stay with me,' he said. 'Never leave me.'

I wasn't quite sure he meant me. I helped

502

him back into bed, where he slept a good long deep sleep, and in the morning — even though I didn't ask any questions — he said the sting was a remedy. And he did look better, brighter-eyed and rested.

*   *   *

It was another early spring. Green came before it was due, running the risk of a late freeze. In the scuppernongs, nubs of green popped out on the trunk of the vine, and fernheads pushed their coiled heads up through the sandy soil of the pine barrens. Something told me the time was ripe for mending my fences.

I went to my mother.

At the edge of the field I called out as usual, and Daddy came with sweets for the children. We talked a minute and then I said I wanted to go inside to see her.

'I don't believe you ought to do that,' he said. 'She won't be ready for it.'

'Maybe she will. You all play out here awhile and let me go in.'

Cee was sitting on her bench by the chimney. Still stubborn, she showed no sign of seeing me at all when I came in. But I was going to love that big old woman even if I had to fight her to do it.

'Hello, Mama.'

She had that hard, stony face that women find for themselves when nothing has worked out as they hoped, and they want it known hope is no longer welcome.

'Mama, I've come to say I'm sorry, and I want you and me to go back to how we were before.'

Her mouth was set, and I thought she might not say anything. But after a minute she cleared her throat.

'And how were we before?' she said.

'We tried to keep each other happy.'

'It sure didn't work.'

'No, but I don't guess that means it was the wrong thing to do.'

She folded and unfolded her hands in her lap.

'I made a big mistake and it broke my heart,' she said. 'I can't go back.'

'What mistake?'

'I put all my eggs in one basket.'

'Well, I've done the same then. And I expect it will break my heart, too, but what other choice did we have?'

'You had other choices,' she said.

'I'm not talking about my husband. I'm talking about my children.'

She raised her eyes to me.

'You taught me that,' I said. 'You were

fierce, remember? You were going to keep us from all harm, no matter what. I'm so sorry, Mamma, that we went and got ourselves into the trouble you warned us against, I'm sorry we didn't do like you wanted. But we couldn't help it.'

'Rhoda — '

'Don't cry. No, you can't, because we've got too much to cry about and it would take up all our time.'

'I was wrong to say those things about him,' she said.

'I don't think you said anything that didn't turn out to be true.'

'I just was hoping you wouldn't have the sorrow — he was bound for trouble, because of the way he is — because he wouldn't ever bow down to anyone — and it's going to be bad, isn't it? It's going to end so bad.'

'No, it won't. I promise.'

'You don't think so? But they have got the reward money in cash now, counted in piles and ready to pay out! Someone's going to turn on him. It could be someone you trust — '

'Everything will be all right. You have my word. Look, here's Sally and Del.'

They were peeping around the corner of the door. No one has ever been able to resist those two — brown-eyed Sally, and Del with his Lowrie eyes of gold-flecked green. They caused hearts to melt. Cee reached out her hand to them, and they came in.

★ ★ ★

When we got home, Henry was standing in the doorway looking out, and I wrapped my arms around his waist.

'I've decided on something,' he said. 'I want you to come with me to the hives.'

'Right now?'

He had never asked me to go with him to the hives before.

'Nectar's running. There'll be work to do before the first honey-flow. Cleaning boxes and maybe rehiving.'

'All right,' I said.

We walked the children to Flora's and then set off toward Back Swamp. He kept his bee boxes in different places so the honey would take the flavor of what was growing in that one spot. The swamp honey had a taste of tupelo and cypress, woods honey of pine. But there was one moving hive, which he carried from place to place, wherever flowers were blooming.

'I made you something — a gift,' he said as we crossed a muddy branch on a two-log bridge. 'It's not much. I wish I had something better. You've gone so long without the pretty things a woman's meant to have.'

'What have I ever wanted?'

'Everything under the sun, I expect.'

'I never asked for anything.'

'Just the same, you have wanted. Not trinkets and such, but other things. Books, pictures. One time you wanted to go to the Atlantic Hotel in Wilmington and hear a band play music.'

'Oh, that was just a fancy. I didn't really want to go.'

'Well, I wanted to take you.'

He started walking faster, with his eyes fixed beyond what could be seen in the lane ahead.

We cut through McNair's field and then struck off through the cane behind the Sampsons. I fell back a few steps, to let him have the lead and be alone.

He had always been alone. He always would be, even in the records of history. He would be written down as a common bandit, and the papers would call him the King of Scuffletown, in that snide tone making fun of him, meaning King of Nowhere. It angered me more than I can say, to think of that. I'd rather have saved him from ridicule than from death itself. What I wanted was for him to be honored, as a man who stood for justice in a time and place where nobody else did. Anyone can do that, but almost no one does. It is a well-known path to ruin, and everyone who ever tried it has been mocked and vilified.

I heard an odd sound as we walked, a low noise that came and went. It would stop a second or two and then return, growing just a little louder every time. I tried to figure out where it came from. I was about to ask Henry if he heard it when suddenly I knew.

This was something no one would believe, and no one but me would ever hear — Henry Lowrie humming. What thought or memory could have lifted his spirits, I didn't know, but he was humming along like a man without a care. Except there was no melody, only a kind of purring sound. By and by, it grew so loud it was no longer a hum but a rich, rumbling droning from deep inside, almost a cry or a moan, but not sad. Not a lament.

He came to a stop and raised both his arms high, with the moan continuing.

I remember Clelon, howling and throwing his arms up when he couldn't make himself understood. But Henry's moan was steady with purpose. He knew what he was doing.

Then I saw his arms beginning to turn black in patches. The patches spread and grew together until both arms and his back too were covered with a pelt that seemed to quiver and twitch.

It was bees. Bees everywhere, covering him, a mantle of bees.

His hum faded and theirs rose, until he and they were singing the same. When he turned to face me, he looked like no man I knew. I would not have recognized him. Only his eyes were visible, the rest of him was crawling with bees.

He raised a hand to signal me not to speak.

The only thing I could think at the time was, those bees were greeting him. He had called to them, and they had come. But they could have killed him if they'd wanted to. And when I think back to it now, I know he was showing me a secret of safety. *Let your guard down, and you will be guarded. Leave yourself open, and a grace will come.*

There were other outlaws, men who could not make themselves a place in the new Union for one reason or another — maybe they were Rebels who wouldn't surrender, or people like us, fooled by the Union's promises and then left out in the cold, or maybe just wild gunmen who got a taste of war and couldn't quit. But all those outlaws rode off somewhere and hid. Henry stayed home. That whole year after Henderson died,

Henry stayed with us. The newspapers said he was hard to find, but he wasn't. He went to church, rode the trains, gave a speech at Union Chapel school. One time he went hunting and a dog belonging to Oakley McNeill fell in with him and treed a raccoon, which Henry then shot. But since game was rightly due to the dog owner and not the shooter, Henry delivered the raccoon to Oakley that night, and took no guard or lookouts with him. The McNeills — or anyone from anywhere around — could have killed him easy.

He lowered his arms, and the bees stopped moving altogether. They looked stunned, barely clinging to his shirt, gathered into clumps like sheep's wool — and some dropped to the ground where they lay in a trance or turned in circles.

'What's happened to them?'

'I gentled them. They've done my bidding.'

'But why?'

'Because they are mine.'

He closed his eyes, breathing deep.

'But from now on they'll be yours,' he said. 'This hive I'm giving to you. I want you to care for them.

One bee flew, and then another, and they began swarming to the box, which was set on a tree stump four yards off the trail. But a single stumbling bee wobbled up Henry's neck and onto his upper lip.

His eyes were still closed. The bee did not move, but poised waiting. He opened his mouth and she entered, and his mouth closed.

It was a trick beekeepers can learn. But there was something else, too, a kind of daring love. She was in his mouth for a long time, until he picked her out and let her fly from his open palm.

He pointed to the bees that now covered the hive.

'There's the present I said I made for you,' he said. 'A glass hive.'

It was like any other hive, a box with a hinged top, except that it was made of windowglass, both the walls and the frames for the combs inside. You could see through it and watch the workings of the bees; and the bees could see out.

He brought me up close to them, and he spoke to them.

'You have worked for me,' he said to them. 'Now work for her.'

* * *

That night when we went to bed, he didn't put out the lamp right away.

'I have figured out what must happen now,' he said.

'What is it?'

'If we decide to leave Robeson County, it can't be by train. All the stations are guarded. We can't go by wagon, the whole county is watching for us, wanting to claim the reward.'

'I'm sure there are people who would help us.'

'None outside the county.'

'So you mean we must stay.'

'I can't do that either. As long as I'm here, the world's at war with Scuffletown. They won't let it be. But if I was to die — '

'Don't say that.'

'It's the only way.'

'I won't listen to it. No, not to any talk of dying at your own hand. I won't.'

'Rhoda, I'm going to need your help.' He took my face in his hands. 'Here's what I'm saying. We'll make it look like I'm dead. We'll make everyone believe it, even in the settlement. Then the trouble will be over, there'll be no more reward, and people can live in peace.'

'But you won't be dead?'

'We'll be alive and well, you and me both.'

'Where?'

'Anywhere. Tennessee — Kansas — California — We'll change our names. Stay moving till no one's looking for me anymore, then find us a good little farm and start all over again, like we just got married.'

I hadn't heard such energy in his voice since the old days before his father died. In the lamplight his face was the handsomest it had ever been, the black hair pushed back from his forehead, his eyes all lit with this idea of making an escape to some untroubled part of America.

'It might work,' I said.

'It will work.'

'But I couldn't go with you right away. People would get suspicious. I'd have to wait awhile.'

'Yes, and then after things quiet down, you can join me. Meanwhile, you can make a crop of honey and have enough money to live on until I send for you.'

I was breathless, knowing the odds were against us but letting myself speculate. *Maybe. Just maybe.*

Then and there, lying side by side, we started plotting his death.

'You need an eyewitness,' I said. 'Somebody who'll say he saw you die, but it has to be someone they'd never doubt. It can't be one of us. And then you need a way to get out of the county in secret. And — why are you smiling at me?'

'You're a smart thing.'

'And tell Boss,' I said. 'We'll need his help.'

'Boss won't like this plan.'

'He might not like it, but he'll help us anyway.'

But we agreed the others couldn't be told. Later they'd know, but for now the fewer people who were in on it, the better the plan would work.

He thought he could also get help from the camp of Federal soldiers still stationed on the river bank, due to pull out any day. A lieutenant there had once offered to be a go-between if Henry ever wanted to turn himself in. We decided he should go that night, and tell the lieutenant he wanted to move out with the troops when they withdrew.

'And if I don't get back by morning, I want you to meet me at Tom's, early. Bring the children with you.'

★ ★ ★

I didn't fall asleep until after midnight. At the back of my mind was a growing fear. Suppose we did escape from North Carolina to start over somewhere else? New names would not disguise us very well, and the hills of Tennessee could not hide us forever. With a

514

wife and children, he would be found.

I must have had a low fever, for I woke with a sick taste in my mouth and clammy skin. But the cause might have been the decision that had come to me while I slept. It wasn't one that would have come to me by day, but I didn't question it because I felt it had risen from deep down, from the earth itself, from the past and from the dead. I got the children dressed, and we set off to Tom's when the sun was just lifting above the ledge of clouds packed down against the horizon. Along the way, I told them what I decided.

'We belong here,' I said. 'North Carolina needs Henry Lowrie.'

But the truth is not something that surprises children. I might as well have said the creek will run and the cock will crow. Polly dropped into sleep in my arms, and the older two tramped along the ruts of the lane, kicking up sand. Overhead the wild grape twined. About us was the luster of Robeson County, morning light stretched thin, black crow on a fencepost, last year's broom grass red under this year's green. In my lifetime all my strongest urges of love or grief or wild fury had come to me in the out-of-doors, under this very sky. What flooded me now was not love and the other rages but *home*. There was nowhere else for me.

We could come up with another plan of some kind. I'd think of something. Applewhite had lived safe in the swamps for years when the law was after him as a runaway. We could go on the way we had been living, at least for a while longer, and see if things got better.

At Tom Lowrie's cabin, his wife, Frances, was cooking breakfast, and she hurried us inside. Her boy, Orlin, stood guard outside with a shotgun, his hard little eyes looking eighteen instead of eight. Another boy who had seen too much. If I raised Del in a western state, maybe he would never get those stony eyes — but then what would he know of himself?

Flora came with her three girls, and Steve's wife, Cath, with hers, but none of us knew why we were there and we didn't talk about it, just busied about with food and children until Orlin came running in.

'It's them.'

Frances looked out and said, 'Oh, Lord. Preserve our souls.'

'What is it, Frances?' I said.

'They have gone and done something.'

They came hollering and hooting like they once used to but had not in many years — slapping each other's shoulders with their caps, rough-housing the way men do when something has happened so good they can't believe it. Tom grabbed Orlin up and hugged him and kissed him, and then went for Frances and spun her around.

'Guess what we got, Frannie. Guess!'

'I don't know.'

'Name the best thing you could wish for.'

'A pardon,' she said.

'No, we don't need one! We got a *safe*. And it's full. Tell them how much it came to, Henry, after you got done counting.'

Henry sat down at the table with all the rest of them crowding around — Boss, Andrew, Steve, Tom, Applewhite. I got him a cup and poured hot coffee into it, and he didn't say anything until after he had taken some.

'It's a good bit of money,' he said.

'How much?' Flora asked.

'Don't tease,' I said to him. 'Just say it out.'

'Yes, well — it's twenty thousand.'

Cath covered her mouth with her hands and Flora burst into tears. Frances thanked God for blessing us.

Twenty thousand dollars. We had been living on the six dollars a month we got by selling honey and scuppernong wine.

'Where is it?' Flora said.

'Where'd it come from?' I said.

Little Orlin was the only one at the table not beaming at the thought of wealth beyond our wildest dreams. He didn't believe, or maybe he had never learned to hope. I looked for Del and saw him shrunk back in a corner, scared to death because he had never seen grown men and women lose themselves in joy.

'Where'd you hide it?' Flora said.

'A good place,' Andrew said. 'Henry's the only one who knows the spot.'

Flora said, 'There isn't any good place for that much money, Andrew. A digger will sniff it out and dig it up. You need to put a guard over it. You need to watch it day and night — '

'It's going to be all right,' Henry said. 'It won't be found.'

I wished I was alone with him. I longed for his smell, and his skin on mine, and his kissing. I kept watching him, waiting for a chance to get him off somewhere alone and tell him we couldn't run away. The boys were drinking brandy now, and someone took out a banjo. They wanted to say that number over and over again.

'Twenty thousand. Twenty thousand, Henry. Did you know it would be so much?' Tom said.

'He knew,' Boss said. 'He planned it out,

nothing left to chance. That's why it went so smooth.'

'It wasn't smooth,' Henry said.

'No, you can't call it smooth when you leave the goods behind,' Ap said. 'A whole other safe, dumped in the middle of the street! But at least it turns out we dumped the right one. When that big mule threw hisself forward and the dray didn't budge, I said let's just take the sheriff's safe and leave the hardware-store safe behind. Why would Mr. McLeod be holding more than a few dollars anyway? But Henry says no, dump the sheriff's and keep McLeod's. How'd you know which one, Henry?'

'He thinks a step ahead of them,' Boss said. 'They thought we'd go after the sheriff's safe, so they put their money in McLeod's back office instead, but Henry's too smart for them.'

'That's a once-in-a-lifetime sight, Orlin,' Tom said to his boy. 'That many greenbacks in one place. When we blew the door off, we didn't believe what we saw.'

'Hell, it's a never-in-a-lifetime sight for most,' Steve said.

'Mr. Henry, did you expect it would be so much?' Orlin said.

'I had a guess.'

I'd never heard anyone call him Mr. Henry,

and it jarred me. 'Mister' was for the older generation of men. But then, Orlin was the younger generation. He reminded me of Boss, or Boss long ago — a boy of promise, whose chances were slipping away. Henry had said he was bright and could make a success of himself, and the men had started giving him little jobs, keeping watch or bearing messages. I could tell from the way Orlin looked at Henry, he would have followed him to the ends of the earth.

'Still,' Applewhite said, 'I don't know why they'd have it in cash. Any man who's got twenty thousand to spend is a man who writes a bank check. Unless it might be on a gambling debt.'

'It's the reward money,' I said.

Steve rubbed his head and said, 'She could be right.'

Applewhite frowned. 'I bet so. They're offering twenty thousand for Henry Lowrie dead or alive.'

'So what?' Boss said. 'I say that makes it better. He collects his own reward.'

'And I say we use it to move out now,' Tom said. 'Maybe that's not what we want to do, maybe we'd like to stay where we have always been, but I say it's time to go.'

'Well, we got the means to do it right,' Steve said. 'We can hire good horses and new wagons, and take plenty of provisions.'

'How soon can we be ready?' Ap said.

'A week, maybe less.'

'Make it less,' Applewhite said. 'Three days.'

They started talking about what route we would follow, how long a journey it would be. No one mentioned the possibility that we wouldn't be allowed to leave, but everyone was aware that might be the case.

'We'll go at night,' Steve said. 'South into the Marion District, where we know places to stay, then west to Georgia. Alabama, Mississippi, Texas. We'll find people along the way who if they don't know us will at least know where we come from and why. We'll make our way to somewhere better just like everyone has always done when it didn't work out for them in the place they started.'

Excitement spread around the table. I saw Henry lean forward, look once at me, and then push his chair back.

'Come on, Orlin,' he said. 'Let's get some air.'

Sally came up to lean on my leg and I put my hand on her head. 'I don't want to go west, Ma,' she whispered.

I thought of Allen Lowrie and the words he once said when I was a girl on his front porch. 'Stay in North Carolina,' he told me.

And now I saw his reason. The people here were ours, and I loved them more than I could say. Escape would be treachery. But maybe it was different for Henry. He had stayed in North Carolina as long as he humanly could, and done for it all that he could, and now he was backed into a corner.

Outside, a gun went off.

No one thought anything of that. A gunshot wasn't unusual. Maybe Henry had shot a squirrel, or maybe he was showing Orlin how to use the pistols.

But then Orlin appeared in the doorway, pale and sick-looking.

'He fell.'

'Who? Henry?' Tom said.

The child looked frantically from one of us to the next, hoping someone would tell him that what he'd seen was not as bad as it looked.

'Who fell, honey?' asked Frances.

'Mr. Henry. He's bleeding out of the neck.'

Boss was the first one out of his chair, and I was so close behind him I pushed him through the door.

I saw Henry lying in blood.

'Get McCabe,' Boss yelled to Tom. 'Steve — Andrew — Ap — someone must have shot him from the woods. Track them down. Somebody take Orlin back inside. Keep all those children inside!'

Boss and I knelt on either side of Henry.

'Henry!' I said. There was more blood than I had ever seen, and somehow his jaw seemed soft with torn flesh.

'Don't make him talk,' Boss said.

'Henry, say something. Are you really shot?'

Boss said, 'Keep your mouth shut, Rhoda.'

'Oh, my God, look, he's really shot.'

Boss said low, 'Henry, tell her to shut up.'

And Henry opened his eyes.

'How bad is it?' Flora called, and he closed his eyes again.

'We need something to stop the blood, Flora,' Boss called. 'Anything.'

'Why did you go and do this *now*?' I whispered.

Boss answered, 'Because Orlin's here.'

And Orlin was a perfect witness. He would be believed because he would truthfully tell what he'd seen.

'I'll get Tom's ox and cart,' Boss said. 'Bandage him up.'

The newspaper spread the word:

'Henry Berry Lowrie was apparently killed in an accident at the home of his brother Tom Lowrie. An eyewitness has been examined by the sheriff and found to be trustworthy since he is a child and can have no purpose in falsifying his account. He says Henry Lowrie was carrying a shotgun when he stumbled and fell at the edge of the porch, whereupon the gun accidentally fired, both barrels discharging into the victim's chin from below. However, the body has not been found, and it is supposed that the family have buried it in the vicinity of Back Swamp or Turkey Branch, as is their custom. In the absence of a corpse, the reward for the capture of Lowrie has not been withdrawn.'

But no one ever saw that wound up close. It was made of deer blood and entrails. I wrapped Henry's head and neck in bandages, which quickly became blood-soaked. Boss and I took him in the cart as far as Turkey Branch, where Henry climbed out.

He stood there looking like a bloody specter. Boss laughed. They both thought it was comical.

'I don't like seeing you that way,' I said. And then I fell to pieces crying.

'I'm fine. Oh, Rho, come on, look here. I don't have a scratch.'

'It's not just the blood.'

'What, then?'

'Henry — I can't go with you.'

He didn't believe me. 'We planned it this way. You wanted to go.'

'I changed my mind. I can't.'

'Now, yes, you can — you're a strong girl, the strongest I've ever known, and you can manage this. The traveling might be hard on you, but we'll have some help — the U.S. Army is going to see us all the way to Virginia.'

'I don't mean it's too hard. I mean I've decided I'm going to stay here. I'm going to keep the children here.'

Henry looked up into the tops of the pines.

'You don't really mean it, do you, Rho?'

'I do. I'm not leaving.'

'Then I'll stay with you.'

'No — I want you to go. And I want you to take Boss.'

'Why?'

'Because, don't you see? You think you're saving Scuffletown — but the truth is, the men you leave behind are going to be killed.'

'That's nonsense.'

'No, she's right,' Boss said. He had moved off to stand away from us, but he turned his head and said, 'After the troops leave Robeson, any member of the Lowrie gang who's still here will be dead inside a year. If not hanged, then shot on the road some night. There won't be a one of us left standing.'

'So take Boss with you, Henry, and both of you go.'

He leaned back against a pine. He unwound the bloody bandages and tried to wipe his face clean.

'All right. For now. But you'll join us later, Rhoda. I'll have my wife and children with me. Is that clear?'

'I'll join you.'

★ ★ ★

We had another death to plan.

'It has to be different,' Boss said. 'So no one will connect it to Henry's.'

He was the only one of us who had much enthusiasm for the second death, his own.

'You could just drown,' I said.

'I'm starting to wonder if you want my life saved at all. And if so, why.'

'Because I remember you. I remember what you were and what you dreamed of being, and I believe that if you can start over in a new place with Henry teaching you, you'll remember those things.'

And I did believe that. He had the sullen rage that will come to all boys if they reach manhood and find an empty horizon. With time, and a chance at real life, he could be himself again.

'It should look like I was killed for the ransom. The killer would be the witness.'

'We couldn't ask anyone to do that. If they were found out, they'd be charged with abetting. And it can't be kin. So where will you find an outsider you trust? Because he'd have to keep the truth a secret forever.'

'I guess there's no one,' Boss said.

Henry said, 'There is someone.'

'Who?'

'In fact, he'd take the risk and jump at the chance.'

'Who are you talking about, Henry?'

'Donohue McQueen.'

'You'd trust *him*?' I said.

'With my life.'

'You think he'll put himself forward as Boss's killer? He'd be hated in Scuffletown forever, and that's the opposite of what he wants.'

'All Donohue wants is the chance to do one noble act. What's said of him afterward doesn't figure into his thinking. If it serves our cause — if it's for the good — he'll do it.'

★ ★ ★

527

And Henry was right about that. Donohue McQueen allowed himself to become the most hated man in Scuffletown.

He went to the sheriff's office, and he said he had killed Boss Strong.

McTeer laughed outright.

'Where's the body?'

'Andrew Strong's house.'

'I'll believe it when I see it.'

Donohue said, 'Let's go then before the women get hold of it and bury it off somewhere.'

McTeer eyed him, starting to wonder if it might be true.

'You're a settlement boy yourself, I'm told. Is that right?'

'I'm part.'

'Because that would make it nice. Boss Strong done in by one of his own. How'd you do it?'

'I shot him in the head. He was lying on the floor at Andrew's place, he was playing on his mouth organ. The others didn't know what happened, they thought his head just exploded.'

'You mean you shot him through the window?'

'No. Through the cat hole.'

McTeer stared. He couldn't decide if Donohue was a stupid fool or a brilliant genius. Who would think of shooting directly through the cat hole?

'Are you sure he's dead? How close did you get to him?'

'Couple of yards.'

At Andrew's cabin, they found no corpse. Flora, who was the only person there, said she didn't know anything. But they found a wet floor, scrubbed with lye within the past hour. They found blood on the wall and bloody clothing under the house. Flora broke down and said yes, Boss had been shot, but his body had been taken away, she didn't know where. McTeer couldn't help concluding that Boss Strong had indeed been killed by Donohue McQueen, given the close range of the shot.

And the next night, a trainload of Federal soldiers pulled out of Moss Neck, all in uniform and looking one just like the next. Nobody counted them or looked under the caps of those asleep by the window.

Epilogue

I have become a figure of mystery in Robeson County. Since I keep to myself, I am not often recognized in person, and sometimes on the street or in a store I overhear people talking about Rhoda Lowrie. There are three things they want to know. When will she remarry? Does she know what happened to Henry? And what has she done with the money?

The first is easily answered. I won't marry again. My husband is still alive. Every year he is more and more alive, not just in my memory but in the history that's the memory of this land. A young person might find it hard to believe that a woman could give up the man she loves and yet still claim to love him. But it can be done. The truer the love, the easier it is to do. And by easy I don't mean painless. I only mean that the love sustains me. For twenty-five years now it has been my mainstay. I have been a married woman all that time.

The money disappeared. I remember Daddy used to tell me, when you go money-digging you must keep quiet. If you talk, the money moves. And all money is like that, liable to turn from you and find another home. The reward of twenty thousand dollars offered by the state of North Carolina for the capture of Henry Berry Lowrie made its way into the hands of the U.S. Army, or officers of that army. The cost of blue uniforms and a train ticket to Richmond was high that night.

As for what finally happened to him, I am not at liberty to say whether I know the answer or I don't. But I can tell some things.

I saw them board the train. More than a few of those soldiers had Indian girls clinging to them at the depot, and no one noticed me. When the train pulled out, the girls all went back to Scuffletown.

Two letters passed between us.

Dear Rho,
I will not write the name of the place
where I am, in case this letter falls into
the wrong hands. But it is a good place. I
think it will do for us fine. I will send the
money for you and the children when I
have it, and that will be in November.
You can send me a letter by way of the
Adjutant General in Lumberton.
H.B. Lowrie.

Dear Henry,
Your brother Tom is dead, he was killed
in July. I don't know who by but I know
it is true because they took a picture of
him and put it in the court house. They
are standing over him with guns and one
man has a foot on Tom like a deer.
Andrew died on Christmas Day. He was
shot in the back of the neck in Pate's,
buying molasses. Steve met up with the
caravaners one night, but they were
bounty hunters, and they killed him with
an ax. I am sorry to have to tell you these
sad events. All the wives are widows now
and need my help. And so I can't come
to join you. I think also I must warn that
you should not come back here. There is
a murderous rage against the Lowries. We
women are safe, so you have no worry on
that account, but there is a great deal of
heartbreak and sorrow among us. Your
children are well.

— Rhoda

I did hope he would write back to me after
that, but he didn't. I know he blamed himself
for what happened here, although I believe it
would have happened no matter what.

And after that, a sort of peace descended
upon us, the peace of a beaten and ruined

land where all the young soldiers are dead.

Margaret and I go down to the river some afternoons, and fish. We live as we hoped to do, in houses near each other. There's memory in the river, she says.

'Do you know where he is?' she once asked me.

I guess I didn't answer fast enough, or else Margaret reads me well.

'No,' I said, 'I don't.'

'You've seen him, haven't you?' she cried. 'I can tell by your voice. Why didn't you say so? Did he come here? Does he still?'

'If I knew anything, I couldn't reveal it,' I said. 'Not even to you or my own children.'

'You could drop a hint.' She looked down into the water, running fast and black before us. 'I bet he's still a handsome man.'

'Margaret, I've told all I can tell.'

'All right. Everyone knows anyway. He's alive. Everyone knows.'

*   *   *

We aren't rich but we survive, me and Margaret. Polly helps. Sal has her own family, and Del is the only one I worry for. He says he will go down to Georgia, following turpentine, since it has died out in North Carolina. Things have been dying out here for a long time, I tell him. Tribes disappeared. A colony got lost. Languages once spoken will never be heard again, and the parakeets will not be seen. I'm telling Del, what's lost is lost — but on the other hand there is always a chance of recovery. Meantime we grieve the departed and know they live, gaining force while the earth slowly grows. We wait.

Allen Lowrie 1795 – 1865

His cousins:
   Heck Oxendine 1841 – 1865
   Boss Strong 1850 –
   Andrew Strong 1848 – 1873

His nephews:
   Jarman Lowrie 1844 – 1863
   Wesley Lowrie 1845 – 1863
   Little Allen Lowrie 1846 – 1863
   Henderson Oxendine 1844 – 1871

His sons:
   William Lowrie 1840 – 1864
   Tom Lowrie 1843 – 1873
   Steve Lowrie 1844 – 1873
   Henry Berry Lowrie 1846 –

We do hope that you have enjoyed reading this large print book.

Did you know that all of our titles are available for purchase?

We publish a wide range of high quality large print books including:
Romances, Mysteries, Classics
General Fiction
Non Fiction and Westerns

Special interest titles available in large print are:
The Little Oxford Dictionary
Music Book
Song Book
Hymn Book
Service Book

Also available from us courtesy of Oxford University Press:
Young Readers' Dictionary
(large print edition)
Young Readers' Thesaurus
(large print edition)

For further information or a free brochure, please contact us at:
Ulverscroft Large Print Books Ltd.,
The Green, Bradgate Road, Anstey,
Leicester, LE7 7FU, England.
Tel: (00 44) 0116 236 4325
Fax: (00 44) 0116 234 0205

Other titles in the
Ulverscroft Large Print Series:

THE FROZEN CEILING

Rona Randall

When Tessa Pickard found the note amongst her father's possessions, instinct told her that THIS had been responsible for his suicide, not the professional disgrace which had ruined his career as a mountaineer and instructor. The note was cryptic, anonymous, and bore a Norwegian postmark. Tessa promptly set out for Norway, determined to trace the anonymous letter-writer, but unprepared for the drama she was to uncover — or that compelling Max Hyerdal, whom she met on board a Norwegian ship, was to change her whole life.

GHOSTMAN

Kenneth Royce

Jones boasted that he never forgot a face. When he was found dead outside the National Gallery it was assumed he had remembered one too many. The man he had claimed to have identified had been publicly executed in Moscow some years before. The presumed look-alike was called Mirek and his background stood up. The Security Service calls in Willie 'Glasshouse' Jackson — Jacko — as they realise that there is a more sinister aspect. Jacko and his assistant begin to unearth commercial and political corruption in which life is cheap and profits vast, as the killing machines swing into action.

THE READER

Bernhard Schlink

A schoolboy in post-war Germany, Michael collapses one day in the street and is helped home by a woman in her thirties. He is fascinated by this older woman, and he and Hanna begin a secretive affair. Gradually, he begins to be frustrated by their relationship, but then is shocked when Hanna simply disappears. Some years later, as a law student, Michael is in court to follow a case. To his amazement he recognizes Hanna. The object of his adolescent passion is a criminal. Suddenly, Michael understands that her behaviour, both now and in the past, conceals a deeply buried secret.

THE WAY OF THE SEA
AND OTHER STORIES

Stanley Wilson

Every story in this collection was written by Stanley Wilson with radio in mind. The BBC has broadcast all of them, and many have been used overseas. All have appeared in magazines or newspapers. The stories range the globe and beyond, from India to Canadian backwoods, from an expedition up the Amazon to a hundred years' journey to the planet Eithnan, from the Caribbean to a rain-sodden English seaside promenade, and from a fishing trawler to a hospital ward. There is frustration, there is tenderness, there is horror, there are tears, but there is laughter as well.

A BRIDE FOR
SIR BERENGAR LE MOYNE

Dora Woodhams

In 1258, seventeen-year-old Emma is
faced with a dilemma: Her father is dying.
He has sent for a comrade in arms, Sir
Berengar le Moyne, to marry Emma if she
agrees — and take her to his demesne of
Bernewelle le Moyne, where she will be
safe from the plots of her older half-
brother Gerold, who plans to marry her to
his only friend Sir Mauger when his father
dies. Emma's eventual decision leads her
into meeting King Henry III, his Queen,
Eleanor of Provence, and Henry's son and
his young bride, at the Royal Hunting
Palace in Rockingham Forest.

Beti Sil

Neath Port Talbot
Libraries
Llyfrgelloedd
Castell-Nedd
Port Talbot

MOBILES
MONA

*Books should be returned or renewed by the last date
stamped above.*
*Dylid dychwelyd llyfrau neu eu hadnewyddu erbyn y
dyddiad olaf a nodir uchod*   **NP56**